COLD SEA RISING

Richard Moran was born in New York City
in 1942. He attended St Francis College, Maine
and the University of Paris. He first wrote
professionally as a military correspondent and
newspaper editor for the American Army in
Europe from 1965 to 1968. Thereafter he spent
four years as an advertising copywriter in New
York.

In 1971 he moved to San Francisco where
he lives now with his wife Kathleen and four
daughters. He taught himself the trade of
carpentry and began to write seriously. *Cold
Sea Rising* was conceived when Richard
Moran's desire to write adventure stories com-
bined with his interest in the earth sciences.
It is the first book in a trilogy of novels he is
planning based on science. The second will be
*Dallas Down*.

RICHARD MORAN

# Cold Sea Rising

Collins/Fontana

First published in Great Britain by
Fontana Paperbacks 1987
Second impression August 1988

Printed and bound in Great Britain by
William Collins Sons & Co. Ltd, Glasgow

# ACKNOWLEDGEMENTS

I am indebted to Dr Garniss H. Curtis of the Geology and Geophysics Department, the University of California at Berkeley, who took time from his busy teaching and research schedule to review the manuscript and interpret and expand upon the terms and principles of geophysics upon which *Cold Sea Rising* is based.

Soledad Allegrotti, the loveliest, youngest eighty-five-year-old lady I shall ever know, was a kind and constant source of optimism who sustainedly nurtured my spirit and never wavered in her faith in my work.

My fullest gratitude is due to Glenna Goulet, who prepared my original draft and retyped the manuscript time and again. Glenna encouraged me through several difficult rewrites.

I'd like to express special appreciation to my literary agent, Frederick Hill of San Francisco. Fred's faith in my novel long buoyed me, and his excellent representation brought the book to the able hands of my publisher.

I wish, too, to thank my editors at Arbor House, Ann Harris and Arnold Erhlich. *Cold Sea Rising* would not have come to fruition without their thoughtful story suggestions and astute editing.

I'd also like to thank Dr Arthur B. Ford of the US Geological Survey, Menlo Park, California. A veteran of ten seasons of research on the white continent, Dr Ford was of inestimable assistance in my research of the topography of West Antarctica.

# NORTHDRIFT
## O.O Nautical Miles

The Soyuz P7 satellite, sixty-five days out of the Tyuratam Cosmodrome in Soviet Kazakhstan, neared the bottom of the world from the north in polar orbit 240 miles above the earth.

Cosmonaut Yurii Ryumin turned from a systems check at the sound of a beeper pulsing from the communications terminal. For the fourth consecutive orbit, the identical message from Ground Control appeared on the computer screen: CONDUCT VISUAL TERRAIN SURVEY 280 SECOND DURATION COMMENCING 1246:10 HOURS ORBIT TIME.

The corners of Ryumin's mouth turned up in annoyance. 'How do they expect us to keep up our work schedule if they keep interrupting us with this asinine chore?' he said to his crewmate, Vladimir Malyshev. 'What is it about a damn fogbank that Tyuratam finds so compelling?'

'It isn't the fog they're interested in, Yura,' Malyshev said. 'They want to know what's causing it. It's spring in Antarctica. There's never any fog this time of year, much less a bank of that size.'

Ryumin shrugged and pulled the accordion-mounted periscope down to eye level, pressing his brow against the headrest. He squinted into the eye sockets and let his vision adjust to the panorama of the 5,500,000-square-mile white continent passing below.

Centred on the south pole, the ice-covered landmass was roughly circular but for a long peninsula jutting north like a finger pointed at the tip of South America.

Everything in the world was north. New Zealand and Australia lay beyond the Pacific horizon, Africa across the South Atlantic, the Asian subcontinent over the reaches of the Indian Ocean.

9

Ryumin switched to medium magnification and began panning west from the pole across the broken, crevassed ice fields. In a moment the 14,300-foot-high Transantarctic Mountains came into the view field. At the western foot of the range the icescape of jagged hummocks resumed, then yielded suddenly to a vast white plateau.

Beneath the dead flat snow lay the horizonless expanse of the titanic Ross Ice Shelf, a solid block of ice roughly the size of Spain.

Ryumin blinked as the blinding surface of the Shelf slowly filled the periscope eye. Lodged against the horseshoe-shaped shores of the Ross Sea facing the Pacific, thirty per cent of the Shelf was aground on the sea floor. And along the semicircular landward rim, a crust of snow-covered ice moored the floating Shelf to the continent.

This brooding colossus of ice stood at the head of the great West Antarctic Ice Sheet, a titanic glacier that held enough fresh water trapped in its towering bulk to raise sea levels around the world over twenty feet. Only the backward pressure of the Shelf restrained the Ice Sheet from surging forward through the Ross Sea and into the Pacific Ocean.

Even in this the last year of the twentieth century, few human beings other than space travellers and research scientists had ever set eyes on the 200,000-square-mile expanse of the Shelf. The men who came to tap the newly discovered mineral riches of Antarctica busied themselves far inland, where strategic metals were mined from cavernous excavations under the permanent ice fields.

For almost forty-five seconds the periscope showed nothing but the passing mass of the Shelf. Then, slowly, patches of dark-grey fog appeared over the ice. A moment later the scan reached the sea and Ryumin stopped the pan. He could see the fogbank clearly now. The swirling wall of vapour began out in the open ocean off the Shelf and ran straight as an arrow towards the towering white cliffs that faced the ice.

Ryumin pressed a button on the periscope cross grip,

and a distance graph flipped over the lenses. He recorded the numbers and punched the coordinates into the on-board computer. He glanced at Malyshev as the calculated length, depth, and breadth of the fog flashed on the screen. 'The bank's almost doubled in size since our last pass.'

Malyshev shook his head. 'There's something very warm under those waves down there, my friend.'

Ryumin swung the periscope along the coast bordering the Shelf. Several miles from the ice an irregular black patch appeared against the snow-covered shore, and he switched to 1000 × magnification.

The close-up lens picked out thousands of small black and white bodies huddled together tightly below.

'The penguins are still there, Vova.'

Malyshev smiled ruefully. 'The warm air must be making them very uncomfortable. You'd think they'd move down the coast.'

'They'll cook first,' Ryumin said with ill humour. He swung the periscope back and began his report to Ground Control.

Two hundred miles below, 80,000 Adélie penguins stood motionless gazing in hypnotic terror out over the heaving waves at the line of dark-grey vapour rising from the sea.

The fogbank billowed out suddenly, and the raucous sound of boiling steam breaking the surface hissed across the water. A chorus of low, plaintive wails washed over the colony.

From the front rank, a single large male strode purposefully forward, covering the hundred yards to the surf line with short, hurried steps. He stopped at the lip of the water and stared out at the angry wall of fog. On the left side of his white-feathered chest, pink skin and tufts of eiderdown underfeathers showed through a long, jagged scar, the trace of a narrow escape from the jaws of a leopard seal two winters before.

Others of his scale-like outer feathers were missing, torn away in fights with males challenging his supremacy. He had won sovereignty over the colony at the age of eight and emerged victorious from every subsequent test of his command for the past sixteen years. He was very old and very wise.

Ten years ago a Norwegian zoologist had observed the penguin for a season as he directed the daily routine of his charges. The scientist had named the great bird Konge, 'king'.

It was Konge who led the sea hunts for the teeming schools of shrimplike krill on which the colony fed and who spearheaded counterattacks when predatory skua gulls raided the penguins' spring rookery. In all matters affecting the welfare of the colony, from the disciplining of neglectful parents to the settling of territorial disputes, the other Adélies deferred to Konge.

He focused his binocular vision on the alien fog and watched with burning eyes until the hissing steam finally trailed off and stopped.

Eighteen days before, a volcanic fissure had split the floor of the sea beyond the coast. The submarine line of seething lava appeared to Konge and the other diving penguins like a huge red sea snake slithering through the dark depths below them.

The fracture was the emerging mouth of a plume, a vertical pipeline of molten magma that rose from the earth's fiery mantle up through the crust beneath the polar sea. The fissure spewed a continuous discharge of bubbling gases and pillow-shaped lava through the sea floor. Day by day it had built itself into a formidable submerged ridge. Hourly it grew longer and higher.

The sea had warmed steadily as the torrid volcanic debris pulsed through the fracture. As it grew hotter, Konge had posted sentries along the beach to keep his charges ashore, knowing instinctively that the heated water would sicken the penguins.

Only the winds howling off the nearby Ross Ice Shelf kept the line of steam and fog billowing above the fracture from blanketing the entire coast in thick grey vapour.

The bitter gusts from the interior pushed against the backs of the penguins, as if to force them into the breaking

12

waves. Hunger, too, urged them forward, for Konge had not permitted krill hunts for twelve long days.

Nursing females had appeared continually before him, flipperlike wings thrust out stiffly in subservience, begging to fish so they could feed their starving hatchlings; to each Konge had signalled no.

He might have given in and permitted the colony to brave the dangerous ocean temperatures, and even the threat of the boiling steam, were it not for the awful bubbles. The hissing globules had the rotten smell of eggs orphaned in the sun, and where they burst at the surface, the noxious vapours had killed any of the penguins who were near.

Perhaps a dozen impetuous yearlings had slipped by Konge's guards the day before, intent on exploring this intriguing new diversion. Their lifeless bodies now bobbed in the surf at the step of the beach.

The bubbles were poisonous hydrogen sulphide, and they rose all along the volcanic tear in the earth. From its first appearance thirty miles offshore, the fissure had lengthened day by day, passing beneath the glistening seaward cliffs of the Shelf and pushing over 200 miles into the bay under the huge slab of ice.

The seawater trapped beneath the underside of the Shelf and the tortured floor of the bay churned violently as more and more volcanic gases and steam belched from the rift. The pressure had been building up by the hour, the vapours screaming for release through the glacial stratum above. As the water warmed, the ice anchors securing the Shelf to the bottom inexorably melted away. By the sixteenth day, only the crustal bridge along the shore linked the ice to the continent.

But to Konge and the other penguins, the Ross Shelf appeared as it always had: a seemingly endless expanse of flat, white ice field stretching south into the wind-scourged reaches of the bay. The Ice looked undisturbed, glistening benignly in the slanting rays of the early spring sun motionless on the horizon.

For uncounted millennia, the return of light and warmth

13

had triggered the life cycles of the penguins and the few other animals native to this brutal land. The spring was short – the flick of a solar eyelash – and the renewal of life demanded precise timing.

Yet this one spring the lifeclock had stopped. The few penguin hatchlings born before the terror began had all starved to death without their nursing food of regurgitated krill. The unhatched eggs lay cold and abandoned in their pebble nests.

When the nurturing sea turned hostile, Konge had charged through the colony, hectoring incubating parents off their nests, signalling his lieutenants to do the same.

Further inshore, thousands of skua gulls stretched their wings nervously, cocking their heads to peer towards the sea with suspicious black eyes. The predators made no move to devour the unprotected eggs.

The great herds of Antarctic seals that inhabited the coasts bordering the Ross Sea had fled to the safety of the open ocean the day the ominous fogbank first appeared. Their rocky lairs along the shore were deserted, hollow and silent without the familiar bellowing of the bulls and calls of the cows.

Konge tensed suddenly. At that moment the breath of this dying season was sucked into an instant of nothingness, one soundless drumbeat of warning. Then through this hushed void rumbled the ominous muffled roar Konge had known would come.

In the dark depths below the Shelf, a great heartbeat of the earth pumped a massive red flood of molten magma up through the plume. As the fiery lava and gases entered the heated seawater, the bay under the Ice began to seethe like a closed iron kettle. Steam and noxious vapours boiled upward, slamming into the lid of the ice above.

Konge wheeled and raced back towards the colony.

As the roar built, the skuas lifted into the polar air in an explosion of terrified and flailing wings.

In seconds, the maddened gases had fanned out below the Shelf, searching for a vulnerable point in the Ice, an escape route into the air above. Where the Shelf met the coast, only the crust bridging the surface to the shore held back the incalculable pressure, and it was here that the first cracks appeared.

Konge reached the first rows of penguins and signalled frantically with his short tapered wings. Down! Down into the snow! Like wheat before a wind, rank after rank of birds flopped over on their bellies, each successive row following the one before it. Still, several hundred penguins remained standing, frozen in shock by the earsplitting sounds of the fracturing ice.

More and yet more vapour hissed through the floor of the bay. A shoreline section of crust bulged ominously. Seconds later a sixty-mile long strip of ice blasted skyward with a roar heard a thousand miles out in the Pacific.

A fusillade of razor-sharp ice splinters fanned across the ice and sea, slicing through the rookery like a scythe. The standing penguins were cut in two, decapitated, chopped off at the legs. They toppled soundlessly into the snow, each small black and white form the centre of a crimson patch.

Four miles away, huge cracks fed rapidly off the jagged hole blown in the Ross Shelf and raced along the shore of the bay, shattering the remaining crustal links to the land. Pressurized gases below shot up into the latticework of sudden fractures and forced the gaps to widen. By inches and then by feet, a deep gorge rapidly filling with turbulent seawater opened between the Ross Ice Shelf and the Antarctic continent.

The Shelf stood steady in the bay, as if bewildered by its sudden independence, too massive to be even minutely affected by the ebb and hurl of the violent water beneath it.

Konge rose, blood seeping from a wound on his right shoulder, his unblinking black eyes taking in the living and the dead. His stare lifted to the massive white cliffs on the Shelf. He had seen something. Movement.

Almost imperceptibly, the Shelf was pulling away from the land. By feet and then by yards the Ice began to drift ponderously to the north, out towards the vast and warm Pacific.

Konge watched for a long time, then turned his attention back to the colony. With voice and wing he commanded his lieutenants, and they hurried off to organize the dazed colony into long lines of march.

Mercilessly Konge shooed birds wailing over their dead mates into the evacuation columns. There was no time for mourning. They must move inland, far inland, and quickly.

The terror at the bottom of the world had just begun.

NORTHDRIFT
2.3 Nautical Miles

The luminous red numerals of the digital display panel began to change rapidly at exactly 6:36 A.M. eastern standard time. Instantly, a bell tone sounded, chiming loudly through the quiet, almost deserted Geodynamics Branch of the Goddard Space Flight Centre in Greenbelt, Maryland.

The lone geologist monitoring data from Goddard's Satellite Communications Group looked up from the detective novel he was reading at the room's control desk.

He had grown used to the constant low murmur of the computer recorders. Around the clock they logged ground survey information telemetered from NASA's network of GRAVSAT probes in orbit a hundred miles above the earth.

The GRAVSATs had been sent up in the mid-eighties to study the planet's gravitational field. Fractures in the earth's crust produce variations called anomalies in gravity readings. Geophysicists and geologists were able to plot subsurface fault lines and seismic zones by studying the GRAVSAT data.

Detectable gravity changes also occur when molten magma moves through the earth's crust. The plastic lava is less dense than surrounding rock and therefore gives off a lower magnetic reading. Scientists using the GRAVSAT surveys could spot magma moving upward and forecast imminent volcanic eruptions and lava flows through submarine rifts.

With few exceptions, data were routinely filed away in the Geodynamics Branch's computer memory banks for later analysis. The bell tone, however, signalled a sudden dramatic change in the incoming gravity readings. The technician walked quickly to the digital display.

He switched off the bell, looked down at the numbers, and whistled appreciatively. The earth's gravitational field normally gave off a reading of 1,000 milligals, units that measure the acceleration of gravity. But now the digital display was registering only 935 milligals.

There would be only one explanation for such an abrupt change: the GRAVSAT mission was reading a huge magma discharge through the earth's crust somewhere below its orbital path. The geologist shook his head in disbelief. The 65-milligal differential simply couldn't be correct.

When Mount Saint Helens erupted in Washington State back in the early eighties, there had been a 30-milligal change. The largest anomaly he'd ever heard of was the 45-milligal differential recorded when Ecuador's Cotopaxi volcano blew its top in a stupendous eruption in the summer of '92.

He reached down and pushed the CONFIRM button on the display board. Again, the reading of 935 milligals flashed. The geologist felt the first knot of foreboding in his gut.

The room's large IBM computer droned to life as he walked to the machine's control console. The computer had begun interpreting the GRAVSAT data and plotting the location of the anomaly the moment the first signals came in from space.

The position of the monstrous magma discharge was flashed on a small green screen. The GRAVSAT was over Antarctica, 10,000 miles away. The eruption was coming from a submarine rift over 200 miles long. The fracture originated in the McMurdo Sound region in West Antarctica at approximately 77 degrees south latitude, 165 degrees east longitude, and ran southwest towards the pole.

He pushed the key marked OVERLAY and a stylized map of the white continent flipped over the chart, picturing the path of the rift directly below the huge Ross Ice Shelf.

As he watched, the single word PROCEDURE came on the screen. He knew the GRAVSAT readings had triggered a special program somewhere in the computer's memory banks.

The screen blinked again and a message block appeared:

6:40 A.M., OCT. 15, 1999. MAJOR GEOLOGICAL FLUX ROSS SEA REGION WEST ANTARCTICA. SUBMARINE RIFT MAGMA DISCHARGE. AREA THERMAL DISASTER POTENTIAL TEN, REPEAT THERMAL RANGE CRITICAL. IMMEDIATE PRIORITY NOTIFICATION (1) DIRECTOR, NATIONAL SCIENCE FOUNDATION, WASHINGTON, DC (2) ADMIRAL WALDO MULDOON RANKIN, USNR (CHAIRMAN, ANTARCTIC CONFERENCE) FALMOUTH, MASS.

The geologist's eyebrows arched. Up to that moment, he had encountered the priority notification only during the Geodynamics Branch's biannual systems drills. But then there had never been a magma discharge great enough to generate the incredible gravity anomaly he had just recorded. The instructions began to blink on and off across the screen and he walked back to the control desk.

He leafed through a thin red directory of priority telephone numbers, found the two he needed and began dialling the number of the National Science Foundation in Washington.

The Astrophysicist Charles Gates turned from the triple-insulated window in the headquarters module of the American Antarctic Research Station at McMurdo Sound and surveyed his fellow scientists seated around the conference table.

'Looks like the wind's dying down,' he said, a swirl of smoke from his omnipresent pipe encircling his grey head. 'We may be able to get an aircraft up soon. Everybody here?' Gates was in Antarctica to study the far reaches of space through the ideal observation conditions of the thin polar atmosphere. He was senior scientist on the ice during the '98–'99 winter season.

The research director, John Michaels, yawned. 'All section heads present, Charlie. In body, anyway. Most of us were asleep.'

Although the rays of the low, motionless polar sun slanted through the window, it was ten minutes to midnight at McMurdo.

Gates snorted. 'I doubt anyone slept through that God-awful roar fifteen minutes ago. Sure as hell knocked me out of bed.'

He sat at the head of the table. 'OK, I want to review what we know so far. Peter, what the hell's going on off the coast?'

The marine geologist, Peter Buxton, lowered a mug of coffee. 'Submarine volcanism. As we're all aware, it started almost three weeks ago. Until today, I wasn't too concerned. We know there've been magma discharges through the McMurdo Sound seabed before.'

'Admiral Rankin's findings?'

'Yes, his geological survey back in '89 turned up evidence of a rift-related volcanism off the Ross Ice Shelf. Dormant at the time.'

'Obviously it is no longer dormant. I want to know how extensive you think the eruption will be.'

'Eruptions, plural, Charlie. There's more than just one vent spewing up lava out there. I've charted widely spaced geysers along a line maybe twenty miles long. The steam columns stop abruptly at the seaward cliffs of the Shelf.'

'Do you believe the rift extends under the Ice?'

'Rankin thought so,' Buxton said.

Gates turned to the only woman present. 'Melissa, what's happening to the Ice Shelf?'

Melissa McCoy had the distinction of being the first human conceived and born on the Antarctic continent. Her father was Admiral Waldo Muldoon Rankin, America's preeminent Antarctic expert, and her mother had been Doctor Ingrid Rankin, a renowned pioneer in the treatment and prevention of frostbite.

Melissa had inherited her parents' love of the white continent. Her unwavering goal throughout school had been polar research, and she'd earned a doctorate in glaciology from the Massachusetts Institute of Technology. In the ten years since, neither marriage nor motherhood had kept her from spending every other winter pursuing her work in Antarctica.

She shook her head. 'I can't be sure until I have a look from the air, Charlie.'

'You want to hazard a guess as to where that sound blast came from? It was ice fracturing, wasn't it?'

'I'm not sure "fracturing" is the word. More like ice exploding.'

'I have a theory about that,' Buxton volunteered. 'If a pocket of gases vented by the rift were to be trapped, confined under the ice, the pressure might have built enough to blow a hole through the Shelf.'

'It's feasible,' McCoy agreed. 'Whatever's happened, I suspect a very large berg or maybe bergs have split off the seaward cliffs of the Shelf.'

Gates held a match over the unlit bowl of his pipe. 'What brings you to that conclusion?'

'A feeling, Charlie. Literally. If you stand still outside

you can feel a sort of grinding through the soles of your feet. I'd say there's a very large section of ice scraping along the floor of the bay on the way out to sea.'

Gates turned to the meteorologist Dick Spaulding. 'What's the wind direction?'

'Due north. If Melissa's right about a large berg calving off the Shelf, it'll be pushed out to sea relatively fast.'

The videophone buzzed next to Gates, and he flipped on the set. 'Yes?'

The face of the marine biologist Ken Kennard looked back from the screen, the paraphernalia of his laboratory slightly out of focus behind him.

'I'm sorry to interrupt your meeting, Charlie, but I thought you'd want to know.'

'What have you got, Ken?'

'One of my thermal sensors monitoring the floor of the bay beneath the Ice Shelf is registering an extraordinary temperature rise in the seawater.'

'How extraordinary?'

'Over thirty degrees above readings just ten miles away.'

Gates let a puff of pipe smoke curl towards the ceiling. 'You suggesting we've got another active vent in the middle of the bay? That the volcanic fracture stretched two hundred miles under the Shelf?'

'I'm simply reporting the data from my thermal sensors, Charlie. You tell me what it means.'

Gates said, 'I will when I know myself, Ken. Thanks.'

The special projects director, Benjamin Cohen, tossed a pencil on the table. 'If we've got a major magma discharge going on out there, shouldn't Goddard be picking it up on their GRAVSAT monitor? I know damn well they've got a gravity probe in polar orbit.'

Gates scowled. 'C'mon, Ben, you know how the game's played. Chain of command bullshit. Data from Goddard's got to go through foundation headquarters in Washington before we get it. Probably another hour or so.'

'We're sitting right here on top of volcanism and we're the last to be told what we're up against,' Buxton spat. 'Goddamn interagency politics!'

Melissa McCoy said, 'Why wait for NASA? All I need is an hour over the Shelf and I can tell you what's happening to the Ice. If Jim's willing to go up in these winds.'

Navy Lieutenant JG Jim Culpepper grinned. 'To get you alone, Melissa, I'd fly into the teeth of a blizzard.'

Melissa was used to sexual innuendo. At thirty-four she was at her intellectual and physical peak. She was both intelligent and beautiful, with her mother's oval face and white-blond hair. Her startling blue eyes reminded many people of her father. There were always ten men for every woman wintering over on the ice, and the passes started the moment the last plane to the outside world lifted off into the darkening sky. By now, after so many seasons in Antarctica, the once disconcerting routine of stalking men had become no more than the vague buzz of mosquitoes. The wolves had metamorphosed into bugs.

Melissa ignored the bright-eyed pilot and looked at Dick Spaulding. 'What do you say? Safe to put a chopper up?'

The meteorologist nodded. 'Winds have been falling off. We're not looking for anything above thirty knots for the next twenty-four hours.'

'OK, Melissa,' Gates agreed, glancing at Culpepper. 'No heroics, you two. Keep the flight within a hundred-mile radius. Agreed?'

Ten minutes later the US Navy Alouette III helicopter rose noisily above the American base, whipping up a swirl of powdered snow as it climbed into the freezing air.

Culpepper adjusted his throat mike. 'You want to head up the coast?'

Melissa shook her head. 'No, too much fog to see what's going on. I'd like to fly southwest and intersect the Shelf seventy to eighty miles inland.'

'Southwest it is,' Culpepper said, banking the Alouette.

Melissa swung a pair of binoculars across the horizon in a slow arc as the helicopter flew inland over the glacial terrain of Victoria Land.

From the air the ice fields below looked forbidding and hostile. Dark yawning crevasses latticed the surface, and huge snowdrifts rose hundreds of feet into the air against jagged ice cliffs.

Why did she come here, she asked herself again. Why had she spent over seven years of her life in this godforsaken place? She knew the answer, of course. Antarctica was her world. It had been since she was a little girl listening to her parents' enthralling stories of the white continent. This was where her work was, where she belonged.

Even the children were off-centre in her life. She loved Kate and Shea, she loved them very much, but it was her research that was her focus, her research that impassioned her, that brought her back again and again to Antarctica.

She'd paid the price for her long absences from her family. There were great gaps in her mother-daughter relationships with the girls. She hadn't been there to teach Shea how to read, and she hadn't been there to hold an infant Kate the nights she woke up crying with teething pains. And she hadn't been there for Josh.

She wasn't sure which day, which month, which year, her husband had stopped loving her. She only knew that when she looked into his eyes, that special place in him was closed to her forever.

She knew she'd lost Josh long before he'd met Anya. Still, his phone call from Moscow had come like a thunderbolt. Hearing him say he loved another woman had left her shaken and depressed for months.

Melissa brought the binoculars up to her eyes. Stop it, she scolded herself. Stop picking at it. Slowly she adjusted the focus and swept the horizon towards the west.

A moment later she froze the sweep suddenly and started forward. 'It's not possible!'

The pilot stared in the same direction. He couldn't pick out anything unusual in the patchwork of broken pressure ridges and random blocks of jagged ice. 'What do you see out there?'

The glaciologist hesitated for a moment, adjusting the

glasses. 'It shouldn't be, Jim, but unless I'm hallucinating, there's open water ahead.'

'C'mon, Melissa, we're over seventy miles from the coast.'

'Here, take a look for yourself,' she said, handing over the binoculars.

The pilot focused and squinted into the distance. He could clearly make out a dark band ahead shimmering in the sunlight. The wavering reflection could only be glinting off a water surface. 'Son of a bitch! Where the hell did that come from?' he asked, handing back the glasses.

'There's salt water under the Shelf for four hundred miles in from the open sea. A lead must have split open all the way to the coast.' McCoy again fixed her binoculars on the silvery phenomenon ahead.

'Can you see how far it runs?' Culpepper asked.

'Not yet. It disappears behind pressure ridges on both sides.' Three minutes later they crossed the last hummocks at the edge of the Shelf.

'Good God!' She had put down the glasses and was staring wide-eyed at the surface below. Channelled between towering white cliffs, a dark ribbon of choppy seawater over ten miles wide stretched through the broken icescape like a black snake slithering across a wrinkled white bedsheet. The lead ran north to south as far as they could see.

'Get Charlie Gates on that radio, Jim.'

Culpepper nodded, his eyes glued on the turbulent river cleaving the Shelf. 'Navy recon to McMurdo.

'McMurdo to navy recon. Go ahead.' Simultaneous two-way radio communication had been introduced in the late 1980s, eliminating the need for tedious 'over' and 'out' instructions between aircraft and ground stations, and the response was loud and clear.

'McMurdo, can you get Dr Gates to the radio? We've got something out here he'll want to know about.'

'Will do, one one five. Give me a minute.'

'We'll stand by, McMurdo.'

The helicopter radio crackled back to life. 'McMurdo to navy recon. I have Dr Gates here.'

McCoy pressed her throat mike. 'Are you sitting down, Charlie?'

'Not yet,' the imperturbable voice came back. 'But I suspect from your tone I'm about to.'

'We're over the southwest rim of the Ice Shelf, Charlie, about thirty minutes from the base. We have open water below.'

There was a pause, then Gates came back on. 'Is it a confined pocket or a sea lead?'

'It's definitely a lead, Charlie, about ten miles across and stretching to the horizon on both sides.'

'How far from the coast are you?'

Melissa looked at Culpepper. The pilot pushed his mike button. 'About eighty air miles, Dr Gates.'

'I don't like it. What's the water surface like?'

The glaciologist scanned the lead with her binoculars. She could see broken ice floes bounding twenty feet or more up the frozen cliffs of the gorge on the crest of whitecaps. 'Extremely turbulent, Charlie. The surrounding snow is pretty quiet. I don't think there's enough wind down there to account for the wave action.'

'That points to considerable depth. What's the median thickness of the Shelf there?'

'This far in from the ocean, I'd say about eighteen hundred feet.'

'Just a moment,' Gates said. 'Let me get my chart.'

The radio crackled for a moment, then Gates was back. 'What's your exact position?'

'One hundred sixty degrees ten minutes east longitude, seventy-eight degrees forty minutes south latitude,' McCoy reported.

'All right, I'd like you to follow the lead south for another thirty miles or so. That will put you over Hardtack Bay.'

Culpepper and Melissa looked at each other. 'How'd you know the lead ran north-south, Charlie?' she asked.

'I think the answer will be apparent when you reach that inlet,' Gates said. 'Call back in when you get there.'

Melissa studied the black finger of seawater below as the Alouette flew above the gaping fracture. The split was littered with jagged, broken ice blocks. In several places columns of steam and dark smoke rose from the chasm. Fifteen minutes later they reached the shore indentation.

She pressed her throat mike. 'We're over Hardtack, Charlie.' She focused her binoculars. 'Oh, Lord!'

Gates's voice was impatient. 'What have you got out there?'

'The rupture roughly circles the bay, then doglegs southwest. No end in sight.'

'I think we both know what that means,' Gates said evenly.

Melissa said, 'The fracture's following the shore of the bay.'

'Exactly. That's not a lead you're over, Melissa. It's a break between the Shelf and the coast.'

Culpepper cocked an eyebrow at the glaciologist. 'You two going to tell me what you're talking about?'

'The Ice, Jim. Unless Charlie and I are very wrong, the Ross Shelf is adrift.'

'You're out of your minds! The damn thing's twice the size of New Zealand!'

Gates's voice came back through his earphone. 'She's right, Jim. The volcanism below must have been intense enough to blow the crustal links between the Shelf and shore.'

'That roaring explosion,' Melissa said.

'Now we know where it came from. You two better get back here fast. We'll need the Alouette to keep track of the drift.'

'I think we should contact my father, Charlie.'

'We'll call the admiral as soon as you get in. Safe return.'

'Navy recon one five,' Culpepper signed off. He looked at Melissa. 'Melissa, if the Shelf drifts north, I mean way north out into the Pacific, won't the whole damn thing melt into the ocean?'

The woman let out a long breath. 'If it moves up towards the equator, it sure as hell will.'

'What if it keeps floating around in the southern latitudes?'

'Then it's big enough to survive at sea for decades, maybe centuries.'

'Any way to tell where it'll head?'

'Right now all we can be sure of is that the Ross Ice Shelf is loose in the Pacific.' She looked down at the titanic, horizonless mass of ice below. 'And the winds are pushing it north.'

NORTHDRIFT
18.0 Nautical Miles

The bluefish had not eaten since the day before and it was ravenous, its senses keenly alert as it searched for food along the southern coast of Cape Cod fifty yards off the beach.

It smelled the chunk of squid at the same time as its eyes caught the bait's whiteness suspended in the gloom two feet off the bottom. The fish dived. The rest of the school was near. Hesitation meant a rival would feed.

On the shore Navy Rear Admiral Waldo Muldoon Rankin was watching dawn pink the eastern horizon when he felt the tug. He let the blue have five yards of line, then set the reel and yanked the tip of the long-surf casting pole backward in an arc.

The line snapped taut, setting the hook. Slowly Rankin brought in the blue, playing him skilfully in the shallow chop, wading into the breakers at the end to grasp the fish under the gills.

He cleaned the fish on the beach, leaving the innards for the gulls and crabs, and headed back down the beach towards his weathered cottage facing the sea.

The sixty-seven-year-old Rankin grimaced as he walked. 'Damn!' Salt spray had got down the neck of his windbreaker and run across the mottled pink and white scar tissue on his chest.

He'd been badly burned during the Korean War when an enemy phosphorus shell ripped into the conning tower of the US submarine *Stingray*. The explosion and fire killed or wounded every officer on the small diesel sub. Despite first- and second-degree burns over most of his chest and arms, the twenty-one-year-old lieutenant JG two months out of Annapolis was the only officer still on his feet. He took command.

29

With the tower riddled with jagged holes, he couldn't drive the *Stingray*. For the next seventy-two hours he'd run south on the surface, fighting through a gauntlet of North Korean gunboats before bringing his boat and crew under the protection of the guns of the UN forces at Inchon.

He'd been awarded the Navy Cross and the first of the many rapid promotions that were to distinguish his career.

The retreating waves left a shattered tree limb on the sand before him, and he stopped to drag the wood up onto the higher beach. The water-polished log would make good firewood. He'd come back later in his jeep to retrieve it.

Rankin had requested pilot training during his convalescent leave, and when the skin grafts healed, he was assigned to the Pensacola Naval Air Station in Florida.

A week before he got his wings, he'd been intrigued by a posting on the 'Available Duty' board. The navy needed pilots for its new SFX Squadron, an elite all-volunteer unit flying support missions into the weather-scourged American Antarctic base of McMurdo Sound. He'd signed up the next day.

From the moment he'd first set foot on the white continent, he was hooked. The next year he'd wangled a job as head of flight operations at McMurdo. Two seasons later he'd been in command of the naval team that surveyed and laid out Antarctica's first earth- and rock-based landing field at Marble Point.

When his crews were bulldozing the airstrip, Rankin had come across mineral traces that the McMurdo lab identified as nickel and chromium. He became convinced that the seventh continent could provide new sources of these and other strategic ores and talked the navy into granting him a two-year sabbatical to study geophysics at Stanford.

The November after he earned his Ph.D., he'd returned to the southernmost landmass, now knowing what to look for and where. Rankin collected rock and soil samples from a vast area of the western part of the continent before the sun set for the winter, then spent the long dark months until spring analysing and cataloguing his specimens. And falling in love.

Doctor Ingrid Bergstrom was a twenty-three-year-old Swedish medical researcher studying frostbite treatments when Rankin met her at McMurdo Sound in the autumn of 1958. He'd never forget his first sight of her striding towards him across the snow, tall and lithe, her light hair and classic face glowing like gold in the last rays of the setting polar sun.

He'd asked her to dinner, and they'd ended up talking and laughing all night. Three months later they'd asked the base chaplain to marry them. Ingrid and he had been luckier than most couples. They shared not only a deep love for each other but a consuming passion for the white continent and its scientific secrets.

They'd been the truest of partners, devoted to each other as lovers, finding identical passion in their scientific work, and Ingrid's death late last year had shattered Rankin. He missed her deeply.

Rankin heard a sudden cacophony of screeches on the beach behind him as the gulls discovered the guts of the bluefish.

That winter in Antarctica he'd identified the locations of nickel, chromium, cobalt, titanium, manganese, and tin deposits. Yet for years afterwards the minerals remained available in more accessible regions around the world and for almost three decades his findings gathered dust at the Pentagon.

When the first shortages of strategic minerals pinched the defence industry in the mid-eighties, Washington suddenly remembered Rankin's discoveries at the bottom of the world. Overnight his intimate knowledge of the Antarctic topography became indispensable. Congress approved his promotion to flag rank.

The largest wave in a set of combers broke on the beach and he sidestepped nimbly up the sand, the white tongue of salt water licking at his boots.

Through the rest of the decade and into the early

nineties, Rankin headed American mineral recovery in Antarctica, coming to enjoy the same semi-autonomy as had Admiral Hyman Rickover, the father of US nuclear submarine development, two decades before.

Although he was then a serving American officer, he took the outspoken position that the riches of the white continent should be shared with the resource-poor Third World nations, a stand that earned him the antipathy of several conservative administrations in Washington.

But Rankin's humanist views weren't lost on the international community. When the Treaty of Christchurch, establishing the Antarctic Conference, was signed in 1994, he was the unanimous choice to become director of resource development.

He retired from the navy with full honours, but few of the Pentagon brass were sorry to see the principled and unyielding maverick go.

Still, he had become a force in Washington, a voice that spoke for an entire continent, and on that last day he spent an hour alone with President Allen in the Oval Office, then was feted on the Hill by committee chairmen from both the House and Senate.

Rankin scrunched his shoulders against the cold onshore wind and glanced out over the grey swells of Nantucket Sound. The rising sun had disappeared beneath an angry cloud bank. There was a storm near, and unconsciously he picked up his pace towards home.

A week after he retired, Rankin was at work in Christchurch in New Zealand. He quickly gained a reputation among conference members as a brilliant administrator and an apolitical man who favoured no single nation or ideology.

As often as possible, he wintered over in Antarctica, overseeing the mining operations firsthand and conducting geological research. But not this past season.

The summer before, a routine physical had uncovered acute leukemia in Ingrid. Most chronic strains of the malady could now be controlled by the highly effective corticosteroid drugs that had evolved through the 1990s,

32

but effective medications for the acute forms of the disease continued to elude medical research.

Ingrid had insisted they not tell Melissa and Josh. The death brush would paint pain and pity on the faces of her family, and she couldn't bear the thought of seeing the sadness and fear in the eyes of her grandchildren.

The doctors had told them Ingrid would have at least six months left when Melissa returned from Antarctica, and Rankin had stayed behind the past season on the pretext of a needed rest. But time had run out for Ingrid.

The end had come quickly the week before Christmas. Ingrid died holding his hand, propped up against the headboard in their small upstairs bedroom looking out over the sea she so loved.

Rankin stopped now on his way up from the beach and looked towards the window of the bedroom where she'd closed her eyes. Ingrid. He could feel her presence up there still, and he always fished within sight of the house so she could watch.

He went up the steps to the grey-boarded porch feeling tired and morose. His soul had soured with Ingrid's death and he battled frequent bouts of depression. He had become especially pessimistic lately about the fate of mankind.

Science could master anything, it seemed, except man's propensity for mindless strife. Billions that could be spent on research were being poured instead into the sinkholes of lavish weapons systems and huge standing armies.

This past September, Iran had invaded Kuwait, and the British-backed Arabs had defended their country with the latest tank-mounted lasers. Tehran's Muslim fanatics had died in roasted waves; the BBC reported 30,000 blackened bodies rotting in the sun of the Persian Gulf.

Yes, science could master anything if man didn't annihilate himself first.

His daughter Melissa's strained marriage also depressed him. He believed himself at least partly responsible and that pained him deeply. He had been thrilled when Melissa first showed an interest in Antarctic research during her middle-school years and it had been the proudest moment in his life when she received her doctorate in glaciology. He'd encouraged her every step of the way, transfusing her with his own boundless enthusiasm and dedication. He could not have known that the fire he had kindled in her would become all-consuming, that in the scheme of things she would come to place her scientific work before her husband and children.

Rankin opened the back door and put the blue and his fishing pole in the pantry, then stripped down to a T-shirt and jogging shorts for his daily three-mile run on the hard sand above the breakers.

Behind him in the house the videophone rang again for the third time in the past hour.

# NORTHDRIFT
## 19.7 Nautical Miles

THE Ross Ice Shelf drifted inexorably north from its Antarctic berth into the cold southern fringe of the Pacific. The largest mass ever to move across the face of the earth advanced steadily on the reefs and small islands in its path, one by one reducing the land specks to pebbles and powder beneath its gargantuan bulk.

The staccato din of ice cracking and shattering as it gouged through rock shot back in earthshaking thunderclaps across the polar shore, setting off huge ice slides in the coastal mountains.

Before it the Shelf pushed a jagged flotsam of broken floes. Along its towering white cliffs rising from the sea, icebergs as big as cities calved off into the angry waves and followed north in satellite course.

Where the ocean floor rose towards the surface, the Shelf cut a deep trench through the submarine sediment, as if a monstrous plough furrowing a field.

A mile ahead of the ice lay the last island outpost fringing the Antarctic coast. Beyond, the deep blue-green waters of the Pacific yawned like a vast highway north towards New Zealand and Australia.

Two hundred and forty miles above, the Soviet Soyuz P7 appeared again over the horizon. Cosmonaut Yurii Ryumin peered down disinterestedly, irritated by the repetitious task of surveying the polar topography.

His mouth clamped suddenly shut and he started against the periscope headrest. He pulled away, wiped his eyes, and looked again.

Across the small cockpit, Vladimir Malyshev arched his eyebrows. 'What is it, Yura?'

'I'm not sure,' Ryumin answered. 'There appears to be

a long crack – a separation – between the Ross Shelf and the continent. You'd better have a look.'

Malyshev cast his crewmate a bemused frown. 'There are always cracks in the coastal ice this time of year, Yura. It's spring down there, remember. The floes along the shore are breaking up.'

'No, no,' Ryumin shook his head. 'It's not in the coastal ice. The separation runs far inland towards the pole. There's something very wrong.'

Curious, Malyshev pulled down his periscope and focused the instrument. Ryumin was right! A dark fissure stood out clearly against the white ice.

The rupture entirely circled the ice shelf from the McMurdo Sound region inland, then back out again far up the coast.

'Quickly, switch on the cameras!'

'What do you suppose has happened?' Ryumin asked, activating the automatic KATE-140 mapping cameras on board.

'I have no idea,' Malyshev answered slowly, his eyes riveted on the black semicircle below.

Five minutes later they were out of range and Ryumin switched off the cameras. 'Some snapshots to send home, eh, Vladimir. Those ought to keep the fellows in photo interpretation busy for a while.'

Malyshev smiled and flicked a switch, alerting Tyuratam, in the Central Asian part of the Soviet Union, that photographs were about to be transmitted.

Unlike the American astronauts, Soviet cosmonauts were discouraged from any but essential voice communication. The Russians were afraid that a slip of the tongue would give valuable technical information to eavesdropping posts monitoring their satellites.

A small red light blinked on, indicating that the Soviet ground station was ready to receive the pictures. Malyshev turned on the phototransmitter and made sure the computer-controlled machine was functioning properly.

Satisfied, he turned to Ryumin. 'I have a feeling we shall be quite busy on our next orbit.'

NORTHDRIFT
20.7 Nautical Miles


Rankin was sautéeing his morning catch in a pan of butter when the videophone rang again. He flipped on the counter-top extension next to the stove.

'Admiral Rankin,' he said brusquely, glancing at the screen as he turned the bluefish. A thin, sallow-complexioned young man in a white lab coat looked back at him. 'Sir, my name is Chester Nelson. I'm a staff geologist with the Geodynamics Branch here at Goddard Space Flight Center.'

'As you can see, I'm cooking breakfast, Mr Nelson.'

'Yes, sir, I know it's early but I've been trying to reach you for over an hour, Admiral.'

'That so?' Rankin squeezed a fresh lemon over the fish. 'All right, what's got you boys at Goddard stirring at first light?'

'You're on a priority one sheet here, sir, to be notified immediately of any geological activity in the Antarctic. There's been a major magma discharge along a submarine rift on the western perimeter of the continent.'

Rankin's head snapped towards the screen. 'What's "major", son? Let me have the numbers.'

'One of our GRAVSAT missions in polar orbit passed over the Ross Sea area at approximately six-thirty this morning our time. Our monitors here at Goddard show a gravity anomaly of nine hundred and thirty-five milligals.'

'Great God in heaven!' Rankin's breath rushed out like an undertow beneath the words.

'We've never recorded anything like it, sir.'

Rankin felt a chill force through the open pores of his skin still flushed and warm from his run. 'Where in the Ross Sea? Give me a specific location!'

'Preliminary data . . .' the geologist's voice squeaked.

He cleared his throat. 'Preliminary data show magma venting along the fissure from the McMurdo Sound area two hundred and twenty miles southwest to approximately eighty-two degrees south latitude.'

Rankin's eyes were blue spear tips. 'Son, I want you to be sure before you answer. Are you telling me the fracture runs under the Ross Ice Shelf?'

'I've confirmed twice, Admiral. I'm afraid there's no question about it.'

Rankin sank back into a cane-bottomed chair like a weighted diver into water. Here, after sixty-seven years, was the core moment of his existence, a vortex that would suck in his decades of geological exploration and research on the white continent, the work that had been not just his career but his life. Here was the nightmare that came to him when his probes into the ocean floor had turned up the volcanic fissure that pointed so ominously from McMurdo Sound towards the unexplored seabed beneath the Ross Ice Shelf.

Fire and ice. One could not exist in the presence of the other. Volcanism severe enough to cause a 65-milligal differential in gravity readings would drastically raise the temperature of the seawater trapped under the Shelf. The more magma that spewed through the torn seabed, the greater the meltdown of the submerged ice anchoring the Shelf to the floor of the Ross Sea.

Rankin felt a wave of adrenaline pump through him. The Shelf sat astride the Antarctic coast like a towering white dam blocking the seaward movement of the land-bound West Antarctic Ice Sheet.

Good God in heaven, if the Shelf broke free of the continent and drifted north out of the Ross Sea, there would be nothing to restrain the titanic glacier behind it. The entire West Antarctic Ice Sheet would surge forward over the sunken bedrock of Marie Byrd Land and slide inexorably into the ocean.

Sea levels around the world would rise rapidly as the Ice Sheet entered the warmer northern waters and began inevitably to melt. How much of an increase was impossible to predict without detailed computer projections; fifteen, eighteen, perhaps twenty feet.

Boston would go under, New York, Washington, New Orleans, Los Angeles, San Francisco. London and all the major European ports would be inundated. Cape Town, Rio de Janeiro, Singapore, Hong Kong, Tokyo, the great port cities of the world would disappear beneath the waves.

Without harbours, global shipping would come to a dead stop. Planes couldn't handle a fiftieth of the commerce, international trade would strangle. Foodstuffs from exporting countries like the United States would rot in warehouses while millions of people across the swollen seas in the Third World slowly starved. Riots, wars, would erupt over precious supplies of grain, powdered milk, cooking oils, rice.

Rankin looked toward the videophone lens. 'Mr Nelson, I want to be contacted immediately if the GRAVSAT readings change. Up or down.'

'Will you be at this number, sir?'

'No. You can reach me through the National Science Foundation network.'

'I'll put it in the computer, Admiral.'

'I appreciate that. Good-bye.'

He rose as the image of the geologist dimmed on the screen. He went to his tiny den and turned on the video transceiver linked by satellite to the bottom of the world. It took only a moment to punch in his personal code that would alert the communications centre at the American base that a priority call was coming in.

'McMurdo Station. Good morning, Admiral Rankin.'

He recognized the young Navy signalman on duty. 'Good morning, Mendez. I want to speak to Dr Gates.'

'Yes, sir.'

The unshaven face of Charles Gates appeared on his screen. 'Hello, Waldo. I was just going to call you.'

'I understand we've got a problem down there, Charlie.'

'Didn't take you long to find out, Goddard?'

'I just got off the phone with one of their people in the Geodynamics Branch. Their GRAVSAT in polar orbit picked up the magma venting. According to the geologist I spoke with, the fissure extends from McMurdo Sound southwest to the middle of the bay.'

'We guessed as much,' Gates said. 'A thermal sensor under the Mid-Shelf has been registering a hell of a rise in seawater temperature. It looks like . . . Hang on a minute, Waldo.'

Gates rose and walked off camera. In a moment he was back. 'Melissa just landed in the Alouette.'

'Where's she been?'

'Over the Shelf. Goddard give you any numbers?'

'They're recording a gravity anomaly of nine hundred and thirty-five milligals, Charlie.'

Gates's face paled beneath his whisker shadow. 'Good God! Are they sure?'

'They're sure. Tell me what's going on off the coast.'

Gates described the geysering, the towering fogbank, and the steadily warming temperature of the sea. Rankin's daughter poked her head on camera as he finished. Her face, red-cheeked from the cold, reminded him of how she'd looked as a little girl coming home from a toboggan ride down the dunes.

'Good morning, Melissa.'

'Hi, Dad.' She peeled off her heavy hooded parka.

Rankin grinned ironically. 'You picked a hell of a season to sign on as the senior glaciologist down there, sweetheart. You're the one in the hot seat now. We're going to need continuous reports on the stability of the Shelf.'

'I'll be monitoring by the hour, Dad. As long as the Shelf's still within helicopter range.'

'Within range? What are you talking about?'

'I didn't tell him,' Gates said.

Melissa's face had the look of a woman who had to tell her father she was about to marry a man he didn't like. 'The Shelf's adrift, Dad. It's moving north.'

Rankin stared incredulously at the image of his

40

daughter. 'You mean a section's split off the outer cliffs?'

'No. The entire Shelf's separated from the continent. I just came back from a flight along the shore of the bay. The break is now about twenty miles across and getting steadily wider.'

'The computer calculation is a continuing northdrift at about six point nine nautical miles per hour, Waldo,' Gates added.

Rankin sat stunned. 'You realize what this means, Melissa. The West Antarctic Ice Sheet is going to surge into the Ross Sea. The oceans are going to rise, God only knows how much.'

'God and I, Dad,' Melissa said softly. 'I did a computer analysis of the water volume of the Ice Sheet last March. If the entire Sheet melts, the level of the world's oceans will go up twenty point six feet. I'm working on a map projection of the land areas that would flood.'

Rankin had the look of a man who'd absorbed so many sudden blows that yet another had no impact. 'You know what this means?' he said, his voice fatigued and strangely flat. 'It won't be just the port cities, the vulnerable fringes of the continents, that go under. We're facing the inundation of vast stretches of coast miles inland from present shorelines.'

Rankin brought a fist down hard on the desk next to the transceiver. 'I just don't understand how my calculations could have been so wrong. How did the Shelf's ice anchors melt so quickly? The crustal bridges to shore were thousands of feet thick. The seawater couldn't have been hot enough to dissolve almost a mile of ice above, not this quickly.'

'It wasn't the heat, Dad. The ice along the shore was shattered by a gas and steam explosion.'

'What!'

Gates said, 'It was an explosion all right, Waldo. The loudest goddamn noise I've ever heard. The sound waves literally shook the base.'

Rankin grimaced. 'None of this makes any sense. You two are familiar with my geological survey of the coast.

41

The magma along the fissure's been generated by a subduction zone, the boundary between the Pacific and Antarctic plates. It would have taken an incredible volume of gases and steam vented all at once to burst through the Shelf.' Rankin went on, 'That sort of big bang is more characteristic of –' He stopped abruptly.

'Of what, Dad?'

Rankin ignored his daughter's question. 'Charlie, Woods Hole is scheduled to run a series of plankton experiments up the coast from you. They start yet?'

'Yeah. They began diving last week at Cathedral Bay.'

'Good. I want the *Alvin* and her escort brought down to McMurdo Sound right away. I'll clear it with their people here.'

The Woods Hole Oceanographic Institution conducted a major part of American marine research and exploration. Their three-man submersible, *Alvin*, could descend to the deepest ocean trench on earth. The craft had a pressure hull, life-support systems, lights, cameras, sonar, hydrophones, and mechanical arms for experiments and sample collection on the seabed.

'I'll crank them up, Waldo.'

'Melissa, if I'm not mistaken, my old mobile drill tower is out in number two warehouse.'

'I think it's still there, Dad.'

'I want you to have one of the Seabeds hook up a Sno-Cat and pull the rig out near the coast. As soon as you're set up, drill into the crust beneath the snow.'

'What am I looking for?'

'If you hit it, you'll know. I'm not playing games, sweetheart. I just want you to reach your own conclusions without any prior bias from me. Fair?'

Melissa smiled. 'You're always fair, Dad.'

Gates said, 'We'll play it your way, Waldo.'

'Charlie, I'd like a moment with my daughter.'

Gates rose. 'Of course, Waldo. I'll keep you advised.'

Melissa's eyes searched her father's as Gates left.

'I'm going to call Josh,' Rankin said. 'We need him.'

Melissa stared at her father. 'For God's sake why?'

'We've got to have the best media voice we can get. Someone who can put news stories and bulletins together fast when the sheet reaches the Pacific and the inevitable meltdown begins. Coastal populations will have to be given a steady stream of news about which shores will go under and when.'

Melissa threw up her hands. 'I understand all that, Dad. But why Josh? He's not the only damn journalist on the planet. I'm not really sure we could work together. God knows, we don't seem to be able to live together.'

Rankin had that stern admonishing look that always froze her in guilt as a child. 'Now, listen to me, Melissa. If our projections don't go out fast and accurately, if they aren't received with instant credence, millions of people could drown. Millions. We need a journalist with an internationally respected by-line communicating our reports. A journalist with media contacts throughout the Pacific. That's Josh. You're going to have to put aside any personal feelings. So will he.'

She was trapped. 'You're right, Dad. I'm sorry.'

'Let's set to work, sweetheart. I'll need that map projection as soon as possible.'

'About an hour.'

'Good. I'll talk to you soon.'

Across 12,000 miles, Melissa blew him a kiss. 'Bye, Dad.'

Rankin returned to the kitchen. 'Son of a bitch!' The bluefish was a black curl in the smoking pan. He took the skillet outside and put it on a railing post for the scavenger gulls to pick clean.

Below, the waves curled and pounded against the beach, the surf constantly washing away and rebuilding the sand and stone hook of Cape Cod. He was suddenly, achingly aware the rising seas would inexorably eat their way up the slope of the dunes and take his home. Melissa's home. Ingrid's home.

There was nothing he could do, nothing any power on earth could do to stop the coming assault of the oceans against the shores and coastal cities of the world.

For a long time Rankin stared out over the grey sea.

A large jut-ribbed mongrel dog, having failed in his night's search for a pliant bitch, paused on the slope of a wooded hill and wailed his frustration into the predawn gloom of Tiburon, California.

In his bedroom a quarter of a mile away, Joshua McCoy shot bolt upright in bed, the raucous howl from below yanking an adrenal trigger in the fear centre of his mind.

For that horrible moment between deep sleep and wakening, the lingering cry of the dog was the howl of the starving wolves that stalked the Hindu Kush mountains of Afghanistan.

He'd been on his first assignment as a foreign correspondent for the *New York Times*, covering a *mujahedin* guerrilla force during the second Soviet-Afghan War, in 1988.

A blizzard had caught the resistance group in a boulder-strewn valley near the Salang Pass, thirty miles north of Kabul. McCoy and two guerrillas became separated and found a cave to wait out the storm.

The wolves came as the snow slackened before dawn. It was only years after savage war had stripped the last bush fowl from the feral countryside that the emaciated wolves took to hunting humans. The animals seemed to know when men where vulnerable.

The three men had no wood for a fire to hold the pack at bay and but two clips of ammunition for their captured Kalashnikov rifles. Their only defence was to wait until the snarling animals were partway into their cavern, close enough to be sure of a kill with a single bullet.

When the *mujahedin* main force returned two days later, there were twenty dead wolves ringing the cave entrance. The men inside had four bullets left.

He'd never forgotten the nearness of the yellow eyes and slavering teeth and the howls that shrieked out of a primeval nightmare.

The cry of the dog finally faded and McCoy's heart slowed.

He'd come back from Afghanistan twenty pounds lighter, new furrows in his face, a sober, thoughtful cast to the green eyes that had witnessed so much human suffering and carnage.

When he stepped off the plane in New York, he'd found that his stories chronicling the struggle of the freedom fighters of Afghanistan had earned him the Pulitzer Prize for international correspondence. His career took off.

McCoy reached for the tissue on his nightstand and wiped the oily sweat of fear from his face.

He'd spent several months in Christchurch in 1989 covering the conception of the Antarctic Conference. He'd come to respect and then form a close friendship with Admiral Waldo Rankin, the beleaguered new director of resource development in Antarctica. A week after they'd met, Rankin introduced McCoy to his daughter, Melissa.

She was an exciting woman, a brilliant polar researcher unafraid to work for long dark months in the most hostile environment on earth, and in bed a lithe, golden-haired goddess as hungry for him as he for her.

They'd fallen in love on their first date and were married in a spartan ceremony at the American Consulate a month later.

They'd had only stolen hours together in Christchurch. Perhaps that had been part of their allure for each other. McCoy had spent far more time with her father, championing a cause they both believed in.

When the industrial nations proposed assigning mineral rights on the basis of production output, a ploy to guarantee the technologically astute countries a disproportionate share of the continent's riches, Rankin had turned to McCoy for help in opposing the manoeuvre.

The correspondent's detailed series in the *Times*, run

with the encouragement and support of the science editor, August Sumner, had exposed the inequities of the proposal. The global outcry that followed had forced the more sophisticated nations to retrench, and when Antarctic mining rights were formally assigned, the resources were equitably shared.

Rankin had given McCoy and the *Times* a large share of the credit for the victory, and McCoy's international stature rose another notch.

He'd covered the American preparations for the manned landing on Mars in 1992. The next year he'd followed up a lead and broke the story of the French genetic engineers who'd discovered a hormone that retarded the aging process. When the cell stimulant was finally synthesized in another year or so, it promised to add a third to the human life-span.

He'd been reassigned frequently during the nineties, posted to Beijing, Cape Town, London. Melissa had continued her own career, spending the nine-month winter seasons in Antarctica every second year. Somehow they'd conceived two children, the births coming the odd years he and Melissa were together.

Shea was born in China; Kate, two years later in South Africa. Despite his misgivings that their small girls needed a mother at home, Melissa had insisted on her regular biannual returns to the ice.

He'd made do with governesses and housekeepers, taking on much of the mother's role himself. He'd learned to mix formulas and kiss away the pain of skinned knees. He'd led a spartan social life, hoarding his free time for the children. After so many years raising Shea and Kate almost alone, he knew his children far better than most fathers. As babies he'd known what each of their different cries meant, when they were tired, frightened, needed changing. Now he could look into their faces and judge their emotions, their moods. They were like little books he read every day, and he loved every page of them.

In 1996 McCoy had been named the *Times* bureau chief in Moscow. Then last year he'd taken over the responsibility for news coverage throughout the burgeoning countries of the Pacific basin as that region replaced the North Atlantic area as the global centre of technology and commerce.

McCoy heard whispers outside his door and a moment later a small face wearing granny glasses peered around the jamb.

'You OK, Daddy?' his nine-year-old daughter asked. 'I heard you yell.'

'Just a bad dream, Shea,' he said. 'I'm sorry I woke you.'

Six-year-old Kate appeared beside her sister. 'What's going on?' she said, her words slurred with sleep.

He laughed and held out his arms. 'C'mere you guys. I need a hug.'

Sisters, yet so different, McCoy mused as his daughters nestled one on each side into the folds of his arms. Shea was highly sensitive, gentle and shy, a beautiful little girl with smooth faultless skin and long straight brown hair. Kate was light-haired, outgoing, boisterous, and afraid of nothing.

His daughters were his joy, and he loved them deeply. When they were very small their constant demands had worn him down at times. It hadn't helped that they'd lived in foreign countries half the time.

Kate ran a hand against his beard stubble. 'What time are we going out on the boat, Daddy?'

McCoy had promised to take them sailing out to the Farallon Islands on the thirty-five-foot catamaran he kept in the Tiburon marina. He looked at the bedside clock; it was almost 6 A.M. No point in trying to get back to sleep.

'Looks like we're all up for the day. We might as well get cracking early. If we can catch the ebb tide, we'll be through the Gate by eight.'

'What about breakfast?' Kate reminded him. 'Soledad isn't awake yet.'

McCoy tousled his youngest's hair. 'Soledad isn't the only one around here who can cook. I will personally prepare breakfast this morning.'

Soledad Allegrotti had come to them as a housekeeper five years before and quickly become a beloved member of the family and surrogate mother to the girls. At eighty-three, she was a woman of extraordinary vitality, with a great, good heart, and one of the wisest people McCoy had ever known.

'But you burn everything!' Kate protested.

He made a mock long face. 'Burn everything!'

'Kate's right, Dad,' Shea chimed in. 'The last time you did eggs Soledad had to buy a new pan.'

'And twenty-seven bottles of room spray stuff,' Kate said, grinning.

He laughed again. 'That many?'

'I could make French toast,' Shea volunteered, her eyes round with the prospect of actually cooking something for her father. 'Soledad taught me.'

McCoy smiled down into her serious nine-year-old face. There was fear in his love for Shea, a fear that she was too fragile to absorb the blows that come in every life. He wondered how long he could shelter her, stand between her and hurt.

He found it bitterly ironic that he had caused his oldest daughter the greatest pain she had known in her young life. His marriage to Melissa had degenerated into acrimonious sniping whenever she was home with them, and the fights always tortured Shea.

Whatever love he'd shared with Melissa had withered long ago. Their long separations had made them strangers, forced and impatient with each other, their lovemaking awkward and increasingly infrequent. They just didn't seem to know each other, and looking back, he doubted they ever had.

The running battle with Melissa surfaced in ugly scenes. He'd swear to himself that he'd never be drawn in again, then the tension would erupt and he'd find himself suddenly in the midst of loud venomous exchanges with his wife. Like so many children, Shea had walked the swaying tightrope between parents who loved her but not each other.

'Okay, Shea,' he said. 'You're in charge of breakfast. Need any help?'

'No, except Kate could set the table.'

The six-year-old somersaulted forward out of her father's arms down the length of the bed. 'I always set the table. Besides, Sundays I shave with dad.'

'Table setting sounds just the job for a cashiered cook,' McCoy said, dodging a pillow Kate sailed at his head. 'After we shave, you can show me where Soledad hides things. Now you guys get dressed and start breakfast while I take a shower.'

The girls jumped down and headed for the room they shared. 'Don't start shaving until I get there, Dad,' Kate said, skipping backward through the door.

'Won't even lather up.'

He rose and stretched. The muscles in his lower back were still sore from a hard set of tennis two days before. Getting old, he thought, crossing the room to pull the curtains.

At forty-one his face was strong, with prominent cheekbones, thick eyebrows arching over wide-set intelligent eyes, and a Celtic nose, once broken. He had a cleft chin, and along the right ridge of his jaw a two-inch-long scar from a skiing accident shone whitely through his fading tan.

His six-foot-one-inch body was broad-shouldered and solidly muscled, although lately he'd been feeling slack about the middle.

He opened the curtains and stepped through the sliding glass door onto a long redwood veranda. They'd bought the hillside house in Tiburon for its panoramic view, and he'd never been sorry.

Beyond the veranda the shadowed expanse of San Francisco Bay stretched south towards the still-dark silhouette of the city. Above the Berkeley Hills the rising sun reddened the eastern sky, and to the west a dough roll of fog fed in through the Golden Gate from the open ocean.

He looked down with petty satisfaction at the silver

snail trails leading across the wood to Melissa's large planter boxes. She'd put in spring annuals last autumn so there'd be flowers to greet her when she returned from the ice. The slimy little bastards were probably devouring the bulbs. Served her right. Dammit, she should have stayed home where she belonged.

He watched a fishing smack beat down the lightening bay past Sausalito on the way to its crab pots off Point Bonita.

The truth was Melissa hadn't really belonged to any of the homes he'd made with the kids over the past years. Heart and mind, his wife never really left Antarctica.

It was Anya who should be here, laughing with the children, singing soft Ukrainian folk songs, sharing his bed.

Ironically, Melissa had introduced them.

It all began when Melissa had been scheduled to leave for Antarctica the same month McCoy was assigned to Moscow as bureau chief for the *Times*. She had rearranged her itinerary so that she could come to Russia for a couple of weeks to organize the apartment and settle the children in school.

While she was in Moscow Melissa had attended a polar symposium at the Russian Antarctic Institute. There she met the newly appointed director, Anna Yegorovna Cherepin.

The professional bond between the two women blossomed into a personal friendship over lunch the next day. That night Melissa brought Anna, or Anya, as they came to call her, home to meet her husband and children. The American family took to the Ukrainian woman immediately, and at the end of the evening they all insisted that Anya return.

McCoy found himself looking forward to Anya's visits. There was an easy rapport between them from the first. They liked the same music and books, and he discovered Anya shared an identical irreverent sense of humour.

He was drawn to her sexually as well. Her deep dark

eyes and the full curves of her breasts and hips conveyed a musky Slavic sensuality.

Neither he nor Anya had planned what happened. There had been no manoeuvring, no eye contact behind Melissa's back, no clandestine rendezvous in a sweaty bed.

They had simply fallen in love, at arm's length, in full view of his wife.

Still, he was a married man and Anya was his wife's friend, and for long weeks after Melissa left for Antarctica they stuffed wedges of ethics and guilt between them. They loved but didn't make love.

Then the month before Christmas, a tornado of news struck with the sudden change in the Russian leadership. McCoy spent a string of sixteen- to twenty-hour days interviewing, writing, and running the frenetic *Times* bureau. By the first of the year he was exhausted, and Anya worried over the fatigue in his eyes and voice. He badly needed a rest.

She'd borrowed a country dacha from a colleague and invited McCoy and the girls out to Peredelkino the following weekend. McCoy had shook his head. The children were going to Leningrad on Friday for a three-day class trip.

Anya had insisted he come anyway. The dacha didn't have a phone. He could read, walk in the woods, relax. Two days later they had driven out to Peredelkino. He could see in her eyes that they would sleep together that night. But her eyes hadn't told him she was a virgin.

Afterward, remembering how timidly she'd returned his kisses at first, how tense and frightened she'd been when he'd held her against him, he wondered why he hadn't known all along.

For two days they gave themselves to each other, devoured each other, and when they drove back to Moscow hand in hand that Sunday night, neither had ever been happier.

With the girls away, his apartment had felt lonely and empty when Anya dropped him off. He'd rattled around

51

for an hour thinking, a dozen emotions washing over him. He would not have Anya confined to the shadows of his life. He didn't want her to be the 'other woman', who spent every Christmas alone.

He must tell Melissa. Tonight. It was not as if he were suddenly jilting her, tossing her aside. There had been nothing between them for years. A divorce would be hard on the children, but he saw no other way. He picked up the phone and put through a satellite call to Antarctica.

Melissa had listened without a word as he told her he loved another woman, that he wanted a divorce. She remained silent for several moments after he finished.

'Are you still there, Melissa?' he'd asked.

'Yes, Josh, I'm still here,' she'd said, a crack in her voice, a crack of pain he hadn't expected. 'You'll have to give me some time to accept all this. Whether or not I agree, we can't take any legal steps until I return. We can't get divorced over the phone, can we?'

'No, we'll have to wait,' he agreed. 'I just wanted to be honest with you, tell you about Anya, and give you a chance to think. I don't want to hurt you, Melissa, not any more than I already have. But I want Anya, I want a chance to be happy.'

She'd sounded on the verge of tears. 'We'll talk about all that in November. Please kiss the girls for me and tell them their mother loves them.'

'I will.'

'Good-bye, Josh.'

Anya began to share his bed three, four, five, times a week. Often she arrived in time for dinner with the children. Many nights she came later, when Shea and Kate were asleep. And every morning she got up at 5 A.M. and left before the girls and Soledad got up.

As wonderful as the nights were with Anya, still none was ever again as perfect as Peredelkino. There was guilt in bed with them in McCoy's apartment. They were adulterers, and after the KGB visited Anya, they knew they would never be anything else.

Melissa arrived in Moscow the following October. They

hadn't talked about the divorce, not a word. By then he'd known Anya would never be allowed to leave the country. They'd never marry.

Perhaps she'd read between the lines in his letters about the children, but somehow Melissa sensed that the threat of divorce had passed, that for the sake of the girls Josh would remain in the marriage. She never asked why. She never mentioned Anya.

Instead, she'd surprised him by announcing she was taking a sabbatical from her research work. She was scheduled to return to the ice the following November, but meanwhile she had a year off and she wanted to spend it getting to know the children.

They agreed she'd take Shea and Kate back to Tiburon. The California schools were better, and the girls had spent too long growing up in foreign cultures. They needed time with their American peers. Josh could fly in as often as possible while he finished up his remaining year at the Moscow bureau.

He hated to admit it, but he'd been relieved when the kids flew home with Melissa. He was increasingly ashamed of what he'd been forced to become, and he found it agonizing to look into his daughters' trusting faces and know he was not the father, the man, they thought him to be.

His mouth tightened remembering the morning after Peredelkino when Anya told him Chirikov's dacha had been bugged. The KGB had taped their entire weekend together. They'd recorded everything.

The Soviet Committee for State Security offered a straight quid pro quo. They would destroy the tapes in return for Mr McCoy's cooperation in certain sensitive matters. If he refused, Anya would be immediately stripped of her position and assigned to obscurity somewhere in the belly of the Soviet Union.

There was no question of spying, the KGB emphasized. Mr McCoy was an esteemed journalist with an international reputation for accurate, perceptive reporting, and they simply wished his personal assessment of certain foreign governments and their leadership.

He risked no disloyalty to America or his country's interests. Indeed, the better Soviet decision makers understood democratic motives, the less chance would exist for East-West discord and the nearer world peace would be. But neither he nor Anya were under any illusion that the KGB would long be content with just his political appraisals. It would only be a question of time before they attempted to set the hook and draw him into espionage.

Yet if he refused to cooperate, he would never see Anya again. He couldn't let that happen, he couldn't lose her. He took the only way out. He arranged a meeting with the CIA station chief at the American Embassy.

McCoy came to an understanding with the US intelligence. He would relay the KGB queries, and the agency would supply the appropriate misinformation. The director himself would fly up to New York and brief the *Times* publisher, Maxwell Chadding.

McCoy's work as a journalist took him to the embassy often, and his visits weren't suspect. During his third session with the station chief, the agent came around his desk with a large, flat suede-covered case.

'I'd like you to pick out something personal for Anya,' he said, opening the lid. 'Something she might wear often.'

McCoy stared incredulously at the array of watches, necklaces, brooches, and bracelets in the box. They were all of inexpensive Russian design, a few gaudy, but most simple, tasteful.

He selected a single large cultured pearl set in the centre of a long silver chain and dangled the necklace six inches from his eyes, scrutinizing the setting. 'Bug?'

The station chief shook his head. 'No, microchip recorder-transmitter. It's a way for Anya to contact us if the normal channels fail. It could save her life, Mr McCoy.'

Anya had never used the microchip transmitter. She'd never had to, thank God. Still the game they'd played for two years was difficult and dangerous.

54

For the first several months the KGB had pumped him about South Africa, where he'd been assigned for almost a year. What was his assessment of the country, the strengths and weaknesses of its people and economy? Was the government likely to send the army north if an insurgency movement broke out in Zimbabwe? Would the United States support Pretoria?

And what did he know of Prime Minister Botha? Did Botha chase women, drink, gamble, was he intransigent, compromising, hard, soft? What motivated the man, what drove him?

During his assignment in Moscow the KGB asked for detailed characterizations of most of the statesmen he had covered and interviewed for the *Times*, particularly the newly elected President Wollcott in Washington.

McCoy had torn up the careful biographies supplied by the CIA and instead sketched portraits that emphasized the strengths and blurred the weaknesses he had detected in the men.

Beyond seeing Anya, that subterfuge was the only satisfaction he found in the obscene business. He was bitter at being used, by both sides, torn that he'd compromised his professional ethics.

And in the end he had lost Anya anyway. Anya.

A young voice erupted behind him. 'Daddy!' You haven't even taken a shower yet and I've already got the bread soaking in the eggs.'

Shea's French toast! He crossed the veranda feeling terrible and bent to the hurt little face. 'I'm sorry, Shea. Really. I let my mind wander. If breakfast is ready, so am I.'

She brightened hopefully. 'What about your shower?'

He picked her up and carried her towards the kitchen. 'I'll be a smelly bear today. C'mon, I'm hungry.'

NORTHDRIFT
28.7 Nautical Miles


The Japanese Antarctic Krill Fishing Fleet steamed steadily east across the Ross Sea at twelve knots, the reinforced steel-plated bows of the four ships slicing effortlessly through the drifting and broken ice floes fifty-five miles off the coast of Marie Byrd Land.

On the wing bridge of the 18,000-ton *Awa Maru*, the fleet's factory ship and flag vessel, Captain Makato Okada scanned the seas with his binoculars.

He frowned. The squadron's diamond formation was flawed. The SS *Wakasa* and the SS *Kumano* were in position off the stern flanks, but the SS *Nikko* had fallen too far behind.

The captain cocked a finger at a bridge messenger, bringing the young sailor instantly to his side.

'Tell the second mate to order the *Nikko* up. She is out of formation.'

'Hai, Captain!' The sailor saluted, disappearing into the bridge house.

Okada was a strict disciplinarian. He was also immensely proud of his small flotilla. The ships had all been manufactured in the modern Mitshubi Works in Kobe, and none was over ten years old.

In the mid-eighties the Japanese had begun commercially harvesting the teeming schools of krill that abounded in the frigid waters off the Antarctic continent. The krill could be fished cheaply, and the Third World nations desperately needed the protein supplement in their diets.

Okada lowered his binoculars and rubbed his nose with a gloved hand. The air temperature seemed several degrees colder than normal for the Antarctic spring.

Ah! I am getting old, he thought. It is well I retire this year. Polar fishing is for younger men.

56

He left the wing for the warmth of the bridge house.

The first mate, Kanji Takahashi, was waiting just inside. It was time for him to relieve Okada on watch. The first mate was tall for a Japanese, almost six feet, and athletically built. He had a ready smile and a quick, lively sense of humour. Both his fellow officers and the men under him liked Takahashi immensely.

The young officer bowed stiffly to Okada in the Japanese naval tradition. As always, Okada was pleased, although it was unthinkable to show it. Too many young men nowadays ignore the old ways, he thought.

'What is the weather report?' Okada asked.

Takahashi read from his clipboard: 'Sea calm, with one-half- to one-metre swells. Overcast, cumulus clouds at eighteen hundred metres. Sea temperature, minus two degrees Celsius. Air temperature, minus twenty-seven degrees Celsius.'

So I was right, Okada thought, the air and sea temperatures are both below normal.

'Sir, we are getting an unusual reading on the radar,' Takahashi said. 'We would value your opinion.'

Okada swore silently. The new satellite-linked radar had been installed on all four ships of the fishing fleet before they left their home port of Yokahama. These sets were a product of Japan's sophisticated electronics industry, computerized, modern miracles, according to the Matsushita Corporation, the manufacturers.

To Okada they were incomprehensible, infernal machines that had vexed him during the voyage to Antarctica. They were full of bugs! Matsushita had apparently expected some shakedown problems. One of their electronics wizards was assigned on board.

Okada followed Takahashi to the small room behind the wheelhouse where the radar was housed. The Matsushita technician was behind the machine, with some sort of testing device in one hand and a folded diagram of the mysterious inner workings of the set in the other.

Takahashi pointed to the small green screen hooded

against intrusive light. A white radius swept the glowing tube, as a second hand would a clockface.

As the radius swept across the nine-o'clock position, small white pips appeared on the screen behind it, glowed for a moment, then faded as the hand moved on. Normal clusters of broken pack ice and drifting floes, Okada knew.

The hand arched past the ten-o'clock mark, suddenly leaving a field of complete white in its wake. Okada watched incredulously as the radius swept through twelve- o'clock, one, two, three. The entire top one third of the screen had showed up white.

The radar's satellite eyes saw a solid object dead ahead stretching across the horizon.

'It showed up twenty minutes ago, Captain,' Takahashi said.

'What is the scanning distance, Takahashi?'

'Short range.'

'Put the set on long range.'

Takahashi reached down and flipped a switch on the console. The screen flickered, went blank for an instant, then the green glow returned. They watched the hand make its sweep. This time almost the entire screen showed white.

'It's a fogbank,' Okada finally said.

'But, Captain, look at the density. Whatever it is shows up as a solid object,' Takahashi gently argued. 'Perhaps an iceberg.'

'Impossible!' Okada fumed, annoyed with the misleading radar and with Takahashi for being fooled by it. 'The long- range capability of this glorious new radar of ours is six hundred and fifty kilometres. That image fills the set. That's then the largest iceberg ever recorded, Takahashi.'

The first mate bowed. 'Unquestionably you are correct, Captain. A fogbank. It is only that the satellite scan shows such a solid density. As it is directly astride our present heading, I felt it was wise to consult with you.'

Okada relented. 'You did the correct thing, Takahashi. If I had not taken a sextant reading myself ten minutes ago, I might not be as certain. We are almost ninety kilometres off the Ross Ice Shelf. Our course parallels the coast. There is no need for alarm.'

'Yes, Captain.'

'Undoubtedly that orbiting piece of space junk above us is misreading ice crystals within the fogbank.'

Okada turned to the technician now replacing a small plate on the back of the console. 'Can't you do something with this cursed machine? Now it's showing immense phantom images!'

The Matsushita expert shook his head. 'I can find nothing wrong, Captain. The satellite feed is functioning correctly. Are you sure of your position?'

Okada went purple with rage. 'How dare you question my navigation? I have commanded ships for twenty-five years. Get off my bridge. At once!'

The technician realized too late he had stepped over a dangerous boundary. They had warned him in Kobe. The captain was from the old school, a regular 'Tojo'. He lowered his head and slunk off the bridge, silently cursing his thoughtless question.

Okada cast the radar a scornful look and went to the large, insulated glass window facing the bow. Takahashi followed silently. The captain lifted his binoculars and scanned the sea ahead. A wall of fog was just visible on the horizon.

He motioned Takahashi to his side. 'There it is. Although I admit this is not the normal season for it, nevertheless you can see for yourself a fogbank lies directly ahead.'

The first mate took the proffered glasses and studied the mist.

Face prevented him from admitting it, but the captain was both surprised and unnerved by the thick vapour ahead. In over three decades of fishing, he had never encountered fog this early in the year.

'Satisfied?'

'Yes, sir,' Takahashi said sheepishly.

'Now, come with me.'

Okada led the way to the small chart room behind the bridge.

'Ring navigation and get an exact fix,' Okada ordered.

Takahashi made the call, jotting down the figures he was given.

'Now plot our position, Takahashi.'

The first mate bent over the chart table and quickly lined in the position of the *Awa Maru* on the transparent overlay. He straightened and gave Okada the answer he expected. 'We are ninety-one kilometres off the Ice; latitude – '

Okada held up a hand. 'Enough. I know your navigation to be superb, Takahashi. The lesson I am trying to teach you concerns computers, satellites. You cannot always trust them. You must use your senses, your own logic.'

'I understand, Captain.'

'That damnable new radar is the perfect example. It would have us believe that is a six-hundred-and-fifty-kilometre iceberg ahead. An iceberg of such size has never existed, never will. The radar is wrong and I am right.'

'I shall remember, sir.'

Okada grunted. 'Good. It is your watch, Takahashi. Signal the fleet to close to two hundred metres and commence the foghorn drill two kilometres before we enter the bank. I don't want any strays. I'll be in my cabin.'

'Yes, Captain.' Takahashi saluted as Okada left the bridge. Normally, the ship's master remained topside during fog conditions, but Okada had been training his first mate to take over his command next year. He wanted Takahashi to assume as much responsibility as possible on this voyage.

Takahashi had the radio operator signal the *Kumano*, *Wakasa*, and *Nikko* to close within two hundred metres and turn on their foghorns. Thirty minutes later the small fleet was in position, strung out in a shallow arc facing the mist.

The minutes crept by placidly. In his cabin, Captain Okada sat cross-legged on a straw mat using a long-handled brush to put the finishing touches on a delicate rice-paper watercolour. He could feel the deep, steady throbbing of the engines and the slight rise and fall of the ship in the swell, the nerves of his body sensitive to every small vibration of the *Awa Maru*.

From the ship to starboard, Okada could hear American love songs blaring from a tape cassette. He much preferred the tranquil strains of traditional Japanese music himself, although he occasionally enjoyed the Western classics. He sighed and added blue to a bird wing.

On the bridge, Kanji Takahashi watched the fogbank loom up several hundred yard ahead. He raised his binoculars and once more swept the line of ships. Each was correctly positioned, their foghorns regularly echoing off the thick mist. Satisfied, he lowered the glasses and stared straight ahead into the thick vapour.

Then the fog was upon them and the bow disappeared into the grey swirls. Instantly the air felt much colder to Takahashi. A chill ran through him. The hair on the back of his neck and on his arms stood up straight. He sensed a presence in the fog. Something was out there!

At that instant the sickening screech of metal ripping and crushing tore through the ship like the scream of a wounded beast. The vessel shuddered and lurched violently as the bow lifted and rose at a forty-five-degree angle, pushing upward into the fog seventy feet above the sea.

Takahashi crashed backward into a bulkhead, his head snapping viciously against the steel plate. As if in a dream, he watched the huge starboard anchor, trailing its broken chain behind, hurtling down at him out of the mist. His quick reflexes took over before his stunned mind could function, rolling his body off the bridge to the deck twenty feet below. He was dimly aware of ice cascading down all around him before he blacked out.

The anchor and tons of jagged ice ripped through the bridge, crushing men and machinery into an unrecognizable mass of torn bodies and twisted metal. The siren used to signal sonar detection of schools of krill went off madly, drowning out the screams and throat-rattling sounds of men dying.

Live electric cables tore from their conduits and swept the decks, flaying the living and dead alike. Great blue-white chunks of ice shattered steam pipes, and jets of furious vapour exploded upward, scalding to death two lookouts in the crow's nest, eighty feet above the deck.

Below, Captain Okada was thrown violently against the steel-plated bulkhead and knocked momentarily unconscious. He fought his way back to awareness, clawing through swirling cobwebs, forcing his eyes open.

He couldn't see! He reached up and realized his face was covered with blood, his forehead badly sliced. He tore a piece of cloth from his shirt, wiped the blood from his eyes, and crawled to the cabin door, sprung open on impact. The passage-way outside tilted crazily upward, the end leading to the bridge now open to the freezing air and fog. He grasped the handrail and weakly pulled himself fist over fist up the corridor to the gaping hole above.

The bridge was an incredible scene of carnage. The men he had left shortly before were unrecognizable in death: decapitated, mutilated, fused into the metal of the rear bulkhead. He gaped incredulously at the sight of the bow disappearing up into the swirling gray vapour. Then Okada became aware of the ice. Great chunks of it embedded in the wreck of the bridge and sliding down the slanting decks.

The radar had been right! But where had it come from? There had never been an iceberg over six hundred and fifty kilometres wide. The largest he'd ever heard of was a fifth that size. They couldn't have struck the Ice Shelf along the shore. He had checked their position himself. He had made Takahashi do the same. They were far out at sea.

Off to port he heard muffled collisions and instantly human screams seemed to come from every direction in the fog. The fleet! The *Kumano, Wakasa,* and *Nikko* had been close behind the *Awa Maru*. They, too, must have struck the ice. From starboard the screech of ripping metal again tore over the sea. Another ship had smashed into the frozen monster hiding in the mist. Helplessly he clung to the twisted stump of the bridge wheel, the awful realization that four good ships were dying at that moment driving him to the point of insanity.

Then, through the blood and tears of frustration, he glimpsed a hand grasp the solitary piece of bridge rail still standing. He stared, frozen to the buckled deck, as Takahashi pulled himself up from below.

'It was in the fog,' Takahashi gasped.

The words snapped Okada back to his senses. He leaped forward and helped the first mate up. For a moment they stared at each other wordlessly.

'I am to blame . . . I . . . ' Takahashi stammered.

Okada gripped the taller man's shoulders. 'No, Takahashi. I am in command. I bear the responsibility. You could have done nothing.'

'I was on watch,' the young officer said woodenly, his eyes dull, vacant.

Okada slapped him hard twice across the face. The first mate leaned back away from the blows, then seemed to steady.

'Pull yourself together, Takahashi. We must get the crew into the lifeboats.'

Takahashi winced. The shock was wearing off. The first mate looked around him, as if he were seeing the destruction for the first time.

'The satellite phone, Captain, we must report our position.'

Okada shook his head and pointed towards the starboard side, where the anchor had torn through the bridge and on into the communications room.

'Even if it still works we cannot get to the set.' Okada said.

Takahashi looked and shuddered. Live electric cables hissed spasmodically in and out of the jagged entrance, like vipers guarding the door to a sacred Hindu temple.

'We must get the crew into the lifeboats towards the stern, Takahashi. The ones forward are now too far above the water,' Okada said, sweeping a hand towards the sharply upward angling bow.

'At once, Captain,' Takahashi said, back in control.

'I'll send the men still inside to you, Takahashi. There is little time.'

Okada disappeared down the open corridor into the bowels of the *Awa Maru*. Takahashi watched him go, then lowered himself to the boat deck below. The footing was treacherous with slivers of ice. The ship suddenly listed to port, the lifeboats swinging out and away from the port side of the vessel, where Takahashi now balanced precariously. He half slid down the sloping deck towards the stern.

The surviving crew had also realized that the forward boats would be useless. There was a knot of terrified sailors at the first aft lifeboat station. Two of the men were heaving ropes at the dories swaying far out over the water, trying vainly to pull the two crafts in close enough to board.

'Idiots!' Takahashi screamed. 'Calm yourselves. You will never bring them in that way.'

The officer's chastisement had an immediate effect. The men stood back. The inherent Japanese respect for authority cut through even panic.

Takahashi pointed to an emergency firebox. 'Get me that axe,' he thundered.

One of the men leapt forward, tore the tool from its mounting, and handed it to the first mate. Takahashi snatched a rope from the deck and knotted it securely around the axe handle. He motioned the men clear and swung the axe in an arc, loosing it finally towards the first lifeboat. It sailed over the top of the craft and Takahashi yanked, snaring the hooked edge of the blade on the inner gunwale. The crewmen rushed to the rail and helped him pull the boat in.

Four minutes later the dory was full and descending in jerks down the sloping side of the *Awa Maru* towards the freezing sea below. The craft at the adjoining station were brought in the same way. Takahashi sent two men to starboard to bring the sailors struggling with the lifeboats there back to the port side. Small groups of seamen appeared from the crew quarters, the galley, the freezer compartments, the engine room. The captain is working fast, Takahashi thought.

Two more lifeboats were lowered into the sea. Now there was one usable dory left, one last chance for escape from the rapidly settling ship.

He questioned several men. All the crew were accounted for, either in the lifeboats or dead. Captain Okada fought his way down the slanted, slippery deck.

'Abandon ship, Kanji. You are in command of the survivors. Keep the boats together, the men as warm as possible. Tell them in Yokahama what happened. Give them my apologies.'

'Captain, no! You must come with us. You couldn't have known. Whatever this evil thing Antarctica has spawned, it is no mere iceberg. You saw the radar.'

Okada's face was incongruously peaceful. 'No, Takahashi. You will warn them what lies in these waters. A killer of fleets! I stay with my ship. Now go.'

Takahashi knew no amount of pleading would change the captain's mind. He was of the old school. He turned sadly and descended the icy deck towards the last lifeboat. They lowered the dory quickly into the sea and pulled away from the stricken, dying ship.

Fifty yards off, Takahashi ordered the small inboard motor cut. The men stared silently back at the *Awa Maru*. They could see Okada clearly on the bridge wing.

The captain faced the boats and slowly brought his hand up to his weather cap. Takahashi stood, tears running down his cheeks as he returned the salute.

A moment later the *Awa Maru* began her final slide into the freezing depths.

'Start the motor,' Takahashi roared.

The lifeboat pulled away quickly from the sinking ship, fleeing the inevitable downward suction that would come when the *Awa Maru* disappeared beneath the waves. Well clear, Takahashi ordered the motor idled once more, and they watched until the final knife edge of the bow slipped into the ice-choked waves.

Silence filled the lifeboat. Takahashi became aware that the men were all staring at him, waiting for his orders. He pulled himself together and looked down about the dory. Several of the fishermen had obvious wounds, blood congealed on their faces. He realized there must be other injuries. At least two of the crewmen looked to be in shock. Yet the worst danger, he knew, was not the injuries of shock but the freezing air temperature. It was minus twenty-seven degrees Celsius.

And there were the other lifeboats to consider. They were somewhere in the fog. 'Keep the boats together,' the captain had said. That was the first thing he must do, before the other dories scattered hopelessly over the Antarctic swells.

Takahashi picked up the bridge bullhorn he had brought aboard and called into the swirling grey fog, his electrified voice echoing off the nearby frozen cliffs of the Ross Ice Shelf.

# NORTHDRIFT
## 33.9 Nautical Miles

Joshua McCoy put a cool box with sandwiches and cold drinks in the trunk of his car, then turned to the open door of the house. 'C'mon, you guys. We don't want to miss the tide.'

Six-year-old Kate skipped out of the door. 'I'm all ready, Dad.'

'Where's Shea?'

'She forgot her windbreaker.'

McCoy heard the phone ring inside, then Shea's trilling, 'Grandpa!'

Kate flew towards the house. He followed her in, wondering why his father-in-law was calling this early on a Sunday morning. Shea met him breathlessly at the door.

'It's Grandpa, Dad. He wants to talk to you, and me and Kate after.'

'Thanks, sweetheart. I'll give you a yell.'

'We can show Grandpa our new school pictures,' Kate said.

'Yeah, good idea!' Shea agreed, and the girls bolted for their room.

McCoy sank into a chair before the videophone. His eyes narrowed in disquiet at the sight of Waldo Rankin's face. The admiral looked drawn and grey, his expression a troubled mask.

'Good morning, Josh.'

'Are you all right, Waldo?'

'I need your help.'

'Anything, Waldo, you know that.'

Rankin's granite jaw thrust towards the camera. 'A submarine fissure has broken through the seabed off the west coast of Antarctica, Josh. The volcanism has shattered the glacial bridges between the Ross Ice Shelf and the continent. The ice is adrift in the Pacific.'

McCoy looked at Rankin incredulously. He was familiar with the Antarctic topography from his work during the Treaty of Christchurch meetings.

'Good God, Waldo. Two hundred thousand square miles of ice! Any chance it'll ground itself, the currents push it back against the shore?'

'Virtually none. The continued northdrift of the Shelf is certain. And that's not the worst of what's coming, Josh. With the Shelf gone from the coast, the mouth of the Ross Sea is wide open. The entire West Antarctic Ice Sheet is going to surge through that huge gap in the coast and slide into the Pacific.'

McCoy felt an adrenal pump start. 'Then we're facing a tremendous rise in sea level.'

'Do you have a chart synthesizer on your terminal?'

McCoy nodded. 'Yes.'

'Melissa has just sent me a computer analysis of the water volume of the sheet and the land areas that would flood if the ice melts entirely into the sea. You keyed?'

McCoy hit the GRAPHICS/RECEIVE button. Rankin's image disappeared and a topographical map of the earth flicked on the screen. Oceans, gulfs, bays, rivers, and large lakes showed in blue. The continents and islands were green.

'You're looking at the relationship of land and sea as it now exists,' Rankin said. 'Here's what we face if the West Antarctic Ice Sheet melts into the oceans.'

Vast strips of the continental shorelines suddenly appeared purple, as did thousands of islands and peninsulars. Florida was almost entirely purple, along with a huge semicircle of the Gulf of Mexico coast.

In Europe, Holland was purple. The colour splashed across the coastal plains of France, Belgium, Germany, Denmark. Around the world, the map showed the sea inundating the land wherever the elevation was below twenty point six feet. The river valleys wouldn't be spared. Purple fingers reached far up the Mississippi, the Thames, the Seine, the Nile, the Amazon.

McCoy felt numb. 'This can't be happening, Waldo.'

Rankin's face replaced the chart on the screen. 'There's no way to stop it, Josh.'

'You said you needed my help.'

'When the flooding begins, so does the panic. On a global scale. The only way to fight that is with the truth, with calm and reasoned analysis of what regions must be evacuated first. There are only so many planes and ships we can use to ferry people from the vulnerable elevations.'

'What can I do?'

'I'll be monitoring the rate of the meltdown, Josh. The computers will give us the coasts and islands that will go under first. I want you to come to Antarctica with me. I want you to be my voice.'

'Antarctica!' Conflicting emotions played across McCoy's face. 'How long?'

'You'd better figure on three or four months.'

McCoy's voice was pained. 'I'll help in any way I can, Waldo, except the way you ask. I can't take off and leave the girls for that long.'

'Josh, I know how you feel and I admire you for it. I've kept my mouth shut all these years but I've always known what Melissa's work has cost you. The responsibility of raising the kids has fallen on your shoulders, and you've borne it virtually alone. You've been a damned fine father, a better one than I was. Still, what I ask transcends the needs of Shea and Kate. I say that as their grandfather, Josh. I say it knowing they'd say it.'

'You're asking me to leave them without an anchor, Waldo. I know goddamn well that with this going on Melissa won't be coming home any time soon. Suppose one of them gets sick, has an accident. Four months is a long time. Look, we have top correspondents in Tokyo, Beijing, Singapore. I could assign any one of them to you, all three if you need them.'

'It's got to be you, Josh.'

'For God's sake, why?'

'We'll be advising nations with coastal populations to begin massive evacuations that will disrupt their countries.

The source of the advisories and bulletins going out must have international credibility because the reports will be impossible for governments to verify on their own. You've got a long track record of consistently accurate and unbiased reporting from Moscow to Christchurch. Your voice will be listened to.'

'I could give you the names of journalists with far more international clout than I, Waldo.'

'Fine. But only recommend men that also have access to the largest communications network in the world and a working relationship with the chairman of the Antarctic Conference – me.'

'Waldo – '

'It's all right, Daddy,' Shea said, Kate framed beside her in the doorway.

McCoy looked at his daughter. 'What's all right, Shea?'

The girls crossed the room. Shea said, 'We were waiting at our bedroom extension to talk to Grandpa. We heard what he said. A lot of people could drown if you don't go.'

'We want you to help Grandpa,' Kate piped in.

'That's a grown-up decision for you girls to make,' Rankin said from the screen. 'I'm proud of you both.'

McCoy drew his daughters to him. 'I could be away a long time, guys. You'd be alone here with Soledad.'

'Hold on, Josh,' Rankin said. 'Everything's happened so quickly that this hadn't occurred to me before, but why not fly the girls down with you to New Zealand? We'll be headquartered in Christchurch and they could stay at my house there.'

'We could see mommy, then,' Kate said excitedly.

'And I could help with your stories, Dad,' Shea offered, her eyes wide behind her thick granny glasses. 'You said I was a good writer.'

'Well, Josh?' Rankin put in from the screen.

McCoy hugged his daughters. 'What are you guys waiting for? Say good-bye to your grandfather and go pack.'

The girls squealed simultaneously, then said in unison, 'Bye, Grandpa!' and bolted for their room.

70

'I'll call August and get the *Times* network geared up worldwide, Waldo,' McCoy said. 'When are you flying down there?'

'I have to stop in Washington first. I don't care for this administration. Bloodless bunch. Still, I wore my country's uniform for over forty years. I want to make sure our government fully understands that a large part of the responsibility for the coming evacuations will fall on American shoulders.'

'I'd like to include the reaction of the White House in my first release, Waldo. I'll hold the story until you've met with the president. Meanwhile, I'll get down to Christchurch.'

'We made a hell of a team during those treaty hearings, Josh. I'm glad we'll be together on this.'

They said good-bye and McCoy stared out over the veranda to the dawn bay. What would all this mean to Anya? The Russians were bound to send a team to Antarctica to monitor the northdrift of the Ross Shelf and the seaward surge of the Ice Sheet. Anya was the Soviet Union's foremost Antarctic expert. Would they send her?

His pulse quickened. The entire white continent was international territory. The grip of Soviet security on its citizens loosened at the bottom of the world.

There was a chance!

McCoy pulled himself back. Later, Anya. He turned to the videophone and punched in the number of the science editor of the *New York Times*.

August Sumner switched off the electric buffer and stepped back to admire the shine he'd just given his 1939 Ford 'Woody' stationwagon. Above the gleaming maroon hood and fenders, the birchwood sides glowed under a new coat of varnish.

The car always reminded him of a Bing Crosby movie set in Connecticut before World War II. The science editor's home fit the same image. The rambling white clapboard house, built in 1790, nestled on four acres of woods near the small New York town of Bedford Hills, forty-five miles north of Manhattan.

'August,' his wife called from the front door. 'Josh McCoy is on the phone.'

He crossed the lawn under the flaming autumn branches of a 200-year-old oak and kissed a flour-speckled Penelope, standing on the stoop. The smell of baking bread wafted from the kitchen. 'Thank you, darling. I'll take it in the library.'

After thirty-five years of childless marriage, they were still in love, each other's best friend and confidant. Penelope smiled. 'Tell Josh I send my love,' and went back to her oven.

The noetic Sumner had been interpreting the physical world for the *Times's* readers for over forty years, and the single library wall not lined with books was covered with framed degrees, awards, and photographs of Sumner with renowned scientists and inventors, many of them personal friends.

He sank into a deep leather chair and turned on the videophone, wondering why McCoy was calling so early on a Sunday morning. It wasn't yet 7 A.M. in California.

'Good morning, Josh.' He surveyed his friend's stricken face. 'Is there something wrong?'

'Very wrong, August, as wrong as it can get. I just got a call from Waldo Rankin.'

He told Sumner about the Ross Sea volcanism, the northdrift of the Shelf, and the coming surge of the West Antarctic Ice Sheet into the ocean.

'If Melissa's computer projections are correct, we're facing a rapid rise in sea levels,' McCoy finished.

'How much of a rise?' Sumner asked.

'Twenty point six feet, August.'

'God help us,' Sumner breathed when McCoy finished. 'Does Rankin have any hope, any hope at all that the ice will drift back against the continent, remain in Antarctic waters?'

'There's virtually no chance of that, August,' McCoy said. 'The Shelf is moving steadily north. Waldo believes the meltdown will begin within days.'

'Days!' Sumner took off the wire-framed glasses perched on his patrician nose and slowly ran a hand back through the grey hair that receded in wavy troughs from his high forehead. 'I've been a journalist and editor for four decades, Josh. I've reported starvation in Africa, genocide in Iran, that nuclear-reactor massacre in Brazil four years ago, tragedy after human tragedy. But this! Huge populations live on remote islands and coasts, far from any possible evacuation harbours or airports. Millions will drown. Millions!'

The two men stared at each other for a moment in anguish.

'We can't save everyone, August,' McCoy said quietly. 'But we're not helpless. Waldo will be feeding me his computer calculations on the rate of meltdown. He'll be able to project which shores must be evacuated first. We can zero in on those threatened populations with our broadcast facilities, hammer away at the urgency to abandon the islands, move inland from the coasts. I recommend we begin immediate twenty-four-hour-a-day situation reports on the *Times* network. We can at least give people a head start.'

'I'm sure the publisher will agree,' Sumner said. 'I'll call Chadding and get our best technical and news teams focused on this at once. Any idea which reporters you'll want? Batrowski and Fleming are both good with the scientific end.'

'Give me a day to see how this shakes out, August. I'll use staff from our Christchurch bureau to start.'

'When are you leaving?'

'I've called the airport. *Times Two* will be serviced and ready in an hour.'

*Times Two* was the plane permanently assigned to McCoy, one of two twin Gates Lear jets that functioned as self-contained airborne news-gathering centres. *Times One* was based in New York. The aircraft proved invaluable when major stories broke in remote areas of the world, where communications were primitive or nonexistent.

*Times Two* was crammed with the latest computer-enhanced media technology, from smart word processors to satellite-linked audio-video transmitters and receivers. From the plane, McCoy could reach anywhere in the world and have live television, still pictures, and printed texts beamed on board.

'Anything you need?' Sumner asked.

'I'd like to use the flight time to do some homework. I'll be requesting global topographical data, any existing studies of the interaction of ice with the open sea, probably some material on submarine volcanism.'

'Of course. I'll have the research department fully staffed by noon. The computers will be programmed to give your requests priority.'

'I'll start pulling the first piece together on the way down, and I'll send it in as soon as Washington reacts.'

The editor nodded. 'I'll get to the office.'

They looked at each other for a moment, both aware what lay ahead was far more than the covering of a story.

Sumner said, 'I wish I had something profound to say, Josh. I think you know how I feel. The *Times* is sending in the best it has. Godspeed.'

'Thank you, August.'

McCoy's image vanished from the screen, and Sumner rose. A wave of depression washed over the editor

Catastrophic change was about to befall the earth, up-heaval that would touch every man, woman, and child on the planet.

And it would be the responsibility of the *New York Times* to warn the world.

The first heavy snow of the year was falling in Moscow, putting a soft gauze mask on the stoic face of the winter grey city. At the Soviet Antarctic Institute on Kalinin Prospekt, thirty-two-year-old Anya Cherepin looked up from her desk at the sound of a knock on her door.

'Enter.'

Sergei Postyshev, her nephew and secretary, charged through the door and crossed the room rapidly. Cherepin knew by her nephew's approach that the eighteen-year-old had something important to tell her. Important to the impetuous Postyshev, at least.

Sergei reminded her unpleasantly of her father. All his life her father had been a kolkhoz, a collective-farm, worker on the wheat-growing lands near Lubny, 120 miles east of Kiev, in the Ukraine. He was a brooding man, with a frostbite-scarred face, who seemed to have been born in his sweat-stiff fur hat, quilted jacket, and rubber boots. He reeked perpetually of fertilizer.

Her mother had died two years ago. She'd been a farm tractor mechanic, as well as the doting mother of three girls and the harried wife of a crude, demanding husband. Anya had watched her mother metamorphose into a tired, sucked-out *babushka*, an old woman, before she was forty.

Anya's two older sisters lived now with their boorish labourer husbands within a few kilometres of the tiny, sagging house where she'd spent her earliest years.

But for a providential gene from God only knew what root of her peasant lineage, she would have shared their fate. To the consternation of her father and the joy of her mother, intelligence tests in her first year of school proved that Anya had a brilliant mind.

She'd been selected to attend a special school for gifted children in Lubny and later sailed through her entrance exams to the earth sciences school at Moscow University. She'd stayed at the top of her class and earned degrees in geology and mineralogy.

Two years after graduation she'd pioneered a method of sound-wave analysis that made possible the identification of ore deposits beneath the permafrost-covered polar lands of the Soviet Union.

When Antarctica was opened up to mining, she'd been assigned to help plan mineral extraction and she immersed herself in research on the white continent.

Cherepin had mastered glaciology and polar meteorology. She'd done psychological profiles of Soviet scientists who'd endured long winters on the ice isolated from the outside world. For two summers she researched the Antarctic marine food chain from the Russian bases at Mirnyi and Molodezhnaya.

Her dedication had brought her to the attention of Vladimir Chirikov, doctor of geological sciences and president of the Soviet Academy of Sciences. Over the objections of her jealous male colleagues, he had named her director of the Antarctic Institute three years ago.

Her nephew represented a compromise in her personal standards. She had always decried the rampant nepotism of the Soviet system and yet six months ago she had submitted to it herself. Her eldest sister, Yulia, had written a tearful letter. Her son, Sergei, was about to be inducted into the army. They wanted to send him to the Chinese border. So far away. He was her only boy. Couldn't Anya find him a draft-exempt job at her institute?

Cherepin was trapped. To her sisters, bogged down in the hopeless mud of the collective farm, she was a goddess living a life they could only imagine. How could she not share her good fortune with her own blood?

She had pulled strings, got Sergei a coveted Moscow *propiska*, a residence permit, and taken him on as her secretary.

'Yes, Seryozha, what is it?'

'Auntie, these photographs have just come in from the Space Flight Center at Tyuratam,' he said, waving a stack of wire-photos. 'They are from our Soyuz P7. You won't believe – '

'Stop,' Cherepin interrupted, frowning. 'First of all, you are to address me as "Comrade Director" in this office. Second, be good enough to speak slowly and intelligibly. Your verbal reports are becoming as incomprehensible as your written ones.'

Postyshev sagged, his face a deep red. 'Of course, Comrade Director. I have forgotten myself,' he said, his boyish exuberance evaporated.

Cherepin felt a pang of guilt. 'All right, Seryozha,' she said smiling, 'what is it that has so dazzled you? Have little green men landed, perhaps?'

'No, the photographs are of Antarctica,' he said warily, not quite trusting the smile. 'Something has happened to the ice.'

'May I see those, please?'

Postyshev handed over the pictures.

Cherepin turned on her desk lamp and looked at the first shot. Her jaw tightened. The photograph showed a dark slash curving around the semicircular landward rim of the Ross Ice Shelf. The line could only be open seawater, black against the surrounding glaciers.

She sat back in her chair, stunned. There could be no mistake. The entire Shelf had broken free of the continent! But how? Thirty per cent of the ice was aground. Something must have happened to the seabed below the Shelf. A submarine quake?

'Seryozha, be good enough to go over to that cabinet against the wall and get me the geological file on Antarctica. Top drawer, to the back, I believe.'

Postyshev rummaged through the drawer and returned with the folder.

There were several Soviet maps and charts, done during preliminary mineral and oil exploration. Cherepin dismissed them out of hand. They were crude compared to the

American study conducted by the US Antarctic expert Rankin.

She spread the American survey out on her desk and scrutinized the Ross Sea area. There were no fault lines indicated. Yet the map did show a dormant volcanic rift beneath the Ice Shelf.

Perhaps the fracture was not so dormant after all. The Ross Ice Shelf was essentially a floating glacier. Certainly it was possible submarine volcanism had melted away the Shelf's ice anchors to the seabed. With these restraints gone, there would be nothing to hold the Shelf against the continent.

She took a pair of calipers from her desk, got a reference from the map, and measured the width of the fracture. About thirty-five miles.

Unconsciously, she drummed the desk top with the calipers. The seawater was trapped in a narrow gorge between the Shelf and the continent. The fierce Antarctic would keep the confined waters turbulent. The wave action would force the ice away from the continent, the constant push of watery hands against the Shelf. What happens then? The winds! Where would the winds off the coast take it?

'Seryozha, I have two urgent jobs for you. First, call Tyuratam and tell them it is my request that their cosmonauts take infrared photographs of the Ross Sea area on their next pass over the ice.'

The young man nodded eagerly.

'Then you are to go to the File Department, Meteorological Section. I want all the graphs of prevailing winds along the western coast of Antarctica. On your way back stop in at the Oceanographic Department and bring me the charts of the ocean floor extending out from the McMurdo Sound region. Do you understand?'

'Yes, Comrade Director.'

'Good! On my desk within one half hour.'

'I'll take care of it.' He spun on his heel and half trotted from the room.

Cherepin picked up the phone.

'Central exchange.'

'This is Institute Director Cherepin. I wish to speak to Comrade Chirikov.'

'Comrade Chirikov is in conference.'

'Get him out of conference.'

'On what authority?'

'Priority one seven five,' Cherepin answered. It was the designation for a crisis beyond Soviet borders. It ranked third behind War Alert and Domestic Emergency.

'Your message will be forwarded. Please remain at this phone.'

She hung up and turned to the window behind her desk. The snowfall was heavier, the flakes swirling against the insulated panes. The international scientific community had known for decades what would happen if the Ross Shelf ever disappeared from the Antarctic coast: the entire West Antarctic Ice Sheet would surge forward through the Ross Sea and out into the open ocean.

The inevitable meltdown of the Ice Sheet in the warm Pacific would bring on a cataclysmic rise in sea levels. How much? Five metres, six metres? There was no way of knowing without a computer analysis. She'd run a projection as soon as she spoke to Chirikov.

It suddenly struck her an observer team would be needed in Antarctica. Perhaps she would be chosen for the mission. Despite the gravity of what she'd just discovered, Cherepin felt suddenly exuberant. Joshua would surely be covering the story of the tremendous geological upheaval in Antarctica.

Joshua. It'd been seven long months since she'd last seen him. Her first thought each morning was of him, and when she closed her eyes at night, his image floated across the threshold of sleep into her dreams.

She would never forget the day Melissa had brought her home to meet her family. She'd found herself flustered and not a little frightened the first time she'd looked into his green eyes, eyes that befriended and yet at the same time aroused her.

As a girl she'd lain awake in revulsion those nights her

brutish father used her mother's body on the other side of the bedroom curtain. She'd sworn no man would ever foul her in that way, and as her mind flowered she'd used her intimidating intellect to keep men off balance, off the scent, off her.

She'd been a twenty-nine-year-old virgin when she met Joshua, used to the predictable pursuits of macho Russian men who stalked her not as a lover but as a trophy. Then suddenly here was this man who offered no machinations, she sensed, sure enough of his own masculinity that he needed no confirmation between the legs of a woman.

He was the only man she'd ever loved, the only man she'd ever made love to. And now (oh, please, God, now) she'd see him again.

Behind her the phone rang.

# NORTHDRIFT
## 52.2 Nautical Miles

Chauncey Dutcheyes sat cross-legged and deathly still on the cold Pacific beach, alternately sniffing and tasting the wind from the far south. He was 128 years old, the oldest human being on Campbell Island 400 miles south of New Zealand.

The ancient Maori native had not moved from the sand for over four hours. His great-great-great-grandaughter Miki was becoming concerned.

Despite her deep respect for his privacy, she left the eucalyptus grove where she'd stood watching and sat silently next to him on the beach.

For some time more Chauncey said nothing. Then he turned to her and took a great breath, the air rattling in and out of his tired lungs.

'Ah, Miki,' he smiled. 'Always you are by my side. Your suitors will become jealous.'

She smiled and reached out to hold one of his spotted, parchment-skin hands. 'Should I spend my time with boys when I could be in the presence of a man?'

'Once a man, little one. Now hollow and useless, like those empty shells on the beach.'

'There is more to a true man than the strength of his physical self, Great-grandfather. The gifts of your mind remain powerful.'

A rasping laugh shook his brittle frame. 'So young and already so wise. Your husband will be a fortunate man.'

She tossed her waist-length dark hair and let a trickle of sand run through her fingers. 'I'll wait for a man like you, Great-grandfather. A deep and good man. And you will dance at my wedding as guest of honour.'

Many men wanted Miki. She had a quick mind and a radiant spirit, a buoyancy that bubbled up out of her like the froth above a breaking wave. When she laughed, her brown eyes danced and a glow shone through her olive skin.

'You are a flame that lights men's lamps,' Chauncey would often tease her.

Now she saw something change in her great-great-great-grandfather's eyes. 'Are you ill?'

He smiled wanly. 'Not in body, child.'

She studied him. 'What is it, Great-grandfather? Why has this sadness come over you?'

He said nothing for a moment. Then he reached out and touched her face. 'An evil thing will soon come from the south, Miki,' he said, a long, boney finger pointing out over the waves beyond the lagoon.

'Is it a storm, a typhoon, Great-grandfather?'

'Were it only that, my child. No, what is to come will strike from the land of ice.'

A chill seized her as she followed his gaze towards the southern horizon and the bottom of the world beyond. Her great-great-great-grandfather's predictions always came true.

Chauncey Dutcheyes was a seer.

The surname Dutcheyes was a legacy more than 350 years old. In late 1642 the intrepid explorer Abel Janzoon Tasman had navigated his two ships, the *Heemskerck* and the *Zeehaen*, along the unknown west coast of New Zealand's South Island.

On December 12 a war party of Maori natives had sallied from shore in outrigger canoes and attacked a small boat launched by the *Zeehaen*. Three of the seven sailors aboard were killed outright by the Maori and a fourth, a fourteen-year-old cabin boy, Gerrit Quast, had been knocked into the sea by a blow to the head with a war club.

Presuming the boy drowned, Tasman had sailed his ships quickly away to the safety of the open ocean. But Quast had only been stunned by the club and was pulled alive from the water by the Maori.

When the youngster regained consciousness on the

beach, the Maori had fallen back awestruck at the sight of the Dutchman's strange violet eyes. Believing Quast's eyes mirrored a powerful spirit within him, the Maori had allowed the young sailor to live.

And it turned out the superstition of the natives was right. Quast himself later believed the gift of precognition had been inherent in him and the blow to the head had triggered the phenomenon. Whatever the source of his powers, it soon became apparent the Dutchman could foresee the future.

He could somehow tell days ahead when storms would come, when the infrequent but terrifying earth tremors would strike, and when enemy attacks were imminent. He could look into a woman's eyes and know if she was with child before she knew herself, and he sensed, too, when death hovered near.

Quast's powers attracked a growing following of Maori who believed he possessed a divine spirit. Alarmed by the young Dutchman's rising influence among his people, the Maori chief ordered Quast put to death.

Before the sentence could be carried out, the Dutchman and 250 of his faithful escaped to sea in outriggers under cover of a moonless night.

Knowing their pursuers would search the warmer waters to the west and north, Quast and his followers fled south towards the frigid southern fringe of the Pacific.

On the tenth day at sea they saw the stationary clouds on the horizon that meant an island lay ahead. Eight hours later they came in sight of the rugged coast of uninhabited Campbell Island.

The island was cold, humid, and windy, and had an area of only forty-four square miles. Yet the rich volcanic soil produced bountiful yields of fern roots and berries, the cliffs provided an inexhaustible supply of seabird eggs, and the surrounding seas teemed with fish and seals. The colony flourished.

The third month on the island Quast took as his wife the beautiful Kalani, and a year later she bore him a son.

When the midwife first looked into the newborn's face

she let out a muffled cry. The infant's eyes had the same purple cast as his father's eyes. It was Maori tradition to give children descriptive surnames, and the boy was named Dutcheyes.

As the child grew it became apparent he possessed the same extraordinary gift as his father; he could foresee the future. When Quast died forty years later, his son assumed the stewardship of his people, and then his son, in turn, inherited the mantle of benevolent leadership.

When Chauncey was born in 1871, the great-grandson of Quast, his violet eyes assured the Maori of Campbell Island that yet another seer had arrived to guide them into the future.

In 1902, when Chauncey was thirty-one, he had shepherded his Maori people to the west coast of the island eighteen hours before a volcanic fissure had split the eastern shore, spewing molten magma over the land and sea near it.

In 1918 and again in 1926, he had warned of devastating typhoons. He knew where the schools of fish had moved when submarine quakes had chased them from their former feeding grounds. He could tell which remote beaches the ever-dwindling seal herds would choose to birth their young.

Year after year, to the present day, Chauncey had served as a wise counsellor and protector of his people. He was not just a leader but a living legend among the Maori of Campbell Island.

Miki felt her great-great-great-grandfather squeeze her hand and she helped him rise painfully from his lotus position in the sand.

'Come, Miki. We must prepare the people. There is little time.'

Together the old man and the young woman walked up the beach towards the village, the cold harbinger wind from Antarctica blowing steadily at their backs.

The official black Volga sedan left Moscow on the Lenin Prospekt, crossed the last of the three auto rings that circled the city like moats, and sped southwest on the Kiev Highway.

Anna Cherepin sat in the back seat staring blankly at the necks of the driver and the plainclothesman from the Kremlin. Her mind was in Antarctica, absorbed with the Ross Ice Shelf that she had confirmed was now a gargantuan rogue iceberg.

The briefcase on the seat beside her bulged with the latest Soyuz P7 photographs documenting the widening breech between the Shelf and the continent. Analysis of the infrared scan she had requested confirmed a huge thermal release into the seawater beneath the ice.

The leather case also contained detailed charts of the currents off Marie Byrd Land and Victoria Land flanking the Ross Sea, up-to-the-hour meteorological observations, and the notes she'd taken before she left Moscow.

Two and a half hours ago Cherepin had told Vladimir Chirikov of the northdrift of the Ice Shelf. The academy president was an avid supporter of her Antarctic research. He grasped immediately the implications of 200,000 square miles of ice loose in the Pacific.

Chirikov had asked her to stay on the line. Several minutes later he'd told an astonished Cherepin they would be meeting with Mikhail Romanov himself, the general secretary of the Communist Party and the chairman of the Presidium of the Supreme Soviet of the USSR. A car would pick her up.

Meanwhile, she had carte blanche to ask the full cooperation of any department of Soviet science she wished. They were placing her in charge of coordinating all available information on what was happening at the bottom of the world.

Cherepin shifted her gaze to the window. Just before Vnukovo Airport was the turnoff for the writer's colony at Peredelkino, where Pasternak was buried and where she had spent the happiest days, and nights, of her life, reliving those hours so many times since, as if taking out jewels to caress.

It was Chirikov who had lent them his dacha for the weekend. She remembered how wrenching it had been to return to Moscow, and how she had said goodnight to Joshua in front of his building and driven the lonely way home to her apartment on Arbat Square.

There were two men from the KGB waiting when she opened her door.

She would always think of the pair as 'Knife' and 'Fork'. Knife was tall and thin, with the sharp angular face of the steppe cossacks. The second man had a medium build and a face with heavy eyelids and a patch of sparse hair that rose from his head in a row of tufts like the tines of a fork.

The questions had been thrust at her without preamble: why was she seeing the American journalist McCoy? Was she not aware that Soviet citizens were expected to report any contact with Westerners to the Committee for State Security? What exactly is the relationship between the director of the Antarctic Institute and the Moscow bureau chief of the *New York Times*?

'We are friends,' she insisted, adrenal fear pumping her voice high. 'My relationship is with his family, his wife and children, as well as with McCoy.'

There was an edge of derision to Knife's voice. 'So you spent the weekend at Comrade Chirikov's dacha with a friend.'

She fought down a bubble of nausea. They had followed her to Peredelkino! 'Yes. I'd been planning the weekend for some time and, two weeks ago I think it was, I invited McCoy to come along.'

Fork fixed her with hooded eyes. 'Why? Why did you wish to take the American to Peredelkino?'

'To give him a rest. He was tired. His work demands very long hours, and he has two small children at home to mind as well.'

Knife turned to Fork. 'A restful weekend in the country. Certainly Comrade Cherepin's explanation is plausible enough.'

'Convincing, most convincing,' Fork agreed.

'However, we must be thorough,' Knife said. 'Perhaps a quick review of the comrade's dossier.'

Fork's voice was guttural. 'Only to be prudent, of course.'

The exchange was too smooth, the repartee too practised, and she realized, sickened, that they were playing a vile game with her, two depraved cats with a cornered mouse.

Knife extracted a file from his shiny black briefcase and began to read: 'Anna Yegorovna Cherepin. Born December 3, 1967, Lubny, Lubny Raion, Poltava Oblast, Ukrainian Soviet Socialist Republic. Mother: Nina Makarovna Dobrotko, mechanic . . .'

And mother! Anya wanted to scream at him. Simple, loving, tender mother.

'Father: Yegor Pavlovich Cherepin, collective-farm worker. Education: Subject entered the Lubny Primary School, September 1, 1974, age seven. Transferred to Gifted Student Program, Lubny Special School, October 15, 1974.'

Anya listened in surreal detachment, making silent corrections in her biography as Knife traced her life from her first schooling to her appointment to head the Antarctic Institute.

She was incredulous at what the KGB knew about her: her earliest friends, her academic performance, every place she'd lived, every job she'd had, every trip she'd taken. There were character sketches from past neighbours and co-workers, political assessments from department heads she'd served under.

Knife flipped to the last page. 'Personal: Subject is not a party member. She is considered apolitical. No known sympathies for nonconformist or subversive groups. Prefers company of scientists and intelligentsia. Subject is unmarried, lives alone.' Interviews with neighbours and colleagues indicate no sexual liaisons.'

There was an unmistakable note of titillation in his voice now. 'Subject may be lesbian or sexually dysfunctional.'

Anya didn't know whether to laugh or cry. *I am neither, you suffocating buffoons!*

'So there we are, Comrade Cherepin,' Knife said, putting down the dossier. 'Certainly your background suggests no ulterior motive for your weekend with the American. You are neither political nor promiscuous.'

'Your saying so is most reassuring,' she said acidly, casting a hard bright smile at Knife.

Then it was Fork's turn to play with the mouse. 'Comrade Cherepin, I simply don't understand,' he said, his face scrunched in studied bewilderment. 'Your dossier is exemplary. How then are we to fathom the tape from Comrade Chirikov's dacha?'

Anya's heart froze. *No! They hadn't, not that!*

Fork pulled a small cassette player from his case. 'From what I've heard of the recording so far, your weekend with McCoy was not precisely platonic.'

'Perhaps Comrade Cherepin can explain what was taking place,' Knife said with a leer. 'Explain in some detail.'

'Yes,' Fork agreed, his eyes running down her body. 'The more detail the better. Shall we listen?'

Anya closed her eyes and shrank inward as Fork turned on the machine.

They'd recorded everything, from the moment she and Joshua had walked in the door. She cursed herself. Chirikov held a high scientific post, he was not a party member. He was suspect. She should have guessed his house would be bugged.

The next three hours were excruciating. Her eyes tightened and filled with tears hearing Joshua's voice. She cringed, agonized that she had given the KGB this weapon against him.

Time and again Fork stopped the recorder and re-wound. 'Here, you see, I don't understand what I am hearing. Could you explain how these sounds came to be made?'

Then he would play again the moments she and Joshua were making love. Her mind wobbled like a top. How could such iridescent moments sound so ugly now?

Anya refused to dignify the prurient farce with an answer. Each time he rewound the tape and put her through the anguish of listening to it, she stared back at him wordlessly and shook her head perplexed.

'Your silence is most unfortunate,' Fork warned her repeatedly.

'Most unfortunate,' Knife invariably echoed.

And they went on grinding her down, their filthy ears sucking in and sullying the most intimate, beautiful moments in her life. At the end they had her where they wanted, wrung out, debased, feeling obscenely naked and vulnerable before them. They told her why they'd come. Then they left.

She burst into tears and for a long time she sobbed uncontrollably. Finally, she stopped and began to pace. She tracked the floor for almost an hour, then threw herself down at her desk and wrote Joshua a letter breaking off their relationship.

She didn't tell him about the KGB or their tape. Only, in a detached tone, that it was best for both of them. Please, no calls, no questions. She'd try to explain some day. Have a lovely life.

She rose and paced and read the letter. Halfway through she screamed silently at the ceiling and tore the sheets into shreds. She fought for control, then sank down at the desk and began again.

She spent the entire night rewriting the letter. Love, anguish, mad schemes, hints of suicide, her desperation poured onto the pages. As quickly as she penned the words she realized he must never read them. Scraps of paper littered the floor around her.

The final version was vague, short, and sterile, an

epitaph chiselled laboriously into a headstone. The weekend had been a mistake; they must never see each other again; please don't try to contact her; good-bye, Joshua.

She ached to tell him how much she loved him, how he'd risen like the sun in her grey life. But that would have ensured that he'd come to her, step further into the KGB trap.

At 5 A.M. she put on her coat and left the apartment. Arbat Square was almost deserted. Four or five early-rising labourers in quilted jackets wandered across from the warren of crooked eighteenth-century streets that fed the plaza.

Anya walked quickly to the Arbatskaya metro station. She felt eyes on her as she fumbled in her purse for the five-kopek fare. She whirled around suddenly. Knife stood half behind a shuttered beer kiosk, his face abashed that she'd spotted him. Then his eyes hardened and he looked past her.

She rode the escalator down. What did it matter if he followed her? They knew she'd go to Joshua, they wanted her to. Knife wouldn't stop her, search her, read the letter.

She clutched her purse tightly and walked to the middle of the vaulted station. Behind her, Knife stepped onto the platform. The letter burned through the leather bag under her arm the eternal five minutes before a train arrived.

Kiev, Smolensk, Kutuzov, the ornate stations of the Moscow metro passed, their heroic mosaics and ponderous chandeliers making each stop appear a small subterranean opera house.

She got off at Bagrationovskaya and walked the five blocks to Joshua's apartment on Kutuzov Prospekt. Knife followed twenty paces back.

Nearing the building she slipped her hand in her coat pocket and gripped the key Joshua had given her. Knife wouldn't know she had it. He expected her to ring, then he would follow her in when the concierge answered.

Anya reached the apartment house, unlocked the door

and shut it quickly behind her. She heard the slap of running feet outside as she pushed the lift button. She caught a glimpse of Knife's angry face through the entry glass a moment before the car started up.

She got off at the fifth floor and walked down the long corridor to Joshua's large corner apartment. She took out the letter and stared at the envelope, a thick cocoon of despair all but suffocating her.

She couldn't, she just couldn't! Her hands twisted, to tear the letter. She stopped and looked at the door, through the door, to his bedroom, to his face. For him, she must do it for him.

Anya knelt and slipped the letter under the door, then turned and fled back to the lift. Knife was standing in the foyer with the concierge.

'That will be all,' Knife snapped at the old woman, then glared sullenly at Anya as the sleepy concierge scratched her grey head and waddled back to her room.

Anya steeled herself and approached him. 'I have given McCoy your message.'

'You were not to speak to the American again without wearing a recorder. You were told.'

'It was a letter.'

'Your written communications to him were to be passed through the Committee for State Security. I could place you under arrest.'

'But you won't,' Anya said, strangely sure of herself. 'You're not certain that's the right thing to do. I am your access to McCoy, and you want him.'

She could see the hesitation in his eyes and she knew she was right. She pulled on her gloves. 'I am going home now. Would you care to share a seat on the metro?'

Knife quivered in fury. 'You think you're very clever, Comrade Cherepin.'

'To have outwitted you? Hardly. It was not that great a challenge.'

She turned and walked out before he could answer. Behind, she heard Knife demand a phone of the concierge.

The landing lights for Vnukovo Airport flashed by on either side of the speeding Volga.

Joshua came to her, of course, the same morning, as soon as he woke and found her letter. And she'd told him about the KGB, as she'd known she would all along. She could live without knowing his love, but not without his knowing hers.

She collapsed in his arms when she'd finished telling him what the KGB wanted. 'The bastards,' he said, 'the bastards,' and stroked her hair.

'They can send me away, Joshua,' she sobbed. 'They can steal our future. But they can't take the love we've had, they can't take away Peredelkino.'

He held her until she quieted. Then he cupped her face in his hands. 'There may be a way, Anya,' he said, making her heart soar. 'I'll need a few days.'

And he'd found a way. She sighed and shut her eyes, willing fate to let them find a way now.

The Volga sped on through the night.

Joshua McCoy led his two daughters by the hand to the gate of the private aircraft terminal at San Francisco International Airport.

'There's your plane, Daddy,' Shea said, pointing across the tarmac to *Times Two* being serviced in front of an open hangar a hundred yards away.

The pilot and copilot were going through the preflight checklist as they climbed the boarding stairs.

'Morning, Josh,' Captain Donald Russell said, squeezing his hefty frame through the small door between the cockpit and the main cabin. Copilot Kevin Mahoney followed.

'Don, Kevin, I'd like you to meet my daughters Kate and Shea.'

'Hi, kids,' Mahoney said with a grin.

'Your dad's told us a lot about you two,' Russell said. 'Do you like to fly?'

'Yes,' Shea answered for both. 'But we've only been on big airplanes before.'

'Do you have soda and snacks and stuff on this plane, Mr Russell?' Kate asked hopefully.

The pilot laughed. 'C'mon, I'll show you where the cold compartment is. I think we have enough Cokes and sandwiches to keep you two fuelled.'

Mahoney clapped McCoy on the shoulder. 'You want a bet on the Forty-niner game this afternoon, Josh?'

'Who are they playing?'

'Shanghai. You give me three points and I'll take the Dragons.'

As the cultures of the Pacific basin had begun to homogenize in the late eighties, American football had been adopted enthusiastically throughout Asia. A pan-

Pacific league was formed, and millions cheered the weekly games.

Handicapped at first by lighter linemen, the Far Eastern teams had learned to hold back American tacklers with a version of *akido*, a passive style of Japanese self-defence. They were more subtle runners than the bigger Americans and their intricate play patterns drove teams from the States wild.

McCoy guffawed. 'C'mon, Kevin. That Shanghai quarter-back Deng Shaoqi can lay the ball on a dime from fifty yards. I'll take the Forty-niners, but I want seven points.'

'Four. For fifty bucks.'

'You've got a bet.' McCoy threw his coat over the back of one of the six roomy, custom-upholstered seats facing each other in twos across the wine-coloured carpet.

In the centre of the cabin, accessible to each seat, was a knee-high console crammed with the latest communications technology. There was a linguistic word processor that automatically translated stories to or from every language spoken around the Pacific, including several Chinese dialects.

Next to the processor was a computer terminal that gave McCoy access to the *Times's* MAINBRAIN in New York. He could key the computer and call up instant data on the economy, population demographics, history, geography, political structure, and leadership of every nation he covered.

There were several other microelectronic communications devices built into the console, including circuitry for the reception of photographs, maps, charts, and other graphics.

Three screens were suspended from the ceiling in tandem. The first was the videophone, and the second, a television monitor that could pick up any station in the world via satellite. The last screen was fed pictures by the camera mounted in the belly of *Times Two*. The lens could scan the surface of the earth below with definition fine enough to recognize individual faces on the ground.

Captain Russell returned from the rear of the plane, where Shea and Kate were busy exploring the galley. 'What's this all about, Josh? All operations would tell us is that you'd called and asked that we get right to the airport and file a flight plan for Christchurch.'

'I'll fill you in when we're airborne,' McCoy promised.

'Fair enough.' Russell turned towards the girls. 'Shea, Kate, why don't you come forward when we're airborne and I'll teach you how to fly a plane.'

'Really?' Shea said, wide-eyed. 'Could we, Daddy?'

McCoy smiled. 'Sure, I'll send them up as soon as we reach cruising altitude, Don.'

'Good,' Russell said, and moved into the cockpit.

McCoy buckled the girls in, and the sleek aircraft taxied to the runway. The takeoff was smooth, and Shea and Kate craned their necks to peer below, absorbed with the ship-dotted bay and the pastel city of San Francisco stretched beneath the banking port wing.

Across the water, the flatlands of the East Bay rose gradually to the first range of hills. McCoy shook his head. When the West Antarctic Ice Sheet melted into the seas, Berkeley, Alameda, Oakland, Hayward, and San Jose to the south would all disappear beneath the waves. So would the low-lying areas of the peninsula on which San Francisco stood.

The jet streaked out over the Golden Gate Bridge and Kate squealed. 'There's the Toys R Us store.' The bridge was three levels now, with a deck of shops, restaurants, and moving sidewalks slung beneath the original roadway and the new magnetic train monorail above, linking San Francisco with Marin, Sonoma, and the northern coast.

The Lear jet neared its cruising speed of 1,200 miles per hour and in minutes the California coast disappeared behind them.

McCoy keyed the videophone. 'What do you say we call Mom?'

'She's sure going to be surprised we're coming, isn't she, Dad?' Shea grinned.

'Surprised and happy,' McCoy said, smiling at his daughter.

It only took a moment for the McMurdo Sound operator to locate Melissa in her research laboratory.

'Hi, Mommy!' Kate burst out as her mother's face appeared on the screen. 'Guess where we are.'

'Hi, sweetheart, hi, Shea. Is that Daddy behind you?'

'Yep,' Kate said. 'Guess where we are.'

Melissa's eyebrows knitted in feigned concentration, 'Goodness, I don't know. Are those portholes I see? Are you out on the boat?'

The girls laughed delightedly. 'Nope,' Kate said. 'Guess again.'

'Let's see, what time is it in San Francisco? Are you in the Neptune restaurant having clam fritters for brunch?'

Kate clapped her little hands in triumph. 'We're in Daddy's plane,' she burst out, unable to contain the news any longer.

'We're coming to see you,' Shea added, bright-eyed.

'Well, that certainly is a surprise,' Melissa said, looking at McCoy curiously. 'Dad told me you were coming down, Josh, but I never dreamt you'd be bringing the girls.'

'They'll be staying at your father's place in Christchurch,' McCoy explained. 'We have no idea how long it will take to get a handle on things down here. Waldo and I agreed it would be a good idea to have the girls near.'

Melissa nodded. 'Yes, of course. I'm glad.' She brightened. 'I can't wait to get my arms around you two. I have nine months' worth of hugs and kisses stored up.'

McCoy felt a pang. 'You two,' Melissa'd said. Because he was a strong man she thought he needed no strokes, that he was self-gratifying. Despite the fact that he no longer loved her, despite the shell that had crusted between his wife and himself, still the sting was there.

'Will you meet us at Grandpa's?' Shea asked hopefully.

McCoy watched a familiar shadow of guilt cross Melissa's face. 'I'm afraid I can't come to Grandpa's right away, Shea,' Melissa said. 'With all that's happening, I have more work to do than ever. Did Grandpa tell you about the ice? Do you understand?'

'It's okay, Mommy,' Shea said, hurt in her small voice. 'We know you have to do a lot of stuff.'

For an instant McCoy hated his wife.

'But you can come to Grandpa's soon, can't you, Mommy?' Kate ventured.

'Yes, sweetheart,' Melissa said. 'I'll come the moment I can get away. We'll go horseback riding and swimming, and I'll take you shopping. You'll both love the stores in Christchurch.'

'Daddy got us all new school clothes last month,' Shea said, then added thoughtfully, 'But I still need gym sneaks, and Kate's playing shoes are a wreck.'

'They are not, they're just ripped a little,' Kate protested.

For several minutes they talked of family things and planned their time in Christchurch.

Then McCoy said, 'Why don't you guys take Captain Russell up on that offer to fly this thing? We could use a couple of trained pilots in the family.'

Shea said, 'We get the hint, Dad. You want to talk to mommy alone.'

He grinned ruefully. 'I should have just said that, shouldn't I?'

'Well, you did tell us to be direct, Daddy,' Shea said with relish in her tone.

'Practise what you preach, Daddy.' Kate wagged a finger at her father.

McCoy grinned. 'You guys just love to catch me, don't you?'

Shea laughed and touched the tip of his nose. 'Yep.'

He squeezed them both. 'Now that you two have thoroughly enjoyed the moment, say good-bye to your mother and beat it.'

'See you at Grandpa's,' Shea said.

'Don't forget about the horseback riding,' Kate reminded her mother.

'Good-bye, my darlings. I'll see you soon,' Melissa promised. She smiled from the video screen as her daughters disappeared through the cockpit door. 'You have such an easy rapport with them, Josh. But then you always did.'

'Not always. There are days when we're eyeball to

eyeball and I'm a wink away from hauling them out to the woodshed. Kate got into my oil paints last week, and I'm going to have to have the walls of her room sandblasted.'

Melissa smiled softly. 'That bad?'

'Soledad headed for the smelling salts when she looked in the door. I think Shea described it best. She said it looked as if a fruit cocktail had exploded.'

Melissa laughed. 'A vivid picture.'

'By the way, I had a little talk with Shea about the birds and the bees last weekend. Nothing specific – I don't think she's ready for the graphics yet. But I thought it was time for some general do's and don'ts.'

'What brought that on?'

'I noticed her making some rather obvious cow eyes at Johnny Goodrow out on the veranda the other day.'

'Not that little boy next door,' Melissa said.

'He's sprouted quite a bit since you've been gone. So has Shea.'

Melissa looked at him quietly for a moment. 'We seem to be having one of those flip-flop conversations again, Josh. You're telling me things a mother usually confides to a father.'

'Yes, well . . .' He let the thoughts trail off unfinished.

Before he could pick up the sentence the words TIMES CENTRAL ON HOLD flashed across the bottom of the screen.

'I have another call coming in, Melissa,' he said. 'We'll phone you from your father's place as soon as we get in.'

'I'll get up to Christchurch as soon as I can, Josh. Honestly, the moment I can get away.'

'It will mean a lot to the girls,' he said. 'We'll talk to you soon.'

'Good-bye, Josh.'

August Sumner's face replaced Melissa's on the screen. 'There's a Reuters piece out of London reporting a fracture through the Ross Shelf, Josh,' the editor said. 'The BBC and several television and radio stations on the continent are broadcasting the story and we've had inquiries at our bureaus in Buenos Aires, Cape Town, and Singapore.'

'Has anyone realized the fracture's actually a break be

tween the Shelf and the continent? That the Ice is drifting north?'

'Not so far. There's a heavy fog in the Ross Sea region. Normal satellite observation is impossible and there are only a couple of all-weather infrared probes that orbit that far south. Yours should be the first definitive story.'

'I'll file as soon as I have the White House reaction from Waldo.'

'Fine. I've alerted all our media outlets – print and broadcast. Your piece will go out immediately. Have a good flight, Josh.'

'Thanks, August.'

McCoy hung up. It would be only a matter of hours now before the world found out about the cataclysm looming at the fringe of the Pacific. He knew there'd be disbelief at first, an inability to accept the terrible truth.

But then, as the oceans began to flood, incredulity would inevitably change to fear and then to panic. No matter if the warning bulletins he issued through the *Times's* media network were heeded and immediate evacuations were begun, there was still simply no way to save all the inhabitants of the planet's low-lying islands and coasts.

McCoy stared dejectedly down at the horizonless expanse of the Pacific below. God help the world – in the next few weeks and months millions of men, women, and children could perish in the rising sea.

The brakes squealed as the black Volga slowed and turned off the Kiev Highway onto a macadam road. The car followed the track through a forest of birch, the headlights turning the trees into silver sentinels against the dark night.

A mile and a half into the woods the Volga stopped at a rustic guardhouse with a log barrier hung across the roadway. Four spit and polish Soviet soldiers stood before the rough pole, their hands resting lightly on AK-47 automatic rifles slung across their chests on leather straps.

A young lieutenant appeared from the lighted guard hut and peered into the Volga. 'Papers, please.'

The officer took their IDs back inside and picked up a phone. The unsmiling guards never took their eyes off the car. Three minutes later the lieutenant returned their identification along with a stamped visitor's pass.

Cherepin saw the floodlights of the party general secretary's compound through the trees. They passed a second inspection at the high steel-mesh gate giving entry through a double fence, and were directed to a side entrance of the ornate dacha.

The sprawling wood house was painted a bright turquoise and carved in the traditional *izba* style. A florid-faced man in the ubiquitous dark suit of the civilian KGB stepped onto the gravel courtyard as they pulled up. He examined Anna's visitor's pass, then guided her inside and down a long hall to a large room, where a fire blazed in a cavernous stone fireplace.

The several men in the room turned to look at her as she entered. She realized uneasily that she was the only woman, and far outranked by everyone else present.

To one side stood Admiral Pyotr Trepkin, the tall,

blue-eyed and blond architect of the modern Soviet submarine fleet, his shoulder epaulets gleaming in the flickering light of the fire.

She had worked with Trepkin on an Antarctic submarine research project and found him technically brilliant, but at the core a hollow egotist drawn to fancy uniforms and women.

Beside him Air Force General Viktor Danilevsky rested his buttocks against the back of an overstuffed chair. An inept series of skin grafts after a fiery fighter-plane crash had left him with a face like a turtle's back. Pink scar tissue traced boxed squares of transplanted skin from his forehead to his chin. The general had the reputation of a drunkard living on his past fame as a pilot.

In a darkened corner Cherepin spotted General Leonid Vlasov, the bearded commander of the 32nd Karelian Division, a crack combat unit often airlifted suddenly to foreign trouble spots. Vlasov was known as a consummate soldier and a strong advocate of the use of Russian military force to solve political problems beyond Soviet borders. The 32nd Karelian had been the most decorated division to come out of Afghanistan. Vlasov's men loved him.

Two civilians were talking before the fire. Premier Grigorii Banyachenko nodded and smiled. Cherepin knew the premier well, meeting with him often on institute matters. The seventy-two-year-old Banyachenko was a pleasant, tired man, looking down the road to his retirement from the ruling Politburo.

Beside the premier, the horse-faced chief of the KGB, Boris Duglenko, regarded her expressionlessly, his thick black hair hanging down over his forehead like a mane. Cherepin had once sat for a torturous hour before the desk of Duglenko answering questions. She looked away quickly.

The only one sitting was the defence minister, Marshal Panel Savin. The grey-haired heavy-boned Savin lounged in his chair like an English peer in the sanctum of his club. Cherepin thought his face oddly pink and smooth for a sixty-year-old man, and even more so for a man with his reputation as a ruthless thirster after power.

Cherepin's loyal patron Vladimir Chirikov waved from the far end of the room and started towards her. She smiled. The short, stout, white-bearded earth scientist always reminded her of a merry elf.

Chirikov kissed her cheeks and stepped back. 'Anya, you should see your face. Such big eyes. You look a country schoolgirl on her first day at the university.' He lowered his voice and nodded towards the others in the room. 'Don't be intimidated tonight. Not one of them has your mind.'

She smiled at her mentor. 'Always the father, Volodya. What would I do without you?'

Admiral Trepkin appeared at Chirikov's elbow. 'It is refreshing to have a woman's face among us, Comrade Cherepin,' he said, his tone that of a self-assured womanizer.

Cherepin forced a smile. 'I hope I am as welcome after I have given my report.'

'Really? Is your news so distressing? I doubt anything you could tell us would be as bleak as some of the things we've been informed of here.'

Marshal Savin motioned them over to his chair. 'I understand you are responsible for our little gathering, Comrade Cherepin,' he said. 'Are your penguins at the south pole rattling sabers at us, perhaps?'

Before Cherepin could answer, the double doors to the hall opened again and the men turned, Savin rising from his seat, as the general secretary of the Communist Party of the Soviet Union entered the room.

Sixty-seven-year-old Mikhail Romanov was a poet cast into the arena with gladiators. He had intelligent, thoughtful eyes and a long, quixotic face that as often as not wore a bemused expression.

He was the leader of Russia by historical accident and he knew his grip on the rudder of his country was tenuous at best. In idle moments he wondered how long it would be before the hardliners deposed him.

103

'So long as they didn't shoot him, he thought, he would find it a relief to step down. He had never sought the job, after all. The Central Committee of the CPSU had picked him, plucked him from his insular world of blueprints and steel skeletons, and made him in a stroke one of the two most powerful men in the world.

He still thought of himself as the engineer he'd been for forty-five years. He'd been a good engineer, perhaps a great one, a passionate builder of city complexes, massive hydroelectric power plants, and soaring bridges.

His projects invariably came in on time and under budget, and he engendered a proud, harmonious spirit among his colleagues and construction teams that was unique in the Russian work force.

He'd been named the Soviet Minister of Light Industry in 1988 and had quickly transformed that office from a bureaucratic bottleneck into a practical, problem-solving post that rejuvenated Russian domestic construction.

The party rewarded him with a seat on the Politburo, and his name began to be touted for higher office. He'd steadily demurred. He was an apolitical man who had joined the party only out of career necessity. He wanted no part of the vulgar infighting that swirled through the ranks of the Soviet leadership.

But Afghanistan had changed everything. The debacle had finally cost over 200,000 Russian lives and hundreds of billions of rubles. The country, even the party, had no further stomach for the ideologues who had occupied the Kremlin and brought Russia to the brink of disaster.

The nation needed a manager, a man of calm reason and foresight, and when the party leader Koriakov was ousted in 1996, the Politburo had turned to Romanov. He could not refuse the call to heal his country.

He'd accomplished a great deal in his three years as general secretary. The country was at peace, agricultural and industrial production were both up, and personal freedoms flourished. He was immensely popular with the people.

But he harboured no illusions that his stewardship of

104

Russia would go on unimpeded much longer. The hardliners in the party, the army, and the KGB were once more restless, increasingly insurgent. Romanov had incurred their wrath by putting a stop to several schemes for foreign intrigue.

It had taken courage, for he had no power base of his own and the militarists were steadily gathering strength. Several of his most vehement opponents faced him now in the room he entered.

Romanov folded his lanky form down into the lone chair before the curtained windows facing the fire. 'Gentlemen, Comrade Cherepin, I believe you all know why we are here. An unprecedented situation has arisen on the continent of Antarctica. I know as little about the south pole as I imagine the rest of you do, with the exception of Comrade Cherepin of course.'

Romanov's eyes sought out Anya seated stiffly at the far end of one of the couches. 'Comrade Cherepin, would you be good enough to describe this unique crisis that has brought us all together?'

Cherepin cleared her throat. 'With your permission, Comrade Romanov,' she said, unfolding a large map from her briefcase.

Romanov motioned to an aide by the door. The man quickly went to a built-in closet, took out a cork-backed easel, and set it up beside the couch. Cherepin pinned the map to the cork and picked up a pointer from the easel tray.

'This is the Ross Sea,' she indicated, 'and this white mass is the Ross Ice Shelf. The Shelf is essentially a floating glacier. Thirty per cent of the Ice is, or was, aground on the sea floor, and along the landward rim a crustal lip of ice and snow extended out over the surrounding glaciers.'

Cherepin ran the pointer around the border of the Shelf. 'This afternoon I received a series of photographs from our Soyuz P7 in polar orbit showing this crustal bridge has been fractured. An infrared scan carried out by the Soyuz on its next orbit confirmed my suspicion that submarine volcanism had broken through the floor of the Ross Sea beneath the Ice. The fracture and undoubtedly the melting away of the Shelf's ice anchors were caused by a huge upwelling of volcanic heat and pressurized gases. The Ross Shelf, Comrade Romanov, has an area of about five hundred thousand square kilometres. It is now drifting out to sea.'

There was a stunned silence in the room.

'How do you know for a fact the Ice Shelf is drifting?' Romanov asked.

Cherepin reached into her briefcase and pulled out the satellite photographs, passing them along the couch to Romanov.

'I have marked them in sequence. If you will notice, shots one through five show a thick dark band around the Shelf. Obviously open seawater.'

Romanov nodded absently, leafing through the photographs.

'We estimate the breach at that point to be almost twenty miles wide. In the time since those last pictures were transmitted, the Shelf would have drifted another seventy kilometres or so to sea.'

'Aren't leads opening in the ice all the time during the spring, Comrade Director?' Trepkin asked. 'Even breaks as large as the present one?'

'The leads of which you speak are caused by normal seasonal shifts of the ice pack. The rupture surrounding the Ross Ice Shelf circles six hundred and fifty kilometres in from the open sea to an area where we know the ice to be over twelve hundred metres thick.'

There was a murmur among the men.

'The other members of the Academy of Sciences I contacted agree there is no possibility the fracture will refreeze.'

Romanov had passed the photographs to the others. General Vlasov studied one, then looked at Cherepin. 'During our training exercises north of Murmansk, I saw many large icebergs pushed up against the coast by the heavy seas. Won't the same thing happen once this Ice Shelf of yours has left the bay it occupies?'

'Unfortunately, no,' she answered. 'Quite the opposite

will take place shortly. The winds in the Ross Sea region this time of year blow steadily to the north. The Shelf can only be pushed farther and farther from the continent. There is no question that this will happen.'

'Do you have any idea where the Shelf is likely to drift?' Romanov asked.

Cherepin shook her head. 'Such a huge mass has never floated on the surface of the sea before, Comrade Romanov. Never in history. It may continue to drift due north towards New Zealand, or it may veer northwest into the Indian Ocean, towards South America. To chart the course of such a monstrous entity is beyond our capability. We have no precedent.'

General Danilevsky shifted impatiently in his chair. He and his Latvian mistress had downed a quart of cognac earlier that night, before he had been summoned from his comfortable Moscow apartment to this remote dacha.

'Why are you so concerned about a damn iceberg, even such a large one?' he said, scowling at Cherepin. 'If this Shelf presents a problem, let me go after it with a few squadrons of MiGs. I'll pound it into ice cubes for you.'

Romanov leaned forward in his chair. 'Do you know who you remind me of, Comrade Danilevsky?'

'Who is that?'

'Hermann Goering, that Nazi Luftwaffe marshal sixty years ago,' Romanov said mildly. 'Reichsmarshall Goering had the same ignorant arrogance about his own air force.'

Danilevsky sank back wordlessly into his chair, the veins of his red forehead pulsing.

'If I might answer the comrade general?' Cherepin asked.

Romanov nodded.

'First of all, Comrade Danilevsky, the Shelf is still in Antarctic waters, where it is protected by the Treaty of Christchurch. The agreement forbids the use of any arms whatsoever on the continent or at sea within eight hundred kilometres of it. The Soviet Union is a signatory of that treaty. Second, it would take every conventional bomb in our arsenals to break up even a fraction of the ice, assuming we were fool enough to attempt such a thing.'

'Fool!' Danilevsky flared half forward in his chair, then felt Romanov's gaze and sputtered out like a wet fuse.

'Comrade Romanov, it must be understood,' Cherepin said, 'there is more than one threat facing us from Antarctica. The more imminent danger is that the Ross Sea volcanism will worsen while the Shelf is still in the waters overhead. A massive eruption of magma during the next few critical days would cause a cataclysmic meltdown of the Shelf and send huge ocean waves seeping north into the Pacific. Low-lying coasts from New Zealand to Siberia would flood far inland.'

Cherepin raised the pointer again to the map. 'The second threat lies here, the West Antarctic Ice Sheet,' she said, running the pointer across Marie Byrd Land.

'As massive as the Ross Shelf is, the Ice Sheet dwarfs it by comparison. The sheet has a surface area of some six million four hundred and seventy-five square kilometres of ice. Exhaustive field studies by both Soviet and Western glaciologists have concluded the Ice Sheet is highly unstable. The natural glacial flow is forward towards the coast, and for millennia only the backward pressure of the Ross Shelf has restrained the Ice Sheet from surging through the Ross Sea and out into the open ocean.'

'Let me understand you, Comrade Cherepin,' Romanov said. 'You're telling us that with the Shelf now drifting north out of the Ross Sea, six and a half million square kilometres of ice is about to enter the ocean?'

'Yes, Chairman Romanov, that is precisely what is going to happen. And as the Sheet begins to melt, the seas will start to rise. My computers at the institute project the world's oceans will go up seven to eight metres.'

Romanov came forward in his chair. 'Eight metres! Then our harbours will flood, our coasts?'

'All the world's seaports are doomed. The principal Soviet cities that will be inundated include Leningrad, Murmansk, Arkhangelsk, Odessa, Sevastopol, Vladivostok. Hundreds of smaller harbours and hundreds of thousands of miles of shore lands will also disappear.'

The men gaped at Cherepin, the crackle of the pine fire as sharp as gunshots against the sudden communal silence.

Romanov's face looked stricken. He had been born and raised in Odessa, on the Black Sea coast. Most of his family still lived there. As a boy, during the starving times after World War II, he had watched the foreign freighters unloading grain, meat, and condensed milk at the city's quays.

'We face food stortages, then,' he said hoarsely, in his voice the fear of hunger that had haunted generations of his peasant ancestors.

He sought out the president of the Academy of Sciences. 'Your people are always analysing potential national disasters, Comrade Chirikov. What will happen to our food supplies when the seas rise?'

Chirikov frowned. 'Forty per cent of the wheat we consume comes in through our ports, Comrade Romanov. So does eighty per cent of the corn, ninety-eight per cent of the coffee and tea, one hundred per cent of the sugar. Eighty per cent of the citrus fruit arrives in ships.'

'Enough,' Romanov said, closing his eyes. 'I want to know only one thing. Will there be famine?'

'No.' The scientist shook his head. 'There will be shortages of almost everything. Our people will have to tighten their belts. We'll all do without. But no one will starve.'

Romanov turned to Banyachenko. 'You spent thirty years managing industries, Comrade Banyachenko. Can our factories continue running without imports?'

'Barely, Comrade Romanov. Perhaps at some sort of maintenance level. We are heavily dependent now on Western technology. We import computers, software, solar panels, fiber optic equipment, robots, microelectronics. Without state-of-the-art imports, our technology will inevitably fall behind that of the United States, Europe, and Japan.'

The KGB chief, Duglenko, boasted, 'We have the largest, most sophisticated intelligence service in the world, Comrade Banyachenko. My agents can produce prototypes of evolving technology in the West and we could then manufacture these devices within our own borders.'

'Provided we have the raw materials, Comrade Duglenko,' Cherepin said. 'Our Antarctic ports will be among the first to flood. We will be cut off from a major source of our minerals.'

Chirikov looked over his glasses. 'Quite so, Comrade Cherepin. However, we are only a couple of years away from being able to synthesize many of these metals. With intensified research, we could fabricate them sooner.'

Romanov probed the premier again. 'You haven't mentioned our energy reserves, Comrade Banyachenko. Can we keep the power on to industry?'

'Yes, we can. Everything west of the Urals is now on nuclear fission. In Siberia and the eastern republics it's a mixture of fission, geothermal, and perhaps thirty per cent still fossil-fuelled.'

Marshal Savin stirred in his seat. 'Certainly we must concern ourselves with the domestic considerations, Comrade Romanov,' he injected. 'However, I suggest that the military implications are far more critical.'

Romanov frowned at the hawkish officer. 'How so, Comrade Savin?'

'We have no large army units beyond the European and Asian mainlands, as you know, Comrade Romanov. However, we will lose a great many defence installations both on our own coasts and abroad: airfields, satellite radar stations, communications posts, a mixed bag. It is the navy, of course, that will suffer the brunt of what is to come.'

'Suffer is an inadequate word,' Admiral Trepkin said. 'When our harbours flood, the navy will be decimated – over the span of some months, I grant you – but inexorably, ship by ship. A quarter of the fleet is still diesel-powered. We will lose these as soon as their oil bunkers run dry. The rest of our vessels are nuclear, but fully half will require some maintenance of their reactors within a year. Without dry docks, this is impossible.'

Chirikov said, 'Chairman Romanov, there may be a temporary if – what should I say – unorthodox answer to the problem of our doomed harbours. It may be the cause of our dilemma is also the solution.'

Romanov regarded Chirikov thoughtfully. 'Go on.'

'If my dear colleague Cherepin's calculations are correct, the Ross Shelf will be well out in the Pacific within a matter of weeks. The ice is perfectly flat on top, like a tabletop. More to the point, like a dock. And, of course, being ice, it floats, rising with the sea. I propose we break sections off the outer cliffs of the Shelf with lasers. I'm talking about large segments perhaps two kilometres by five. These could then be positioned off our Pacific coasts and used as floating harbours with quays and access roads hewn out of the ice cliffs at the level of a ship's deck. We have used such ice docks in Antarctica for several years now.'

Romanov was intrigued. 'And how would you move these docks all the way north the length of the Pacific to our Siberian shores? I doubt a tugboat exists powerful enough to pull a mass of ice some ten kilometres square.'

'We don't need tugboats, Comrade Romanov. We have the Mirnyi engines. We use them to move large icebergs away from our coastal facilities at our Antarctic base of Mirnyi. I sent you a full report.'

Romanov nodded. 'I recall your report. However, I suggest you brief the others.'

'Of course.' Chirikov adjusted his old-fashioned bifocals. 'The Mirnyi engine has a very simple chemical-mechanical operation. When we have a large body of ice we wish to move out to sea, we hew out a cavern within the rear of the iceberg below the water line, an engine room if you will. The Mirnyi engine is installed with a drive shaft extending out through the ice to twenty-four-metre propellers. Cylinders of liquid freon are stored in the ice around the engine room. The freon is then pumped under high pressure into heat exchangers submerged in the water. As the freon leaves the zero-degree iceberg and hits the warmer seawater, it turns into gas, expands rapidly, and spins turbines that drive the propellers. The freon is then recycled into liquid form and used again and again. We're quite proud of the Mirnyi engine. The West has nothing like it.'

Marshal Savin's eyes were suddenly riveted on the scientist. 'How fast can these engines of yours move the ice?'

'Five to six knots per hour once underway, perhaps eight with a current flowing in the same direction.'

Savin thought for a moment. 'Even at the latter speed, it would take some time for these ice stations of yours to reach the Siberian coast. What's to prevent them from melting under the equatorial sun, as Comrade Cherepin says will be the fate of the Ross Shelf?'

'Plastic, Marshal Savin,' Chirikov said. 'Specifically, Plastic R-16. It comes in liquid form and hardens to an even coat on contact with the air. An inch thickness of R-16 will simultaneously reflect sunlight and thoroughly insulate whatever's under it from the air above. We spray it around construction sites in Siberia to keep the ground from turning into a quagmire every spring.'

The bearded General Vlasov spoke for the first time. 'I'm familiar with R-16, Comrade Marshal. We use it to make tank paths when my division is manoeuvring across frozen rivers.' He looked at the academy president. 'It is simple enough to spray from helicopters.'

'Won't these ice stations also melt from below?' Savin asked.

'The problem is manageable when we're dealing with only ten square kilometres,' the scientist said. 'We simply suspend heavy plastic sheets down into the water from the edges of the ice. During the small initial meltdown, a cocoon of cold water will form below. The fresh water of the Shelf is lighter than the salt water and it will remain near the ice above. The melting underneath will slow and almost cease as this pool becomes colder and colder.'

Romanov rubbed his hands lightly together and considered Chirikov's scheme. It was an outlandish idea, yet apparently quite plausible. And he had to admit he found the concept brilliant.

He nodded at Chirikov. 'Very well then. You may begin preparations to bring these ice stations of yours north to our—'

'No!' Marshal Savin was on his feet, his normally unflappable face animated.

Startled, Romanov stared at Savin. 'I beg your pardon, Comrade Marshal. What did you say?'

'Not north to Siberia, Comrade Romanov. East to the shores of America, west to the coasts of Japan, China, Southeast Asia, Australia!' He whirled to face the others. 'Do only I see what is before us? Think! Ice stations we can navigate through the sea at will with no need for fuel. Stations two kilometres by five with sides as steep and deep as the largest harbour. Stations that are perfectly flat on top!'

Admiral Trepkin shot forward in his chair. 'Ports we can move anywhere in the world!'

'Yes!' Savin slammed a fist into his palm.

'Two kilometres by five! And flat! We could land our largest planes,' General Danilevsky bellowed.

'Yes!'

General Vlasov's eyes shone. 'An area that large, room for troop barracks and armour dumps.'

'Yes!' Savin turned back to Romanov. 'Comrade Romanov, never has such an opportunity for strategic gain been thrust before us. We have it within our power to place fully equipped Soviet military installations off San Francisco, Los Angeles, Tokyo, Shanghai, Hong Kong, Singapore, Manila, Sydney. They cannot attack us in international waters without provoking all-out war. When they lose their harbours, their navies will be paralysed. They will have no defence against our lasers, missiles, planes, and invasion troops poised off their coasts. The West will be forced to yield whatever concessions we demand. The Pacific, Comrade Romanov, will become a Soviet mare nostrum.'

Romanov felt numbed by the sudden turn the conference had taken. The last thing he wanted was a risky military venture. Yet, even as party general secretary he realized he hadn't the power to thwart the plan alone. He'd have to rally the support of moderates in the Presidium. Best to feign enthusiasm and play for time.

'Comrade Director Cherepin,' he said. 'How long will it take for the Ross Ice Shelf to reach international waters?'

Cherepin was dazed, her mind brutalized by what she

had just heard. They wanted to turn the pristine ice of the Ross Shelf into stations of war.

'Approximately sixty-two hours,' she murmured.

Romanov turned to General Vlasov. 'Is your Thirty-second Karelian Division presently equipped and ready for an airlift to the Shelf?'

'My paratroopers are fully trained and supplied down to the last bootlace, the last cartridge, Comrade Romanov,' Vlasov said fervently. 'We are in the midst of mountain manoeuvres and morale is at a high point. My Mongolians beg to go into action.'

'Where is the division now?'

'In the high Altai Range in the eastern Kazakh Republic, north of the city of Alma-Ata.'

Romanov turned to General Danilevsky. 'Is the air force capable of airlifting Vlasov's division to the southern hemisphere, to Antarctica, in under three days' time?'

Danilevsky mopped the cognac-scented sweat from his forehead. 'We have the necessary planes assembled at Tashkent, in the Uzbek Republic. Antonov-30 troop transports held in reserve should we have to go back into Afghanistan a third time. These planes are kept fully serviced. We can take off as soon as the Thirty-second Karelian Division is brought to the airport.'

The chairman looked at Chirikov. The scientist appeared as stricken as Cherepin, appalled at the prostitution of his plan for the ice docks. 'How long would it take to separate several ice stations from the Shelf?' Romanov asked.

'Only a few days. Once scored with a laser beam, the ice tends to fracture on its own along the line of the heat ray. It's the same principle as cutting a pane of glass. However, very large lasers are needed. I doubt machines of this size could be airlifted.'

Cherepin knew there was an ice-cutting laser at Mirnyi. Chirikov was taking a chance, making a brave attempt. She slid her hand over his on the couch and squeezed gently.

'I believe I have a solution,' Admiral Trepkin offered. 'Our nuclear attack submarine *Mezen* entered the South

Pacific through the Drake Passage two days ago. She steams submerged at sixty knots. Given her present position, she could be off the ice in perhaps sixteen hours. She's armed with anti-aircraft laser tubes mounted through her deck. The *Mezen* could cruise below the Shelf firing upward along a line until a section of the ice is separated. We've used this manoeuvre before to clear areas for our subs to surface through the northern ice packs.'

Romanov looked at Chirikov. 'Would this work?'

The scientist nodded wearily. 'Yes.'

Romanov rose and faced the fire, his head bent, his back to the silent room. This mad scheme of Savin's offered the hardliners just the sort of strategic coup they were searching for. Its success would erase the debacle of Afghanistan, all the other mistakes. The militarists would fight his opposition tooth and nail. He would try. What else could he do? He turned finally and faced the group.

'I shall bring Savin's plan before the Presidium. I wish to hear other opinions.'

'May I suggest that certain steps be taken in the interim, Comrade Romanov,' Savin said.

'Such as?'

'Vlasov's Thirty-second Karelian Division should be flown to Tashkent and prepared for an airlift to Antarctica. The *Mezen* must be ordered south as well.'

'You are assuming the Presidium will approve, Comrade Marshal.'

'I am. Still, neither action I recommend commits us irrevocably.'

Romanov nodded and rose. 'Very well, issue the necessary orders. But I emphasize, Comrade Savin, no further action is to be taken until the Presidium has made a decision.'

Savin's voice was oily. 'Naturally, Comrade Romanov.'

Romanov exchanged a stare with the officer, then faced the others. 'I shall have rooms assigned to you here at the dacha. We'll meet again after the Presidium meeting.'

He made to leave.

Cherepin suddenly found herself on her feet, horrified at her own audacity. 'Comrade Romanov.'

Romanov turned and looked at her.

'If the airlift to Antarctica is approved, I believe I should accompany the mission.'

'For what purpose, Comrade Cherepin?'

'The expedition will need a scientist familiar with glaciology, someone to monitor the Shelf's drift speed. Regional meteorological conditions should also be observed firsthand and figured into the calculations.'

Romanov hesitated.

'If I could just have a moment of your time, Comrade Romanov,' she said quickly. 'I'm sure I could convince you.'

He shrugged. 'Very well, Comrade Cherepin. I shall send for you after I've arranged the Presidium meeting.'

Romanov turned and left the room. The military and government leaders followed, hurrying off to phone subordinates in Moscow.

Cherepin found herself alone with Chirikov. The academy president sighed dejectedly. 'A turn of events I did not foresee, Anya. I could use some air. Will you walk with me?'

The snow had thickened. The harsh lights along the perimeter fence were diffused through the swirling flakes as they left the dacha and walked slowly across the courtyard.

She took his arm. 'It's monstrous. I wish I had never told them.'

Chirikov patted her hand. 'Anya, it would hardly have been possible for you to conceal five hundred thousand square kilometres of ice drifting north into the Pacific. If there is any blame, it is mine. I told them about the Mirnyi engines.'

'What will happen, Volodya, if Savin succeeds with his ice stations?'

The scientist sighed. 'The West will be forced to make concessions. To disarm, certainly. Economic pressure will follow. Then political demands. Slowly but inexorably the democracies will be strangled.'

'Then the coming millennium will be communist.'

'You are mistaken, Anya. Not even we live under communism. Marx, and the Greeks before him, envisioned communism as a utopian society, communal harmony, the sharing of wealth, and the withering away of the power of the state. Does that sound like the system we live under in the Soviet Union?'

A guard dog barked and yanked at his chain somewhere off through the dark snowy trees. 'Is there no way to stop them?' she asked.

'None. Savin was right. Once the ice reaches international waters and Vlasov's airborne division takes possession, it would be an act of war for the West to attack.'

They walked several steps in silence. 'Suppose the Americans were told of Savin's plan before the Shelf drifts beyond the protection of the treaty?' she asked.

'If they brought pressure to bear before the ice stations became a *fait accompli*, perhaps Romanov and the other moderates could rein in the military. But it is an idle dream, Anya. You said yourself there are only sixty some hours left before the Shelf crosses the treaty boundary. There's no way to warn the Americans in time.'

She stopped abruptly. 'I have a way, Volodya.' She told him about the pearl pendant Joshua had given her.

His face froze. 'No, Anya! I cannot allow you to attempt such a thing. If they intercept the message, you'd be shot.'

'Comrade Cherepin,' a voice called through the snow from the blur of the dacha behind them. 'The Comrade Romanov will see you.'

She gripped his arms. 'It's the only way, Volodya. They must have special scanners to pick up the transmission. It's only five thousandths of a second long. They won't be monitoring the phones of Romanov himself.'

Chirikov hesitated, his face torn by indecision.

'Comrade Cherepin!'

She pushed Chirikov in the direction of the dacha. 'Buy me two minutes, Volodya.'

'You are a brave woman, Anya.' He turned and walked towards the voice.

She tore off her gloves and found the pendant through

her thick fur collar. She turned the clasp 180 degrees and sensed more than heard the minute hum of the tiny battery as the recorder switched on.

She took a deep settling breath and began. 'This message is for Joshua McCoy. I shall soon be with you. I have found a way.'

The thick Russian snow muffled her words as Anya told McCoy of Savin's plan to bring America and the West to their knees.

## NORTHDRIFT
### 74.6 Nautical Miles

The black, dart-shaped aircraft broke through scattered clouds at 8,000 feet and throttled back, nosing down towards Andrews Air Force Base outside Washington, DC.

Admiral Waldo Rankin had always loved the sensation of flying a fast, responsive plane. After four decades he felt the same sustained rush he'd experienced the first time he'd taken the stick during his flight training at Pensacola.

The SR-96 he was flying was one of the world's fastest aircraft, capable of almost four times the speed of sound at altitudes of more than 100,000 feet. The latest successor to the early U-2 intelligence probes, the SR-96 had been especially adapted for Rankin's Antarctic research.

The plane could survey 90,000 square miles an hour with its cameras, meteorological and marine monitors, and multiple sensor systems. Below the tail was a thematic mapper, a sensing device that could scan the earth's surface at seven different frequencies of infrared radiation and distinguish mineral deposits in the earth.

The SR-96's onboard thermovision was designed to detect the heat of molten magma rising through the planet's crust. It was the thermovision that helped Rankin plot the subduction zone stretching through the Ross Sea.

Rankin brought the jet down smoothly and taxied to a hangar belonging to the National Science Foundation. He made sure the plane would be serviced and refuelled for takeoff again that evening and then put through a call to foundation headquarters.

'Afternoon, Admiral,' the director, Kevin Florence, said. 'I tried to reach you at the Cape. The satellite operator told me all your incoming systems were shut down.'

'I needed some time without interruptions, Kevin. I wanted to go back over my geological rescarch.'

'Find anything?'

'A few hints. I need more data to be sure.'

'You coming to Washington?'

'Just landed at Andrews. What's the latest from McMurdo?'

'I talked to Charlie Gates about half an hour ago. The magma discharge up through the submarine fissure is apparently increasing. The water temperature's gone up two degrees, and there's almost nonstop geysering offshore now.'

'Damn! White House know about all this yet?'

'We've got a problem there, Waldo. I called the president's national security advisor, Samson Fisk. He just didn't grasp the seriousness of the situation at all. When I told him about the Shelf, his reaction was, "I'm not going to take time from the president's busy schedule to bother him about some damn iceberg floating around the bottom of the world. I'll try to arrange a meeting next week." Then he hung up in my ear.'

'You have the number of his private line?' Rankin asked.

Florence gave it to him.

'I'll get back to you, Kevin.'

Rankin stabbed at the digits and a moment later a reserved female voice answered. 'Samson Fisk's office.'

'This is Admiral Waldo Rankin. I wish to speak with Mr Fisk.'

There was a pause. Rankin guessed she was checking a list of individuals Fisk would accept calls from.

'I'm sorry, Admiral. Mr Fisk is in conference.'

'Young lady, unless you want to find your ass in a computer pool in the sub-basement of the Pentagon tomorrow morning, you'll tell your boss I'm on the phone.'

The cool voice was suddenly unsure. 'Uh, just a minute, Admiral.'

A moment later the security adviser came on. 'You have a very forceful way with the ladies, Admiral Rankin. I'm confused though. Assigning people to the Pentagon would seem beyond your purview. You are retired, are you not?'

'Only from the navy, Mr Fisk. I'm calling regarding the crisis in Antarctica.'

'I've already informed Mr Florence I'll set something up next—'

'No, Mr Fisk. You will inform the president today. I want to meet with him and the entire Security Council as soon as possible.'

'Well now, Admiral, that just isn't goin' to be possible. The man's hosting the prime minister of France at the moment. If you think I'm going to kick Madame LeClerc's fashionably wrapped ass out of the Oval Office so you can tell the president about some problem you've got in Antarctica, you better think again.'

'It's hardly my problem alone, Mr Fisk. You don't seem able to grasp what's happening in Antarctica. The Ross Ice Shelf has broken free of the continent. It's drifting north into the Pacific. The entire West Antarctic Ice Sheet is going to follow the Shelf into the ocean. The ice will begin melting rapidly when it reaches the warmer northern latitudes. There's going to be a tremendous rise in sea levels, Mr Fisk.'

For the first time doubt edged Fisk's voice. 'Florence never said anything about a rise in sea level.'

'You didn't give him a chance.'

'Maybe I can arrange something after the diplomatic dinner tonight.'

'That's not good enough. I see the president within two hours or I'll go through the Joint Chiefs. General Lowe is a personal friend of mine.'

'Are you threatening me, Admiral Rankin?'

'You're goddamn right I am.'

Fisk wavered. 'Where can you be reached?'

'National Science Foundation. Geophysics Section.'

'By God, this better be as important as you say it is, Rankin. You may be out of government service, but there are still ways to reach you. Do I make myself clear?'

'I've never had a problem understanding people like you, Fisk. You have two hours.'

Rankin hung up and caught a cab into the city. The security adviser was only the first roadblock he'd have to clear. The American response to the Antarctic upheaval must be swift, and there was but one way to get Washington's attention fast.

He was going to scare the hell out of the president of the United States.

The USS *George Washington Carver* glided smoothly south towards Antarctica 120 feet below the surface, its nuclear engines propelling the ballistic missile submarine through the water at over forty knots.

The 18,750-ton, 559-foot-long *Carver* was larger than a battleship and armed with Trident missiles and silent-running torpedoes. There was not another submarine in the world that could match the size, speed, and electronic wizardry of the giant cigar-shaped ship.

For the past two days the American submarine, with a 160-man crew and a dozen civilian technicians onboard, had been following the Soviet Oscar class submarine *Mezen* in a top-secret test of the new antisonar devices installed during the *Carver's* last refitting in New London.

The *Carver's* huge hull had been coated with sound-absorbent paint formulated to suck up the sonar pulses emitted by searching enemy subs. The silhouette of the sail had also been altered, and the entire contour of the *Carver* could be changed in seconds by shifting computer-controlled sheathing built into the exterior plates. Soviet vessels could bounce sonar pulses off the *Carver* from 500 yards and not know the American sub was there.

So far the new technology was working perfectly and the Russian craft ahead had not the slightest clue that the *Carver* was on her tail.

Several hours ago the *Mezen* had surfaced, stayed above for twenty minutes, then dived again. Instead of resuming her leisurely course west towards the Indian Ocean, the Russian sub had veered south and doubled her speed. The *Carver's* skipper, Captain Christopher Carol, knew the *Mezen* had gone up for a satellite communications check. He was also sure she'd received new orders changing her heading.

Carol sat in a red upholstered chair in the *Carver's* control room mulling over his quarry's course change when he felt a tap on his shoulder. The officer of the deck was standing next to him. 'Captain, the *Mezen's* going deeper,' Lieutenant Commander Gerald Travers said.

The *Carver's* orders were to shadow the Soviet sub for a solid week. If they weren't detected during those seven days, the planners at Naval Operations in the Pentagon could be certain that the newly developed sonar screen lived up to its expectations. It would be a major breakthrough for the American submarine service.

'Have you plotted her angle of dive?'

'Yes, sir, about fifteen degrees.'

'Speed?'

'Forty knots, Captain.'

Carol said, 'If the *Mezen* maintains her present speed and heading, she'll reach the Ross Sea in another twelve hours or so.'

'They may be on a scheduled run to one of the Soviet bases on the continent,' Travers offered. 'Mirnyi or Novolazarevskaya.'

Carol shook his head. 'I don't think so. The course change is too abrupt. And they're steaming at flank speed. Why?'

The captain stood and stared at the white blip of the *Mezen* on the sonar screen. 'What the hell could be so important at the bottom of the world?'

Anya Cherepin followed the KGB factotum down a dacha corridor to the personal suite of the party general secretary, Mikhail Romanov, and waited as the aide knocked discreetly on a carved oak door.

'Enter,' the Soviet leader's voice answered from within. The KGB man opened the door, then closed it quietly behind her and withdrew.

Romanov stood behind his neatly ordered desk as she entered. He gestured to a facing chair and smiled. 'Please make yourself comfortable, Comrade Cherepin.'

Cherepin's eyes took in the room as she crossed to the chair. Scale models of bridges, dams, industrial complexes, and yet unbuilt futuristic cities were arrayed on scattered side tables. The pine-panelled walls were thick with framed photographs, some of various building projects but most displaying the smiling faces of men, women, and children she assumed to be the general secretary's family and friends.

Romanov waited for her to be seated before sitting again himself. 'May I offer you some tea?' he asked.

Nervously, she shook her head no. She'd heard that Romanov was a consummate gentleman, considerate to underlings. Still his manners were so starkly atypical of the Soviet elite she had known that she felt disoriented, awkward.

He looped a pair of wire-frame glasses around his ears and opened a dossier on his desk. She caught the first letters of her name on the tab.

'I see you are from Lubny, Comrade Cherepin. I spent almost a year working on the steel-rolling plant there as a young man. It is a lovely region, especially in the spring, when the land is green with wheat shoots.'

Her foremost memories of home were of the long bitter winters and hot dusty summers. But his words brought back a picture of those few weeks in April and May when the weather was temperate and the farmlands were verdant with budding crops.

'Yes, Comrade Romanov, the spring is a good time of year in the Ukraine.'

For several minutes Romanov made polite small talk, inquiring about her family and career.

He studied her file again. 'You've been to Antarctica twice, I see. Your research work there is most impressive. You've made some important contributions to Soviet polar science.'

She risked a small smile. 'Thank you. For me it is hardly work to serve the state in such a way. My research brings me so much gratification in itself.'

He smiled back. 'That is how I feel about my own career.' His hand swept an arc, taking in the trappings of office around him. 'I mean to say, the engineering work I pursued before all this.'

He scanned the papers on his desk once more, then rose and began tinkering with a bridge model on a side table. 'Ordinarily, I would have no hesitation granting your request to accompany the airlift to Antarctica. Assuming the Presidium approves the – what should I say – adventure?'

She caught the distaste in his voice.

'Unfortunately, circumstances make it difficult for me to allow you to go. Indeed, to permit any trip beyond our borders.'

Her heart was a stone anchor in her chest. He was going to deny her the mission.

'Comrade Duglenko was quite insistent I refuse you,' Romanov said evenly. 'He raised certain questions about your loyalty to the state. I believe you know why.'

Anya looked at her hands.

Romanov settled again behind his desk and sighed heavily. 'Tell me about your relationship with this American journalist McCoy. What is the truth of the matter?'

125

She hesitated.

'I assure you, Comrade Cherepin,' he said kindly, 'what you tell me will not go beyond this room.'

She looked at his guileless face, the face of a father, and believed him. Her caution and her awe at his position fell away and the emotional words poured out. She told Romanov how she had first met Melissa McCoy, how she'd become a close friend of the family. Finally, her voice rising and falling fervently, she told him how, inexorably and before she knew fully what was happening, she'd fallen in love with Joshua.

Her words became bitter as she described the KGB bug at Peredelkino, the trap they had sprung, and the demands they'd made.

Revulsion shadowed Romanov's face as she finished and there was open empathy in his gaze. 'What you have told me is all too familiar, Anna Yegorovna,' he said, crossing the boundary of familiarity to use her given name for the first time.

He nodded towards a trifold frame of family photos on the corner of his desk. 'Years ago, before I was elected general secretary, my daughter Nina fell in love with a young Dutch diplomat. He was only a junior embassy official. Nevertheless, I was a member of the Politburo, and the KGB found the liaison a threat.'

He focused sadly on his daughter's picture. 'They declared her young man *persona non grata* and ordered him out of the country. It crushed Nina's spirit. Later she married, had children. Still . . .' His voice fell off and he inclined his head towards his chest. 'Still, she has never been the same. The light had left her eyes.'

His pain emanated across the desk and for a moment Anya felt the detached grief of a stranger at a family funeral. Romanov raised his head and studied her. 'How can you possibly go, Anna Yegorovna?' You can't parachute onto the ice with the airborne troops.'

'I wouldn't have to, Comrade Romanov. The transport plane I would go in could put me down at our Antarctic base at Mirnyi after the jump. From there I can take a helicopter out to the ice.'

Romanov's eyebrows arched. 'Antarctica is an international zone. What is to keep you from defecting, from joining your American lover?'

'"Defect" implies going over to an enemy, aiding and abetting those that would harm my country, Comrade Romanov. That I would never do. I love Russia, the real Russia, deeply.'

'Yet you would go to your American if you could.'

'Yes,' she answered, then closed her eyes and waited for his damnation.

Instead he regarded her mildly. 'You are brave to admit such a thing to me, Anna Yegorovna. I am, after all, the general secretary of the Communist Party of the Soviet Union, the foremost defender of the state.'

'I think you are first a human being, Comrade Romanov,' she answered softly.

For a long moment their eyes held each other across the desk. Then he reached forward and deliberately closed her dossier.

'I will tell you frankly that I am vehemently opposed to Savin's entire scheme,' he said finally. 'I believe this military thrust he proposes will ill serve our country, regardless of whether it succeeds or fails.'

He sighed wearily. 'Yet it is probable the Presidium will back the marshal, despite my position. If the plan is approved, you may accompany the mission.'

Her heart flooded and she started forward impulsively to hug him, then caught herself and perched at the edge of her chair. 'Comrade Romanov, I haven't the words—'

He held up a restraining palm. 'There are no words necessary, Anna Yegorovna. Let us just say I am doing this for my Nina. Now, do you wish anything else?'

Her mind raced. She needed a telephone. An untapped, long-distance phone. She suddenly hated the thought of deceiving the decent man before her. Then she rationalized it was Savin who was betraying Romanov, betraying Russia with his mad scheme. If she could thwart the marshal by sending the micropulse, she would be serving the party leader, serving her country.

'I must call my office and make preparations, Comrade Romanov. If I might be allowed a phone.'

'Of course.' He rose. 'There is a direct line to Moscow in the anteroom.' He came around the desk and took her hand. 'If it is to be, I wish you a safe journey to Antarctica, Anna Yegorovna. I hope you have an opportunity to see your American again.'

She left Romanov's office in a daze, not daring to believe it was true she was going. The anteroom was deserted. Her hands trembled as she reached for the receiver.

A dacha operator was on the line instantly.

'This is Director Cherepin. I wish to place a call to the Antarctic Institute in Moscow.' She gave the number.

A moment later she was put through to her nephew.

'Have you met Comrade Romanov yet?' Sergei asked breathlessly.

'Yes, I've just left him,' she said. 'I shall be away from the institute for a while, Seryozha. There are several things that must be done in my absence.'

She gave him a list of routine administrative chores. As she finished, she placed the pendant against the mouthpiece and turned the pearl 360 degrees. In five seconds the micropulse would go out, riding the telephone microwaves.

'When are you coming back?' her nephew asked.

She felt a minute pulse of electricity jump from the receiver to her ear. She closed her eyes. It was done. Sergei's voice sounded far away.

# NORTHDRIFT
## 84.3 Nautical Miles

Melissa McCoy fought to keep her eyes open as she worked in the snug, overly warm drill hut. Despite the sub-zero Antarctic winds howling across the ice outside, the heat of the equipment had brought the interior temperature above seventy.

She'd lost track of the number of core samples she'd examined since the McMurdo Sound Seabees had pulled the rig out near the coast eight hours ago. Down fifty feet, retrieve a cylinder, down another fifty feet; she had reached the 600-foot level without finding anything unusual. The cores of Antarctic earth were all frozen as solid as rock.

The drone of the drill retreating back up its shaft with yet another cylinder was hypnotic. Her eyelids fluttered. The ringing of a small bell startled her. It signalled that the drill head was about to emerge from the casing. She straightened and yawned as she reached for her work gloves.

Her yawn turned to a gape as the final few feet of pipe backed up out of the shaft. Instead of the usual ice crystals and bits of frozen earth and rock, an incongruous sheen of oozing, steaming mud coated the stainless-steel tube.

Melissa turned off the drill motor, peeled off a glove, and reached out to touch the dripping sediment as the bit made one last slow revolution.

The mud was hot!

She checked the computer monitoring the drill motor. The heat output was normal. She looked around the hut, searching for a loose wire or faulty electrical switch that might have conducted current down the shaft to melt the icy core. Nothing.

Her nostrils caught a whiff of steam. It had the odour of sulphur. Sulphur! She reached for one of the long insulated cylinders used to carry core samples and slipped the hot tube of Antarctic earth inside.

She picked up the mobile phone and in a minute was through to Charlie Gates. 'I need a Sno-Cat out here right away, Charlie.'

'Find something?'

'Yes. I think I found exactly what my father expected.'

Joshua McCoy glanced up from the word processor as the videophone buzzed in the cabin of *Times Two*. He stabbed at a button on the console and the image of a man with a square face and flaming-red handlebar moustache appeared on the screen.

'Good afternoon, Mr McCoy. My name is Levitt Merrill. I'm senior duty officer today at the Central Intelligence Agency Communications Centre here in Langley, Virginia.'

McCoy regarded the man quizzically. 'What can I do for you, Mr Merrill?'

'Are you alone, sir?'

McCoy glanced towards the rear of the plane, where Shea and Kate were busy exploring the small galley. 'Yes.'

The officer's voice was perhaps a quarter of a second out of synchronization with his moving lips, and McCoy guessed the call was going out over a scrambler, a device that garbled conversation so that the words spoken were intelligible to only the two phones in direct communication.

'We received a micropulse communication from the Soviet Union about twenty minutes ago,' Merrill said. 'The message is for you.'

McCoy stared incredulously at Merrill. 'What the hell . . .' Then he remembered. The pendant! Anya!

'Control here in Langley has authorized immediate transmission to you, sir. Would you please prepare to receive on zero five seven point three frequency.'

McCoy reached forward and keyed the computer. 'Go ahead, Mr Merrill.'

'The communication will go out in five seconds, Mr McCoy. Good-bye, sir.'

McCoy flipped off the videophone and a moment later the words INCOMING RECORDING flashed on the computer screen. There was a soft whirling sound, then AUDIO READY appeared below the first message.

He hadn't heard Anya's voice in seven months. McCoy listened in growing disbelief as she told him of the meeting at Romanov's dacha and Marshal Savin's plan for the fortified ice stations.

Her words were rushed towards the end. 'I'm going to try to accompany the airlift. I hope . . .' She stopped in midsentence, then said in a louder voice, 'Tell Comrade Romanov I am coming.' Her tone lowered again. 'Joshua, I have—' The tape ended.

For a moment he sat numbed. Then he reversed the audio and listened to the capsule again.

Was this incredible scheme possible? He knew several countries were experimenting with engines using heat exchangers as their power source. Certainly airfields could be laid out on the pancake top of the Shelf. And it would be relatively easy to hew docks and access tunnels through the sheer cliffs edging the ice. Dammit, if the Presidium approved the plan, that bastard Savin could pull it off! Especially after the West lost its navies.

McCoy switched on the videophone and keyed the *Times's* international operator. 'Yes, Mr McCoy?'

'I want to speak to Admiral Waldo Rankin. You can reach him at the National Science Foundation in Washington. If he's not there, try the White House.'

Admiral Waldo Rankin had not been in the White House since his retirement ceremony from the navy, and he'd almost forgotten the aura of power and history that seemed to exude from the rooms.

The summons to 1600 Pennsylvania Avenue had come quickly. A deferential secret service agent found him retrieving research data from a computer in the Geophysics Section of the National Science Foundation.

There was to be a Security Council meeting in half an hour, the young agent told him. The admiral's presence was requested. A car waited outside. Twenty minutes later the president's naval aide guided Rankin down the red-carpeted corridor of the West Wing of the White House.

Halfway down the wide hall a White House assistant carrying a black briefcase met them. 'Admiral Rankin, you have an urgent international call. If you wish, you may take it in the Appointments Lobby.'

'Thank you, son.' He turned to the naval aide. 'I can find my way to the Cabinet Room, Commander. I've been there before.'

'Certainly, sir.'

The assistant opened the door to what had been the press lobby under President Kennedy and placed the case on a Chippendale table. It snapped open to reveal a video screen built into the top, with the receiver and dial face below. He extended a telescopic aerial.

'Mrs Wollcott doesn't allow permanent phones in the formal rooms,' he explained and left, closing the door quietly behind him.

Rankin picked up the receiver and the face of a White House operator appeared on the screen. 'I'm Rankin. I understand you're holding a call for me.'

'Yes, sir.' The screen went blank, then the face of Joshua McCoy came on.

'Waldo, have you seen the president yet?'

'I'm just about to, Josh. There's a Security Council meeting in ten minutes.'

'I'm glad I caught you before you went in. I just got off the phone with CIA Communications. They relayed a message from Anya Cherepin in Russia.'

Rankin cocked an eye. The strong friendship Josh and he had first established in Christchurch transcended their relationship as father and son-in-law. They'd always been up front with each other, and when Josh came back from Moscow two years ago, he'd told him about Anya and the compromising position he'd been forced into by the KGB.

He hadn't approved of Josh's romantic entanglement. How the hell could he when his own daughter was involved? Still, he'd understood. He knew the root of Melissa's failed marriage was her compulsive absorption with her research work. Her long and frequent absences – the whole focus of her life, really – had made it all but inevitable that Josh would seek in another woman the love and companionship that simply weren't there for him at home.

'Anya's message concerned a high-level session just held at Romanov's dacha outside Moscow,' McCoy went on. 'The meeting was called to formulate a Soviet response to the northdrift of the Ross Ice Shelf, and Anya attended as head of the Antarctic Institute.'

'Their coasts are threatened along with those of the rest of the world,' Rankin noted. 'I'm hoping the Soviets will cooperate in the evacuation of Third World ports and shorelines. We could use their air transports and ships.'

'I'm afraid there's not much chance of cooperation,' McCoy said. 'The Russians are bent on taking strategic advantage of what's happened, Waldo. They're planning a military occupation of the Ice.'

'What on earth do they hope to gain by that?' Rankin asked incredulously.

McCoy told him of Savin's scheme to position

offensively armed ice stations off the coasts of the Western powers.

'Their Presidium hasn't approved the plan yet, but Anya feels certain they will. If she's right, Soviet paratroopers will land on the Ice within three days.'

Rankin let out a long breath. 'Great God in heaven.'

'These Mirnyi engines, Waldo. Have you heard about them?'

'Yes, the Soviets have been using them in Antarctica for the past couple of years. Ironic. Generating power with freon heat exchangers is one of the few technological innovations the damn Russians have come up with. Usually they just steal from the West.'

'Can they use the engines the way Savin plans?' McCoy asked. 'Ten square kilometres is one hell of a mass of ice.'

'They've already moved bergs close to that size. Yes, the Mirnyis could power those ice stations right up off our coasts.'

There was a discreet knock on the door, and the presidential assistant poked his head in. 'I'm sorry to interrupt, Admiral, but the president will be leaving the Oval Office shortly for the Council meeting.'

'Thank you,' Rankin said. 'Josh, I'll get back to you.'

'Good luck, Waldo.'

Rankin recognized most of those present as he entered the Cabinet Room.

'Waldo, how the hell are you?' he was greeted just inside the door. He shook the extended hand of Admiral Chester Rogers, chief of Naval Operations.

'Good, Chester, and you?'

'Fine, fine. Put on a few pounds since I last saw you, but otherwise fit,' he said, thumping a generous midsection. 'Desk job will do it to you every time.'

Rankin smiled. 'You just need a little exercise, Chester. Hell, if I didn't jog along the beach each morning, I'd put on some seal blubber too.'

It was obvious Rogers's stocky frame would never be trim. He had a massive bulldog face to match, closely cropped brown hair, and a tough mouth capable of the saltiest vocabulary in Washington.

'Who the hell in this town can find the time to jog?' Rogers said, laughing. 'They keep me ass-deep in paperwork. The only exercise I get is swimming through the crapola.'

Rankin grinned and turned to survey the room. 'Quite a school of big fish we've got here.'

Rogers waved an arm. 'The vice-president; all the Joint Chiefs; the old man's security adviser, Fisk; Bancroft from State; Axworth from Defence; and Whitcomb from the CIA. You know Florence, of course.'

Rankin nodded.

'Do you mind telling me exactly what the hell's going on, Waldo? All I've been told so far is that there's some huge iceberg or something loose in the South Pacific.'

Before Rankin could answer, the two men were joined by the CIA director, Clyde Whitcomb. The director's sharp nose, balding pate, and dark protruding eyes gave him the perpetual look of a startled bird of prey. Behind his back he was known as the Buzzard, a reference to his insatiable appetite for unsavoury Washington gossip as much as to his appearance. He was universally disliked.

The year Rankin had retired from the navy, Whitcomb had tried to have an Agency electronics surveillance team stationed at McMurdo Sound. Rankin had blocked the intelligence incursion, invoking the provisions of the Treaty of Christchurch forbidding military or political activity on the continent. Whitcomb still harboured a grudge.

'I'm rather surprised to see you at a Security Council meeting, Admiral,' Whitcomb said, a thin smile parting his lips. 'I'd come to regard your loyalties as more international these days.'

Rankin's face darkened. 'My position as chairman of the Antarctic Conference doesn't transcend the obligation I have always felt towards my country and its security.'

'Your policy statements on mineral extraction in Antarctica could hardly be considered pro-American,' Whitcomb taunted him.

Admiral Rogers stepped between the men. 'I hate to break you two chums up, but what say we grab seats before the old man gets here.'

Rankin glared at the CIA director as Rogers nudged him away. 'I'd like to kick that bastard's ass from here to McMurdo Sound.'

'He wants to get a rise out of you, Waldo. That's how he gets his jollies. One of these days someone is going to strangle the ugly creep.'

They sat down at the conference table. 'Tell me about Wollcott, Chester. I've never met him. What kind of a president is he?'

'I spent some time in the Oval Office during the naval appropriations hearings a couple of months ago. I got the feeling he isn't comfortable with the big decisions. He must have called in Fisk or had him on the phone eight, ten, times before he could finally make up his mind to cut that new carrier we requested.'

The conversation in the room died away. Everyone rose as the chief White House usher, Jason, appeared in the doorway, his sixty-four-year-old ebony face noble and expressionless.

'Gentlemen, the president of the United States.'

John Stans Wollcott crossed the Cabinet Room with the broad strides of a man six foot six inches tall. Despite his gangling frame, he walked with a smooth, almost graceful gait, as if his muscles were aware they were moving the most powerful man on earth.

At forty-six he had auburn hair that had yet to sprout its first strands of grey and an oblong face that showed few of the usual worry or laugh lines of a man in his middle years. He had the nose of an Arab falconer, ridge-boned and boldly hooked, set between hard hazel eyes and tufted reddish brows.

His narrow lips parted in a perfunctory smile as he acknowledged the men in the room with an impersonal nod and folded himself into the presidential seal-embossed chair at the head of the Cabinet table.

As the others took their seats, he appraised them one by one. With the exception of Admiral Rankin, whom he knew only by reputation, he had already taken the measure of each of the individuals seated before him.

Vice-President Glenda Roberts was the only woman there. She was a former Berkeley dean and California senator. Her independent positions often clashed with the official White House line. The other members of his Cabinet were loyal, predictable, most, like himself, Republicans and men of substantial private means. Two of them had been advisers during his successive terms as governor of Delaware. The military Chiefs he considered a notch below his civilian Cabinet.

He looked towards his national security adviser. 'Sam, I've got half the diplomatic corps in this town drinking my booze and waiting for dinner with Madame LeClerc,' he said, adjusting the stiff shirt front of his white tie and tails. 'What's this sudden urgency about Antarctica?'

Samson Fisk was a rare combination of successful academic and businessman. He had begun his career as a Russian history professor at Yale and had been named head of the Soviet Studies Department at the University of Chicago at the age of thirty-one. A Ph.D. in international relations, he'd moved on to the Hoover Institution, a conservative Stanford think tank, and then abruptly, at thiry-five, he left the campus circle for the business world.

He'd taken over a small microelectronics firm in Texas in the mid-eighties and built it into the giant Southwest Technologies conglomerate that now did several billion dollars' worth of business each year.

The foundation of his business success was his early realization that Russia represented a vast market for his technological products. He'd forged close commercial ties with Moscow through the unorthodox expedient of being willing to barter where other countries demanded cash.

Fisk had traded his computers and microelectronic processors for Russian timber, diamonds, sable pelts, even Czarist artwork. When he, in turn, sold the Soviet goods on Western markets, his profits were twice what a straight cash deal would have reaped.

While he did business with Moscow and was welcome at the Kremlin, he was virulently anticommunist, a political sentiment he kept masked from all but a few powerful friends in American government. Only a handful of men knew that several of Fisk's salesmen and technicians abroad were US intelligence agents.

John Stans Wollcott was one of those who knew. The Republican president had named Fisk his national security adviser a month after his election.

'I apologize for the assault on your liquor cabinet, Mr President,' Fisk said, loosening a button on the formal jacket that stretched across his barrellike torso. 'I'd hoped to bring the Security Council together on this at a more convenient time. However, Admiral Rankin here insisted rather forcefully that we have some sort of global crisis on our hands. I think it appropriate he explain why we're sitting here instead of at the dinner table.'

Rankin ignored Fisk. 'I'll leave it to you to judge the urgency of the matter I bring before this council, Mr President. At six thirty-six A.M. Washington time today, one of NASA's geological survey satellites in polar orbit detected the movement of magma through the seabed off the western coast of Antarctica. The GRAVSAT data show a two-hundred-and-twenty-mile-long volcanic fissure has split open the floor of the Ross Sea. Both satellite observation and reports from American scientists at our McMurdo Sound Research station confirm that violent thermal activity has set loose an immense body of ice into the South Pacific. The Ross Ice Shelf, a floating glacier some two hundred thousand square miles in area, is now drifting north away from the continent.'

The incredible size of the ice brought stunned expressions to several faces.

The owlish secretary of state, Miles Bancroft, peered at Rankin through his thick, horn-rimmed glasses. 'Am I to understand this shelf is one single block of ice?'

Rankin nodded. 'The largest single mass of ice that's ever entered the ocean.'

'How fast is it drifting?' Bancroft asked.

'The Shelf is moving out to sea at approximately six point nine miles per hour,' Rankin said. 'At this moment, it has drifted almost ninety miles north.'

Bancroft's expression remained sceptical. 'What evidence is there that the ice link between the Shelf and the shore won't re-form?'

Rankin turned to the director of the National Science Foundation. 'I think you should answer that, Kevin.'

'The proof, Mr Secretary, is in the GRAVSAT readings,' the brawny, Irish-faced Florence said. 'The latest data show magma continuing to vent from the submarine fissure. The water between the Shelf and the coast will grow steadily warmer. The ice bridges will not re-form.'

'The northdrift is irreversible,' Rankin said, 'as is the chain of events that will shortly follow in Antarctica.' He described the West Antarctic Ice Sheet and the glacial studies that projected the Ice surging out into the Pacific through the suddenly open avenue of the Ross Sea.

Vice-President Glenda Roberts raised a pencil. 'I'm not a glaciologist, Admiral, but it occurs to me that two and a half million square miles of ice must contain an incredible amount of water. Aren't we facing a drastic rise in sea level when it begins to melt?'

Rankin looked across at Roberts, then turned deliberately towards the president. 'When the entire Sheet has melted into the ocean, the world's sea levels will rise twenty point six feet.'

There was a shocked silence in the room.

President Wollcott's fingers fidgeted unconsciously with a Mars rock cuff link. 'How long will it take, Admiral, for the Sheet to melt?'

'I can't give you a definitive answer, Mr President, not at this moment. There are several variables involved.'

'Such as?'

'Meterological conditions, ocean currents, marine factors that will determine how quickly the Ice reaches the temperate latitudes. There is also the worsening volcanism in the Ross Sea to consider. If we're lucky, the meltdown won't be complete for decades.'

'And if we're unlucky?'

'The waters of the Ross Sea will continue to warm as

magma is ejected through the ocean floor, and both the Ross Shelf and the Ice Sheet will begin melting rapidly in a matter of days, perhaps hours.'

'Admiral Rankin, are you telling us we're about to lose our port cities, our shorelines?' Fisk asked incredulously.

'That is exactly what I am telling you,' Rankin said evenly.

The president stared stonily across the table. 'If the volcanism worsens, are we then facing a sudden ocean flood, Admiral? An abrupt inundation of our coasts?'

'No, Mr President. Whatever the rate of meltdown, the continental United States will have a margin of warning. It is the islands and shores in the southern hemisphere that will go under first. Gradually the rising seas will inundate our western coasts and those of Canada, and across the Pacific the ports and low-lying areas of Siberia, Japan, and China. It will only be a matter of time, of course, before the Indian and Atlantic Oceans crest. A coastal strip from Maine to Georgia will go under, most of Florida and the rim of the Gulf of Mexico. In Europe, Holland will disappear beneath the waves, as well as the ports of every country bordering the sea.'

'And the human loss, Admiral Rankin?' Vice-President Roberts asked, her voice barely above a whisper. 'Have your calculations told you how many people are imperiled?'

'Millions, Madame Vice-President. Millions.'

The Security Council members sat dumbfounded, their eyes riveted on Rankin.

'There won't be a harbour left on the planet,' Admiral Rogers said, a crack in his gruff voice.

Rankin gathered himself. The Council would have to absorb a second blow. 'I'm afraid there'll be one country with naval ports, Chester. Not just berths for their ships but fully equipped harbour installations fortified with landing fields, anti-aircraft lasers, and armoured combat troops. Military stations several square miles in area. Stations of ice.'

He described the Minyl engines. Then he laid out

Marshal Savin's plan to confront a navyless West with floating Soviet strongholds in strategic positions off the coasts of the Pacific powers.

The Security Council members listened motionless, ashen faced.

'The plan's preliminary steps have already been taken, gentlemen,' he finished. 'The Russian Thirty-second Karelian Division, a unit trained and equipped for polar operations, has been ordered to their military airfield at Tashkent. As soon as there is final Presidium approval, the division will be airlifted to Antarctica. Their troops will seize control of the Ross Shelf the moment the Ice crosses the boundary of the Treaty of Christchurch.'

A burst of outrage and consternation filled the room.

Axworth, the secretary of defence, was on his feet, his reed-thin pin-striped body quivering in indignation. 'This is tantamount to a declaration of war, Mr President.'

Air Force General Edgar Garvin pushed his 220 pounds up beside Axworth. Garvin's square, thick-browed face was flushed. 'I recommend the Strategic Air Command be put on full alert, Mr President. Our MX missile system must go to readiness level yellow. Perhaps to red.'

The chairman of the Joint Chiefs frowned impatiently. General James Lowe had been serving as a military attaché in Beirut the night terrorists levelled the American Embassy with a huge car bomb. The explosion blew both his arms off at the elbows.

He had fought the army's attempts to give him a medical discharge for over two years and finally won by enlisting the support of most of the senior officers he'd served under. Lowe had a brilliant analytical mind, and the men he'd worked for unanimously endorsed his argument that his discharge would be an unnecessary loss to the army.

Lowe had risen rapidly through the officer corps, unhampered by his two prosthetic arms. He was a calm, reasonable man who hated war and the death and destruction it brought.

He raised a plastic palm toward General Garvin. 'Let's

142

go easy here, Ed. Their Presidium hasn't approved the Savin plan yet. Beyond that, I find it hard to accept the plausibility of such a manoeuvre. Admiral Rankin, are you certain the Soviets have the capability to move a mass of ice thousands of feet thick and several square miles in area the entire length of the Pacific?'

'The concept is entirely viable, General Lowe. I've seen the Mirnyi engine in use in Antarctica moving huge bergs away from Soviet shore installations along the Indian Ocean coast. The engine is capable of exactly what the Russians intend.'

Samson Fisk ran a hand through his thinning blond hair. 'Mr President, I'd like to point out we don't even know where Admiral Rankin's rather incredible information came from. How can we be sure we're dealing with a solid piece of intelligence here?'

'A valid point, Sam,' Wollcott said. 'Admiral Rankin, may we know your source?'

'I'm sorry, Mr President, you may not. The intelligence came from an individual who is still in the Soviet Union. A leak would cost that person his life.'

Clyde Whitcomb's voice was indignant. 'Are you suggesting the members of the Security Council cannot be trusted?'

'No, Director Whitcomb, I am simply maintaining no valid need to know exists here. I am an American naval officer of flag rank. Surely my information requires no further qualification.'

'You are a goddamn *retired* naval officer, Rankin,' Whitcomb said furiously. 'Mr President, my own people within the Soviet Union report no such intelligence about any Russian airlift to Antarctica.'

'My source was present when the decision was made, I can tell you that much,' Rankin said.

'This is getting us nowhere,' the president said angrily. 'Clyde, I want your intelligence cells in Russia on this immediately.'

'Goddamn waste of time.'

Wollcott flushed. 'That's a direct order! General Lowe,

I want increased satellite surveillance over their military airport at Tashkent.'

The president turned to Rankin. 'I'm going to assume for now your information is accurate, Admiral, and that the Soviet Presidium will approve the plan. However, until I have verification from our intelligence sources, I shall not initiate any overt American response.'

'What about SAC?' General Garvin asked.

'They will continue at green level. None of our military units will go on alert until I am personally satisfied that the Soviets intend to move troops onto the Ross Shelf and carry through this ice station scheme Admiral Rankin has described.'

Garvin shook his head silently in disagreement.

'And if you receive verification, Mr President?' Samson Fisk asked.

Wollcott looked across at the chairman of the Joint Chiefs. 'General Lowe, have we the means to oppose a Soviet force if they move to occupy the Shelf?'

'Yes, Mr President, and no.'

'I beg your pardon?'

'We have the troops, sir, the Eighty-second Airborne, One Hundred and First Airmobile, Seventh Marine Amphibious, all rapid deployment outfits. But we don't have the transport planes. The Pentagon has been trying to get Congress to authorize appropriations for additional troop and cargo aircraft since the early eighties. Each year the requests have been pared from military authorizations.'

The flush had spread from the president's neck to his hairline. 'Do you recommend, General, that we let the Soviets waltz onto the Shelf unopposed?'

'I can put four or five thousand men on the ice in twenty-four to thirty-six hours, if you so order. But I'd have to strip every command from Asia to Europe, including domestic, to do it. Worse, those boys would have to go in only lightly armed. Men or matériel – we can't move both. The Russian airlift capability is ten times our own. They could not only land the Thirty-second Karelian

144

but also laser tanks, missile batteries, choppers. They'd chew us to pieces!'

Wollcott's eyes sought out Rogers. 'Do we have any naval forces in the area?'

'Nothing except the USS *George Washington Carver*, an Ohio class Trident submarine. She's been trailing a Russian sub for about two days now. At last report the Carver was approximately thirteen hundred miles south-east of New Zealand.'

'Trailing?'

'Yes, sir. We're conducting a test of the experimental antisonar devices developed in New London. Basically the same technology we've equipped the Stealth aircraft with.'

Wollcott shook his head. 'Assuming Admiral Rankin's right, we're not going to stop a Soviet division with one submarine. I want contingency plans from the Pentagon.'

'Mr President,' Vice-President Roberts said. 'Until we know one way or another about possible Soviet military manoeuvres, shouldn't we be concerning ourselves with the coming sea level rise? That appears to be the more certain threat at the moment.'

'I'm coming to that, Glenda.' Wollcott looked at his security adviser. 'Sam, I'm appointing you head of an ad hoc Antarctic Crisis Group. I want evacuation plans for the port cities and endangered shore areas, including possible population resettlement areas. You're to come up with estimates of the impact of a sea level rise on coastal industrial centres, agricultural regions, transportation, communications, and food distribution.'

'I'll put my staff to work immediately, Mr President.'

'Admiral Rankin, I trust I can rely on you keeping the Crisis Group advised of any further intelligence you receive, as well as of developments in Antarctica.'

'Of course, Mr President. I'm leaving for Christchurch immediately after this meeting. As chairman of the Antarctic Conference, however, it must be understood that the status bulletins I issue on the Shelf will be available to every nation.'

'Including the goddamn communists, Rankin?' Whitcomb spat.

'There are millions of lives in the balance, Director. I have no intention of letting people drown because their ideology is at odds with our own.'

'This is not the moment for political distinctions, Clyde,' Wollcott chided Whitcomb. 'I'll put the US Information Agency and our communications satellite network at your complete disposal, Admiral.'

'Thank you, Mr President, but I must decline. To use an American government agency to disseminate my reports would make them suspect to some nations. We can't afford the delay in evacuations that might cause. I've arranged to send my advisories out through the *New York Times* Pacific bureau chief, Joshua McCoy. Mr McCoy has a reputation for veracity, and the reach of the *Times's* media network is worldwide. As an American citizen, however, I'll also keep you advised of any further intelligence I receive on the Soviet airlift.'

Wollcott rose. 'Very well, Admiral, I'll trust your judgement.' He looked around the table as the others came to their feet. 'I have the prime minister of France waiting. General Lowe, I'd like those contingency plans by morning. Director Whitcomb, you will contact me the moment you receive any intelligence on a Soviet move to the Ross Shelf. Sam, I want you to work up that analysis of coastal evacuations as soon as possible. Gentlemen, good evening.'

Samson Fisk came around the table to Rankin's side as Wollcott left the room. 'Naturally, Admiral, your reports to the president will come through me.'

Rankin snapped his briefcase shut. 'I expect direct access to the Oval Office right down the line, Mr Fisk. Understood?'

The security adviser's pale complexion reddened as Rankin spun on his heel and moved through the door. Fisk collected his notes and walked towards his office. He had clipped the wings of more than one eagle on his trek to the right hand of the president of the United States. He'd find a way to bring Rankin down.

Charlie Gates was waiting with John Michaels, the research director, and Peter Buxton, the marine geologist, when Melissa McCoy entered the McMurdo Sound lab carrying the insulated cylinder.

She put the tube down carefully on a long table and unscrewed the top. A small cloud of sulphuric vapour rose from the case and dissipated into the air.

The men stared incredulously at each other.

'If I didn't know you were using a shallow capacity drill, I'd swear by the smell you'd reached the asthenosphere,' Buxton said.

The asthenosphere is a plastic zone of the earth's mantle sixty to 125 miles down, where rock is close to the melting point.

'Were you watching the temperature in the shaft?' Michaels asked. 'It doesn't take much to heat steel in the confined space of that pipe.'

McCoy shook her head. 'I dozed a bit during retrieval, but I checked the computer monitor after the drill head came up. The laser heat in the shaft never went above normal. The core wasn't warmed by the machinery, John. There's something heating up the crust beneath us. Something my father knew I'd find.'

Buxton stared out of the window towards the Ross Sea. 'There hasn't been any geysering for several hours now. The GRAVSAT data we're receiving show that the magma discharge along the fissure has concentrated at one dominant sea-floor vent under the Ice – in the middle of the bay about two hundred and twenty miles from us. I'm convinced a submarine volcano is building out there.'

Michaels's eyes narrowed. 'If you're right and there is

a large cone rising from the sea floor, that would mean a considerable magma source.'

'That's what I'm getting at. We've been assuming the magma was being generated by a relatively shallow subduction zone. But let's consider what we know so far. First, an active fissure opens up off the coast; next, satellite observations turn up a major vent over two hundred miles away; and now, Melissa's found evidence that magma's rising under the continental landmass as well. I don't see how a subduction zone could account for the incredible volume of molten material being spewed up.'

Gates studied the geologist. 'What are you suggesting, Peter?'

'I think I know what Admiral Rankin suspected when he asked Melissa to bring up a core from the crust,' Buxton said. He turned to the woman. 'Will you see if you can reach your father?'

She nodded and went to the videophone.

'Charlie, we've got to find out fast how big the magma chamber is,' Buxton said. He looked at Michaels. 'John, have you run the seismograph tapes yet?'

'Haven't had a chance, Peter. I've been tied up computing the drift-path data on the Shelf.'

'Put that on hold and plug in the seismograph readings.'

'I'll run the tape on the shallow tremors first. It'll take a few minutes.'

The McMurdo Station communications centre located Admiral Rankin preparing for takeoff from Andrews Air Force Base. Melissa told him quickly about the hot core sample as Gates and Buxton gathered behind her.

'What do you think, Peter?' Admiral Rankin asked tersely.

'All the evidence points to a gargantuan magma source somewhere under McMurdo Sound, Admiral.'

'I agree. I spoke to the people in the Geodynamics Branch at Goddard about ten minutes ago. Their GRAVSAT data show that lava discharge is increasing rapidly through that vent under the Ice. Have you got a fix on the main magma chamber yet?'

'We're running the seismograph tapes now, Admiral.'

Molten magma moving in a subterranean chamber produces continuous miniquakes in the surrounding dense rock that can be detected by seismographs on the surface. The quakes plotted by the seismograph trace the outline of the magma chamber in the crust, like an X-ray showing a cavity in a tooth.

John Michaels hurried over with a computer printout. 'These are the shallow readings,' the research director said. 'I'll have the deeper tremors charted in a minute.'

Buxton scanned the sheet and shook his head grimly. 'The main chamber is directly under that dominant vent, Admiral. A line of feeder dikes is supplying magma to the submarine fissure and to another smaller reservoir that runs under the station.'

'Son of a bitch!' Michaels's voice came from the other side of the room, where he stood reading the second computer printout. He rushed back to the videophone, his face flushed. 'I have the graph of the intermediate to deep quakes, Admiral, five to fifty miles down.'

'What does the profile show?'

'A vertical conduit of molten magma about four miles wide rising through the crust beneath McMurdo Sound. The source has to be somewhere far down in the mantle.'

Rankin's face was an iron mask. 'About three thousand miles down, I'd say.'

The scientists in the laboratory stared back silently at Rankin.

'I need one further piece of evidence to be sure,' he said. 'Peter, as I recall, there's a computerized spectroscope in the lab there.'

'You want to run a spectral analysis for helium three,' Buxton said.

'Immediately! Melissa, will you pull that core out of its casing?'

'Of course, Dad.' She went to the sink and used a piston-shaped plunger to ease the sediment from the tube.

Rankin said, 'John, you run the spectral analysis.'

'Right away, Admiral,' Michaels took a sliver of the core from Melissa McCoy and brought it to the lab's spectroscope.

Gates searched for his pipe. 'Forgive an ignorant astrophysicist, Waldo, but what will the helium-three level tell us?'

'A great deal, Charlie. Volcanic material that has risen recently from great depths is significantly higher in the helium-three level than lava deposits at the surface. The more helium three in a sample, the deeper the source of the magma.'

Michaels finished running the spectral analysis and strode rapidly across the room. He stopped, wordless, in front of the videophone and handed Buxton the printout.

The geologist read the numbers and looked up sharply. 'These can't be right!'

'I ran the sample twice, Peter.' Michaels insisted. 'They're right.'

Buxton let the printout fall to his side as he stared silently back at Rankin. 'I've never seen anything like this, Admiral,' he said finally. 'The helium-three level is over a hundred and fifty times normal surface readings.'

'I think we have our evidence, Peter,' Rankin said, his voice toneless. 'A plume has broken through the crust beneath the Ross Sea!'

A sudden exhalation of pipe smoke came from Gates's mouth. 'A plume! You mean one of those hot spots through the mantle, like the one that built up the Hawaiian Island chain?'

'That's right, Charlie,' Rankin said. 'The potential volume of lava that could be erupted through the Ross Sea floor is virtually incalculable.'

Melissa's hands flew to her face. 'Dad, the Shelf! Its right over the main vent!'

'From the GRAVSAT data, I'd be willing to bet that vent's building itself into a submarine volcano, Admiral,' Buxton added.

'I agree,' Rankin said. 'The next couple of days will be critical. The sheer volume of magma rising through the plume makes an eruption inevitable. Peter, do you think there's a chance those secondary dikes feeding the fissure could reopen?'

'There hasn't been any geysering for the past few hours, but, yes, it's possible,' Buxton answered dispiritedly.

'If magma's siphoned off along that rift, it would relieve the pressure under the dominant vent. Buy us some time,' Rankin said. 'We have to know if that fissure is still active.'

Gates said, 'That's why you wanted the submersible *Alvin* brought down here, isn't it Waldo? You intend to dive on those vents!'

Melissa took a step towards the video screen. 'Dad, no! I won't let you!'

'If the geysering starts up again, we'll have our answer and I won't need to go down, sweetheart. But let's cross one bridge at a time. Charlie, better have an evacuation aircraft readied out at Marble Point Field. I'm going to issue a bulletin for all member nations of the Antarctic Conference to prepare to pull their mining and research people out of West Antarctica in a hurry. They're holding my plane. Contact me immediately if there's any change in the rate the magma is venting.'

The admiral said good-bye and one by one the men filed out to begin assembling the research material they'd accumulated during the past year in Antarctica.

Melissa McCoy remained sitting silently alone in the lab. She rose finally and walked over to a window facing the coast. For a long time she stood there motionless, staring out beyond the shore, willing the geysers to erupt again through the heaving grey surface of the polar sea.

Joshua McCoy parted the curtain and looked in on his daughters napping in the tiny sleeping alcove at the rear of *Times Two*.

As always, his eyes softened, and he stood there watching their little faces so peaceful and fragile in sleep. They looked the babies they'd been so short a time ago. Six-year-old Kate the more so, but Shea too, although at nine she would have been indignant that he still thought of her that way.

He bent and kissed them both lightly, loving the feel of their little girl breaths against his face as his lips brushed their skin. It was one of the small magic moments that gave meaning to his life, made the sacrifice and worry of fatherhood eminently worthwhile. He wondered again how Melissa could possibly find more reward in her work than in the tender experience of their children.

A chime on the midcabin console signalled an incoming call and he walked back to the video screen. The head that appeared was encased in a visored helmet joined at the neck to a silvery flight suit. McCoy recognized the Antarctic Conference logo on the helmet front.

'I've been expecting your call, Waldo. Where are you?'

'Over Colorado, Josh. We don't have as much time as I'd thought. I've ordered all research and mining posts in West Antarctica readied to pull out on an hour's notice. I'm particularly concerned about Melissa and our people at McMurdo.'

McCoy stared at the video screen. 'What's happened?'

'What I feared most, Josh.'

Rankin told McCoy about the discovery of the plume and about the submarine volcano that satellite surveillance had now confirmed was rising from the sea floor towards the underside of the Ross Ice Shelf.

152

'That plume is a virtually limitless magma source,' Rankin finished. 'If there's a major volcanic eruption, billions of tons of ice will melt within milliseconds. There'll be a sudden cataclysmic rise in sea levels, starting in the southern hemisphere.'

McCoy let out a long breath. 'Good God, Waldo, we're going to need evacuation planes, helicopters, ships. What was the White House reaction at your meeting? Can we expect the help we need from Washington?'

'The president's set up an Antarctic Crisis Group under Samson Fisk. Fisk's drawing up plans for the evacuation of our coasts. I expect him to authorize the immediate use of military aircraft and ships when I explain our latest findings on the plume. If there's any foot-dragging, I'll go right to the president.'

'How did the Security Council react to Anya's information?'

'It stunned them, of course. Still, Wollcott's a cautious man. He wants verification from our own intelligence sources. Understandable. I don't know what action he'll take once he gets it. Short of total war, our military options are limited.'

'I'll punch in the information on the plume and the preparations in Washington and get my first piece right out, Waldo.'

'Thanks, Josh. I'll keep you informed. See you and the kids in Christchurch.'

McCoy watched Rankin's image fade from the video screen. Then he turned to the word processor and began writing the story that would tell three billion people the earth was about to change forever.

The narrow dirt road snaking up into the steep hills of Campbell Island was rutted and stony. The Maori natives struggled slowly in a long line up the winding grade towards the mountain caves where Chauncey Dutcheyes held court.

The first of the islanders had already reached the high camp and were staking out resting places among the large volcanic boulders that offered shelter from the cold winds. A hundred yards up the slope, Miki stood in front of a barn-sized cavern, directing the unloading of a truckload of food and kitchen supplies.

From a spring down the slope, a bucket line of men and boys passed jugs of water hand over hand to be stored in the main cavern and in smaller caves along the cliffs.

The evacuation was going well, Miki mused, warmed by the total trust the Maori people had shown in her great-great-great-grandfather. The ancient prophet had called the islanders together and in a few terse sentences had told them what was to come.

A great wave would rise from the south, he'd said, from the far land of ice. The wave would be twice again as high as the greatest tsunami that had ever come against their island. At midday tomorrow, Chauncey had warned, the lowlands of Campbell would vanish beneath this towering wall of water. The Maori must climb to the safety of the mountain caves.

The last of the foodstuffs was moved into the cool depths of the cavern, and Miki followed the bearers in, showing them where to store the canned goods and perishables. She thanked the men as they filed past. The last, a teenager she had once tutored, stopped and gave her a questioning grin. 'So much food, Miki. How long will we have to stay up here in the caves?'

'I don't know, Laika – until the water goes down.'

'Does Chauncey Dutcheyes know?'

'Yes, I'm sure he knows. He'll tell us when he's ready.'

The boy shrugged. 'I don't mind, however long. There is no school up here. We can play rugby all day.'

She laughed. 'You've got your fondest wish, haven't you. Now shoo and let me finish my work.'

Laika grinned and ambled out of the cavern entrance. Miki went back to her inventory, moving perishables nearer the cool stone walls and noting what supplies they still needed to feed the islanders in the days or perhaps weeks ahead.

She was lifting a fragile case of eggs to a ledge when she felt a presence behind her. She looked back. The seal hunter Kleech stood near one of the arching walls staring at her.

Kleech was a loner. He hunted and lived by himself, coming into town only when he needed groceries or whisky. Each morning he set out in his motorized skiff to hunt seals in the green waters off the coast.

The flesh of his catch he left for the other predators of the sea. All Kleech was after were the seals' pelts, which he sold to the fur traders who came down from Christchurch twice a year.

This was not the first time Miki had caught the hulking fisherman watching her, although always before there had been someone else around. A shiver rippled down her spine.

She took a grip on herself, and faced him. 'I don't like you sneaking up on me, Kleech! Is there something you want?'

He motioned with his chin towards the egg crate. 'I've come to help, to move boxes.'

She forced a smile. 'I don't need any help, but thank you for volunteering. There'll be another truck up soon. You could unload.'

He straightened and moved towards her. 'Why do you dislike me, Miki? You avoid me always.'

She looked past him down the long cavern hall towards

the entrance. She knew he could catch her before she made it outside. 'It's not that I dislike you, Kleech. We simply have different interests. Besides, you keep to yourself.'

He stopped two steps from her. 'You have lived in Christchurch and now a Maori fisherman is not good enough for you. Is that not how it is? How many fine white men did you lie with, Miki?'

Her eyes flashed. 'You're a pig, Kleech! Get out of here!'

He was on her before she could move, one hand twined in her long dark hair while the other pawed at the top of her wool sweater. She turned her head and bit savagely into his wrist, spinning away from his grip as he screamed and let go of her hair.

Her sweater ripped as she fell to the cavern floor. Before she could get up, he was over her, his lips parted at the sight of her breasts, his hands pinning her shoulders to the dirt. She could smell the caked seal blood beneath his nails.

Miki closed her eyes as he brought his face down towards hers.

A sudden command echoed from the cavern hall. 'Kleech! Stop!'

They both recognized the voice of Chauncey Dutcheyes. Kleech cursed and came to his feet. Miki sprang up and ran to her great-great-great-grandfather.

The old man's piercing purple eyes gripped the shark hunter. 'In days past you would have been banished forever from our island for what you have tried to do!'

Kleech's face was a mixture of maddened frustration and fearful awe of the frail seer. He had the strength to snap the back of this damn old man with his bare hands. Yet Chauncey was a powerful mystic and to attack him would be to court dark trouble.

'I warn you to stay away from my great-granddaughter, Kleech.'

The seal hunter moved towards the cave entrance. 'Your powers do not frighten me any longer, old man,' he spat,

156

his retreat giving the lie to his bravado. 'Tomorrow we will all drown under the great tsunami. What is there left to fear from you?' He turned and lumbered from the cavern.

Chauncey stroked his great-great-great-granddaughter's hair. 'Are you all right, Miki?'

She hugged him tightly. 'Yes, because you were here.'

He put his arm around her and they walked towards the bright oval of sunlight at the cave mouth.

'Was Kleech right, Great-grandfather?' she asked in a small voice. 'Are we all to die tomorrow?'

'Many people will perish, my child, many,' he said, his luminescent eyes staring ahead. 'Yet death shall not come here to Campbell.'

'But the tsunami will kill others? How many others?'

'Tomorrow, Miki. Your answers will come tomorrow.'

The Ross Ice Shelf drifted inexorably north, its huge mass dominating the ocean and air as no other floating entity had in the history of man.

A great flock of whirling, diving skua gulls circled overhead, confused by the changed position of the Shelf, their bewildered cries melding with the sound of waves breaking against the chiselled white cliffs.

A pod of baleen whales approached the immense iceberg and swam inquisitively along the perimeter, as perplexed as the skuas by the emergence of the Ice into the open sea.

The Shelf had been born on land millions of years past, gradually pushed out into the Ross Sea by the pressure of glaciers growing behind it, and the underside of the iceberg held tons of rocks and soil picked up as the Ice scraped over the Antarctic ground.

Now the thin bottom layer of ice containing the earth and stone began to melt in the warm seawater, and a great grey-brown cloud of silt was released downward out of the Ice.

A young male baleen spotted the filmy debris and dove to search the murk for plankton. The four-year-old whale glided beneath the ice and, finding no food, pushed upward, poking his nose curiously into the underside of the Shelf. The heavy snout dislodged a three-ton boulder, and the great marine mammal watched as it slowly descended into the depths.

A quarter of a mile away his mate heard his delighted clicks and swam towards the source, finding him again nudging the Ice. She watched as he bumped upward: once, twice, another large rock popped out of the Shelf and spiralled down, a trail of air bubbles following it into the gloom.

The female caught on at once and, squeaking her

enjoyment, joined her mate in this new game. The rest of the pod circled, and news of the intriguing sport was passed along with sentences of clicks and squeaks.

Twenty-nine hundred miles beneath the swimming whales, far down in the planet's fiery deep mantle, the earth's intense heat generated continuous convection currents that forced the plume of molten magma up towards the Antarctic surface. Four miles wide, the plume rose as a vertical red river of viscous rock that coursed through the crust and emptied into a great subterranean reservoir six miles beneath the bay from which the Ross Shelf drifted towards the open sea.

As if a snake dead but for its head, the 220-mile fissure stretching out to McMurdo Sound had quieted to sporadic quivers, only occasional bursts of steam jetting from the line of lava ducts. The magma discharge was concentrated now below the dominant vent that had grown over the hours into a submarine volcano.

More and more molten rock pulsed up from the plume, and the continuously erupting mountain rose inexorably from the ocean floor.

Like a dagger probing a soft belly, the rising volcano pushed its peak higher and higher towards the Ross Ice Shelf drifting above.

# NORTHDRIFT
## 124.2 Nautical Miles

August Sumner tightened, then released the knotted muscles at the back of his neck as he read the *Times's* wire service story from Tokyo. It was 12:30 A.M. Monday morning in New York.

Consternation was building in Japan over the sudden, inexplicable disappearance of the country's Antarctic Krill Fishing Fleet. A Japanese infrared oceanographic survey satellite had photographed the separation of the Ross Shelf from the continent, and officials were openly speculating that the drifting ice and the vanished ships were connected.

The intercom on Sumner's desk buzzed. 'Yes?'

'Toby Watts at the Pacific desk, August. A story just came in from Josh McCoy. You asked to be called.'

'Thanks. Read it to me, will you, Toby?'

Sumner listened to the graphic word picture McCoy had painted of the Ross Sea plume and the increasing volcanism under the northdrifting Shelf.

A messenger walked through the editor's open door and handed him a sheaf of satellite photographs of West Antarctica he'd requested from the *Times's* files. 'Thanks,' Sumner said, signing for the pictures.

'I was interrupted, Toby. Could you read me those last paragraphs again?'

'He describes the probable ocean flooding, then he goes on, "Such a rise would inundate most of the Florida peninsula, much of the lower Mississippi River system, and the Chesapeake and San Francisco Bay areas, among other low-lying coastal stretches of the United States.

"'The great seaports of New York, London, Buenos Aires, Cape Town, Hong Kong, Tokyo, and Los Angeles could become, like today's Venice, cities of canals, as the

160

rising seas inundate every street, structure, and open space less than twenty-six feet above the present sea level.

"'Beyond the paralysis of the world's great seaport cities, the global effects of the now apparently inescapable flood on fishing, commerce, and agriculture along the earth's rich coastal plains would be devastating.

"' The largely pastoral country of Holland, already forty per cent below sea level, would disappear entirely beneath the rapidly encroaching North Sea.'"

Sumner nodded grimly at McCoy's mention of the plight facing the Netherlands. The Amsterdam press corps was not averse to sensationalism. God only knew what the reaction would be when they picked up McCoy's warning. The editor had a vivid picture of Dutch farmers fleeing their fields, so vulnerable behind the country's network of dikes.

McCoy went on to report that President Wollcott had ordered an Antarctic Crisis Group set up under the national security adviser, Samson Fisk, and plans were being drawn for the evacuation of American port cities and shores.

The rest of the story concerned the close monitoring of the volcano rising from the sea floor under the Shelf by both NASA's GRAVSAT probe and the American scientists at McMurdo Station.

Watts finished. 'The word's around we're gearing up to get out a special edition, August,' Watts said. 'I take it I've just read the reason.'

'You have, Toby. Send up a messenger. I have maps, charts, and corollary material to run with McCoy's piece. His story and two satellite photos on the front page. I'll leave the inside layout to you.'

'What sort of space are we talking about?'

'I haven't totalled it. Several hundred column inches at least.'

'Damn, August, I'm going to have to hold over some people from the night side.'

'Whatever it takes, Toby. Those are Chadding's words.'

'Got a headline?'

'How did McCoy flag the story?'

'He sure as hell didn't mince words: "Earth on Brink of Freezing Flood."'

'That's your head, Toby,' Sumner said. 'Run it!'

*Times Two* was an hour northeast of New Zealand when the cabin console blinked to life and a news release from Reuters crawled up the video screen.

Joshua McCoy glanced at the dateline, assumed it was a local story, and turned back to the word processor to resume work on the evolving Antarctic story.

Shea McCoy interrupted the game of Martian checkers she was playing with her sister, Kate, and peered curiously at the screen.

'Where's Campbell Island, Daddy?'

'I don't know, sweetheart,' McCoy answered absently. 'I'll look it up for you in the atlas as soon as I'm finished here.'

Shea read silently for a minute. 'What's a tsunami?'

'A huge wave,' McCoy said. 'What's usually called a tidal wave at home.'

'This story says there's going to be one tomorrow,' Shea said.

McCoy looked up at his daughter and smiled. 'I think you misunderstood something in the story, sweetheart. Tsunamis form very suddenly, usually without warning. You can't predict them.'

'Well, this old native man can, Daddy. He says a tsunami will come tomorrow from some place called the land of ice.'

'What?' McCoy moved over beside his daughter and hit the reverse button below the video screen. The story backed up to the beginning.

CAMPBELL ISLAND: THE VILLAGES, FISHING BOATS, AND FARMS OF CAMPBELL EMPTIED OF MAORI NATIVES TODAY AS RESIDENTS ABANDONED THEIR DAILY ROUTINES AND FLED TO SANCTUARY IN HIGH MOUNTAIN CAVES.

THE MASS EXODUS WAS LED BY A 128-YEAR-OLD SEER, WHO WARNED HIS PEOPLE TO EVACUATE THE LOWLANDS OF CAMPBELL BEFORE A TITANIC TSUNAMI SWEEPS OVER THE SEA-LEVEL FIELDS OF THE ISLAND TOMORROW.

LOCAL MYSTIC CHAUNCEY DUTCHEYES IS BELIEVED BY THE MAORI TO HAVE EXTRAORDINARY PREDICTIVE POWERS. HE IS CREDITED IN THE PAST WITH FORECASTING REGIONAL TYPHOONS, VOLCANIC ERUPTIONS, AND EARTH TREMORS. HE IS SAID TO BE ABLE TO ENVISAGE EVENTS DAYS OR EVEN WEEKS INTO THE FUTURE.

THE ISLAND SAGE INSISTS THE TSUNAMI WILL COME FROM THE 'LAND OF ICE' AND REACH CAMPBELL, 400 MILES OFF THE SOUTHERN TIP OF NEW ZEALAND'S SOUTH ISLAND TOMORROW MORNING.

McCoy stared transfixed at the last sentence as it moved towards the top of the screen. Land of Ice! Could this Chauncey Dutcheyes be forecasting a tidal wave from Antarctica? A colossal flood surge from a sudden meltdown of ice?

'See, Daddy,' Shea said triumphantly. 'The story does say they'll be a tsunami tomorrow, doesn't it?'

'You were right, that's what it says,' said McCoy with a smile, tousling Shea's hair. 'Will you monitor the console for me while I go up and talk to Don a minute?'

'Sure, Daddy,' Shea said, her back straightening at the responsibility.

McCoy pushed through the cockpit door and tapped the pilot on the shoulder. Russell peeled off his earphones.

'Do you know where Campbell Island is, Don?'

'Affirmative, Josh. It's about twenty-three hundred miles southwest of our present position.'

'They have an airport there?'

'Yeah, an old SEATO strip, Southeast Asian Treaty Organization. It's an alternative emergency field for flights between Christchurch and West Antarctica.'

'Change our destination. I want to land on Campbell,'

'You're the boss, Josh, but do you mind my asking why?'

'There's a very old prophet on that island, Don, and if he's right about what he foresees, a million people could drown tomorrow.'

NORTHDRIFT
155.5 Nautical Miles

The secluded dacha of the party leader, Mikhail Romanov, throbbed with activity as speculation grew that the Presidium would momentarily approve the Soviet airlift to Antarctica.

Military and civilian messengers scurried in and out of the chaotic house, phones rang constantly, and helicopters plied the roped-off courtyard like dragonflies over a pond.

The parking lot was a hodgepodge of official cars. Two sleek black ZIL limousines waited nearest the dacha entrance, their MOC licence plates evidence that the $100,000 automobiles belonged to the party Central Committee members.

Next to the posh, long-bodied ZILS were parked the bulky, pregnant-looking Chaikas, the chauffeur-driven limousines of Russia's second-echelon leaders. Finally, eclipsed by their expensive neighbours, a jumble of utilitarian Volgas found space among the trees fringing the courtyard.

Inside the dacha the mood was tense, volatile. The men had spent the hours since their first meeting making preparations for the anticipated airlift, and most of them were red-eyed, fatigued to the point of flash temper.

A KGB aide passed the word that the Presidium had reached a decision, and the military and civilian leaders assembled again in the conference room. As they waited for Romanov to appear, the only sounds were coughs from throats irritated by smoke, vodka, and endless cups of strong tea.

At last the general secretary was announced, and the men stood up as Romanov entered the room. His face was expressionless as he lowered himself into a chair.

For a moment he surveyed the others silently. Then his

gaze sought out Marshal Savin. 'Despite my opposition, the Presidium has approved your plan, Comrade Marshal,' he said. 'The Thirty-second Karelian Division is to occupy the Ross Shelf as soon as the ice has drifted beyond the boundary of the Treaty of Christchurch and entered international waters.'

'Very good, Comrade Romanov,' Savin said with satisfaction.

'"Very good," Comrade Savin? We shall see.' Romanov looked at the others. 'The Presidium approval was not unconditional. Several members expressed grave reservations about this entire Antarctic venture. If the mission fails, if something goes wrong, each of us in this room will be called to account, regardless of one's individual enthusiasm for Savin's plan. Have I made myself clear?'

The men shifted uneasily.

Romanov pressed the bridge of his nose in fatigue. 'Very well then, we shall proceed. Have the military preparations been completed, Comrade Marshal?'

'They have. General Vlasov's Thirty-second Karelian is at this moment in flight to Tashkent. They will land in approximately one hour. Vlasov, Chirikov, and Cherepin have already arrived.'

'What support have you assigned the Thirty-second?'

'I have attached two companies of T-77 tanks equipped with lasers, four SAM anti-aircraft batteries, three batteries of Frog wire-guided surface-to-surface missiles, and a squadron of Mi-30 gunships.'

'Do you consider these forces sufficient?'

'The Thirty-second is only the spearhead. When the ice stations are operable, we will land ground troops in support of the airborne. Further, Admiral Trepkin has ordered the amphibious transport *Ivan Rogov* south from Vladivostok. The *Rogov* carries twelve hundred naval infantrymen, armoured personnel carriers, and air-cushion landing craft.'

'Has General Vlasov prepared plans for the actual jump?' Romanov asked.

'He has. The Thirty-second Karelian Division is to

come down in a rectangular formation. Fifteen hundred men on the sides, one thousand at each end. One flank will descend close to the sea cliffs, thus securing a beachhead for the landing of the naval infantrymen and supplies. Once the paratroopers are down, the tanks, missile batteries, and dismantled helicopters will be assembled and operational within three hours.'

'Does Vlasov anticipate any problems landing on the ice?'

'The Thirty-second has made many jumps onto snow and ice fields before, Comrade Romanov. There is no difficulty there. However, there is one factor involved that the division has not confronted before.'

'And that factor is . . .?'

'Fog. The last series of photographs from our Soyuz P7 shows a blanket of fog now covers the Shelf extending to sea perhaps eight kilometres.'

'And yet Vlasov still plans to go in, to jump blindly?'

'Not blindly, Comrade Romanov. Several years ago we developed a homing device enabling our airborne to jump during snowstorms. It will work equally well in fog. The instruments are equipped with both a radio homing instrument and pulsing high-intensity lights. They will be placed around the drop zone, and the transports coming in above will position themselves using the audio signals. Once through the upper layers of mist, the parachutists will come down using the lights as guides.'

Romanov stared silently at Savin for a moment. 'How do you intend to get these homing devices onto the Shelf, Comrade Marshal?' he finally asked.

'The instruments are already available in Antarctica. They are used during resupply drops in winter, when there is twenty-four-hour darkness on the continent.'

'Yes, yes, but how do you propose to position these things on the Ice.'

'By helicopter. A long-range Mi-32 transport helicopter left our base at Mirnyi two hours ago carrying the instruments and extra fuel.'

'Enough fuel to reach the Shelf? It is a long distance, is it not?'

'It is, Comrade Romanov, and we have planned accordingly. Halfway to the Shelf, on the coast of Wilkes Land, there's a French research station – Dumont D'Urville. Once within range, the helicopter will radio the French that they have lost their bearings and are low on fuel. International cooperation is merely common courtesy in Antarctica. The French will refuel our helicopter, and it will continue on to the Shelf.'

'Won't the French be suspicious, Comrade Savin? Such a navigational error is almost unthinkable,' Romanov said.

'Not in the special circumstances of Antarctica. The proximity to the magnetic south pole often disrupts instruments, even more so during periods of sunspot activity. Solar flares have been occurring for the past week. The French will merely assume our compass was thrown off.'

The KGB chief Duglenko smiled thinly. 'Perhaps there will be less Gaullist pomposity at the Quai d'Orsay when the French find out what we were really up to.'

Romanov frowned and turned to Vladimir Trepkin. 'How do naval preparations stand, Comrade Admiral?'

'Our submarine *Mezen* is approximately ten hours from the northeastern quadrant of the Ross Shelf, Comrade Romanov. As soon as she arrives, she will dive beneath the Ice and begin cutting loose the segments for our ice stations with her lasers.'

'There is no risk this manoeuvre will violate the provisions of the Treaty of Christchurch?' Romanov asked. 'After all, if we flout international law, our men aboard the ice stations could be considered pirates and attacked in the open sea by the West without fear of provoking war.'

'So long as we do not land military personnel on the ice before the Shelf crosses the treaty boundary, there will be no violation.'

'Very well, Comrade Trepkin. Comrade Danilevsky, is the air force prepared to carry out its part of the mission?'

'Everything is in order,' the general replied. 'My

Antonov-30s will take off as soon as the scientific party and the paratroopers are aboard.'

'How many aircraft are involved?'

'I have assigned twenty-five of the Antonovs for personnel transport and sixteen Ilyushins for the armour and other equipment.

'These planes have a twelve-thousand-mile range, do they not?'

'That is correct.'

'I should like to hear the flight plan, Comrade Danilevsky. Where do you intend to refuel?'

'At Mossamedes, in Angola, Comrade Romanov. The airlift will then head directly west over the Atlantic towards Saint Helena Island. Beyond Saint Helena, at approximately twenty degrees west longitude, the flight will turn directly south. Four hours later the Thirty-second Karelian will drop onto the Ross Ice Shelf. Aerial tankers accompanying the flight from Angola will then refuel the transports, and the planes will return to Mossamedes.'

'And the American reaction to a flight of forty-one Russian aircraft the length and breadth of Africa? What do you suppose this will be, Comrade General?'

'They know by now, of course, that the Ross Shelf is drifting north into the open sea. When their satellites follow our planes flying south across Africa, they will strongly suspect our destination. When the airlift leaves Mossamedes, their military will be certain.'

'This does not concern you?'

'Not overly. They will undoubtedly ask Cape Town to scramble reconnaissance aircraft when we approach the borders of Angola. However, both the Americans and the South Africans are familiar with our planes. They'll realize the Antonovs and Ilyushins are transports, not bombers.'

'You believe neither the Americans nor the South Africans will attempt to impede the flight, force the aircraft down, or worse?' Romanov challenged.

'On what pretext would they threaten our planes, Comrade Romanov? The airlift violates no international law.

No state of war exists. So long as we don't violate proscribed air space, South African for instance, there is simply no alternative for the Americans but to track the airlift passively with their satellites.'

There was a crackling silence in the room while Romanov considered Danilevsky's plans. He had to admit the hard-drinking general had answered his arguments. There seemed to be no loopholes in his scheme. Was there anything he'd missed? A possible reaction to the Soviet move he had not anticipated?

Romanov turned to the KGB chief. 'Have there been any indications of American military preparations, Comrade Duglenko?'

'Our satellite military reconnaissance network shows no sudden or unexpected activity on the part of their armed forces, Comrade Romanov. Our operatives within the United States report none of the American rapid deployment forces have gone to alert. Normal training, security, and leaves continue. It is the same at their bases abroad.'

'I have your assurance then, the Americans will not oppose the airlift?'

'I am not clairvoyant, Comrade Romanov, but no, I see no signs they will confront us militarily.'

'And politically?'

'This is to be expected, of course. What form their counteractions may assume will undoubtedly surface shortly.'

Romanov rose from his chair. 'So, all would appear ready. I emphasize one thing above all, gentlemen. If at any point the airlift provokes an armed response from the West, the mission is to be terminated. No strategic advantage we could possibly gain with these ice stations would justify the provocation of World War Three. I am returning to the Kremlin. We meet next in Moscow.'

The CIA director, Clyde Whitcomb, was reading an intelligence estimate of Soviet long-range air transport capacity when his intercom buzzed.

'Yes?' He yawned. It was 5:15 in the morning.

'Assistant Director Burrows is here, sir.'

'Send him in.'

Whitcomb had assigned Burrows to pinpoint the Russian 32nd Karelian Division. The assistant director entered briskly and handed Whitcomb a pink folder. 'This just came in from one of our agents in the Kazakh Republic, Clyde. That Soviet airborne unit left the capital city of Alma-Ata several hours ago by air.'

'Destination?'

'Tashkent.'

Whitcomb slammed the folder down on his desk. 'That son of a bitch Rankin was right. Dammit, he's made us look like fumbling amateurs. I'd like to know where the hell he's getting his information.'

'Directly from Romanov's dacha, sir. When you came back from the White House, I checked incoming intelligence.' Burrows handed Whitcomb a copy of the micropulse message from Cherepin to McCoy. 'This was in your morning briefing file.'

Whitcomb's eyes widened as he read. 'Who the hell is Anya? And why is this *New York Times* correspondent Joshua McCoy receiving this sort of information – over one of our communications satellites, no less?'

'Anya Cherepin, sir, director of the Soviet Antarctic Institute,' Burrows said. 'She and McCoy were lovers while he was the *Times's* bureau chief in Moscow a couple of years ago, before you took over the agency. The KGB caught them on tape, made the usual threats and demands. McCoy came to us.'

172

Burrows went on to explain how the CIA and McCoy had crafted a steady stream of disinformation to blunt the KGB intelligence probe. 'The micropulse was sent out over a recorder-transmitter we supplied for Cherepin. This is the first time she's used it.'

Whitcomb waved the paper in his hand. 'But how did Rankin get hold of this?'

'McCoy's his son-in-law. Beyond that they've been close friends and philosophical colleagues since they met in New Zealand about ten years ago.'

Whitcomb pushed back his chair. 'So that's it. Rankin's got a pipeline right into the goddamn Russian strategy sessions.'

Burrows shrugged. 'That's about what it amounts to, sir.'

Whitcomb tapped the desk with a pencil. 'I won't have Rankin beating us to the president with any further intelligence on the Soviet airlift, assuming the bastards go ahead. Alert our people in Tashkent immediately. I want to know if so much as a moth flies out of that airport.'

'I'll keep you current,' Burrows promised, turning to leave.

'And get me Samson Fisk at the White House,' Whitcomb said as his assistant reached the door. 'Right away.'

President John Stans Wollcott slumped on a flowered couch in his pyjamas and dressing gown watching Samson Fisk stride across the Yellow Oval Room on the second floor of the White House.

'I assume this couldn't wait another hour until I got up at seven, Sam,' he said, running an annoyed hand through his tousled hair.

'I thought you'd want to be informed immediately, Mr President. I've just received a call from Clyde Whitcomb. The CIA has confirmed that the Soviet Thirty-second Karelian Division is in flight to Tashkent. The unit will undoubtedly leave from there for Antarctica.'

Wollcott rose and stared out over the southern grounds

towards the floodlit shaft of the Washington Monument. 'Admiral Rankin's intelligence was correct, then.'

'I consider this confirmation that the Soviets intend to seize the Ross Shelf. I believe they'll carry out Marshal Savin's plan for the ice stations as soon as their Presidium gives final approval, Mr President.'

Wollcott threw back his head. 'Dammit, how the hell could we have spent hundreds of billions on weapons systems over the past couple of decades and still manage to come up criminally short of something as militarily basic as transport planes? What the hell good does it do to have a rapid deployment force if we can't get the troops to where they're needed?'

'Assuming their Presidium approves Savin's scheme, Mr President, there are several responses open to us beyond sending in combat troops of our own.'

Wollcott looked at his security adviser. 'You're never at a loss for options, are you, Sam? What are you recommending?'

'We could call in their ambassador. Scatter a few threats, such as cutting off their access to our computer networks. I mean a total blackout: industry, banks, the universities. We might even suggest we'd rearm the Afghani insurgents. The Karelian Division hasn't crossed their borders. Strictly speaking, they're not committed yet. They can back down without a public loss of face.'

Wollcott shook his head wearily. 'Past presidents have been down that road, Sam. It didn't work for Carter, it didn't work for Reagan.'

Fisk's face remained bland. He'd fed Wollcott the fodder. 'There is, of course, a stronger alternative.'

'I'm listening.'

'High-stakes poker, Mr President. We hit the Russians between the eyes with a bluff they don't dare call. Make the price of occupying the Ross Shelf and splitting off those ice stations appear so expensive they're forced to fold.'

'Spell it out, Sam.'

'Twelve of our laser battle stations are in duty orbit. I

suggest we let the Soviets know we would not hesitate to use directed energy weapons against their troops if they go ahead with an airlift to Antarctica.'

Fisk was referring to the $120 billion network of laser-armed satellites the United States had assembled above the earth in 1992. The huge weapons had been ferried in several large sections to their orbit altitude of 800 miles by the space shuttle, NASA's reliable work horse developed back in the early eighties.

The battle stations had been developed to neutralize Russian missiles in the event of war. The lasers were designed to intercept and destroy Soviet rockets during their vulnerable boost phase as they rose through the atmosphere above the Russian countryside.

The lasers employed incredibly smooth, thirty-foot mirrors to aim and focus deadly flashes of electromagnetic radiation at an enemy.

The ultraviolet rays were capable of burning through any metal yet forged on earth. Directed towards humans, the lasers would turn men into heaps of cinders in milliseconds. The 5,000 troops of the 32nd Karelian Division would simply vanish as dust in the wind were one or more of the monster weapons turned against them.

Wollcott's face was incredulous. 'You're talking about pulling the plug on the whole damn planet, Sam! If I take out one of their divisions with our directed energy weapons, what's to prevent the bastards from tossing a couple of nuclear eggs at one of our military bases in the States? Where does it stop after that!'

'I'm proposing we bluff with the battle stations, Mr President, not actually use them.'

Wollcott's voice was hesitant. 'You know the Russians' psyche, Sam, their inferiority complex in relation to the West. What do I do? Buzz Romanov on the hot line and tell him I'll turn his troops into Russian Rice Krispies if they occupy the Ice? Hell, direct pressure only gets their backs up. Makes them absolutely intransigent.'

'I'm well aware of that, sir. I propose to pass on the

threat obliquely. A controlled "leak" to the media should message across.'

'Go on.'

'I believe I have the perfect shill for our poker game, Mr President – the *New York Times* correspondent Joshua McCoy.'

'The journalist who's acting as Rankin's media voice now?'

'Yes, sir. A couple of years ago McCoy had an affair with a Russian polar scientist named Anna Cherepin. She's head of their Antarctic Institute, and we know now that she was the mole that supplied McCoy and Rankin with the first intelligence on the Soviet plan to occupy the Ross Shelf. As far as we know, she got the information out without being detected.'

Wollcott rubbed his eyes. 'I won't pretend to know where you're leading, Sam. What does all this have to do with your media plant?'

Fisk told the president about McCoy's double-agent role in Moscow. 'The point is, sir, the KGB continues to believe they've compromised McCoy. They're unlikely to suspect he'd cooperate with an American intelligence manoeuvre, not so long as they have a file on his activities in Moscow to hold over his head.'

'But McCoy will cooperate with us.'

'I doubt it, Mr President.'

'Sam, this is the most convoluted conversation I have ever had,' the president said, exasperated. 'I have to assume you're zigzagging to some logical conclusion.'

'McCoy won't play our game, but we have a friend at the *Times* who will. A friend who will see that Mr McCoy writes the story we want.'

'A friend? I assume you mean the publisher, Chadding.'

'Precisely, Mr President. McCoy will be physically isolated at the bottom of the world. Information on outside developments will have to come to him funnelled through the *Times* communications centre. Chadding can forward the facts we supply without McCoy having access to any sort of verification.'

Wollcott toyed with the belt of his dressing gown. 'How much would you tell Chadding?'

'Just enough to draw him in, make him think he's part of the show. Chadding's not a fool. Still, he's a fierce patriot. When we tell him what the stakes are, he'll do whatever the White House asks.'

Wollcott mulled over what the security adviser was proposing. It was a dirty business, manipulating the media, not that he'd been entirely innocent of the manoeuvre during his career. The point was moot in any case. With a military response out of the question, his hands were tied. If an alternative appeared, he'd cancel Fisk's stratagem. In the interim he could see no option. The intrigue would buy time.

'I have reservations, Sam. We're screwing with the Constitution here.'

Fisk regarded the president impassively. He knew what Wollcott's next words would be.

'Yet I don't have any better ideas. The moment we receive word that their Presidium has approved Savin's plan, inform the *Times* we are ready to resist with the laser battle stations.'

The security adviser came to his feet. 'I'll call Chadding.'

'One more thing, Sam. Keep me at arm's length from this. Nothing on paper.'

'Of course, Mr President.'

Fisk could not suppress a grin as he rode down in the elevator. The ploy Wollcott had approved was devised to block a Soviet airlift to the Ross Shelf; yet its intricacies were not confined to that end alone.

When the Russian ice station threat had been removed, he would slip the word off the record to select friends in the media that it had all been a bluff. It would go unsaid but implied that Rankin and McCoy had cooperated fully in the scheme, using Rankin's role as chairman of the Antarctic Conference and McCoy's position as a trusted *Times* correspondent to further the ruse. Neither man would have a shred of credence left after they'd been

177

exposed as willing participants in an American political manoeuvre.

The security adviser's eyes shone as he left the White House.

The Russian military airport at Tashkent was a tangled web of planes, troops, helicopters, and matériel. Anya Cherepin stood on the VIP balcony of the terminal building with her gloved hands behind her back and the fur collar of her polar parka pushed up about her neck.

She watched the movement below impassively. Long lines of Mongolian troops shuffled patiently across the tarmac, transferring from the transport helicopters of the 32nd Karelian Division to the air force's long-range Antonov-30s

Over their bulky uniforms the men wore white camouflage coveralls. Their boots, belts, helmets, and weapon stocks were also snow-hued, leaving their brown faces the only splashes of colour in the columns.

The first step in the Soviet airlift to Antarctica was going well. Two hours ago a squadron of giant, squat Ilyushin cargo jets had lifted off for the refuelling depot in Angola on the southwestern coast of Africa, their cavernous bellies crammed with dehydrated food, polar clothing, armoured vehicles, and ammunition.

Vladimir Chirikov appeared on the balcony beside Cherepin. 'You should have had lunch with me, Anya. The Uzbek cooking has an Oriental flair to it. A treat after the boiled cabbage of Moscow restaurants.'

She smiled wanly. 'I couldn't eat, Volodya. The excitement. Perhaps it's dread.'

He frowned. 'Dread? Why do you say that?' He looked round surreptitiously and lowered his voice. 'You got the information out. Now that the Americans know, they won't allow our troops to take the Shelf. You'll see. The airlift will be turned around in Angola.'

'I must send another message. Tell them of the final approval of the Presidium.'

His eyes widened. 'Anya, please, I beg you! You got away with it once. But you said yourself it was unlikely that Romanov's phones were monitored. This is entirely different. A military airport! You are tempting fate.'

'Are you going to help me, Volodya?'

He looked at her a moment, then shook his head and sighed. 'Who else is there? What shall I do?'

'Keep an eye behind me and nod as I speak, as though I were talking to you. And time me; the tape is only three minutes.'

She turned the setting and began telling McCoy of the final Presidium approval of Marshal Savin's plan and the refuelling stop in Angola.

'I'll be landing at Mirnyi, Joshua,' she finished. 'From there I can slip away. There's an Antarctic Conference weather station twenty kilometres up the coast.'

Chirikov's hooded eyes stared at his watch face. 'Five seconds, Anya.'

'Goodbye, Joshua. Soon. I'll see you soon.'

She squeezed Chirikov's arm, took a deep breath, and went inside to a phone cubicle. She called her nephew Sergei at the Antarctic Institute and passed on several mundane instructions for ongoing projects. Two minutes into the call she circled the setting and placed the pendant against the phone. Thirty seconds later she hung up.

Cherepin walked slowly back to the balcony, where Chirikov was watching the last of the troops going up the ramps into the large transports. They descended the stairs to the field and walked to the command plane parked nearest the terminal.

Ahead, General Leonid Vlasov was talking with two of his military aides at the foot of the ramp. He turned as they walked up. 'So, Comrade Chirikov, Comrade Cherepin, you are ready for our little adventure?'

'Quite prepared,' Chirikov answered.

'Good! When my Thirty-second Karelian has taken the Shelf, there will be much for your scientists to do. We must have the ice stations operational quickly, yes?'

Cherepin gave Vlasov a perfunctory smile and hurried

up the stairs into the plane, Chirikov following two steps behind.

She didn't notice the two men standing slightly aside from a knot of 32nd Karelian officers fifty metres away. They wore the white camouflage coveralls of the division, but they looked somehow odd, uncomfortable in the uniforms. One man was sharp-faced, the other showed tufts of hair that jutted like fork prongs from the front of his cap, and they watched Anya intently as she boarded the aircraft.

Ten minutes later the command plane roared down the runway and rose into the swirling flakes, the other twenty-four Antonov transports carrying the 5,000 troops of the 32nd Karelian Division lifting off one by one behind.

Anya Cherepin stared out of her small window lost in thought. Within an hour they would cross the Soviet border. Then south. South across Africa, south to the bottom of the world. Below, the Russian countryside grew blurred in the low clouds, then finally disappeared from view.

Shea and Kate were in the cockpit eagerly searching the sea ahead for the first lights of Campbell Island when the videophone buzzed in the cabin behind.

'Your source certainly gets around, Mr McCoy,' Levitt Merrill, the CIA communications officer, said from the screen. 'This time the micropulse came from the Uzbek Republic.'

'Tashkent?' McCoy asked.

'Within ten miles, certainly.'

'Thank you, Mr Merrill.'

'Message is on the way.'

McCoy listened apprehensively to Anya's second tape. He prayed that the KGB wasn't monitoring the phone she was using. God help her if she were caught.

When the tape ended, he sat silently for several minutes. If she reached the Antartic Conference weather station on the Antarctic coast, he could get her out. But she'd have to make it that far on her own.

He shook off his foreboding and put through the call to the admiral. The cabin video screen flickered and the helmet-framed face of Waldo Rankin appeared.

'I'd been holding out hope the Presidium would turn Savin's plan down,' Rankin said when McCoy'd finished reading Cherepin's message. 'I'd thought Romanov would be able to keep a tighter rein on the military.'

McCoy outlined Anya's escape plan.

'When the time comes I'll order a chopper from the weather station to mount air reconnaissance over the ice towards Mirnyi,' Rankin assured him. 'We'll bring her in.'

'What do you think Washington's reaction will be when you tell them the Soviets are going ahead?'

'I pray cool heads prevail. I'm not worried about the

Pentagon. Jim Lowe will keep the saber rattling under hand. It's Samson Fisk who bothers me. I don't trust the man's instincts. Unfortunately, he's got the president's ear.'

McCoy felt the cabin pressure changes as *Times Two* descended on the approach to Campbell.

'You'll probably beat me into Christchurch, Waldo. I'm going to make a little detour.' He told Rankin about the story of the ancient island seer.

'It's a hell of an unconventional lead to be following, I know. Still, this is one I couldn't leave alone.'

'Only mediocre men do the conventional, Josh,' Rankin said. 'I'll only be in Christchurch long enough to refuel, myself. I have to round-trip Antarctica. I'm going to run a thermovision scan of the seabed above the plume.'

'You've just flown all the way from Washington, Waldo,' McCoy protested. 'Now you want to fly another forty-five hundred miles – to Antarctica and back.'

'It's got to be done. I can finish the scan and be back in New Zealand in three hours. Good luck on that island, Josh. Give the kids a hug for me.'

'I will, Waldo. Grab some sleep when you're done.'

Rankin's face faded from the screen and a moment later Shea and Kate raced back through the cockpit door.

'Daddy, Daddy, Campbell Island's right ahead of us,' Shea said breathlessly.

'We saw the lights!' Kate added, hopping excitedly from one leg to the other. 'Captain Russell said to tell you we're going to land in ten minutes.'

McCoy smiled at his daughters. 'OK, guys, buckle in and we'll have a look at this island.'

'It's too dark, Daddy,' Kate said as she and her sister flopped into seats beside their father and drew seat belts across their laps. 'You can't see anything but some lights.'

McCoy grinned at his six-year-old. 'I just happen to have a magic TV camera on board. A camera that can see in the dark.'

Kate's eyes widened. 'Magic? Really?'

McCoy tweaked her nose. 'Watch.' He leaned forward

and turned on the television camera built into the belly of *Times Two*, then switched to an infrared lens and focused on the black horizon ahead.

The corner of Shea's mouth wrinkled up in a half smile. 'You're always saying things are magic, Dad. It's really an infrared camera, isn't it?'

'Infrared to some, magic to me,' her father insisted.

'Look! Hills!' Kate said as the screen showed Campbell's volcanic heights rising gradually from the surface of the sea. The lowlands of the island slowly appeared below the slopes.

McCoy punched the request TOPOGRAPHICAL MAP: CAMPBELL ISLAND into the computer and instantly a colour print of the island flicked onto the screen.

There were high cliffs facing the western and southern coasts, while the eastern shore was deeply indented with several bays.

'Do they speak English on Campbell?' Shea asked.

McCoy didn't hear his daughter. He had suddenly noticed something. Hurriedly he keyed EXPAND MAP BORDERS. Now the island was pictured at the centre of a large area of the South Pacific. To the northwest was Australia, to the north New Zealand, to the northeast Polynesia. But to the south there was nothing.

Nothing but empty sea between Campbell and 200,000 square miles of drifting ice.

'I don't think we need to wait for CIA information of Rankin's information, Mr President,' Samson Fisk said of the intelligence just received at the White House. 'His source was accurate about the mobilization of the Thirty-second Karelian. We must assume the airlift has left Tashkent, with Presidium approval, to seize the Ross Shelf.'

'Then you recommend we proceed with the laser ploy?'

'I think it essential we move at once, sir. The Kremlin must believe we are ready to use our laser battle stations the moment their troops land on the ice.'

Wollcott hesitated a moment, still uncomfortable with Fisk's unsavoury ploy, then sighed resignedly and nodded. 'Very well, get the story out.'

There was a phone call waiting when Fisk reached his White House basement office several minutes later. 'Clyde Whitcomb on four,' his secretary said.

The CIA director's voice was agitated. 'One of our intelligence satellites is monitoring a large formation of Russian troop transports flying south out of Tashkent. It could be – '

'The Thirty-second Karelian?' Fisk interrupted smoothly. 'It is. The Soviet Presidium has approved the airlift to Antarctica.'

Whitcomb sputtered.

Fisk twisted the knife. 'Admiral Rankin informed us half an hour ago. You're coordinating intelligence for the Crisis Group, Clyde. I'll leave it to you to advise the Joint Chiefs and the Cabinet Secretaries.'

A thin smile crossed the security adviser's face as he hung up, cutting dead the string of curses.

## NORTHDRIFT
184.6 Nautical Miles

Joshua McCoy stood at the top of the boarding ramp to *Times Two* and looked out over the moonlit airport of Campbell Island.

Despite the hour, there were men working. Fifty yards away two mechanics laboured over the engine of a Cessna under bright portable floodlights. In the distance a fuel trailer moved towards a Quonset hangar, where several other small aircraft were being serviced.

It struck him the planes were being readied to evacuate their owners at first light, before the tsunami Chauncey Dutcheyes had predicted swept over the island.

Shea and Kate appeared on the ramp beside him. They descended the stairs and walked towards the long, low whitewashed terminal. They were almost at the building when the doors opened. The woman who strode out was beautiful, an apparition in a bright-blue sweater and yellow wool skirt. She walked towards them with a fluid grace, the effortless gait of women of the Pacific islands.

McCoy judged her to be about five two, with long dark hair billowing in switchback waves to her waist. Delicate sun-lightened lashes curled over liquid brown eyes and a small nose. Her teeth were milk-white against her almond skin.

She came to a stop before them. 'I've been waiting for you.'

'I beg your pardon?' McCoy said.

'I'm Miki Dutcheyes. It is my great-great-great-grand-father who predicted the tsunami. He told me three hours ago a newspaper correspondent would be arriving at the airport in response to the story I wrote. You are a journalist?'

186

'Yes,' he said hesitantly. 'I'm Joshua McCoy of the *New York Times*. These are my daughters, Shea and Kate.'

Miki smiled at the girls. 'Welcome to Campbell.'

'You sent out that news release?' McCoy asked.

'Yes. I thought the international media would spread Great-grandfather's warning, and the thousands of people in the path of the tsunami could be warned in time to flee to safety.'

For a moment bitterness tinged her voice. 'There hasn't been a word about the tsunami on radio or television. Nothing in the videopaper. The international press has turned its back on Great-grandfather's vision. The Pacific is on the brink of a cataclysm and no one will listen.'

'I will,' McCoy said.

'Dad's a good listener,' Shea assured Miki earnestly.

The woman's smile returned. 'I'm sure he is. A far better listener than I am a hostess. May I offer you and your daughters some refreshments, Mr McCoy?'

'If you'll call me Josh.'

'Of course. And I'm Miki.'

She led the way to an unpainted ramshackle hut off to the side of the terminal. They walked through a glass-beaded curtain into an interior flickering with shadows from several alcohol-fuel torches. Across the room a huge, ancient aquarium gurgled air bubbles through its surface.

'Cosy,' McCoy said, his eyes adjusting to the dim light.

'It's the atmosphere the tourists expect, the few visitors we get,' Miki said with a smile. 'Can't have a remote South Seas island bar with formica tables and electric lights, can we?'

Behind the bar a heavyset greying Maori man in a flowered shirt was deep in conversation with a squealing, buxom woman. He plodded down the duckboards, beaming a smile.

'Miki, it is good to see you. How is your great-great-great-grandfather?'

'Fine, Cecil,' she said as they found a table. She introduced McCoy and his daughters.

'Ah, you must have come to write about the tsunami, Mr McCoy,' the bartender said. He stole a glance at the woman down the bar and lowered his voice. 'I shall be going up to the caves after the charter flight leaves at dawn, Miki. All the private planes will be gone by then, too. You understand. It's business.'

Miki followed Cecil's eyes towards the woman now busily reapplying makeup. 'I've understood you for years, my friend,' she said laughing. 'Just don't wait too long. Do you have any of your Cecil Specials prepared?'

'Yes, yes, a whole pitcher in the cold box.'

'You can't come to Campbell without tasting Cecil's fruit punch,' Miki said, and smiled at the girls.

'What's in it?' Shea asked.

'Papaya,' Cecil said, 'and pineapple juice, one squeezed orange, a dash of lime, a little coconut milk. And on top, my secret ingredient.'

The bartender bent towards the girls. 'Orchid petals. Do you ever hear of such a thing!'

'Real orchid petals?' Shea asked, her eyes wide.

'As real as Campbell,' Cecil replied with a grin.

'Better bring us four of those,' McCoy smiled.

'Good, good,' Cecil said, and lumbered back towards the bar.

'Can we go see the fish, Dad?' Kate asked, her eyes glued on the gurgling aquarium.

'Sure, if you promise you won't dive in.'

The girls laughed and scooted for the tank.

'You have lovely children, Josh,' Miki said.

'Thank you, Miki,' he said, smiling back. 'Tell me, your story was well written, professional. Are you a journalist?'

'I edited the student paper at the Canterbury University in Christchurch the year I graduated. I wanted to be a correspondent, like you.'

She smiled wistfully. 'But Campbell called me back, and now I help my great-great-great-grandfather look after our people.'

188

'Any regrets?'

'None. I'm needed here. Really needed. That makes my life very worthwhile.'

Cecil set down punch drinks before them and brought glasses to the girls staring wide-eyed into the bubbling fish tank.

'I have to ask you the obvious question, Josh,' Miki said. 'You're the only journalist to respond to my story. Why?'

McCoy sipped his punch. 'Your great-great-great-grandfather predicts the tsunami will come from the far south, the "land of ice". I have no idea how he knows, or even if he does, but there's been a tremendous geological upheaval in Antarctica. The Pacific is on the verge of exactly the sort of cataclysm Chauncey Dutcheyes foresees.'

He watched the subtle changes in her face as he told her what was happening at the bottom of the world. There was a slight twinge along her jaw when he described the northdrift of the Ice Shelf and the sea-level rise that portended. And when he pictured the plume beneath the Ross Sea, an anxious flicker bothered her eyes for a moment. But she kept her emotions in check.

She regarded him coolly when he finished. 'You would actually use what my great-great-great-grandfather told you in a story?'

'In the past few years science has come to recognize the gift of precognition. My mind is open. I came here to learn more about Chauncey Dutcheyes and his visions.'

Her eyes softened. 'Most off-islanders think it's so much native rubbish.'

'Tell me about him, Miki.'

Her voice was fervent. 'I believe Great-grandfather is one of those handful of individuals found from time to time who are finely tuned to the vibrations, the pulse of the earth. Much more so than the most precise instruments and monitors of science. He senses the vagaries of nature, Josh. He can read the earth as you or I might read a book. And he's been unfailingly right about these things for over a century.'

189

'About what things?' McCoy prodded.

'The weather, for one. Great-grandfather always pulls his outrigger out of the water a day or two before we get a good blow. Often the meteorologists here at the airport would be insisting there was no possibility of a storm for at least a week: barometer rising, winds gentle, sea oily calm. Yet there would be Great-grandfather preparing for foul weather.'

'Did he warn everybody?'

'His actions were enough for the other Maori, Josh. He never had to utter a word. Everyone cleared their craft of the water with his. Except for a few old island hands, the whites on Campbell thought it was all native mumbo jumbo. But it wasn't! There'd be a weather inversion or some freak atmospheric conditions and a sudden typhoon would come tearing through.'

'Do his gifts, powers, whatever you'd call them, extend beyond weather prediction?'

'Yes. One day when I was a very small girl I came across him on the beach alone, head up, sniffing the sea wind. "Pele speaks," he said, pointing off to the northwest. Nothing more, just those two words.'

'Pele? The Polynesian volcano goddess?'

'That's the one. This was the first time I realized his vision reached far over the sea. Right enough, the next day our teacher told us a Mount Saint Helens had erupted in your American northwest. The volcano blew at the exact hour I found him standing on the beach.'

'I've got to meet your great-great-great-grandfather, Miki,' McCoy said. 'Will he see me?'

'Under ordinary circumstances, no, Josh, he wouldn't. He believes off-islanders carry cultural diseases. He views the world beyond Campbell as beyond redemption, corrupt to the core, rife with immorality, avarice, twisted human values. He is constantly on guard less these vices infect our people.'

'I can't say I blame him.'

She smiled. 'He'll see you, though, once I've spoken to him. He trusts my judgement.'

'Thank you, Miki. I take that as a great compliment.'

'More an observation. There is always truth in the faces of children. I saw quite clearly the love and light that shine in your daughters' eyes as they look at you. Their eyes told me all I need to know about Joshua McCoy.'

All life below the Ross Ice Shelf was dead. The dragonfish, mysid shrimp, isopods, and zooplankton had boiled and suffocated as the waters trapped under the Ice seethed with super-heated gases, steam, and black volcanic debris.

Almost continuous eruptions of molten magma had now built the dominant vent into a submarine mountain thrusting up over 1,600 feet above the sea floor. The summit of the volcano was within 200 feet of the underside of the Ice, and directly over the peak, a huge, hollow cathedral dome had been thawed out of the southern flank of the Shelf.

A deep rumbling emerged from the tortured summit and seconds later a great dark jet of lava fragments and furious gases shot up through the water and stabbed into the centre of the ice dome, like a hot poker into wax.

The scorching steam bored 800 feet farther through the monstrous slab above, and when the raging fountain subsided finally, only 300 feet of ice capped the immense pocket of pressurized gases below.

The surcease was fleeting. The plume had only paused to refill the reservoir beneath the ocean floor and a quarter of an hour later the muffled boom of upwelling magma came again from the crater. The second eruption was huge. Great showers of volcanic glass rained down on the sea around the mountain, and boulders of pillow lava rolled down the slopes, building the cone still higher and wider.

The ice roofing the dome could not hold. A circular patch of Shelf 3,000 yards across disintegrated upward like a rock-salt blast from a shotgun. Instantly a mushrooming cloud of boiling steam and black ash hissed madly into the

Antarctic sky and rose quickly to 50,000 feet. Within minutes warm volcanic debris began to fall over the drifting Shelf and the western coast of the continent. It settled on the Ice in a gritty blanket, and a thin band of steam like a carpet of vapour began to rise as the upper surface melted.

When the eruption subsided an hour later, the pocked crest of the volcano was barely ten yards below the rapidly melting southern edge of the Ross Ice Shelf.

The *New York Times* publisher, Maxwell Chadding, waved August Sumner to a chair facing his large mahogany desk. On the walls of his spacious office were the memorabilia of three decades spent as a fund raiser and national commmittee man for the Republican Party, including photographs of Chadding with GOP presidents back to Richard Nixon.

'Thanks for coming right up, August. I know how swamped you are.'

'I needed an excuse to get away from the phones, Max. What can I do for you?'

'I've been going over the foreign media. I can't remember when a story has generated the worldwide reaction McCoy's piece has. Bulletins on radio and television; the papers from Toronto to New Delhi are hitting the streets with special editions. According to our Moscow bureau, *Pravda* redid its front page in the middle of the press run.'

'The competition is going to have to rely on our coverage exclusively for some time,' Sumner said. 'Even if they had reporters down there, correspondents with Josh's credentials are few and far between.'

'You're both doing a hell of a job on the story, August, but that's not why I asked to see you. I just got a call from Samson Fisk in Washington.'

'Was he peddling the official line as usual?'

Chadding's jowly face was grim. Fisk hadn't told him that the laser threat was a ploy – only that it was in the national interest that the *Times* make public precisely how and with what weapons the American government would respond to a Soviet seizure of the Ross Shelf.

'There's no way to ease into this, August. President

Wollcott is prepared to use our laser battle stations against the Soviets.'

The editor stiffened. 'In the name of God, why?'

'You're aware there's a Soviet airborne division in flight to Antarctica?'

'Yes, Josh filled me in several hours ago.'

'Fisk claims that the lasers are the only way to stop the Soviets from seizing the Ross Ice Shelf,' Chadding said.

Sumner shook his head. 'Max, if we parboil a division of Soviet soldiers in a cauldron of Antarctic seawater, aren't the Russians likely to put their intercontinental missiles on red alert? After that, one miscalculation by either side and its *Götterdämmerung*!'

'I brought up the point,' Chadding said. 'I had to listen to a five-minute lecture on the Russian psyche. Fisk believes they'll bluster and bully but stop short of actual hostilities. They can't afford another Afghanistan. You know the logic.'

'Yes, I've come up against that line of reasoning before, Max,' Sumner said. 'I find it simplistic. Worse, it's dangerous to assume the Soviet leadership has been cowed by Afghanistan. On the contrary, they may view this as a chance to recoup all and more.'

Chadding shrugged. 'The point is Washington just doesn't see any other way militarily to deal with this. And there's no time for diplomacy.'

'All right, I'll concede this country has to react. We can't just let the Soviets seize the Ross Ice Shelf unchallenged. But why the laser weapons? Can't we simply threaten to send in frontline combat troops?'

'I asked Fisk that same question. His answer was rather sobering. We just don't have the transport planes to get our rapid deployment forces down there in time, and the Russians know it.'

'I thought we doubled military aircraft production under President Reagan,' Sumner said.

'We did, but we're still two to three years away from anything like parity with the Soviets.'

'Is there some reason we couldn't knock off their

195

occupation forces with conventional bombs? I know damn well our new Graphite B-6 bombers have the range to fly the forty-five-hundred-mile round trip from New Zealand to the Shelf. The Russians would be sitting ducks on the Ice.'

'You know the topography of the Shelf, August. Deep snow covers the Ice. Bombs would have a greatly diminished effect. On the other hand, directed energy beams can be swept across the surface like fire storms. Even were the lasers to miss troops and armour, they would still melt the Ice right through and drop the whole Russian show into the sea.'

The science editor sighed wearily. 'You've painted one hell of a grim picture, Max.'

'Fisk wants McCoy to write the story. The White House believes Josh's credentials sit well with the Russians.'

Sumner's tired mind wasn't searching for any subtleties in Fisk's reasoning. 'The laser threat involves the Ice Shelf; it's part of Josh's story in any case.'

'I agree. I'll arrange to have his piece go out directly from *Times Two* to all media – print and broadcast.'

The intercom on Chadding's desk buzzed. He stabbed at a button. 'Yes?'

'Washington, Mr Chadding.'

'Tell them one minute.'

'Yes, sir.'

'August, this is a story I wish we didn't have to print. But we do. Tell Josh I know it will be a tough one to write.'

Sumner rose. 'I'll tell him.' The two men locked eyes for a moment, then the science editor turned and left the room. Behind him he heard Chadding tell his secretary to put through the Washington call.

Sumner took the lift down and folded himself into the chair behind his desk. For a long moment he looked with aversion at the phone on his desk.

Then he punched in a video call to *Times Two*.

The Oscar class Soviet submarine *Mezen* cruised slowly through the freezing polar depths 200 feet beneath the northeastern corner of the drifting Ross Ice Shelf.

Captain Oleg Sadovsky looked from the sonar screen to his senior lieutenant, Stepan Burmistenko. 'Plot?'

Burmistenko studied the illuminated chart on which the exact position of the vessel was marked by a tiny red pip of light. 'Approaching two kilometres from the outer ice cliffs. Ninety seconds to firing mode.'

Sadovsky turned to his gunnery officer. 'Open laser ports.'

'Aye, Comrade Captain.'

A grating sound came from the deck above as the round outer doors to the anti-aircraft laser tubes slid open.

Sadovsky shook his head at Burmistenko. 'I tell you, Comrade Lieutenant, we are under the strangest orders I have ever received. Why would they want us to break these huge segments of ice loose from the Shelf? Why must they never explain?'

Burmistenko shrugged. 'It has always been so in our navy, Comrade Captain. The admirals equate brains with rank. We lower-grade officers haven't the intellect to fathom command decisions.'

Sadovsky smiled ironically. 'Yes, I suppose they do reason that way. We –'

A sudden metallic thud boomed through the sub, echoing madly about the confined steel spaces.

'Stop engines!' Sadovsky roared. In two great steps he was at the sonar screen. 'You imbecile,' he shouted at the helmsman. 'You have brought her up too close to the ice!'

'No, Comrade Captain, we are well below the Shelf – sixty metres minimum,' the sailor protested.

'Then we have struck a downward pinnacle. How could the sonar have missed it?'

Again the helmsman disagreed, staring at the sonar repeater before him. 'With all respect, the bottom of the ice is dead flat. There are no downward irregularities.'

Sadovsky snapped, 'Three-hundred-and-sixty-degree scan!' For several moments he watched the screen intently as the sonar swept a circle around the sub. A small white blip appeared on the tube at the six o'clock position. The captain and the sonarman exhanged puzzled looks. The radius inscribed another circle. This time the object was well below the *Mezen*. Whatever had struck the sub was plummeting towards the bottom.

Sadovsky straightened. 'Sea ice drifting downward,' he said, his voice unsure.

The first officer caught the hesitation. 'Look at the rate of descent, Comrade Captain. Would ice sink that quickly?'

Sadovsky frowned. 'There is a layer of fresh water beneath the Shelf. Sea ice, with its salt content, is heavier. A freak event. Still, we took a good bang. Have the damage-control officer check all the controls that go through the hull. Also the Fathometer exterior casing. Let's make sure we've not developed any problems before we get under way again.'

At the edge of the ice above, the male baleen whale surfaced for air. Several other members of the pod circled curiously, watching him. He had been playing his new game for hours. Popping boulders out of the underside of the Shelf and watching them plunge into the depths with their intriguing trains of silver bubbles.

And now there was a new dimension to the sport. He had dislodged a rock with his snout just as a long, strange shape had passed directly below him. The metallic sound as the boulder collided with the shape was unlike anything he had ever heard in the oceans before. The other whales, too, had picked up the boom of the rock striking the *Mezen*.

There was an excited round of clicks from the huge

mammals. Four whales dove under the Shelf in unison. The male now had an audience to perform for. He swam rapidly towards the patch of rocks he'd discovered several thousand yards in from the edge of the ice, focused on a boulder dark against the translucent bottom of the Shelf, and began thumping it with his 1,500-pound snout.

The other whales joined in around him. More boulders were jarred loose and descended towards the *Mezen*. The biggest of these, a ridge-edged rock as large as a car, tore into the submarine's starboard hull, rupturing the pressure plates above the control room. A sphere of sparks like ball lightning erupted from a tangle of live electrical conduits suddenly exposed to the sea.

Damage alarms went off wildly as freezing salt water poured into the control room. The systems board that monitored the status of the *Mezen's* intercontinental ballistic missiles lit with a string of red lights.

Burmistenko paled as he looked at the board. 'Comrade Captain! The ICBM controls have shorted!'

'Go to emergency bypass!' Sadovsky screamed above the sound of the seawater rushing in.

The lieutenant flicked on the backup system. The red lights blinked off. Except one. Burmistenko punched at the backup button. Again and again. The light stayed on.

'One of the missiles won't respond, Comrade Captain. It's on sixty-second countdown!'

'Call the missile room! Tell them to disarm manually!'

Burmistenko grabbed the phone. It was dead. 'Communications are out!'

'Start engines,' Sadovsky bellowed at the officer of the deck. 'We must get out from below the ice!'

Above, the largest of the whales, an elderly, forty-five-foot male covered with barnacles, had been poking unsuccessfully at a huge boulder for several minutes. His excitement turned to anger when the rock wouldn't budge. Finally, he turned his huge body and slapped at the dark shape in the ice with his massive tail. The boulder broke loose and started downward.

A moment after the sub's screws began to turn again,

the rock struck the horizontal rudder, jamming it in the dive position.

The *Mezen* knifed towards the bottom.

In the control room, the crew was thrown violently forward. Water sloshed neck-deep towards the bow. Captain Sadovsky fought his way back up the angling deck to the rudder controls.

With every ounce of strength he tried to force the rudder back to the level cruise position. It was impossible. The boulder had wedged the steel steering plate against the hull. 'Stop engines,' he screamed. It was a useless order. There was no one at the control to obey.

The *Mezen* dove, without human design, down into the depths of the Ross Sea.

Stepan Burmistenko stared at the missile countdown clock, numb to the screams of his shipmates and the water rising around him.

He realized he was going to die. Yet he felt strangely calm, detached. Ten seconds left now. He wondered which American city the SS-N-34 missile had been targeted for. What matter? The warhead would detonate at the instant of impact with the ice above.

Four seconds, three, two. A roaring shudder shook the *Mezen* as the engine of the SS-N ignited and the fat missile rose ponderously through the deck of the dying submarine.

Burmistenko knew it would be only moments now. He suddenly saw the face of his dead grandmother. He was a small boy again in her care while his parents were at work. She was lighting candles before her icons. She turned to him and held out her arms. He felt a great peace envelop him.

At that instant the SS-N struck the titanic frozen slab above, crushing the guidance computer in its nose. To the crippled brain of the missile, the weapon had reached its target.

In milliseconds Stepan Burmistenko and the *Mezen* and the pod of whales ceased to exist, torn into countless shreds of animal tissue and steel fragments as the thermonuclear warhead detonated against the bottom of the Ice.

Above, the northeastern corner of the Ross Shelf disintegrated upward in a titanic thunderclap of maddened blast waves. Thirty-three thousand square miles of solid ice, one-sixth the entire area of the Shelf, was instantaneously metamorphosed into boiling steam, hissing meltwater, and billions of needlelike shards of blue-white ice.

An immense mass of radioactive vapour, water, and ice mushroomed into the freezing polar atmosphere. Higher and higher the saturated cloud boiled, as if a malignant growth sprouting out of control from the tortured ocean.

At 10,000 feet, gravity prevailed. The billions of tons of water and fragmented ice ejected into the air, a flood suspended in the sky, reached the apex of the eruption, paused, then fell again towards the violent sea below.

The water came down with the force of a mountain dropping into the sea. A towering, foaming ripple eighty miles across rose from the lip of the impact area and raced outward. To the south, the crest slammed into the remaining body of the Shelf, raised the roaring ice cliffs, then fell back upon itself. To the north, there was nothing to break the path of the spumous rim of water. As the volume from the blocked southern side swiftly backed up behind it, the gargantuan ripple rose into a tsunami that hovered 280 feet above the level of the ocean.

A continuous avalanche of seething, frothing white water cascaded down its sides as the largest wave ever to swell the surface of the polar sea raced north from the bottom of the world.

Joshua McCoy was typing the last sentence of his story into the word processor of *Times Two* when Miki Dutcheyes bounded up the ramp with his laughing daughters.

Kate ran to him and leaped into his lap. 'Daddy, daddy, Miki showed us a beach where the seals come out of the water. There must have been about a million zillion of them.'

'More like a thousand, Dad,' Shea said, throwing her little sister a condescending look.

The story McCoy had just written had left him deeply depressed. Still, he forced a smile. 'I'm glad you two had a good time.'

'The bestest time ever,' Kate bubbled.

'Mr Russell and Mr Mahoney are down at the beach, Dad,' Shea said. 'They said to tell you they'd watch us if we wanted to come back for a while.'

'Just another hour, please, Daddy,' Kate implored.

McCoy took Kate's chilled hands in his own, 'It's cold on the beach. Another hour and I'll have to thaw you guys out over the heater.'

'Oh, Dad, please, please, please,' Kate pleaded.

He didn't have a chance. 'Okay. But only an hour. Then you two take a nap without any gripes. Promise?'

Kate hugged him, then jumped from his lap and raced with Shea towards the door.

'Only an hour, Dad,' Shea promised as they reached the head of the ramp. 'We promise.'

Miki looked at McCoy as the slap of the girl's shoes faded across the runway. 'Something's happened, hasn't it?'

McCoy nodded glumly. The call from Sumner had

stunned him. He wasn't sure which he found more appalling: the Societ move to occupy the Ice or the American counterthreat to use the laser battle stations.

He gestured towards the word-processor screen. 'I've just finished the most frightening piece I've ever written. God, I don't want to send that damn story out!'

'May I read it?' Miki asked.

McCoy swung the screen towards her and backed up the story. Miki followed the text as it crawled from bottom to top.

CAMPBELL ISLAND: SPECIAL TO THE *NEW YORK TIMES* —THE GEOLOGICAL UPHEAVAL NOW SHATTERING THE WEST ANTARCTIC COAST WAS OVERSHADOWED TODAY BY A WHITE HOUSE DECISION TO DIRECT THE INTENSE HEAT OF ORBITING AMERICAN LASER WEAPONS AGAINST THE ROSS SHELF SHOULD THE SOVIET UNION ATTEMPT TO LAND MILITARY FORCES ON THE ICE.

PRESIDENT WOLLCOTT HAS DECIDED TO EMPLOY THE DIRECTED ENERGY BEAMS ABOARD US LASER BATTLE STATIONS IN SPACE IF THE RUSSIANS CONTINUE WITH PLANS TO OCCUPY THE SHELF WHEN IT REACHES THE OPEN SEA BEYOND THE NEUTRALITY ZONE OF THE TREATY OF CHRISTCHURCH, THE *TIMES* HAS LEARNED. THE SOVIET UNION IS BELIEVED TO BE PREPARING TO SEPARATE HUGE SECTIONS OF ICE FROM THE SHELF, BLOCKS SEVERAL SQUARE MILES IN AREA, AND TURN THESE INTO FORTIFIED 'ICE STATIONS', USING A REVOLUTIONARY POWER SOURCE CALLED THE MIRNYI ENGINE TO PROPEL THE IMMENSE FLAT-TOPPED ICEBERGS THROUGH THE SEA.

ONCE IN POSITION OFF THE COASTS OF THE US AND ITS PACIFIC ALLIES, THE STATIONS, SERVING SHIPS AND SUBMARINES AND BRISTLING WITH AIRCRAFT, MISSILES, AND TROOPS, WOULD BE USED TO COMPEL THE WEST TO GRANT POLITICAL AND COMMERCIAL CONCESSIONS, PERHAPS EVEN TO CAPITULATE MILITARILY.

A SOVIET AIRLIFT OF POLAR COMBAT TROOPS AND MATÉRIEL IS PRESENTLY EN ROUTE TO ANTARCTICA. THE FORCE IS REPORTEDLY NOW FLYING SOUTH OVER AFRICA AND IS EXPECTED TO REACH THE ROSS SHELF SOMETIME TOMORROW.

THE SOVIET UNION'S AIRLIFT CAPABILITY IS VASTLY SUPERIOR TO THAT OF THE UNITED STATES AND WILL ENABLE THEIR MILITARY TO FERRY IN ARTILLERY, ARMOURED VEHICLES, HELICOPTERS, TANKS, AND VAST STORES OF AMMUNITION. IN SHARP CONTRAST, THE US IS CRITICALLY SHORT OF THE LONG-RANGE TRANSPORT PLANES NEEDED TO AIRLIFT ROBOT TANKS, LASER BATTERIES, AND OTHER LARGE, HEAVY MILITARY ARMS TO AS REMOTE A REGION AS WEST ANTARCTICA.

*TIMES* SOURCES BELIEVE THAT IF BATTLE ERUPTS OVER THE 200,000-SQUARE-MILE SHELF, IT WILL COME WITHIN HOURS AFTER THE ICE DRIFTS ACROSS THE TREATY OF CHRISTCHURCH BOUNDARY.

SHOULD PRESIDENT WOLLCOTT SANCTION THE USE OF LASERS AGAINST SOVIET TROOPS ON THE SURFACE OF THE SHELF, IT IS CONSIDERED INEVITABLE THAT THE TREMENDOUS INHERENT HEAT OF THE WEAPONS WILL MELT A VAST EXPANSE OF THE ICE INTO THE OCEAN.

HUGE WAVES OF MELTWATER WOULD SWEEP NORTH INTO THE PACIFIC. IN THE INDUSTRIALIZED NATIONS, WITH SOPHISTICATED COMMUNICATIONS AND THE MEANS TO IMPLEMENT RAPID EMERGENCY EVACUATIONS, IT IS LIKELY THE INHABITANTS OF LOW-LYING SHORE AREAS COULD BE MOVED TO SAFETY BEFORE THE SHORES WERE INUNDATED.

IN THIRD WORLD COUNTRIES, HOWEVER, COASTAL POPULATIONS WOULD BE DOOMED TO MASS DROWNINGS. MILLIONS, PERHAPS TENS OF MILLIONS, WOULD PERISH ON COASTAL PLAINS, ON LOW-LYING ISLANDS, IN RIVER DELTAS, AND IN ISOLATED SETTLEMENTS ALONG VULNERABLE SHORES.

THERE CAN BE NO QUESTION THAT PRESIDENT WOLLCOTT IS AWARE OF THE GRAVE CONSEQUENCES OF USING THE LASERS AGAINST THE ROSS SHELF, ALREADY THREATENED WITH A RAPID DISSOLUTION INTO THE SOUTHERN SEAS IF THE VOLCANISM ALONG THE COAST OF ANTARCTICA WORSENS.

HE IS EVIDENTLY CONVINCED THAT THE US CANNOT HALT THE DEPLOYMENT OF SOVIET ICE STATIONS WITHOUT RESORTING TO THE DIRECTED ENERGY WEAPONS.

Miki read on in silence, shaking her head at McCoy's description of the Mirnyi engine and the Soviet plan to blockade the major ports of the Pacific powers with the ice stations.

'It's terrifying,' she said with a shudder when she finished.

McCoy hit the TRANSMIT button and sent the story out. For a moment he stared dejectedly at the blank screen. 'I wonder whether the tsunami Chauncey foresees will be caused by American laser fire,' he said absently.

'I don't know,' Miki shook her head. 'He hasn't told me yet.'

Their backs were to the cabin door when McCoy suddenly felt the hair rise on the nape of his neck. He turned and stared into the face of Chauncey Dutcheyes.

It could be no one else. The ancient Maori was clad only in sandals and tattered woollen shirt and trousers. Yet McCoy was struck at once by the nobility of that aged face and the almost palpable spirituality that radiated from his frail frame.

Miki followed his gaze and leapt to her feet. 'Great-grandfather!'

The seer's compelling purple eyes embraced McCoy as Miki introduced him. He shook his head at the American's offer of a seat.

Miki studied Chauncey's grim visage and reached out to lay her hand against his hollow cheek. 'What's happened, Great-grandfather? What have you seen?'

205

Chauncey's voice was cracked and hoarse with age, yet there was still strength and passion behind his words. 'The tsunami comes,' he told them, sweeping a hand towards the lagoon and the open ocean beyond. 'The wave is three hours to the south.'

Miki's face froze. 'Some of our people are still in the lowlands.'

'I have sent runners, little one. All will reach the mountains in time. All except four.'

He turned to the American. 'We must evacuate our hospital here, Joshua McCoy. Most of the patients can be treated in the high caves. But four need oxygen to breathe.'

'We have oxygen onboard,' McCoy volunteered. 'I'll fly your people out to the hospital in Christchurch.'

Chauncey rested a hand on McCoy's shoulder. 'Thank you. There is another thing. The patients are afraid they will die forgotten in an alien place. I am the solace of my people. They have asked that I go with them.'

'I'll be honoured to have you on *Times Two*, Chauncey,' McCoy said.

Miki gaped at her great-great-great-grandfather. He had not been more than a day's sail from Campbell in over a century. 'If you fly to Christchurch, Great-grandfather, I shall go with you.'

'I knew this would be your wish, Miki. Come then, we must gather our people from the hospital.'

'I'll have the plane fuelled and ready to take off as soon as you get back,' McCoy promised.

'We shall return in one hour,' Chauncey said. 'While we are gone, I ask you to warn the islanders and shore dwellers beyond Campbell.'

'Of course,' McCoy agreed. 'I'll send out an all-media bulletin immediately. Where will the tsunami come ashore?'

'The great wave will strike the south of New Zealand after it passes Campbell. The coastal cities of eastern Australia must also be evacuated. The tsunami will move north, then against the islands of New Caledonia. Before the sun rises tomorrow, the shore lands of the yellow races beyond the equator will flood.'

'China, Japan?' McCoy's voice was incredulous.

Almost imperceptibly, Chauncey nodded. 'Even these. Spread your warning, Joshua McCoy.'

Chauncey and Miki left for the hospital. McCoy glanced at his watch as they crossed the tarmac. Rankin should have finished his thermal survey of the Ross Sea floor and be back in Christchurch by now. He punched in the number for the office of the chairman of the Antarctic Conference in New Zealand.

A secretary answered, then Rankin came on the screen. 'Josh, I was about to call you. Charlie Gates at McMurdo just reported a tremendous explosion off the coast. Too much fog for them to see what's happening, but we have to assume there's been a volcanic blowout beneath the Ice. We'll have to issue immediate evacuation warnings for the islands and coasts below thirty degrees south latitude.'

'I think we'd better extend the evacuation area beyond that, Waldo,' McCoy said. He told Rankin of Chauncey Dutcheye's warning that a huge tsunami was sweeping north from Antarctica.

As McCoy finished, the words NASA PRIORITY INTER-RUPT flashed at the bottom of the screen.

'Hang on a minute, Josh,' Rankin said. 'I requested satellite reconnaissance a few minutes ago. This should be it.'

The video went blank for several minutes, then Rankin was back, his face a grim mask.

'Your island seer is right, Josh. NASA just picked up the tsunami. There's something else. The NASA probe is monitoring a huge cloud of fallout above the Shelf. That wasn't a volcanic eruption below the ice. Whatever blew was nuclear.'

'Nuclear!'

Rankin stared at his friend. 'That's not just a tsunami coming at us, Josh. It's a two-hundred-and-eighty-foot wall of radioactive water.'

President John Stans Wollcott took his seat at the head of the Cabinet table and nodded towards his national security adviser. 'All yours, Sam.'

'Thank you, Mr President,' Fisk said. 'Madame Vice-President, gentlemen, as you've already been informed by Clyde Whitcomb, Admiral Rankin's intelligence source within Russia has confirmed that the Soviet airlift to Antarctica was approved by their Presidium.'

He swivelled his chair to face the CIA director. 'Clyde, where is the airlift now?'

'On a southwest heading: at the moment, over Zaïre in Central Africa,' Whitcomb answered.

'Is it the agency's position that the Soviet airlift to Antarctica is irreversible, Clyde?' the president asked.

'That is our evaluation, sir. My staff analysts estimate that the Russian occupation of the Ross Shelf will begin within forty hours.'

'In other words, they intend to seize the Ice the moment it drifts beyond the neutrality zone of the Treaty of Christchurch.'

'My people are convinced this is the Soviet plan, Mr President.'

'The sons of bitches!' the chief of Naval Operations spat, his omnipresent unlit cigar bobbing furiously. 'Once they take the Shelf, it's only a matter of time before their goddamn ice stations appear off our Pacific ports. The bastards will have us by the short hairs!'

No one disputed Admiral Rogers's pessimistic assessment.

Fisk surveyed the dour faces around the long table. 'Mr President, I was informed twenty minutes ago that the *New York Times* story containing our laser threat was just released to the world media. I believe it's time we told the Crisis Group of our manoeuvre.'

Wollcott nodded.

Fisk described the American warning that orbiting directed-energy weapons would be used if the Soviets attempted to occupy the Ross Ice Shelf. Vice-President Roberts and several cabinet members wore expressions of distaste when he finished his account of the media plant.

Secretary of State Bancroft glared at the security adviser. 'May I ask why the Crisis Group was not consulted before you implemented this scheme of yours?'

'To put it bluntly, Miles, we couldn't risk a leak. Letting a piece of information like this loose in Foggy Bottom is all but the equivalent of publishing it in the *Washington Post*.'

The secretary reddened. 'How dare you! My people are thoroughly professional, capable of observing to the letter any and all requirements of secrecy. I demand an apology!'

'If there is an apology due, it's owed by the military,' Fisk countered. 'Oh, it's fine to blame our lack of critical transports on a tight-fisted Congress. But if the Pentagon had spent its budgets on nuts and bolts military hardware, like troop carriers, instead of expensive, redundant missile systems and bogeyman satellites, we would not now be in this dilemma.'

General Lowe looked across calmly, refusing to be baited. 'Ricocheting around the blame for our position will not change it, Mr Fisk,' he said, his voice as precise as the movements of his stainless-steel fingers sorting papers on the Cabinet table. 'Personally, I should like to discuss what options are left open to us. We have no guarantee, after all, that this newspaper plant of yours will work. Or is there something further you haven't told us?'

Fisk felt himself cornered. He could sense Wollcott awaiting his answer with the others. 'The manoeuvre will work,' he insisted. 'I have studied the Soviets for years. They won't dare chance the use of our lasers against their troops.'

'What makes you so certain?' Lowe probed.

'The historical record!' the security adviser said heatedly. 'The soul of the average Russian is scarred far deeper by past wars than any Westerner can imagine. Afghanistan is only the latest bloodletting they have been through. They will not risk a war that could spread to their homeland. They cannot face such a possibility again.'

'I disagree,' General Lowe persisted, unconsciously rubbing one plastic palm against the other. 'The militarists in the Politburo badly need a victory to atone for Afghanistan, to regain the initiative as well as their countrymen's confidence. I believe they will gamble the lives of their airborne troops, even a retaliatory strike against their homeland, to win the Ross Shelf.' Lowe's face and voice were expressionless as always, yet there was a chilling conviction in his words. 'The strategic advantages the Soviets would gain by deploying those ice stations are simply too enormous for them to allow the opportunity to pass. The Thirty-second Karelian Division will not turn back, Mr Fisk.'

President Wollcott cut in impatiently. 'Gentlemen, we are beyond the hour for debate. I wish to know if there is any recourse open to us should the Russians ignore our laser threat and continue on to occupy the Ross Shelf.'

'There are the South Africans, sir,' Director Whitcomb suggested.

'What are you talking about, Clyde?'

'I think everyone is aware the Soviets have been arming the black liberation armies on South Africa's borders for years now. The Boers are trigger-happy as well. Pretoria would probably jump at an excuse to knock out those Russian planes. They could claim a violation of air space, insist they thought they were coming under attack. They have more than enough F-18s to do the job.'

Vice-President Roberts looked at Whitcomb in shock. 'Have you gone out of your mind, Clyde? The Russians aren't fools. They would consider an attack by the South Africans on their planes as an assault by us. And rightly so. We would have an identical reaction if Cuban aircraft brought down one of our unarmed formations. You're suggesting an act of war!'

Whitcomb started to protest, then thought better of it.

'Does anyone else wish to be heard?' Wollcott asked evenly.

The members of the Crisis Group looked back at the president in glum silence.

'It would appear we are unanimous in our assessment of the situation. There are no options. Unless I am presented a viable alternative, we'll stay with Sam's strategy. As for now, I remind you that Soviet military manoeuvres are not the only threat we face.'

The president looked down the table at the director of the National Science Foundation. 'Kevin, what's the geological situation off the Ross Sea coast?'

'There has been a major deterioration, Mr President,' Florence said. 'Our research scientists at McMurdo Station have confirmed that a plume, that is, a vertical pipeline of molten magma, has broken through the floor of the Ross Sea. The plume has built up a submarine volcano beneath the Shelf, and there's already been an eruption through the surface of the Ice.'

'This plume represents a greater volcanic threat than was originally thought to exist down there?'

'Far worse, sir. The discharge potential of a plume is simply incalculable. If magma continues to be vented through the sea floor at the present rate, at least a partial meltdown of Antarctic ice is inevitable during the next couple of days.'

Wollcott dragged his hands down his face. 'Then we face a sea-level rise sooner than expected.'

'Yes, Mr President, we do.'

Wollcott's eyes sought out Fisk. 'Sam, what is the status of your evacuation plans? Can we begin moving our people inland from the coasts?'

'Yes, sir. My staff has prepared a master schedule to withdraw the inhabitants of the threatened port cities and shorelines, beginning with the Pacific coast. We estimate we can move the endangered population within twenty-four hours.'

'Where are these people to go?'

'Most will be sheltered temporarily on mothballed military installations, Mr President. In empty barracks and tent cities. The overflow will be housed in schools and government buildings until resettlement can begin.'

'Food, water, clothing, that sort of thing?'

'Truck convoys will be organized to bring supplies inland from existing coastal distribution sites, sir. We will require an interim nationalization of the trucking industry, the corporate food-market chains, perhaps clothing and other suppliers.'

A presidential aide opened the Cabinet door and crossed quickly to the president's side. He handed Wollcott a single sheet of paper and withdrew.

'There are several other draconian measures we must take,' Fisk went on. 'Immediate gasoline rationing for one. We -- '

The sight of the president's ashen face as he looked up from the paper stopped Fisk in midsentence.

Wollcott's voice was hollow. 'Gentlemen, I have just been informed by Admiral Rankin that there has been a thermonuclear explosion beneath the Ross Shelf.'

There was shocked silence in the room.

'The detonation has melted down a huge section of the Ice.' The president looked down at the paper. 'There is a tidal wave almost three hundred feet high racing north from the Ross Sea.'

Pandemonium broke out.

Secretary of Defence Axworth's voice rose above the tumult. 'Did Rankin identify the source of the detonation, Mr President?'

The President quieted the room with a restraining hand. 'Unknown at this time. Clyde, General Lowe, I want every resource of our civilian and military intelligence networks focused in on the Ross Sea. This may be some sort of Machiavellian Soviet manoeuvre. I want to know what blew up under the Ice and I want to know fast.'

The chief of Naval Operations came to his feet. 'There are hundreds of naval and commercial vessels in the threatened latitudes, Mr President. Those ships must be warned immediately.' He yanked the chewed butt of the cigar from his mouth. 'I ask your permission to withdraw.'

General Lowe rose beside Admiral Rogers. 'I must also ask persmission to leave, Mr President. Several American military commands are situated on low-lying coral islands in the South Pacific. These vulnerable army posts and air force bases must be evacuated forthwith.'

A second aide approached Wollcott and bent to his ear. The president nodded and wearily pushed back his chair. 'Gentlemen, I have a phone call holding from the prime minister of New Zealand.'

'Shall I start the evacuation of the Pacific coast, Mr President?' Samson Fisk asked.

'Yes, immediately.' Wollcott looked across at the chairman of the Joint Chiefs. 'General Lowe, our military forces are to aid in the movement of refugees wherever possible.'

'Every assistance will be rendered, Mr President,' Lowe said.

The president's eyes swept the room. 'Glenda, gentlemen, you all have your areas of responsibility. I wish to be kept current.'

Consternation hovered behind as the president left the room.

Kanji Takahashi forced his saltwater-swollen eyes open and once more checked the line of lifeboats strung out across the freezing sea on rope tethers like beads on a necklace.

Nine ice-laden dories held the survivors of the Japanese Antarctic Krill Fishing Fleet; four had been launched by the SS *Awa Maru*, three from the *Kumano*, and two from the *Wakasa*. There were no boats from the *Nikko*, and after calling through the bullhorn for almost three hours, Takahashi had given up. He presumed the *Nikko* was lost with all hands.

The first mate had ordered the dories to alternate at the head of the tow, shutting down the engines of the others to conserve fuel. There was little else positive he could think to do.

Of the 165 men who'd sailed with the fleet, only fifty-two had made it to the lifeboats.

Takahashi surveyed his shipmates as the line of small craft rose and fell on the undulating crest of the sea. The hours in the boats had taken their toll; a third of the men were curled into motionless fetal positions, while the faces of most of the others were dull, emotionless masks.

They had been in the lifeboats over a day now and had stirred only once, when the sound blast from a tremdendous explosion had come from over the horizon an hour and a half ago.

The Soviet missile had detonated on the other side of the Shelf, over 400 miles away, too far for them to see the mushroom cloud. Still, the sea had suddenly rushed toward the northeast, sucked away by the titanic tsunami, and minutes later a hail of small ice fragments had fallen on the dories.

The men were too exhausted to speculate long on what had happened, most assuming a ship had struck the ice and blown up.

The fog lifted slightly, and the first mate turned to stare through the patchy mist at the seemingly endless wall of ice that was drifting past three miles away.

His mind wandered back to the time when as a boy he had scaled Mount Fuji with his father, an elating experience that had left him with a taste for the high slopes. He'd joined the respected Sakura Tozan Club during his student years and was considered a competent climber.

If the ice cliffs he stared at now were facing a land glacier instead of a drifting iceberg, his mates and he might have ascended the palisades for sport. Certainly, the 120-foot rise would not present too difficult a challenge to an experienced *tozansha*.

As he watched, a swirl of vapour moved slowly across the white palisades, revealing in its wake a dark perpendicular shadow stretching from the water line to the top of the ice. Even at this distance Takahashi knew the shadow to be a vertical crevasse. Undoubtedly, wave action had undermined that stretch of the cliff and a wedge of ice had collapsed into the sea.

At its narrowest point the fracture formed what mountaineers called a couloir, an ice gulley relatively easy to scale because the close walls offered handholds and footholds on both sides of the climber.

A sudden thought crossed Takahashi's mind. The radar on the *Awa Maru* had measured the ice to be 400 miles across. What had Captain Okada said, that the largest iceberg he'd ever heard of was only a tenth that size? If this wasn't an iceberg, what was it?

There was only one answer – one body of ice in the world the size of the white behemoth before him. The Ross Ice Shelf! Was it possible the entire Shelf had somehow drifted to sea?

Takahashi knew the Americans maintained robotic research stations on the Ross Shelf, unmanned data-gathering posts. He had examined several of them through binoculars as the *Awa Maru* worked up the coast last season. Most had antenna towers. That meant radios!

'*Soo desu ka!*' he screamed, bolting to his feet. 'There is a way!' The other survivors in the lifeboat pulled back startled, their eyes wide and afraid. Had Takahashi gone mad?

The first mate ignored the cowering crew. For a moment longer he squinted intently at the crevasse, then bent and yanked open the equipment locker built into the stern.

He had what he needed!

He pushed aside the water bottles and food packets and one by one extracted the instruments he would use. First came the three razor-sharp harpoon heads. They were designed to fit over the rounded ends of oars and were a deadly dissuasion to the sharks that habitually harassed small boats in the warmer Pacific to the north.

The harpoon tips could replace the hollow ice screws and pitons he normally used to ascend glaciers. He examined the short-handled axe used to chop sea ice off the gunwales and added it to the harpoon tips. It would serve well to hew handholds and footholds on the sides of the frozen upper gully.

He was about to close the locker when he found a box of assorted fishhooks and sturdy line and added it to the heap of tools. Some of the hooks were one-eighth-inch steel and could easily support a man's weight. Laced to the boot tips point-down, they would serve in place of crampons.

He shut the locker and looked into the faces of the men around him. He would need two volunteers to scale the ice wall with him if his plan were to have a chance.

He reached into the zippered pocket of his thick parka and withdrew the flare pistol he had guarded carefully against the ruinous sea spray. The cartridge slipped in easily and he slammed the fat barrel shut, aimed the weapon down the line of wallowing dories, and pulled the trigger.

The explosion of gunpowder and the awful scream of the thick projectile just a few feet over the boats ripped through the freezing air.

Grim faces appeared suddenly out of the fur-lined necks of parkas white with hoarfrost.

Takahashi picked up the electric bullhorn. 'Bring in your boats.'

One by one the inboard motors coughed reluctantly to life, and in twenty minutes eight dories had assembled in a rough semicircle facing the first mate's boat. He signalled them to turn off the engines.

Takahashi willed his voice to be strong. 'Men of the fishing fleet. We are a thousand miles from the nearest shipping lanes, two thousand from any inhabited land. If we are to be saved, it must be by your own hands.'

The first mate pointed off towards the black scar striping the face of the Shelf. 'Look there, all of you, at that dark line breaking the cliffs.'

The men squinted towards the ice.

'That is a vertical crevasse,' Takahashi went on. 'It can be easily climbed, like going up the inside of a chimney. I, Kanji Takahashi, shall scale the ice. I need two of you to go with me.'

For the next five minutes he told them of the radar reading, the unmanned American outposts and radios he knew to dot the Shelf, and, finally, his plan to climb the frozen cliffs.

When he'd finished, there was silence among the men, the only sound the lapping of the frigid waves against the boat.

Shiroki Ushiba, the only university graduate among the crew, leapt to his feet in a dory launched from the *Kumano*.

'The first mate is right!' he yelled. 'There could be a research station up there somewhere. At least we should try. It is better than slowly freezing to death.'

The others looked uncomfortably at Ushiba.

In the bow of Takahashi's craft, a sixteen-year-old cabin boy, Harumi Aoki, rose. 'I am with you.'

'So, it is good,' Takahashi said, smiling. 'With three of us we have a chance.'

It took almost fifteen minutes to transfer the men in the first mate's dory to the other boats and to bring over

217

Ushiba, along with extra harpoon heads, axes, and strong hooks.

He made sure his own waterproof compass was secure deep in a zippered pocket of his parka and gave a second from the dory stores to Aoki. The great flat expanse of the Shelf's surface was featureless and it would be all too easy to circle lost in the fog that shrouded the ice.

The cook Konuma contributed a string net of dried fish, his demeanour humble, as if he were provisioning a samurai for battle.

When the preparations were complete, Takahashi looked across at the sombre men who had elected to stay in the dories. 'If we find help, we shall come back for you,' he said. 'Believe there is hope. Faith will keep you warm when the fire in your blood flickers low. It is no disgrace that you stay. It is enough some of us try.'

Forty-five minutes later the lone dory was one hundred yards off the towering cliffs. Close up, the white palisades appeared insurmountable to Ushiba and Aoki, and their hearts sank at the prospect of scaling the dizzying heights thrusting coldly out of the sea.

Takahashi scanned the interior of the crevasse with his binoculars. Very near the V-shaped tip of the fracture an ice ledge four or five feet wide jutted from the foot of the cliff.

It would be a tricky manoeuvre. The timing would have to be just right. Takahashi explained his strategy to the two crewmen. They would catch a swell beyond the cliffs, and the first mate would then gun the motor, racing on the wave crest into the gorge.

When they were close enough, Ushiba and Aoki were to leap for the ice ledge. Takahashi would then cut the motor, allow the dory to retreat from the crevasse with the outward surge, then charge again through the slim opening and jump himself.

The first mate showed his men how to tie the thick fishhooks to the tips of their boots. Each man also carried an axe, harpoon heads, and a hundred yards of strong nylon line coiled around his middle.

They were ready. Takahashi positioned the dory in front of the crevasse entrance and turned to study the waves approaching the cliffs. He waited for a long, regular swell, and as the crest approached the stern, he yanked open the throttle and the small boat shot forward on the summit of the wave.

In seconds they were through the mouth of the ice gully. Ushiba and Aoki squatted tensely at the port gunwale, waiting for Takahashi's signal to jump.

Ten yards from the ledge the first mate throttled back, then threw the motor into reverse. The propeller dug into the foaming water and slowed the dory, keeping it from the roaring maelstrom at the apex of the gorge.

'Now!' Takahashi screamed. As one, Ushiba and Aoki flew for the ice. The hooks dug into the ledge as they landed and fell forward onto the solid surface.

They'd made it!

The broken wave retreated in a rush from the gorge, pushing Takahashi and the dory before it. The first mate circled out from the cliffs and positioned himself a second time facing the ice fracture.

Once more a high swell arched towards the boat and again the dory tore ahead into the face of the cliff. He jumped for the ledge a second too late and for a moment thought he would slip off the ice into the sea, but four strong hands fastened onto his parka and pulled him the final few feet to safety.

The three men lay in a heap for several moments, their breath coming in laboured spurts. Finally, their chests calmed and Takahashi stood and examined the couloir. The walls of the gully were latticed with cracks and small fissures. The ascent would take time, but it should not be too difficult.

'I shall go up first,' he said. 'I'll drive in the harpoon tips as I climb and we'll string safety ropes from these. But your main support must come from the toeholds and handholds I'll chop in the cliff face. Remember, keep three points of contact, two hands and a foot or the reverse.'

The crewmen nodded.

Takahashi turned to face the cliff. When he was thirty feet up, he drove in the first harpoon head with the back of his axe and called down for the next man to begin the ascent.

For almost an hour they struggled upward, sometimes gaining twenty-five or thirty feet at a time, often only ten or fifteen. Wherever they found a seam of ice large enough, they rested.

Once, Aoki slipped and plunged downward towards the waves. Takahashi had been alert, though, flipping the line instantly over an axe embedded in the ice and bracing himself against the cliff. The rope had seared his gloves, but he managed to hold on until the cabin boy could dig in his fishhook talons. Aoki crawled over the lip of the ledge and collapsed beside Takahashi, breathless and ashen faced.

Finally, the first mate scrambled over the top and let out a victorious shout. Aoki and Ushiba heard the unmistakable yell of triumph and hastened one after the other up the rope the last few yards to the flat summit of the Ross Ice Shelf.

They gaped in disbelief at the grey moonlike terrain.

The gritty volcanic ash covering their boot tops extended into the mist as far as they could see. The fog and ash seemed to merge at the close horizons. The first mate took a few paces forward, stripped a glove and bent to feel the gritty debris.

'It is the same powder that fell on the boats,' Takahashi said, bewildered.

Ushiba moved to join the first mate. He dipped a gloveless hand into the ash and brought his fingers to his nose. 'Sulphur!'

'What?' Takahashi asked, sniffing his own hand.

'It has a sulphuric odour,' Ushiba said. 'It's volcanic ash!' He ground the powder between his fingers. 'If there was a volcanic eruption along the coast somewhere, it might have shaken the Shelf loose from the land.

Takahashi was ecstatic. 'You see, I was right! I'll

wager there is a research station nearby.' His enthusiasm was infectious, and the others joined him in an impetuous dance, arms around one another in a whirling ring.

Suddenly the dancers fell backward in a tangled heap, their laughter caught in their throats, their faces white at the ghostly apparition that fluttered up out of the ash.

'What was that?' Aoki stuttered, his body trembling.

A skua, barely alive after flying through clouds of volcanic debris, had used the last of its strength to struggle into the air from the grey powder, fleeing the threat of the stomping feet. It hovered a moment, then dropped again.

Takahashi crawled forward to where the bird had fallen into the ash. He reached into the depression and slowly retrieved the dying skua. 'We are not alone up here, my friends,' he said, holding out the small, limp body.

Aoki reached out and stroked the barely moving breast. 'Poor thing, it can't breathe in the dust.'

Takahashi laid the labouring bird down. 'It is beyond help.'

The three men rose and shook themselves off. It did little good. A grey film clung to their clothes. The climbers exchanged wary looks.

The first mate pulled the net of salted fish from his parka and passed pieces of the stiff fare to his companions. 'We must eat. There may be miles of walking ahead of us. We'll need the energy.'

The men munched unenthusiastically on the fish, startled every few minutes as another convulsing skua roused the ash around them. They realized the ice plateau was carpeted with the birds beneath the volcanic powder.

When they'd finished eating, Takahashi uncoiled his rope again. 'There may be crevices hidden under the ash,' he explained as they tied each other together.

The line secured, the men exchanged forced smiles. 'A month's wages to the first one to spot a research station,' Takahashi promised.

He took a compass bearing, and single-file, the Japanese started off across the Ice Shelf as the death throes of thousands of choking birds stirred the powdery graveyard around them.

Mikhail Romanov blanched behind his Kremlin office desk as he finished reading the translation of the *New York Times* story handed him by the KGB chief, Boris Duglenko.

He laid the translation down deliberately. 'How do the Americans come to know about the Mirnyi engines, the ice stations, the rest of Savin's plan?'

'There is only one possible explanation, Comrade Romanov. The information was passed to the Americans by one of us present at the meeting at your dacha,' Duglenko said.

'Do you know who?'

'Anya Cherepin,' the KGB chief answered, a hint of triumph in his voice. 'You will recall, I warned you about her, about allowing her to accompany the airlift.'

Romanov picked up a calculator from his desk and absently began punching in a geometric progression. 'What leads you to Cherepin?'

'A simple process of elimination, Comrade Romanov. All of us but two meeting at your dacha were either high government officials or general officers of the armed forces, men long trusted and far above suspicion. Only Cherepin and Chirikov were there as outsiders, individuals of unknown loyalties.'

'And of these two you single out Cherepin. Why?' Romanov asked.

Duglenko nodded towards the translated newspaper story on Romanov's desk. 'That story was written by the *New York Times* correspondent Joshua McCoy. As you know, he and Cherepin were lovers while he was the *Times* bureau chief here in Moscow. Somehow she has got information on Savin's plan out to McCoy.'

'Has she been in contact with Western agents, then?'

Duglenko shifted uneasily. 'Not that we have observed. We don't know how she did it, not yet. However, I have ordered her placed under close surveillance. It is only a matter of time before she makes a misstep. When she does, she will be arrested immediately.'

Romanov unconsciously calculated the dimensions of a steel-bridge span. Certainly he could not condone Cherepin's actions, if indeed it was she who had passed Savin's plan to the Americans. What she had done could only be considered treasonous.

Yet there was a greater treason in Savin's plan, a treason against Russia's peace, against a world betrayed for millennia by the schemes of military madmen.

And if Cherepin had committed treason, she had also given him a strong and vital argument to use against the hardliners in the Presidium. Perhaps his colleagues would reconsider the wisdom of Savin's scheme once they knew it was not to be the riskless military manoeuvre the marshal had insisted it was.

The intercom buzzed on Romanov's desk. 'Yes?'

'Marshal Savin is here, Comrade Romanov. He insists the matter is of the highest urgency.'

'Very well. Send him in.

Romanov turned back to the KGB chief. 'You are to keep me informed, Comrade Duglenko.'

'On your orders, I could have Cherepin arrested immediately.'

'Your evidence is circumstantial. If Cherepin makes contact again, then you will act. Not before. Have I made myself clear?'

'I understand, Comrade Romanov,' Duglenko said, and turned to leave.

The gilt doors at the far end of Romanov's massive office opened and Marshal Pavel Savin entered. The suave officer nodded at Duglenko as they passed in the middle of the long marble hall.

'You said the matter was urgent,' Romanov said as the marshal halted before his desk.

'Most urgent, Comrade Romanov. Two hours ago communications with our nuclear attack submarine *Mezen* were suddenly broken. We have not been able to re-establish contact. I regret to tell you that we must consider the *Mezen* lost.'

Romanov came to his feet, his eyes ice tongs gripping Savin. 'Lost? What does that mean, "lost"?'

'Sunk, Comrade Romanov. There can be no other explanation. Engine trouble alone would not have affected the microwave transmitters on board. The *Mezen* carried two radios, as well as an emergency radio, and each of these has an independent power source.'

Romanov's jaw worked. 'Why do you assume the submarine is sunk? Couldn't there be a communications problem? Isn't it possible a relay satellite malfunctioned, or there is some computer problem at our receiving station?'

Savin lowered his eyes. 'There is something else. At the moment we lost contact, there was a thermonuclear detonation beneath the Ross Ice Shelf at the exact position of the *Mezen*. We believe her reactor blew up.'

Romanov sank slowly back into his chair. 'How many?'

'I beg your pardon, Comrade Romanov?'

'How many men did the *Mezen* carry?'

'Officers and ratings, two hundred and forty-two,' Savin said uncomfortably.

Romanov closed his eyes and rubbed the lids with his fingertips. 'Two hundred and forty-two human beings turned into radioactive dust.' He looked up at Savin. 'So now the dying begins. How many more Russians will this mad scheme of yours cost us, Comrade Marshal? Hundreds, thousands, millions? Tell me!'

Savin spread his hands. 'The loss of the *Mezen* is only an aside to my plan, a freak event. Navigating below drifting ice is the most dangerous course a submarine can take. Obviously the *Mezen's* captain made a mistake and it cost his ship. We cannot allow this one setback to deter us from our critical mission.'

'Why are you so certain the *Mezen* perished at her own

hand, that she was not the target of a torpedo run or some other hostile action?'

'Because whatever caused the explosion, the consequences will be far costlier to the West than to us. Knowing this, they would never have fired on the *Mezen* while she was still beneath the Shelf.'

'We lose a submarine and it is our adversaries that suffer? What tortuous logic is this, Comrade Savin?'

'The thermonuclear blast caused a partial meltdown of the Shelf, Comrade Romanov. A huge tidal wave of radioactive ice fragments and meltwater is moving north towards New Zealand and Australia. If the wave continues its path, our oceanographers believe it will devastate the southwest Pacific islands and coasts as far north as Japan. The democracies will lose ports and coastal installations throughout the region.'

Romanov punched random numbers into the calculator as he assimilated what Savin had told him. 'How does what's happened affect your plan for the ice stations?'

'With the *Mezen* gone, our territorial claim on the Shelf must be pressed by the airborne; they must make their drop the moment the Ice drifts beyond the boundary of the Treaty of Christchurch. As for separating the ice stations, I have ordered large lasers disassembled and airlifted south immediately from our Pacific port of Vladivostok.'

'How easily the solutions roll off your tongue, Comrade Savin. I only wish I could be as glib.'

The marshal remained silent as Romanov rose and walked to a large window overlooking Red Square. He stared down at a shuffling line of black-shawled *babushki* sweeping their twig brooms across the floodlit cobblestones below.

Lost in thought, Romanov watched the *babushki*. Would the loss of over 200 men reinforce his cause in the Presidium? Would the tragedy second the American warning that only war and death lay ahead?

He dismissed the conjecture bitterly. There was blood in the air now.

The hardliners would insist that the loss of the *Mezen* committed them irrevocably to their course. 'We cannot allow our gallant sailors to die for no purpose.' He could hear the patriotic harangues ringing through the Presidium already.

'Hold the Thirty-second Karelian in Angola until I have met with the Presidium,' Romanov ordered without turning.

'We cannot afford a long delay, Comrade Romanov. The Americans – '

'Get out! Leave me at once.'

Savin made to speak, thought better of it, and retreated through the tall doors at the far end of the room.

One of the old women looked up at his silhouette in the lit window and pointed with the shaft of her broom. The others lifted their wrinkled faces to stare.

Romanov imagined the question in their shadowed eyes.

What is to come, Mikhail Romanov? What is to come for Mother Russia?

# NORTHDRIFT
## 247.6 Nautical Miles

Admiral Waldo Rankin reached across the stack of marine charts and satellite reconnaissance photographs on his desk at the Antarctic Conference headquarters in Christchurch and stabbed at the intercom button.

'Yes?'

'Joshua McCoy is here, sir.'

'Send him in.'

Rankin rose as McCoy strode across the room, and the two men embraced warmly.

'Josh, damn, it's good to see you. I'm sorry I couldn't get to the airport, but I'm swamped here. Did my housekeeper meet you?'

'Yes. Mrs Moriarty is a lovely lady, Waldo. The girls took to her right away. She bundled them under her wing and the three of them went off as if they'd known one another all their lives.'

'I'll get out to the house and see Shea and Kate as soon as I can,' Rankin said. 'God, I've missed those two.'

'They've missed you too, Waldo.'

'Did you get those Maori islanders to the hospital all right?' Rankin asked as they sat.

'Yes. Chauncey Dutcheyes and his great-great-great-granddaughter Miki are getting them settled in.'

'According to the latest satellite data, Chauncey's prediction of the path of the tsunami couldn't have been more accurate,' Rankin said.

'Then the wave will come ashore to the south?'

Rankin nodded. 'The latest computer projection shows the centre hitting the coast somewhere between Invercargill and Dunedin, two hundred and fifty to three hundred miles below Christchurch. Both cities and the extending shore areas are being evacuated.'

'How bad will it get here?'

'The surge this far north should be twenty or thirty feet above high tide. Christchurch is fortunate though. The Banks Peninsula stands between the city and the direction of the tsunami. The worst of the wave will break up before it can reach the urban areas, although the port and the lower elevations will flood.'

'Any change in the radioactivity readings?' McCoy asked.

'Yes, the level continues to go down the farther the wave moves north from Antarctica. Still, that huge wall of water carries enough contamination to poison badly the coasts it floods.'

McCoy shook his head glumly. 'Any idea yet what exploded under the Shelf?'

'I talked to General Lowe at the Pentagon about twenty minutes ago. One of our hunter subs was tracking a Soviet submarine down there. The Russians disappeared off sonar at the moment of detonation. Either her reactors blew or her control system went haywire and a missile got loose. The Soviet navy isn't suicidal. Whatever happened, Washington is satisfied it was accidental.'

'Did our sub survive?'

'Yes. They were about thirty miles away under the Shelf. They got knocked around pretty thoroughly but the ice above saved them from the worst. If they'd been submerged in the open sea, they wouldn't have had a chance.'

McCoy asked, 'How much of the Shelf was melted down?'

'Almost a sixth. There's an immense volume of melt-water coming at us in the tsunami and it could get far worse in a hurry. That dominant vent through the floor of the Ross Sea has built itself into a formidable submarine volcano. During my reconnaissance flight the thermo-vision screen on board the SR-96 glowed like a TV close-up of the face of the sun.'

'How far has the volcano risen from the seabed?'

'About twenty-seven hundred feet. The summit has

penetrated the Ice. Several hours ago an eruption punched a three-thousand-foot hole up through the Shelf about twelve miles from the trailing edge. I can see only one chance that the volcano wouldn't blow itself apart when the pressure builds again.'

'What's that?'

'If the secondary vents along the fracture reopen, that might drain away enough molten material to bring down the stress in the main magma chamber. I have to know if those smaller vents will open again, Josh. Our airborne monitors can tell us when an eruption is taking place but they can't anticipate it. I'm going to dive on that fracture and get a firsthand look. I've ordered the submersible *Alvin* to be readied in McMurdo Sound.'

'I'm going with you, Waldo.'

'Now hold on.'

McCoy shook his head adamantly. 'If you order a sudden Pacific-wide evacuation of the coasts, the media will have to be alerted immediately. Even lost minutes could cost thousands of lives. Getting the warning out is my job and I have no intention of trying to do it from a safe retreat two thousand miles away.'

The phone rang on Rankin's desk.

'Connie Anderson in Operations, Admiral. You asked to be notified when the tsunami neared Campbell. The wave is closing in on the island now. We have satellite coverage.'

'Thanks, Connie. Punch me in, will you.'

Rankin flipped a switch, and a video screen on the wall came to life.

'Dear God in heaven!' he said as they stared at the live television transmission from satellite cameras high above the South Pacific.

No sight either man had ever seen prepared him for the image on the monitor. The tsunami stretched from horizon to horizon as it raced northward, towering above the ocean like a mountain range rising from a level plain. From the summit, streams of froth and spray trailed behind over the sea as if smoke from a line of prairie fire.

Before it, the titanic wave pushed incalculable tons of fractured ice, ranging from small fragments to jagged icebergs the size of city blocks.

Seconds later an island took form at the top of the picture.

McCoy came forward in his chair. 'Campbell,' he said, half to himself, his eyes riveted on the screen.

For an insane moment the tsunami appeared to hover over Campbell's southern coast. Then the furious hump-backed sea engulfed the lip of the island and rolled in a maddened foam-flecked flood over the lowlands.

As they watched, buildings were swept up like tiny cardboard boxes and carried before the huge arching wall of water. Rankin reached out and switched the video to close-up.

A mile ahead of the wave a stampede of sheep, dogs, cats, and pigs raced up towards the safety of the highlands. Birds, chickens, and ducks fluttered through the dust overhead, flying in the same direction.

Moments later the wave reached the steep slopes of the island's highlands and split into twin surges like a white-water river forking around a boulder in its bed.

The tsunami boiled over the opposite shore and out across the ocean again, carrying with it a flotsam of smashed homes, boats, trees, crops, and the corpses of hundreds of animals and birds that had started for the highlands too late.

Rankin looked at McCoy. 'Seen enough?'

McCoy exhaled a long breath. 'Yes, Waldo. More than enough.'

'We've just had a preview of what's in store for the southern tip of New Zealand in about an hour, Josh,' Rankin said, turning off the monitor. 'After that the east coast of Australia, New Guinea, the shores all the way north to China and Japan.'

The intercom buzzed again. 'Dr Gates is calling from McMurdo Station, Admiral.'

'Put him on.'

Charles Gates appeared on the videophone screen, his

face tired and unshaven. 'The submersible tender *Lulu* just dropped anchor out in the sound, Waldo. I thought you'd want to know right away.'

'Thanks, Charlie. How are conditions down there?'

'We're holding our own. Smoke and ash are continuing to vent from that submarine cone, but there haven't been any magma eruptions for a while.'

'You getting any radioactive fallout?'

'Negative. The explosion took place on the other side of the Shelf, about three hundred and twenty miles northwest, as near as we can tell with satellite triangulation. The offshore winds should keep the nuclear cloud well out to sea.'

'First break we've had,' Rankin said. 'Ask the captain of the *Lulu* to ready the *Alvin* for a dive, will you, Charlie? I want to go down as soon as I get there.'

'When are you coming in?'

'Couple of hours. I'll call you from the air.'

'Melissa and I will meet you at the airport.'

Rankin hung up and buzzed his secretary. 'I need a car downstairs right away, Peg.'

'Yes, sir.'

Rankin rose. 'You sure you want a piece of this, Josh?'

For a fleeting moment McCoy envisioned Shea and Kate, their faces pressed against a window watching for him to come up Grandpa's drive, waiting for a father who would never return from an icy tomb beneath the Ross Sea. He stood. 'No, but I'm going anyway.'

Twenty minutes later Rankin and McCoy crossed the tarmac at Christchurch Airport and scaled the boarding ladder to the SR-96's tandem cockpits. The canopy lowered and a shrill whine began to build within the huge turbojets.

The winged black projectile eased out on the runway, paused to gather power, then flashed down the narrow concrctc ribbon and into the Pacific sky.

Above Pegasus Bay it banked sharply and hurtled south towards the bottom of the world.

# NORTHDRIFT
## 251.8 Nautical Miles

August Sumner leaned back wearily in his chair and pored over the international news summary just hand- delivered to his office. McCoy's bulletin of the titanic tsunami sweeping north from Antarctica had ignited the media and focused the attention of the press around the world on the southwestern part of the Pacific.

Radio and TV in Christchurch were reporting that the evacuation of the eastern coast along the lower half of New Zealand's South Island was almost complete.

The Australian shoreline from Sydney north to the Great Barrier Reef was being abandoned, and islanders in the Tasman and Coral Seas were fleeing to higher ground.

Beyond, refugees were streaming inland along the swampy coasts of New Guinea. The Philippine government had declared a state of emergency and ordered its citizens to evacuate vulnerable shores from Mindanao to Luzon.

A Chinese satellite in South Pacific orbit was broadcasting live television pictures of the tsunami. Long columns of evacuees clogged the shore roads from the newly acquired province of Hong Kong all the way up the coast to Shanghai.

There was consternation in Japan when the government in Tokyo announced a squadron of amphibious aircraft had been dispatched to search for the small boat without a radio on which the young emperor had gone sailing the day before.

The most ominous reports came from the low-lying coral islands in the path of the giant wave. Mobs were storming airports on the Solomon Islands and the atolls of New Guinea, searching desperately for planes to fly them to safety.

The interdepartmental phone buzzed on his desk. 'Yes?'

'Lynn Rotando over at the international desk, August. You asked to be notified when reaction to McCoy's laser piece started coming in.'

'What have you got, Lynn?'

'A sudden outbreak of brush fires, August, from Africa to Indonesia. Our laser threat has half the world believing the final battle between the superpowers is at hand, that man is on the edge of Armageddon. International restraints have simply crumbled. The feeling in a score of capitals seems to be, 'The end is near. It's time to settle scores once and for all.'

'Have any hostilities broken out?'

'It seems to be confined to sporadic shooting so far, but things could heat up quickly. We have a report that South African guerrillas under Nukomo are preparing to cross the border from Botswana and march on Pretoria.'

Sumner shook his head slowly. 'Good God.'

'South Africa isn't the only flash point, August. Radio Indonesia has announced suddenly renewed insurgent attacks against several cities and military posts on its outer islands. And in South America gunboat fire has been exchanged between Chile and Argentina over those islands they're both claiming at the tip of the continent.'

Sumner's direct line to the *Times* Satellite Reception Centre in New Jersey began to buzz insistently.

'I've got another call, Lynn,' Sumner said. 'I want you to keep me informed.'

'Will do, August.'

The editor flicked off the intercom and picked up the phone. 'Sumner.'

'Ilona Feratti, August. We've just received a bulletin from New Zealand. The tsunami struck their South Island about twenty minutes ago.'

Sumner came forward in his chair. 'They get everybody out in time?'

There was a break in Feratti's voice. 'A bridge collapsed under the heavy refugee traffic on one of the evacuation routes out of Invercargill,' she said. 'There were people backed up for almost a mile.'

Sumner felt his gut turn to stone. 'Sweet Lord, Ilona. How many?'

'They don't know for sure. The tsunami swept everything out to sea.' Feratti's voice finally broke. 'They think as many as six thousand people drowned, August.'

Sumner put down the phone.

The dying had begun.

Kanji Takahashi stopped for the sixth time in the past hour to clean the interminable clumps of ash-laden snow from his boots. Behind him, Ushiba and the sixteen-year-old cabin boy, Aoki, staggered up to him and dropped down into the volcanic dust blanketing the surface of the Ross Ice Shelf.

They had been trudging over the grey moonlike terrain for hours now. The soggy ash clinging to their boots and trousers made their progress increasingly difficult and exhausting. The cold, too, sapped their energy.

'First Mate, are you sure there's a research station up here?' Ushiba asked again, discouraged and tired. 'I have seen nothing. No roads, no sledge tracks, no radio towers, not even garbage.'

Takahashi threw a clump of sodden ash at the student. 'A few hours' march and you are giving up. What happened to the brave adventurer who left the boat with me?'

He tried to keep his voice light, but his own fatigue and exasperation were creeping in. The futility of their search so far was beginning to tax even his indomitable spirit.

Aoki surveyed the broken, swirling mist. 'I think the fog is lifting a little,' he said, the enthusiasm of youth still in his voice. 'I saw a patch of sky a while back.'

Takahashi looked up. 'Maybe the winds are starting to move the fog. I'm going to take a look at the sea.'

'What difference does it make if the mist clears?' Ushiba whined when Takahashi was out of earshot. 'It will just be blown back again in a few hours. No one will ever find us up here.'

The first mate gingerly approached the lip of the ice palisades towering above the freezing Ross Sea. He had kept his little group within a few hundred yards of the edge of the Shelf, reasoning that if a research station were nearby it would be close to the water.

He shielded his eyes from the glare of the sun, diffused by the thin mist, and scanned the panorama below. Broken ice floes filled the turbulent waters. The irregular waves were choppy and flecked with foam. There was no sign of a ship or plane or anything else that promised the slightest succour to the marooned Japanese sailors.

Willing his face into a smile, Takahashi walked back to his companions. 'The fog is lifting. It's a good sign,' he said with a conviction he didn't feel. 'Come on, we'll find the station. It's only a matter of time.'

They began their slogging march again. As long as they kept moving, kept a modicum of faith, they would be rescued, there was hope, Takahashi told himself.

They had gone only a few hundred yards when the first mate suddenly held up a gloved hand. He stood perfectly still, an ear cocked upward.

Ushiba and Aoki strained their senses towards the patchy fog. 'What do you hear, First Mate?' Aoki whispered.

'Quiet!'

Then all three of them heard it. The sound of a motor. 'A plane!' Ushiba yelled.

'Shut up!' Takahashi rasped hoarsely. He listened intently. It wasn't a plane. The rhythm of the engine was different. Then he saw the dark shape through the mist, coming in from the south.

'It's a helicopter!' Takahashi shouted. 'Wave your arms! Wave! Wave!'

The three stranded fishermen flung their arms frantically from side to side, screaming at the top of their lungs.

The huge Russian Mi-32 transport helicopter glided in over the awesome line of cliffs facing the Ross Ice Shelf. Through the breaks in the swirling fog, the three men aboard could see the grey blanket of volcanic ash covering the ice plateau below. The vista didn't surprise them. The same gritty powder had fallen on the coast of Victoria Land as they flew over en route from their base at Mirnyi.

The pilot, Valerii Levitsky, spoke into his throat mike. 'Keep your eyes open for a likely landing spot. The surface is completely flat, but there may be crevasses beneath the ash. Look for depression lines. I don't want to smash the undercarriage.'

'Yes, Comrade Lieutenant,' Private Maxim Gordov answered.

The third man aboard sat sullenly in the rear of the aircraft. Ivan Morozov, a KGB agent, took orders from no mere air force lieutenant. He had been sent to Antarctica as a watchdog over the numerous and valued Soviet scientists conducting various experiments on the isolated seventh continent. Even at the bottom of the world, the Kremlin kept an eye on its citizens.

Most of the time, though, there was little or nothing for the Soviet security men to do but write endless reports. Boredom was rampant. An assignment to Antarctica was always a penance for a past misdeed.

Morozov's reports of conversations of questionable ideology among the scientists had generated no response from Moscow. He doubted they were even read. At the same time, he was treated as the informer he was by the researchers at the base. Conversation ceased when he entered a room, laughter died on lips. He was a scorned outsider in a tiny, closely knit community.

His fate had sired a raging feeling of impotence, a black hatred of everyone and everything that surrounded him.

Private Gordov suddenly stiffened and pointed downward. 'Something moved, I saw it! It was red . . . a coat . . . a man!'

The pilot turned the helicopter into a tight circle. 'Are you sure?'

'Yes. At least I think so. He was there and then he was gone in the fog.'

Morozov moved up to the window next to Gordov.

Halfway through the turn both men saw the movement below. There were two, no three, men standing in the ash waving.

From some primal core of his brain, an instinct raced along a chemical path to the thought centre of Aoki's mind. He reached into a pocket, pulled out a stiff, dried fish, and held it up, as if the offering of food to the helicopter would lure it down.

In the circling aircraft, Morozov, too, reacted instinctively. He saw a gun. It had to be a gun. He grabbed an AK-47 automatic rifle from a cabin rack and opened the hinged window.

The three Japanese below stared at the weapon barrel in disbelief an instant before it erupted in orange flame. They dove for the grey powder around them. Aoki wasn't quick enough. The Russian bullets ripped through his chest. He dropped like a weighted bundle of rags into the ash.

The pilot yanked back on the stick at the sound of the automatic fire. The helicopter swooped up into the fog and disappeared towards the sea.

Takahashi rose to his hands and knees, his face white beneath the ash. 'Why?' he screamed at the retreating sound. 'Why, why, why, why?'

He crawled to where Aoki lay in a heap in the grey powder. Ushiba came up beside him. Silently they gazed down at the sixteen-year-old cabin boy.

Aoki was dead.

The smell of cordite and the wind from the open window behind him horrified Lieutenant Levitsky. The firing had come from his helicopter! He turned his head. Private Gordov was staring open-mouthed at the KGB man, still holding the weapon.

'Are you insane?' Levitsky screamed. 'Why did you shoot at those men? They were unarmed.'

Uncertainty passed across Morozov's eyes. Had he made a mistake? If he had, his life was over. He would end up in Lefortovo, the KGB prison in Moscow. He couldn't admit he'd been wrong. He'd have to bluff it out.

'One of them pointed a pistol at us. Didn't you see it?'

Private Gordov was too young, too naive, as yet to stand in awe of the KGB. 'I think it was a fish.'

It was such a plain, straightforward, if absurd, statement that Levitsky recognized it instantly as the truth.

'Put that weapon away immediately, you fool!' he ordered Morozov.

'I don't take commands from – '

'Put it down,' the pilot screamed. 'You're in enough trouble.'

Morozov's bravado dissolved. Levitsky's anger cowed him. He replaced the weapon in its rack. Gordov quickly ran the small chain beneath the trigger guard and snapped the lock. Morozov would have to overpower the pilot to get the key.

'I'm going back,' Levitsky announced. 'You may have killed or wounded them, whoever the devil they are out here on this ice.'

He turned the craft back towards the Shelf, crossing the ice cliffs close above the ash.

Takahashi stood looking down at Ushiba cradling Aoki in his arms. Blood and ash mixed on the still teenager's punctured chest. 'They've killed him,' Ushiba sobbed hysterically. 'He was only a boy and now he's dead. Why did they shoot him? Why? Why?'

Before the first mate could answer, he heard the helicopter coming back. The murderers were making another run at them!

'There they are!' Private Gordov shouted, gesturing excitedly downward.

Levitsky saw the coloured jackets of the Japanese vivid against the grey powder, and slowly he began to bring the giant helicopter down.

The gale-force wash of the props cleared a circle of ash from the ice surface, suddenly exposing hundreds of skua gulls slowly suffocating in the fine volcanic powder.

The only instinctive fear in the skuas' tiny brains worse than the fear of death was a horrible death.

First one, then fifty, then six hundred birds, burning the last of their adrenaline, rose in a cloud of wings. The frenzied skuas tore skyward, twisting as they ascended to avoid the helicopter.

As quick as the reflex actions of the birds' eyes were, still they saw the whirling aluminum blades above as only a blur. Almost 200 of the large gulls were sliced into slivers by the knife-sharp props.

A rain of beaks and feathers and flesh was instantly sucked into the air intake vents of the aircraft's engine. It sputtered and coughed, then died.

Frantically the pilot tried to restart the engine, his hands flying as he changed the air-fuel mixture. It was no use. Even if the vents weren't hopelessly clogged, the helicopter was too close to the surface for any manoeuvre to have a chance.

It tilted forward at a fifteen-degree slant as it lost altitude, and the tip of one of the twenty-six-foot-long aluminum props dug into the ice a second later.

The mutilated blade shook the aircraft unmercifully. The stick leaped from Levitsky's hands and the aircraft swooped back upward out of control, turning on its side in the air. For an instant the wounded machine seemed to hover impossibly in the grey fog. Then it plunged downward into the scattered ash.

Takahashi grabbed Ushiba, spilling Aoki's body into the powder, and ran as fast as he could propel his stunned shipmate. Behind them the helicopter burst into flame. For almost half an hour there was only the roar of the flames and the crackling and snapping of the metal as the fuel-drenched aircraft hissed and burned.

As the fire died, Takahashi approached the smouldering wreck. A blistered hammer and sickle insignia was still visible on the blackened fuselage. Russians! But why would they attack us? he wondered vacantly, his emotions spent.

The first mate suddenly felt bewildered, lost. He felt he was slipping into shock. Dead ashes, dead birds, dead Russians, dead Aoki, dead everthing. He fought for control and started back towards Ushiba. He had taken only a few steps when he stumbled over something in the ash. He bent down. It was a long black metal box, thrown from the helicopter on impact. He strained and turned the heavy box over. The lid was crumpled. It wouldn't budge. He kicked at the top; once, twice, the chest flew open.

Inside were orderly rows of green plastic cylinders. There were Russian words printed on the tubes. Small antennas protruded out of the ends. He picked up several and walked back to Ushiba.

The university graduate looked at Takahashi with uncomprehending red eyes. Rivulets of tears had cleared channels through the ash mask on his face. Aoki's body lay at his feet, where he had dragged it.

'How do we bury him here?' Ushiba asked forlornly, gazing about at the desolate Shelf.

Wordlessly, Takahashi knelt and began scooping ash over the already half-covered body of the cabin boy. In a moment there was only a grey mound of volcanic powder, as lifeless as the form beneath it.

The first mate rose and suddenly remembered the green cylinders he had dropped into the ash beside the grave. He knelt and retrieved one.

'Didn't you tell me once that you could read Russian?' Takahashi asked the only university graduate among the crew of the fishing fleet.

'Yes,' Ushiba answered dully, his numbed mind finding nothing strange in the question.

'What does this say?' The first mate asked, holding out the cylinder.

Ushiba looked at the Cyrillic lettering. His mouth fell open. Life returned to his dark eyes. 'Signal flares,' he said. 'They're a military type. They also emit some sort of radio signal when they're activated, a homing device I think.'

The student rotated the green tube. 'It says the flare has a night visibility of twenty-five kilometres and the radio signal range is one hundred and fifty kilometres.'

Takahashi let out a great whoop. 'We're saved, Ushiba,

we're saved,' he screamed, dancing a mad jig around his stunned shipmate. 'We'll set a line of them along the sea cliffs. The flares will be easily visible against the dark ash.'

It took the two Japanese almost twenty minutes to drag the heay box of flares across to the edge of the Shelf. Ushiba bent, swept the layer of volcanic ash from the chest, and extracted one of the long, bulky cylinders, handing it to Ushiba. The student mentally translated the Russian.

'So. It is simple, First Mate. We pull off the short end, turn it, and strike the butt against the flare tip. It is similar to the ones we used for night boat drills on the *Kumaru*. It will burn for four hours.'

Takahashi took the tube from Ushiba, yanked the striker free of the cylinder, reversed it, and brought the tip down sharply across the butt. The flare burst into a sizzling green light. A steady beeping sound pulsed from the tube.

The men stared at it in awe.

'I'll do one now,' Ushiba said, breaking the spell. He grabbed a cylinder from the box and managed to get it lit on the second strike. The fishermen stood facing each other, each enveloped in his own sphere of green light brilliant against the grey fog.

'Now there can be no doubt the searchers will find us!' the first mate exulted, his confidence restored.

The two cold, filthy Japanese castaways hugged each other, the life light rekindled in their eyes.

# NORTHDRIFT
256.8 Nautical Miles

Charles Gates and Melissa McCoy watched from the control tower at Marble Point Field as the black jet above circled the Antarctic base like a hawk searching the ice for a snowshoe rabbit.

The radio speaker crackled to life. 'SR-96 to Marble Point tower.'

Gates reached for the mike. 'Tower to 96. Go ahead, Waldo.'

'Looks awful damn bleak down there, Charlie. The glaciers are covered with ash from horizon to horizon. You guys have taken quite a beating.'

'The last eruption dropped about eight inches on us.'

'How's the field? Can I put this bird down?'

Gates focused binoculars on the end of the runway. Two Sno-Cats had just finished their ploughing and were lumbering off the apron. Behind them the landing strip of steel-mesh mats was streaked with scars of ash-blackened snow and ice, but it was clear.

'There's a six-knot crosswind, Waldo, gusting to fifteen. We haven't time to cover all the ice patches. It starts to get pretty slick about halfway down the runway.'

'Okay, Charlie. We're coming in.'

'Melissa and I will be waiting in hangar two.'

The landing gear hummed down as Rankin lined the jet up with the narrow strip and lowered the flaps. 'Hang on, Josh. This could get a little dicey.'

'Ready when you are, Waldo,' McCoy answered from the rear cockpit.

The SR-96 whistled in over the ice and set down, the motors screaming as Rankin reversed engines. Near the middle of the runway the aircraft skidded sharply to the left on a glassy finger of frozen snow.

For a moment McCoy thought the plane was out of control, but Rankin played the stick skilfully and the jet slowed and straightened out 500 feet from the end of the steel strip.

Rankin taxied back to the tower-hangar complex. They were still forty yards away when the hangar doors cranked open. The reconnaissance probe nosed into the cavernous building and the doors closed quickly again behind them.

Off to the side, two maintenance workers were servicing the giant C-200 Hercules transport plane that would ferry the station's research party to Christchurch in a week for spring rotation to the States.

Gates and Melissa approached as the jet's engines died.

The two men climbed down and Rankin folded his daughter into his arms. 'God, I've been worried about you.' He clung to Melissa a moment, then held her at arm's length. 'You look tired. And skinny. Didn't your mother and I teach you about sleeping and eating?'

'Neither has been on schedule the last couple of days, Dad.'

She embraced McCoy and kissed him lightly on the lips. 'Hello, Josh,' she said tentatively, awkwardly thrusting her hands into her parka pockets, wishing too late she'd put them into his. 'Did the girls have a good flight?'

'They loved it,' McCoy said. 'I know you're under a tremendous work load with all that's happened, Melissa. Still, I hope you'll get up to Christchurch to see them as soon as you can. They need you.'

'That's a nice thing to hear, Josh – that I'm needed, even if it also makes me feel guilty,' she said. She wanted to ask him if he needed her too. But she knew the answer to that.

'Going for a hike?' McCoy grinned, gesturing towards the knapsack on Melissa's back.

She smiled. 'I don't dare take it off. I have the only copy of literally all my research on computer tapes in there. There's no time to gather my original notes. They're filed away in laboratories all over the base. Everything but what I carry on my back will be lost when McMurdo goes under.'

Despite his insulated flight suit, McCoy shivered slightly

in the freezing hangar. 'Do you ever get used to the cold down here, Melissa?'

'It's only twenty below, Josh,' she said. 'Spring weather. You ought to be around in July, when we have a hundred-and-thirty-mile-an-hour ice blizzard tearing through.'

She'd like him around then, she found herself thinking. She'd like him naked under the soft down quilt on her bed, his body warm and arousing, his maleness shielding as the Antarctic wind howled outside.

She looked at him out of the corner of her eye, surprised at the desire that had suddenly welled within her. God, what was this all about? Did she want him again now because she knew he didn't want her? Because he was a challenge again, a husband metamorphosed back into an alluring sexual stranger? Or was her hunger so strong because he had come to her world, where he tiptoed and she walked surely? Did her control make her the pursuer?

Rankin introduced McCoy and Gates.

'Come on up to the tower,' Gates said. 'We've got a pot of coffee brewing.'

They climbed the spiral stairs to the tower, and Gates handed around steaming mugs. As they sipped, a navy signalman crossed the room from the communications area and tapped McCoy on the shoulder.

'Mr McCoy?'

McCoy lowered his cup. 'Yes.'

'I have a message for you from the *Times* office in New York, sir,' the signalman said, handing McCoy two computer-typed sheets.

'Thank you,' McCoy excused himself and began to read. By the time he finished, his lips had compressed into a thin hard line.

Melissa watched him over the rim of her mug. 'What is it, Josh?' she asked.

McCoy waved the printout. 'It's from my editor, August Sumner. For the past several hours he's been receiving growing reports of military mobilizations in Africa, Asia, and South America. President Wollcott's laser threat has spawned a sense of doom all over the world. Millions of people are convinced that the superpower struggle over the Ross Ice Shelf will escalate rapidly to total war. To total nuclear annihilation.'

'Countries have begun to choose sides,' Rankin said sadly, his voice barely audible. 'Now the fanatics will fan the war fever, drag out old enemies, old scores to settle. God help us. Within hours we may face wars on every continent.'

There was nothing to be said and they sipped their coffee in the thick silence that followed, each lost in his or her own morose thoughts.

Finally Rankin broke the quiet. 'I don't give a damn if the whole world's going mad, I came down here to dive on that volcanic drift and that's what I intend to do.'

'How long do you figure you'll be down, Waldo?' Gates asked.

'That depends on how long it takes to collect steam samples, Charlie. I'll have to run a chemical analysis of the vapour from at least two separate vents.'

'What will that tell you?'

'If there's a high proportion of sulphur gases relative to chloride gases – that's pretty good evidence magma's rising through the crust beneath the rift. And, of course, the opposite applies. If there's a low sulphur content, we'll know the dominant vent in the middle of the bay is draining away the magma.'

'Then the chemical analysis will be enough to tell you whether the rift under McMurdo is still volcanically active?' Gates asked.

'In theory. To be sure, we'll put out a submarine seismometer. When molten magma moves through the crust, it produces swarms of microquakes. If there's seismic activity beneath the fracture, there's a good chance the magma conduits down into the plume are still open.'

'What if you find the magma tubes are closed, Dad?' Melissa asked.

'Without the string of rift vents acting as safety valves

to relieve the pressure within the volcano, we can expect that submarine mountain to blow itself apart within the next day or so.'

A deep rumbling began to build in the distance, as if a train were coming from over the horizon. They could feel faint vibrations throbbing through the steel-plate flooring of the tower.

'Another eruption,' Gates said. 'Sounds like a small one though.'

McCoy picked up a pair of binoculars and looked out across the field. 'Where's the volcano from here?'

'Southwest, Josh,' Melissa said. 'You'll see the ash column rising in a minute or two. Depending on the winds, we'll get the volcanic fallout in about an hour.'

Helicopter pilot Jim Culpepper appeared at the top of the stairs. Gates introduced him.

'Chopper's ready any time you are, Admiral,' Culpepper said.

'How long will it take you to fly us out to the dive site and make the return trip?' Rankin asked.

The pilot shrugged. 'Forty-five, fifty minutes.'

'I don't want you flying through a sky full of volcanic debris. You'll be cutting it mighty close.'

Culpepper grinned. 'No sweat, Admiral. Don't worry. I'll get the Alouette back here before the ash starts coming down again.'

Rankin regarded the pilot thoughtfully. 'I hope to hell you know your machine, son. All right, crank her up. I want to take off in five minutes.'

'You got it, Admiral.' Culpepper disappeared back down the stairs to the hangar.

Rankin turned to Gates. 'Who's the skipper of the mother ship out there?'

'Sam Crocker. Good man.'

'Get him on the radio, will you, Charlie.'

A moment later the voice of the *Lulu's* master came through the wall speaker. 'Captain Crocker here, Admiral.'

'What's your dive status, Captain?'

'We're in position about three miles off the fracture ridge. There's been sporadic geysering, sir. You understand why I don't want to bring my vessel any closer.'

'Of course, Captain. Is the *Alvin* ready to go down?'

'She's all checked out, prepared to dive the minute you shut the hatch. We have another problem out here though.'

'Let's have it.'

'Eight- to ten-foot seas. There's no way a chopper can set down under these conditions.'

Rankin swore under his breath.

'There is one alternative,' Crocker went on. 'Your Alouette has a cargo hoist. It's a tricky manoeuvre, but you could be lowered by winch.'

'I don't see we have any choice, Captain. We should be over your deck in about twenty minutes.'

Rankin hung up and turned to McCoy, 'You heard. You didn't contract for this kind of operation, Josh. It could turn into a one-way trip.'

'We're going to see this through together, Waldo. I'm making that dive with you.'

Melissa gathered herself. 'I'm going too, Dad. I've been down in submersibles a dozen times on research dives beneath the Shelf. I know the systems.'

She held up an adamant palm as her father's jaw began to work. 'Now don't waste time arguing. You know you can use me.'

Rankin sputtered. 'You bet I'll argue! It's going to be dangerous down there, damn dangerous. Two lives are enough to risk.'

'Your father's right, Melissa,' McCoy said. 'We can't put both our lives on the line. Think of the girls – Kate and Shea would be alone.'

'You don't believe I think at all of the children, do you, Josh?' Melissa shot back. 'I mean ever!'

'This is not the time, Melissa,' McCoy said. 'We're talking about a specific decision here.'

Melissa set her hands on her hips. 'I think the real reason you're both against me going is that I'm a daughter and a wife. Translate that into a woman.' Her eyes flared. 'Let me remind you both that I'm also a scientist, a glaciologist with a job to do. If I'm going to calculate the meltdown accurately, I'll need submarine temperatures and salinity readings, data the *Alvin* can provide.'

'We could run your tests,' Rankin offered weakly.

'No, Dad. I'll do my own work. You can't deny me the chance to conduct my research simply because you two perceive me as your personal vulnerable female. Dammit, I'm going!'

Rankin and McCoy looked at each other, surrender conceded in their eyes.

The noise of the helicopter engine starting whined up from the hangar below.

'You're right, Melissa,' Rankin admitted. 'You're a scientist, and a damn fine one. Unless Josh has a further objection, you go.'

McCoy looked at his wife. 'Neither one of us can pull back, can we? Too many lives depend on my doing my job, and you doing yours. I guess that gives us the right to risk the future, for us and for the kids.'

Rankin put down his coffee cup. 'Sounds like Culpepper's ready. Let's get cracking before that ash cloud arrives.'

Melissa hooked an arm around both of them as they headed for the stairs. 'Stop worrying, you two. The *Alvin* is as safe as a car.'

# NORTHDRIFT
## 279.5 Nautical Miles

The newscaster had been on the air continuously for over eight hours. His face was lined with strain, his red eyes sunk behind shadowed half-circles of fatigue.

'Ladies and gentlemen, I understand we have gone to a live global transmission. For those of you now joining us around the world, I am Reginald Chamberlain of the Australian Broadcasting Network in Sydney. I shall be reporting the progress of the Antarctic tsunami up our eastern coast here.'

He smiled thinly and hoped the camera wasn't picking up his shaking hands. 'I shall continue coverage as long as I am able to remain on the air. I ask you to forgive any transmission difficulties, as I am quite alone here at the station. Sydney's been evacuated, along with the entire eastern Australian coast as far north as Cairns. Our studio cameras and other equipment are fully automated, of course, and I hope to carry on without technicians.'

He looked down at the news copy on his deck and bit the inside of his cheek. 'I am saddened to have to tell you that the death toll from New Zealand's South Island is now approaching eight thousand souls. It's estimated a further four to five thousand lives have been lost on ships and islands so far engulfed by the wave.'

Chamberlain started suddenly in his chair as a word processor printer rat-a-tatted to life on the desk to his left. He reached over and tore the finished news copy from the machine. He scanned the story and looked up. 'The tsunami is reported nearing Cape Howe, two hundred miles south of Sydney. I shall switch now to live satellite coverage.'

The picture flickered, then a wide swath of the Tasman Sea coast of Australia appeared on the screen. The

251

towering wave stretched across the tube, billions of tons of blue-green water sweeping north at almost 400 miles an hour.

Before it, the curling, frothing palisade pushed a tumbling flotsam scoured from the landmasses it had already overrun.

Human and animal corpses littered the trough at the step of the wave, bobbing as if in a macabre dance through the blocks of jagged ice, uprooted trees, shattered lumber, and the tangled debris of dozens of drowned islands and coasts.

'Oh, dear God!' Chamberlain's pained cry came over the audio as the wave advanced on and then swallowed up a rusty tramp steamer, the scale of the vessel against the monstrous tsunami making it appear a child's bath toy.

A moment later the left flank of the immense wave rolled over the Australian coast at Cape Howe. The maddened liquid wall raged inland, obliterating the work of man and leaving a wide path of levelled, featureless shoreline behind.

For almost a quarter of an hour the satellite camera followed the tsunami as it advanced up the eastern shore of Australia, the torn voice of Chamberlain describing the small towns and settlements being drowned.

The wave inundated the city of Wollongong, forty miles below Sydney, and then disappeared beneath a cloud formation drifting over the coast.

The picture switched back to the newsroom in Sydney.

'If any of you watching remain near the coast to the north, I implore you to get to higher ground inland at once,' Chamberlain said. 'You must not consider your homes safe because they were beyond the reach of past tidal waves. This wave is three times the height of the worst tsunami ever recorded. It's cresting at almost three hundred feet. Please, if you are near the shore, evacuate at once.'

Again the word processor clicked to life. He read the copy and looked back at the camera, a fatalistic calm settled on his face. 'Ladies and gentlemen, the tsunami has reached Botany Bay on the southern edge of the city. Sydney Airport's gone under. I have only a few moments now.'

A roar began to build in the background.

'Carolyn, if you're watching, you saw the lab report. You know why I've stayed. Better this way than to linger. Kiss the children.'

A crescendo of sound boomed through the microphone. The newsroom began to shake.

Chamberlain's face was calm, an infinite sadness in his sunken eyes.

'Good-bye. God bless – '

The picture tilted crazily forward, then went blank.

The Alouette helicopter hovered for a moment, then began to lower towards the submersible tender, *Lulu*, below. The pilot, Jim Culpepper, looked down anxiously as the vessel tossed on the ten-foot waves combing McMurdo Sound.

'You sure you want to try this, Admiral?' Culpepper asked above the throbbing of the engine. 'That deck's going up and down like a yo-yo.'

'Got to be done, son,' Rankin said. 'Bring us as close as you can.'

Joshua McCoy moved to the door and buckled on the lift harness. Rankin started to object.

'Save your breath, Waldo. I'm going down first. I have twenty-five years on you. If this doesn't work, if I break a leg or something and get knocked out of commission, the world can afford the loss. But we can't lose you.'

'He's right, Dad,' Melissa McCoy said. 'If you smash yourself up, the entire meltdown early-warning system goes down the tubes.'

Rankin conceded. 'All right, Josh, you go first. But no heroics.'

Culpepper brought the Alouette down slowly, bucking the strong winds howling out from the ice-shrouded coast. He levelled the aircraft sixy feet above the wallowing *Lulu*.

'I can't take her any lower or I'll risk hitting their radio mast.'

'Okay, son, hold her steady as you can,' Rankin said. He checked McCoy's harness. 'You'll have to jump the last six or eight feet, Josh.'

'Watch the roll,' Melissa warned.

Lieutenant Culpepper put the helicopter on computer pilot and came back. He yanked the handle and shoved back the door. The polar air streaming into the helicopter was numbing. He switched on the hoist, and the winch arm hummed out through the open port, its load hook suspended over the tossing catamaran below.

McCoy attached the harness ring. 'Ready any time, Jim.'

Culpepper put the winch in gear and McCoy started down. A knot of sailors waited on the *Lulu's* fantail as he descended: forty feet, thirty, twenty.

'That deck is pitching badly,' Melissa said, worry in her voice.

Eight feet above the deck McCoy looked back up at the Alouette and drew a finger across his throat.

'Stop the winch!' Melissa shouted to Culpepper.

The harness bucked sharply then began to swing McCoy in a shallow arc as the line stopped feeding out. He undid the chest and waist straps and waited for the *Lulu* to roll to starboard. The port deck angled up towards him. Now! Six hands cushioned his fall as he landed on one knee on the deck.

Relieved of McCoy's weight, the helicopter rose suddenly, then the computer settled the aircraft back into position above the tender.

Rankin said, 'Go ahead, Melissa. I'll come last.'

The woman descended quickly, then dropped lithely to the deck from six feet above. She landed standing, finding a triumphant look in McCoy's direction irresistible.

The Admiral followed minutes later, landing in a crouch. The Alouette circled once, then headed back towards Marble Point.

Rankin, Melissa, and McCoy followed a sailor to the bridge. 'Welcome aboard,' Captain Crocker greeted them. 'Charlie Gates briefed me on your mission. I can't say I envy the three of you making this dive. You pick the wrong stretch of fracture to probe down there, and one of those vents could go up in your face.'

'I want to make it clear before we dive, Captain, that if anything goes wrong, there's to be no attempt to recover the *Alvin*,' Rankin said. 'The geysering could start again at any time. There are only three of us. You have forty men to worry about aboard this ship. Understood?'

'Understood, Admiral.'

'Good. Has the chemical analyser on board the *Alvin* been programmed to make the sulphur tests?'

'All set. All you need is a small steam sample and you'll have a readout in a matter of seconds. The submarine seismometer you requested is also on board. It's stored on the hull amidships, accessible to the manipulator arm.'

'I appreciate your thoroughness, Captain,' Rankin said. 'Let's get under way.'

They left the bridge for the *Alvin's* berth between the twin hulls of the catamaran. The submersible was built especially for ocean-floor research. It could carry a three-man team of scientists to the deepest depths of the sea and was equipped with multiple camera and exterior lighting systems.

'What's that tray on the bow for?' McCoy asked, pointing at the *Alvin*.

'It's an equipment shelf, Josh,' Melissa said. 'It carries traps, corers, temperature probes. On the right, those are vacuums and samplers. A manipulator arm controlled from inside the cabin lets us collect marine life and bottom sediment.'

The three put on insulated survival suits and shook hands with the launch team. Then they slipped into contoured seats, and the heavy hatch slammed home over their heads, plugging the pressurized hull. They ran a final surface-phone and systems check, then Rankin ordered the mooring lines cast off.

'We're going down,' Rankin said, setting the dive planes. 'Keep an eye on the cabin pressure, Melissa.'

The *Alvin's* propellers began to turn, and the ping of the bottom-sounding sonar echoed through the tiny craft as the submersible angled down into the freezing depths of McMurdo Sound.

'God, it's beautiful down here,' McCoy said, staring out through a porthole at the luminescent specks of blue, green, red, and yellow marine life drifting upward like an inverted hail of coloured confetti.

256

At 600 feet the *Alvin* entered a deepening twilight. Rankin turned to Melissa. 'About time for the hull lights.'

She reached forward and flipped a toggle switch on the control panel. The bright illumination from the exterior floodlights reached 200 feet out into the dark depths.

For half an hour the *Alvin* descended towards the floor of McMurdo Sound. Then the pitch of the sonar pinger changed suddenly and Rankin studied the screen. 'There's the fracture ridge. Six hundred yards ahead.'

McCoy glanced at the calibration marks at the edge of the screen. 'Some of those mounds along the ridge summit must be four or five hundred feet above the sea floor.'

'At least,' Melissa agreed. 'And we're over two hundred miles away from the dominant vent!'

'Ready the manipulator arm, Melissa. I'm going to want some steam samples.'

Melissa swivelled her chair to face the controls for the mechanical arm and turned on the power.

'Anything I can help with?' McCoy asked.

'The controls for the television camera to your right, Josh,' Rankin said. 'I'll talk you through.'

It took McCoy only a few moments to familiarize himself with the camera's operation. Slowly he panned an arc of sea before *Alvin*, adjusting the focus and contrast.

'Closing in on the ridge,' Rankin said a moment later. 'Two hundred yards.'

Vague shapes appeared at the bottom of the television monitor.

'What the hell are those?' McCoy asked. 'Looks like a pile of cement sacks.'

Rankin squinted at the screen. 'Pillow lava. It forms when magma from great depth is erupted under water. The lava comes out of the vents like toothpaste from a tube, then breaks off and rolls down the slopes as it hardens.'

The lava fragments became a field of volcanic rock as the *Alvin* approached the slope of the ridge. Rankin brought the submersible around and they began to cruise slowly down the spine of the fracture. For twenty minutes the *Alvin* moved through the dark sea like a robot fish, Melissa, Rankin, and McCoy absorbed in monitoring the TV screen and the rows of sensor gauges that crammed the compact cabin.

'Water temperature's rising,' Melissa said abruptly, looking at a digital reading on the control panel.

'Television picking up anything, Josh?' Rankin asked.

McCoy slowly ran the camera focus to infinity. There was blurry movement in the distance, almost off the screen to the left. He panned the camera over. 'There's some sort of disturbance ahead. Water motion. On the port side.'

They stared at the monitor as McCoy eased the camera focus back. The eerie forms surging in the murk were suddenly clouds of black smoke, billowing up out of the fracture like coal fumes from a smokestack.

'Vent!' Rankin said. 'Here's where it gets tricky. Melissa, as soon as I get the *Alvin* in position, ease a vacuum siphon out into the steam column. Give the siphon five seconds to collect, then bring the arm back and we'll lift away.'

Melissa practised the manoeuvre as her father nosed the tiny craft down towards the vent.

'We're as close as I dare,' Rankin said, using the *Alvin's* two small lift propellors to maintain position in the turbulent waters near the volcanic opening.

Quickly Melissa swung the manipulator arm around and stabbed the tip of the vacuum siphon into the boiling column of steam. The three waited, their eyes glued to the control panel screen, as a vapour sample was sucked back to a vacuum chamber for computer analysis.

Five seconds later the words ANALYSIS COMPLETE flashed on the tube and Melissa withdrew the siphon. The steel tube steamed as it folded back through the cold seawater to the *Alvin*.

Rankin lifted the submersible away from the vent, then keyed the computer. The figures representing the chemical composition of the gases flashed on the screen. He looked at the numbers and shook his head. 'I don't like it. The percentage of sulphuric gases is relatively low.'

258

'Then the magma has stopped rising?' McCoy asked.

'It has along this section of the fracture, I'd say. I was afraid of this. The main flow is obviously feeding up into the dominant vent. These ancillary ducts will die off soon, like atrophied fingers robbed of their blood supply.'

A deep rumbling throbbed through the half-inch-thick steel plates of the *Alvin's* hull, and the submersible suddenly heeled far over on its port side. Rankin's hands flew to the controls and slowly the vessel righted itself.

'What was that?' Melissa asked, her eyes wide.

'Steam eruption,' Rankin said. 'Not far off.'

'I thought you said these vents were cut off from the plume, Waldo,' McCoy said.

'I'm sure they are, Josh. Still, there are huge gas and steam pockets trapped under the ridge. They'll continue to erupt until the pressure is relieved.'

The buzzing of the surface phone startled all three. Rankin reached for the mike. '*Alvin.*'

Captain Crocker's voice sounded strangely tinny, almost ethereal through the small cabin speaker. 'You all right down there, Admiral?'

'Took a shaking,' Rankin answered. 'No damage I can see.'

'You people must live right. There's a geyser shooting up four or five hundred feet into the air about three quarters of a mile from your position.'

'We figured it was close, Captain.'

'How much more time will you need?'

'We still have to set out the seismometer and test one more vent,' Rankin said. 'Another hour and we'll start up.'

'We'll be ready to retrieve the moment you surface,' Crocker promised.

Rankin hung up and started the submersible along the fracture again. They covered about a quarter of a mile, then once more he brought the craft to a standstill above the ridge.

'Let's get that seismometer positioned.' It took them several minutes to place the instrument on the irregular summit of the volcanic mound and make sure it was functioning properly.

McCoy studied the Richter scale graph that appeared on the computer screen. If there were any tremor activity beneath the ridge, impulses from the seismometer would record the movement on the graph. The lines across the screen remained perfectly flat. There was no sign of harmonic tremors.

'Strike two, Waldo,' McCoy said. 'No seismicity registering at all.'

'Looks like the movement of magma has ceased completely beneath the ridge,' Melissa added glumly.

Rankin nodded. 'We'll sample one more vent, then start up.'

Twenty minutes later the television camera picked up movement along the ridge ahead of the *Alvin*.

'Steam column to starboard, Waldo,' McCoy said.

Rankin lowered the submersible towards the foot of the black fountain as Melissa folded the manipulator arm out.

The vacuum siphon probed the jetting steam. Seconds later the computer analysis again showed the vapour composition to be relatively low in sulphuric gas.

Rankin shook his head. 'Strike three. That's all the confirmation I need. There's no question the plume has stopped ejecting magma through the fracture ridge. Everything's being drawn up into that dominant vent. We can . . .'

Rankin's last words were lost in a sudden explosion of sound. All three were thrown violently to the deck as the *Alvin* shot upward like a cork from a champagne bottle. McCoy caught a glimpse of the Fathometer spinning crazily just before the cabin lights went out. Then, as abruptly as the *Alvin's* dizzying ascent had started, it stopped. For a moment the only sound was the muffled roar of the steam column subsiding back into the vent.

'Waldo, Melissa?' McCoy's anxious voice came from the pitch blackness.

'I'm alright, Josh,' Melissa said, then, 'Dad? Dad?'

Silence.

260

McCoy bent, his hands out before him, and searched across the tiny cabin towards where the admiral's chair should be. The contoured seat was empty.

'He's fallen,' McCoy said, kneeling towards the floor plates.

Melissa fought for control and lowered herself. Her hands swept the deck towards the stern. There was only the feel of the cold stainless steel. 'He must have been thrown towards the bow, Josh.'

McCoy inched his way forward. His hand touched a shoe. 'I've got him, Melissa.'

'Easy, Josh, don't move him,' Melissa said, crawling towards McCoy's voice.

McCoy found Rankin's neck and pressed his fingers against the carotid artery. The admiral's pulse was weak but regular. 'He's alive.'

'Thank God!' Melissa reached her father's still form. 'He must have struck his head as he fell.'

McCoy probed the admiral's head gently with his fingers, Rankin's nose and cheeks were sticky. In a moment he found the wound, a deep gash at the hairline on the right side of Rankin's head.

'Your father's got a bad cut on his forehead, Melissa. Feels like he's still losing some blood. Got anything for a pressure bandage?'

Melissa's hands flew to the zipper of her insulated dive suit. She tore a swath of cloth from her shirt underneath and folded it into a tight square, then found McCoy's hands in the dark.

'The emergency power switch is on your side,' Melissa said. 'Let me take Dad and I'll talk you through the panel buttons.' Melissa cradled her father's head in her lap as McCoy rose to his knees.

'The panel's on your left facing me,' Melissa said.

McCoy's hands probed the cabin wall. His fingers brushed across a smooth glass face. 'I've got the sonar screen.'

'Move your hand slowly towards the bow,' Melissa said.

McCoy inched his touch along a trail of instruments and

gauges. He felt a coiled wire and followed it to a hand microphone. I'm at the radio.'

'Okay, the power switch is set into a metal face plate about eighteen inches above the set,' Melissa said.

McCoy found the plate. 'I've got it,' he said, then took a breath and flipped the switch. A row of dim lights flicked on around the rim of the cabin.

McCoy squinted, focusing his eyes in the sudden glare, and looked back to where Melissa was examining her father's wound.

'He's got a deep gash, but the pressure's stopped the bleeding,' she said. 'There's a first-aid kit next to the radio.'

McCoy knelt with the kit and helped Melissa bandage the admiral's head. Then he adjusted Rankin's dive chair to a reclining position, and they lifted him into it.

Melissa pulled a wool blanket from a locker and covered her father, then sat back worriedly in her chair. 'There's not much more we can do for him down here, Josh. I feel so helpless.'

'Waldo's a tough old bird,' McCoy said, wanting to lift her spirits. 'It'll take more than . . .' His voice trailed off and he cocked an ear towards the bow. 'What was that?'

'What?' Melissa's eyes searched the forward cabin.

'Listen!'

Then they both heard it. A gurgling, dripping sound.

Melissa's hands flew to her face. 'Oh, dear God. We've got water coming in!'

McCoy watched a rivulet begin to flow across the deck plates from the base of a bulkhead panel. He knelt and put his ear to the steel.

For the first time there was an edge of fear in Melissa's voice. 'Can you tell how bad the leak is, Josh?'

'Sounds like a steady flow. Hard to tell how much.'

'The hull connector's behind that panel,' Melissa said, her face pale. 'The seal must have ruptured.'

'Any way to get to it?' McCoy asked, straightening up.

She shook her head slowly. 'No, Josh. No way. Not from inside the cabin. Try the radiotelephone.'

McCoy cupped the microphone. '*Alvin* to *Lulu*. Do you receive us on the surface. *Alvin* to *Lulu*.'

Melissa searched the control panel as McCoy's calls continued unanswered. She found the emergency beacon buoy switch and pushed. Nothing. No sound of the beacon's rocket motor firing. She flipped again, and again, then slumped down.

McCoy abandoned the phone. 'Any way to get the power back?'

'Not unless we can find the short or the loose cable connection that caused the failure. There are over five miles of electricity wiring in the *Alvin*, Josh. Where do we start to look?'

'How much air have we got?'

She shrugged. 'Several hours. What difference does it make? The seawater coming in will flood the cabin long before then. We have an hour, Josh. Maybe two.' She shivered. 'It will be very cold at the end.'

McCoy reached across and gripped her shoulders. 'We're going to find a way out of this. There must be something we can do!'

'We can open the sea cocks and make it quicker,' Melissa said. 'But nothing else. Nothing, Josh.'

For a long moment they stared at each other across the tiny cabin.

'Have you ever thought about dying?' Melissa said finally.

'Melissa – '

'I'm not being maudlin, Josh. I really want to know how you feel about death. Do you believe there'll be an afterlife? I don't think I've ever asked you that.'

He looked at her a moment. 'Yes, I believe we go on to something else. Another dimension. Not necessarily physical.'

'Do you envision some sort of heaven, Josh? Do you see angels and harps and fleecy clouds?'

'Sure, part of me still holds on to that image. You know my mother. I couldn't have grown up in a house with that lady and not retain those childhood impressions.' He smiled ironically. 'Then there's the part of me, the cold logical part, that knows my body will return to its base elements when I die. Nothing in the universe is ever lost. My atoms will start up the chain again.'

Melissa shivered. 'I believe that too. That parts of me will have a new life form. I wonder if it will hurt. If I'll get eaten by something.'

McCoy stared at the water creeping over the soles of his dive boots.

'Are the girls religious?' Melissa asked. Then, 'How awful I don't know that. A mother doesn't know how her children feel about God.'

'I've taken them to church a few times,' McCoy said. 'Not often enough. And I've answered their questions when they had them. I think they'll make a rational choice when they're ready to confront religion.'

Tears welled up in Melissa's eyes. 'I've missed so much of their lives. I've been so selfish.'

'You did what you had to, Melissa, we all do. I've known all along how vital your work is to you. And you've achieved great advances in glaciology, in science. Sure, the kids have paid a price for your research. But it has brought something worthwhile, knowledge that will ultimately benefit the world.'

She fought the tears. 'I wanted to do it all, Josh. To be a mother and a scientist too. I'd have liked to but I couldn't. I couldn't be there for Shea's first day at school and be in an Antarctic laboratory at the same time. I couldn't commute from a glacier to Kate's third birthday party.'

'You were there for the important things that happened,' McCoy said, reassuring her. 'If you weren't there in person, you were there in spirit. And don't forget the years you spent three hundred and sixty-five days with them, every hour you had.'

'But I denied them years too, Josh.' She snatched her knapsack of research tapes off the cabin console and shook it viciously. 'I've traded years with my children for the reels of plastic in this bag . . . this goddamn bag of beans.'

264

He grasped her shoulders. 'Melissa, I'd rather the children have had less time with you than had their mother a lesser woman. They've always gained from you, they'll always need you. I mean that.'

Her lips trembled at the corners. She could not hold back the question. 'But you don't need me any more, do you, Josh?'

Before McCoy could find the words, Admiral Rankin groaned suddenly across the tiny cabin and brought his hand up to his head. He winced as he found the bandaged wound. 'What happened?'

Melissa knelt at his side. 'There was a steam eruption, Dad. You were knocked unconscious. Don't try to talk for a while.'

'Of course I'll talk,' Rankin said groggily, pushing himself up into a sitting position. He winced as the blood coursed from his head.

'Dad, please, you should be lying down,' Melissa said with concern.

Rankin squinted at his daughter's face, her features dim in the thin glare of the low-watt emergency bulbs. 'What's wrong with the lights in here?'

'The primary power's down, Dad,' Melissa said. 'There's a short or a broken connection somewhere in the system.' She looked away, not wanting to tell her father the rest.

McCoy put his hand on Melissa's shoulder, and his eyes met Rankin's. 'There's a leak in the bow, Waldo. We're taking in water.'

'Good God!' Rankin pulled himself into a sitting position and stared down at the seawater darkening the foot of the cabin wall plates.

'Did you send up the beacon buoy?' Rankin asked Melissa.

'I tried, Dad. It wouldn't eject.'

'It's got to have a manual trip somewhere,' Rankin said. 'It can't be that much different from the locator buoys we used in the navy.'

'What good's a buoy going to do us, Waldo?' McCoy

said. 'We'll be long drowned before any help gets down here.'

'The help isn't coming down, Josh. We're going up. The buoy is propelled to the surface by a liquid-oxygen rocket. At our depth it will take about two and a half minutes. As soon as the buoy makes contact with the air, a flare goes off and a radio beacon starts transmitting.'

'That gets us found,' McCoy said. 'But how does that get us up?'

'There's a thin lead wire that feeds out as the rocket buoy rises, Josh. There's a telephone line woven into the wire. The other end is spliced to four thousand feet of lift cable in an exterior locker on the conning tower. All the *Lulu* has to do is reel in the wire, hitch our cable to their winch, and up we go.'

McCoy grinned. 'That's beautiful, Waldo. God, that's just beautiful!'

'Have you any idea where the manual trip is, Dad?' Melissa asked.

'The release has got to be somewhere near the firing tube,' Rankin said.

Melissa's eyes searched the shadowed cabin rim. 'The tube is on the right side of the tower,' she pointed upward. 'About there, I think.'

Rankin squeezed over next to Melissa and oriented himself down the keel line of the submersible. 'Move your hand about eighteen inches to the right, Melissa,' he said. 'There, that plate.'

Rankin turned to McCoy. 'Josh, there's a tool kit in that red drawer in the panel to your left. I need a ratchet screwdriver and a flashlight.'

McCoy handed over the tools and watched with Melissa as Rankin unscrewed the six-by-six-inch steel plate set into the hull. Rankin handed the plate to McCoy and flashed his light into the dark square above.

His face lit up. 'There she is, by God! The trip is almost identical to the one on my last sub.'

Melissa's hands flew to her face, her fingers folding into a prayer tent before her nose and mouth.

Rankin reached up into the hull. 'Brace yourselves,' he said to Melissa and McCoy. 'There'll probably be quite a kick in a sub this small.'

Rankin gripped the edge of a panel with one hand and yanked a small lever at the base of the rocket tube. Instantly, a roaring explosion echoed deafeningly through the *Alvin's* cabin as the rocket fired and whooshed upward. The tiny submersible rocked violently in the turbulent wake of the missile.

Despite their ringing ears and the sickening motion of the *Alvin*, all three grinned hugely at one another.

'We're going up,' Rankin said, beaming. 'All we have to do now is wait.'

The water rose nine inches in the cabin before the sudden voice from the telephone speaker startled them all fifteen minutes later.

'*Lulu* to *Alvin*. This is Captain Crocker. Are you receiving *Alvin*?'

Rankin sprang for the phone. 'This is Admiral Rankin, Captain.'

'Admiral, thank God! We've had you dead in the water on sonar for almost an hour. What's happened?'

'A steam eruption knocked our primary power. We're on emergency systems.'

'You're fortunate it wasn't lava that erupted, Admiral. I wouldn't be talking to you now.'

'Not so fortunate, Captain. We're taking water.'

'Damn! How bad is the leak?'

'Bad. You've got to get us up fast.'

'I can't bring you up too quickly, Admiral, or I'll risk snapping the cable.'

'I want you to red-line that winch, Captain Crocker.'

'If that line parts, you'll run out of oxygen before we can get another cable down to you, Admiral Rankin. You know that.'

'We have no choice. Now start reeling us in,' Rankin said.

Five minutes later the *Alvin* lurched suddenly forward, then began rising steadily through the inky depths.

McCoy read out the depth changes on the Fathometer: 'Thirty-nine hundred and eighty feet . . . thirty-nine hundred forty . . . thirty-nine hundred.'

Crocker's voice cracked again from the radiophone speaker, '*Lulu* to *Alvin*. We'll have you up in about half an hour.'

Rankin picked up the microphone. 'Captain, I'm ordering the immediate evacuation of all research bases and mining operations in West Antarctica. I ask you to pass my instructions to Antarctic Conference headquarters in Christchurch.'

'Your order will go out immediately, Admiral.'

'As soon as that's done, ready your vessel for sea, Captain. The moment you berth us you're to head the *Lulu* north at flank speed.'

'Is the situation that critical, Admiral?'

'A major eruption is inevitable. The plume has stopped feeding the vent fracture. All the magma's being channelled into that volcano building in the middle of the bay. That mountain's going to blow before the Ice Shelf can drift beyond the range of the molten fallout. We're facing a major meltdown.'

The cabin leak worsened as the submersible rose. By the 600-foot level, there was almost three feet of seawater sloshing across the deck plates of the *Alvin*.

The rising water forced the three up onto the conning tower ladder. They talked quietly, reassuring one another. Then at last the tower broke through the waves, and sunlight splashed into the cabin.

'Let's get out of here fast,' Ranking said, his hands whirling the hatch-lock wheel. A sudden whooshing sound came from above as the cabin vented.

Rankin thrust his head up through the hatch, bracing against the rim as the *Alvin* wallowed heavily in the ten-foot seas.

The *Lulu* was 200 yards away. A motorized dive boat was already beating across the sea towards them. Rankin climbed out of the tower and reached an arm back down. 'C'mon you two, get out of there!'

McCoy boosted Melissa to her father's grasp, then pulled himself through the hatch. A breaking wave tore the cover from his hand before he could shut the hatch.

'Leave it, Josh!' Rankin shouted against the sound of the waves and wind.

The three clung to tower braces as the ocean seethed around the *Alvin*. The largest in a set of combers rolled over the submersible, sending a deluge flooding down into the open cabin. The *Alvin* listed to port.

The lifeboat from the *Lulu* slapped across the wave crest and throttled back ten feet off the sub. Two men in wet suits dove from the bow and swam towards them.

A megaphone crackled from the lifeboat. 'Ahoy aboard the *Alvin*. We can't come any closer in these seas. Jump clear. The men in the water will assist you. Repeat, jump clear.'

'Josh, you'd better jump first with Dad,' Melissa said. 'He's still rocky. He could pass out when he hits the water.'

'I'll be fine,' Rankin objected.

'Melissa's right,' McCoy said, gripping Rankin's arm. 'Let's go!'

Rankin hesitated a moment, then turned to Melissa. 'Jump the instant we're clear of the hull.'

Rankin and McCoy linked arms and leapt feet first into the cold choppy sea. They trod water a moment, waving at Melissa to jump, then the divers reached them and boosted them up into the grasp of the lifeboat crew.

Melissa stood poised on the lip of the tower. Her leg muscles flexed and her balance came forward on her toes. Her adrenal glands began secreting, anticipating the shock of the cold water. Then she froze, her face suddenly stricken.

She straightened and cupped her hands towards the lifeboat. 'My tapes!' she shouted across the waves. 'I left my tapes in the cabin!'

The men in the lifeboat couldn't hear her words. They could only see that she was hesitating. That she was still on the sinking submersible.

Melissa gestured frantically towards the open hatch. 'I've got to go back,' she shouted against the cacophony of the wind and the sea and the lifeboat engine. 'It's my life's work. My life's work!'

Rankin and McCoy watched in horror as Melissa disappeared down the conning tower. Rankin grabbed the megaphone from the boatswain. 'Melissa, come back! For God's sake, come back!'

As his words echoed off the hull, Melissa's weight moving forward in the cabin pitched the bow down violently. The conning tower stabbed into the sea. A large bubble of air burst from the submerged hatch.

For an impossible moment the submersible hung on its side at the crest of a wave. Then the tiny craft slid down the foam-flecked slope of the comber and rolled keel up in the trough.

'Melissa! Melissaaaaaa!' Rankin's anguished voice tore across the freezing sea as the *Alvin* sank slowly into the dark depths of McMurdo Sound.

# NORTHDRIFT
## 283.5 Nautical Miles

Anya Cherepin cursed under her breath as she left the suffocating hot and stinking Antonov-30 troop transport parked on the runway apron of the Mossamedes Airport in Angola, West Africa.

The sight of the pale, weak, silently pleading faces of the Mongolian paratroopers in the plane had infuriated her. She crossed the tarmac under the broiling African sun with quick, angry steps.

The Antarctic-bound 32nd Karelian Division was going nowhere for now. The airlift was being held up on the ground while the Presidium in Moscow debated the wisdom of continuing Savin's plan to seize the Ross Ice Shelf.

An exasperated General Vlasov and his staff had helicoptered off to Soviet Military Assistance Command headquarters in the comparatively cool highlands eighty miles away.

Cherepin found the senior Russian medical corps officer slumped in a humid corner of the field's main hangar, fanning himself with his service cap. 'Captain Abakumov, the men have got to be taken off the planes. They must be put in the shade and given saline solution,' she said, her eyes flashing. 'I demand they be moved at once.'

Abakumov had been dragged away from his comfortable job at a senior officers' hospital outside Tashkent to join this mission. He considered the Mongolians savages. He was not about to jeopardize his entire career by ordering them off the planes on his own initiative.

'This flight is classified top secret,' he said stubbornly. 'How long do you suppose we can keep it that way with Mongolian paratroopers stumbling all over the field?'

Cherepin shook her head. 'The men are suffering from

heat exhaustion, Comrade Captain. They are already dangerously weak. Leg and abdominal cramping are become widespread.'

The captain's eyes took on a nervous flicker. 'I simply do not have the authority to move the men from the transports.'

'Then call General Vlasov and get it!'

'These are hardened soldiers, after all, quite used to privation. Until I am ordered otherwise, the men must remain in the aircraft.'

'Then I wash my hands of responsibility,' Cherepin said heatedly. 'I hope when we are over the Ice Shelf, Comrade Captain, that no more is required of these men than a simple descent.'

Abakumov was swept by indecision. 'One moment, Comrade Director. Perhaps the troops can at least be given the saline solution. It is something. How long will it take?'

Cherepin shrugged. 'We would have to requisition a supply from the Angolans, then distribute the liquids to – how many? – five thousand troops? I would need perhaps two hours.'

The Soviet medical officer threw up his hands. 'I don't know if there is that much time. If we are still on the ground when the salt solution arrives, the distribution can take place. If we are ordered to take off in the interim . . .'

Cherepin looked disdainfully at the captain. 'Then you would not ask for a delay to such an order, explain the weakened condition of the troops?'

'Believe me, Comrade Director, such a request would not be well received. You must remember these are airborne combat troops. We do not coddle them. I have no intention of challenging orders on the basis of their discomfort.'

Cherepin shook her head sadly. 'Discomfort! A poor choice of words, Comrade Captain. I shall order the salt liquids. The rest is in your hands. And God help you!'

She walked towards the temporary division headquarters

set up in a rusty Quonset. Chirikov emerged from a side door as she neared the building. He spotted her and hurried across the tarmac.

'Anya, have you heard yet?' Chirikov said.

She shook her head. 'Heard what, Volodya?'

'Orders have just come in from Moscow. The Presidium has given final approval to Savin's plan. The airlift will commence any time now.'

She reached out and grasped his hands, her voice trembling. 'Is it true, Volodya? Do I dare believe it's true?'

Chirikov's eyes softened. 'We'll be in Antarctica before this day is out, Anya.'

She closed her eyes, her emotions soaring. She was going to make it! This was the last leg of the flight. Once on the ice, escape would be easy. Nothing was ever locked. A motorsledge with a full tank of gas and she'd be gone.

As sudden as her exhilaration, a wave of melancholy washed over her. Must her happiness come hand in hand with triumph for Savin and his monstrous plan? Must her future with Joshua cost the defeat of decent men of peace like Mikhail Romanov?

'Walk back to the plane with me, Anya,' Chirikov said.

She suddenly remembered the stricken paratroopers in transports. 'Volodya, most of the men in the planes are suffering from heat exhaustion. I was on my way to find saline solution for them.'

Chirikov shook his head. 'There isn't time. General Vlasov is expected to return any moment, and we'll be taking off as soon as he arrives.'

'But, Volodya, the men are badly – ' Anya stopped in mid-sentence, her eyes riveted on a man in an officer's uniform coming out of the headquarters building. Silhouetted against the building, the hair tufting from the man's head looked even more like the prongs of a fork than that night in her apartment.

Fork! What was he doing here? Her heart beat crazily. What else could he be doing here but following her? Had they intercepted one of her micropulse messages? No, she would have been arrested immediately. But they must suspect. If they searched her, they'd find the transmitter.

'I have something to do, Volodya,' Anya said. 'I'll see you on the plane.'

'Don't be too long, Anya,' Chirikov called after her as she turned and walked away from the headquarters.

She forced herself not to hurry her steps. A hundred yards away she paused and darted a look back over her shoulder. Fork hadn't followed. She slid behind a parked truck and walked quickly towards the fringe of the airport.

She stopped in front of the eight-foot-high perimeter fence and unclasped the pendant. Through the steel mesh she could see the lush African jungle creeping to within ten feet of the wire.

If she threw hard enough, the pearl and its tiny transmitter would disappear forever into the thick green foliage.

Anya set her feet and brought her arm forward with all her strength. Halfway through her throw the sudden raucous blare of the airport loudspeakers jarred her off balance. The pendant flew out of Anya's hand at half speed and arched weakly towards the fence. She watched in horror as the necklace snared on the barbed-wire top.

'Attention all personnel of the Thirty-second Karelian Division,' the loudspeaker ordered. 'Ten minutes to takeoff. Return to your aircraft at once.'

Anya stared up mesmerized. As the pendant swung slowly, the white pearl caught the sun and reflected the light like a beacon dangling from the barbed wire. Her senses whirled. Surely the pendant was visible all over the base.

She tore her eyes away, willing herself to be calm, to think logically. When she looked again, the pearl hung still and dull against the high background of wire and sky. She would be a hundred times more visible climbing the fence to retrieve it.

Anya turned and walked towards the command plane parked 300 yards down the runway. She didn't look back.

When Anya was small in the distance, an officer with a

sharp face stepped out from behind an equipment shed and lowered a pair of binoculars. He pulled a small radio from his belt, spoke several words, then walked towards the fence where Anya had stood.

Four minutes later a Russian jeep bearing Fork and a ladder arrived at the fence. Knife went up quickly and yanked the pendant off the barbed wire. The loud-speakers came alive again as the two sped across the tarmac towards their plane.

'Transport doors close in two minutes. All division personnel board your aircraft. Repeat, board your aircraft.'

Ten minutes later the long file of troop transports lifted off one by one into the fierce African sky and formed up for the flight south to the bottom of the world.

Anya Cherepin rested her head against her seat in the command plane and closed her eyes. There was nothing to stop her now. In a matter of hours, a day or two at the most, she'd be with him, with him forever. For the first time since Joshua left Moscow, she felt warm inside.

In a transport 600 yards behind the command plane, Knife locked the door to the officers' lavatory and put Anya's pendant on the sink shelf. Then he took a magnifying glass and a jeweller's pick from a small case and began probing the setting.

Ten minutes later Knife found the transmitter.

Joshua McCoy twisted slowly at the end of the hoist line as he was winched up from the fantail of the *Lulu* to the Alouette helicopter hovering above.

His eyes found the sea off the tender's bow where Melissa had gone down in the *Alvin*. For a horrible moment he wondered whether the tiny submersible had reached the dark bottom yet, or whether Melissa was still drifting down through the dimming twilight, as lifeless as the freezing sea that had claimed her.

A dull, empty ache of shock and disbelief gripped him. He had seen it happen but it couldn't have happened. Not to Melissa. Not to Shea and Kate and him.

Merciful God, why hadn't he told her he loved her? Why hadn't he at least given her that? He tried to remember Melissa's words in the *Alvin*. He wanted to tell the children what she said, tell them how much their mother loved them, how she suffered when her work took her away.

It tore at him that he must gather his daughters in his arms and tell them their mother was dead. What words would he use? Would he promise them their mother wasn't lying drowned in the black bowels of the sea but radiant in heaven, watching over them, keeping a place for them? What would he tell them?

McCoy rose the last few feet to the helicopter. Rankin had gone up first, and he helped McCoy swing inside, then slammed the cargo door shut. The pilot waited until the two men were strapped into their seats, then headed the Alouette towards the Marble Point Field on the Antarctic shore.

McCoy glanced at Rankin. The admiral's face had aged ten years in the hour since Melissa's death. 'You all right, Waldo?'

Rankin sighed heavily, his eyes red and brimming with

tears. 'She never let me down, Josh. She tried so hard never to let me down. I wonder in the end if that didn't kill her.'

'What are you talking about, Waldo?' McCoy said gently.

'Melissa went back for her research tapes. There wasn't any other reason.'

McCoy studied his hands. 'I know that, Waldo. I knew it the minute I saw her turn for the hatch.' He looked at Rankin. 'But why do you blame yourself for what Melissa did?'

'Because it was I who encouraged Melissa's interest in science from the time she was a little girl, Josh. When she was growing up, half my letters to her from Antarctica were some sort of lesson or test. To please me she became a superachiever, a twice-dedicated scientist. She came to live for her work – and in the end she died for it.'

McCoy gripped Rankin's arms. 'Waldo, Melissa loved her work. It gave meaning and purpose to her life. You didn't transfuse that dedication into her. It was there all along.'

The pilot swivelled his seat towards them and handed Rankin his earphones and throat mike. 'You have a call from Dr Gates at McMurdo, Admiral.'

Rankin closed his eyes for a moment. Then he nodded slowly and reached forward for the set. 'Hello, Charlie.'

'I think you know how I feel, Waldo,' Gates said. 'Melissa's been like a daughter to me these past long months on the ice. I'll treasure her memory.'

'Thank you, Charlie.'

'Are you on your way in?' Gates said.

'We should put down in about twenty minutes,' Rankin said. 'Have your people started boarding the Hercules yet?'

'Good Lord, Waldo, they're still packing their research material. There are boxes of computer tapes that have to go.'

'There isn't time, Charlie. I want everyone out to the airfield immediately. Tell them to carry what they can.'

'You're going to hear screams, Waldo; most of the research we've done down here is impossible to duplicate.'

'Can't be helped.'

Gates conceded. 'All right, I'll start everyone for the airfield immediately.'

Twenty minutes later the Alouette lowered towards Marble Point. McCoy gestured towards the rutted track leading out from the research station. 'Here they come.'

Below, an incongruous convoy of ski-fronted half-tracks, snowmobiles, Sno-Cats, and motorized sledges snaked across the ice towards the hangar complex.

The Alouette set down near the control tower, and Rankin and McCoy hurried up the stairs to where Charlie Gates was directing the evacuation.

'How's it going, Charlie?' Rankin said.

'The last strays are coming in now, Waldo,' Gates said.

The sound of a sudden booming explosion rumbled across the ice from the northeast. They turned to stare as a huge dark ash cloud billowed up above the horizon.

'That volcano could blow itself to bits any time now,' Rankin said. 'Get your people on that plane as fast as you can, Charlie.'

'I'll be another ten minutes or so, Waldo. You and Josh might as well take off first.'

'Very well. We'll circle until you're safely up.'

Minutes later the black reconnaissance jet screamed down the icy strip and lifted into the sky above the heaving surface of McMurdo Sound.

Rankin banked the aircraft and they circled high above Marble Point. As they watched, the Hercules transport plane rolled down the runway and rose ponderously above the sea at the end of the field.

Rankin watched the transport lift off, then dove the black jet towards McMurdo Sound. 'Let's say good-bye to Melissa, Josh. Just one last time, let's say good-bye.'

Below McCoy could see the *Lulu* steaming north at flank speed.

Rankin levelled the plane and skimmed the waves where

the *Alvin* had gone down. He banked, throttled back, and returned more slowly. The men stared down silently at the grey waves, each lost in his own remembrances of Melissa.

Then Rankin edged the stick forward and the SR-96 shot north towards Christchurch.

President John Stans Wollcott stared out of the bulletproof French doors to the Oval Office lost in second thoughts. Each hour that passed without a Russian response to the American laser threat left him more unsettled.

What bothered him most was that he had no fallback position. If the bluff failed, he'd be left without any political or military response short of war.

He had no illusion his leadership of the free world would remain viable. The calling of his empty hand would destroy his international credibility. He'd be crippled in the foreign arena for the remaining years of his presidency.

The intercom buzzer startled him out of his dire musings. 'Yes?'

'They're waiting for you in the Cabinet Room, Mr President.'

Wollcott picked up his phalanx of aides and Secret Service agents at the door and walked briskly down the corridor. The Antarctic Crisis Group rose as a body as he entered the door.

'Let's get started, Sam,' he said irritably before the others had sat back down. The dark reality he had forced himself to face was beginning to eat at him. 'I want the domestic situation first.'

'Yes, Mr President,' the security adviser said, lowering himself into his chair. 'The evacuation of our Pacific coast is going relatively well, although there have been some problems.'

'So I understand. The governor of California informed me he's placed the state under martial law.'

'This was necessary to deal with the situation in the Los Angeles area, sir. The freeways to the east are clogged with refugee traffic. The governor ordered vehicles stalled or out of gas to be shoved off to the sides of the roads. In a number of cases armed drivers resisted. The National Guard was forced to open fire. There've been perhaps a dozen deaths.'

'Goddamn nuts!' growled Axworth, the secretary of defence.

'It's gone more smoothly in the rest of the port cities: San Diego, San Francisco, Seattle,' Fisk went on. 'There's been some looting, mainly in the Bay Area.'

'That's not the only problem around San Francisco,' Clyde Whitcomb injected.

'If you mean the trouble at San Quentin, I'm coming to that, Clyde,' Fisk said. 'There was a mass prison-break attempt while the inmates were being loaded onto evacuation buses, Mr President. Fifty or sixty men got away. The police believe most of them will drown when the Bay Area goes under.'

'Good riddance,' Whitcomb scowled. 'The cops should have left them all behind.'

Vice-President Roberts stared contemptuously at the intelligence chief. 'Those prisoners are human beings, Clyde, no matter what their offence.'

Fisk ignored the exchange. 'The worst loss of life so far has occurred in the Seattle area. A ferry jammed with evacuees overturned in Puget Sound. There were several hundred people on board. We have no fatality reports yet. However, given the perilous currents in those waters, we must assume most of the passengers drowned.'

The president paled. 'God help us, how many thousand more will die, how many millions of Americans will become homeless? Against the Russians at least we can try. We can reason, bluster, fight if we have to. But in the face of nature we are powerless. We have no human means to resist a rising sea.'

'At least we can do something for the evacuees, Mr President,' Fisk said. 'Tent cities have been erected at our military installations from the Mexican border north to Canada. Most will be sheltered at the larger bases:

Twenty-Nine Palms Marine Corps station, east of LA; Travis Air Force Base, east of San Francisco; Fort Lewis, up in Washington State.'

'I want no effort spared for those refugees, Sam,' Wollcott said. 'Food, blankets, medicine, baby formulas, everything goes to them on a priority basis. Commandeer civilian aircraft and trucks if you have to, but take care of those people.'

'Yes, Mr President,' Fisk said.

Wollcott turned to the CIA director. 'Clyde, the last agency briefing I received reported the Russians had taken off from Mossamedes. Where is the airlift now?'

Whitcomb glanced at a note bfore him. 'Our latest satellite surveillance places the Soviet transports on a southwest heading towards the Atlantic coast of Africa, Mr President.'

'They're on course for Antarctica, then,' the president said.

Whitcomb nodded. 'Our analysts don't believe there's any doubt about that. They're going to take the Ice.'

General Lowe broke his silence. 'Mr President, it is now obvious the Russians have called our laser bluff. They either don't believe we'll use space weapons against them, or they've decided the strategic gain of the Ross Ice Shelf is worth any risk. It's time to end the hoax. We must reassure the world that the United States will not use directed-energy fire against the ice.'

Samson Fisk shook his head vehemently. 'How are we to know the Soviets aren't simply testing our resolve to the final limit, Mr President. It will take seven or eight hours for their aircraft to reach the Ross Shelf from Angola. We can't give the Russians those hours, not when they may yet turn back at the last minute if we stand firm.'

Lowe's voice was bitter. 'Perhaps you are unaware that half the governments on the planet have gone on a war footing since the announcement of our laser threat, Mr Fisk. The world is in the grip of the mad tenet that Armageddon is at hand and this is the time to settle scores with old rivals. We've had intelligence reports of a dozen unstable regimes ready to launch preemptive nuclear strikes against their enemies.'

'What are we really talking about here, General?' Fisk countered. 'An Arab-Israeli war, an Indian-Pakistani war, a North Korean-South Korean war? Bad, tragic, no one questions that. But can we measure any one of these conflicts against the strategic emasculation of the United States?' Fisk turned to Wollcott. 'I recommend we not retreat one inch from our laser threat until and when the Soviets seize the Shelf.'

The President looked at each man in turn. Both Lowe and Fisk had valid arguments. Yet he was not the president of the world. He was the president of the United States, and his first responsibility was to his country. He made his decision.

'I'm sorry, General Lowe, but I cannot withdraw our ultimatum to the Russians. At the moment our laser threat is our only weapon and I must use it in the defence of this nation.'

Lowe came to his feet. 'I believe your decision will cost countless innocent lives, Mr President. God knows how many people will die in the next few hours. I cannot in conscience continue as chairman of the Joint Chiefs. You have my resignation, sir.'

Wollcott bristled. 'You are flirting with dereliction of duty, General.'

'Call it what you will, Mr President,' Lowe said firmly, gathering his papers.

Wollcott stared fixedly towards the end of the long Cabinet table as the chairman of the Joint Chiefs stalked out of the room.

'Mr President,' Kevin Florence's voice broke the awful silence that followed. 'May I remind the Crisis Group that the Soviet airlift is not the only threat we face from Antarctica.'

The others turned to stare at the director of the National Science Foundation.

'Admiral Rankin believes the volcano rising through the Ross Sea will erupt within twenty-four hours. He sees little chance the Ice Shelf will escape the fiery fallout that follows. The meltdown of the Shelf would make the question of Soviet ice stations academic.'

'Can you guarantee that the eruption will come while the Shelf is still within range of the fallout?' the President challenged stonily.

'No one can predict with absolute certainty what the forces of the earth will do, Mr President. There is no guarantee.'

'Then I will not withdraw the laser threat, Mr Florence. I can do nothing if the oceans flood. But until that happens, I have no intention of letting the Soviets seize the Shelf while there is still the slightest chance the Ice will escape.'

The members of the Crisis Group averted their eyes as Wollcott rose and glared around the table. 'I see nothing further to discuss.'

The waiting screen of adjutants closed behind him as the president turned his back and strode tight-lipped from the room.

The party general secretary, Mikhail Romanov, once more scanned the urgent message he'd received from the Satellite Reconnaissance Office at the Antarctic Institute as he waited for Marshal Pavel Savin to cross the wide marble floor of his office.

Savin stopped a pace from Romanov's desk, the traces of a triumphant smirk at the corners of his mouth. 'You sent for me, Comrade Romanov?'

Romanov regarded the marshal silently for a moment, not bothering to hide his distaste, then pushed the report from the institute across his desk. 'Have you seen this yet?'

Savin glanced down at the letterhead. 'I've read the report.'

'Then why have you ordered the airlift to continue south to Antarctica? Those transports must be turned back to Mossamedes at once. Satellite reconnaissance shows the West has evacuated its research and mining bases in West Antarctica. They would hardly have taken such a step were their scientists not convinced the Ross Sea volcano was in a preeruptive stage. We cannot risk putting our troops on the Shelf, not until the ice has drifted beyond range of the volcanic fallout.'

'The only unacceptable risk is to delay the occupation,' Savin countered. 'If we hold the Thirty-second Karelian in Africa for even a day, we give the West twenty-four hours to exert new military and political pressure on us, perhaps even to send their own forces south from Australia or New Zealand.'

Romanov slowly shook his head. 'I've never understood men like you, Comrade Savin. Men so ready to order other men to all but certain death. We are talking about the lives of five thousand Russian soldiers.'

'No, Comrade Romanov,' Savin spat. 'We are talking about power, about the backbone to use it, the ability to rise above squeamish concern for the few in order to bring victory to the masses.'

Romanov rose, shaking with fury. 'The masses! What masses? The widows and orphans of the men you send to their deaths? Or are the masses you invoke the survivors of a thermonuclear war set off by this monstrous gamble of yours?'

Savin's eyes were flat and dangerous. 'My plan will succeed without war. Once those ice stations are armed and in position, America will be forced to her knees within six months. When my victory comes, I'll remember your opposition. And I will be sure the Politburo remembers.'

Savin spun on his heel and strode rapidly across the wide marble floor towards the door.

'I will fight you, Comrade Savin,' Romanov flung after him. 'This is not the end of it. I will fight you every step you take!'

Savin stopped at the door. 'Fight me? With what? The Politburo has passed the baton to me. You are toothless, Comrade Romanov. Gum your tasteless gruel and leave Russia to the rule of men.'

Romanov sank slowly into his chair as the door closed behind Savin. The marshal was right. He no longer had the power to stop the airlift. In less than six hours the 32nd Karelian would descend on the Ross Ice Shelf.

Romanov's eyes fixed on the ominous report from the Antarctic Institute. God help them, five thousand men would jump into hell.

Joshua McCoy brought a fist down hard on the top of the cabin console in *Times Two*, then reached forward and flicked off the word processor in angry frustration.

His story on the huge Antarctic tsunami wasn't coming together. He couldn't concentrate, couldn't think for more than a minute without his mind's eye drifting back to the sight of Melissa disappearing beneath the sea in the *Alvin*.

Telling Shea and Kate their mother was dead had been the hardest thing he'd yet had to do in his life. Their stricken faces were still vividly before him, their broken sobs still in his ears.

He'd held them for hours, then had to put them through the second ordeal of leaving. It tore him apart to go, but he'd had no choice. The tsunami story had to be written. People must be told what had happened in the South Pacific, what would happen to every coast on earth when the coming volcano eruption melted the Ross Ice Shelf into the sea and the oceans rose around the world.

McCoy had ordered *Times Two* north from Christchurch to get a firsthand look at the devastation wrought by the mammoth tsunami. They'd followed the wreckage-strewn path of the giant wave from the shattered tip of New Zealands's South Island across the Tasman Sea to the eastern coast of Australia.

The voice of Captain Don Russell came through the cabin speakers. 'We're approaching Sydney, Josh. We'll be over the coast in a minute or two.'

McCoy fished through the console drawers for his binoculars. Where the devil did the girls put them? He found the glasses as Russell's pained voice came from the cockpit. 'Great God in heaven! The whole port's gone.'

McCoy stared through the binoculars in disbelief. Sydney's miles of docks and warehouses had been swept away. The spans of the Sydney Harbour Bridge and the Gladesville Bridge had also disappeared, their tilted, twisted towers mute evidence of the awesome power of the 300-foot wave.

He searched for the beautiful Opera House complex that had soared gracefully above the waters of Port Jackson inlet. The world-renowned edifice was gone – only jagged concrete fragments littered the shore where the striking building had stood.

Russell lowered *Times Two* over the silent city. The taller stone and steel buildings still stood downtown, but they had been gutted to the thirtieth floor by the towering tsunami. McCoy watched the wind blow streams of paper and shredded plastic through the glassless windows.

'I wonder if they got everybody out in time?' Russell said, his voice barely audible.

'Almost four million people lived in or around Sydney,' McCoy said. 'A city that size has thousands of old people living alone, thousands of recluses, thousands who are blind and can't see television, who are deaf and can't hear radio and loudspeaker warnings.'

The aircraft circled Sydney once more, then McCoy hit the switch to the cockpit intercom. 'I've seen enough, Don. Let's head up the coast.'

*Times Two* continued north along the flattened shore of Australia, then veered towards New Guinea. The second largest island in the world had taken the brunt of the wave and even now, hours after the tsunami hit, the swampy shores remained flooded forty miles in from the sea.

McCoy spoke by radiophone with Red Cross head-quarters in Port Moresby. The death toll was estimated at 30,000 and rising hourly. They would probably never know how many of their people had perished when the tsunami swallowed up the hundreds of small villages that had rimmed the southern coast.

Although the back of the tsunami had been broken against the shores of New Guinea, an immense surge of radioactive meltwater continued to wash north towards the Philippines, China, and Japan.

For almost an hour McCoy conducted radiophone interviews with government disaster directors in Manila, Singapore, and Tokyo. Evacuations from the threatened coasts to the north were reported going well.

Yet he'd come away from the interviews deeply troubled. The men he'd talked to had all conveyed the sense of fatalistic doom that enveloped the countries of the Far East.

Russian and Chinese missiles were rumoured to have been armed and readied on their facing launch pads. For the first time in almost twenty years, artillery fire had been exchanged across the Korean Demilitarized Zone. And from the Indian border to the outer islands of Indonesia, cities had begun to burn as insurgent guerrilla movements went on a now-or-never rampage of suicide attacks.

McCoy started the story again and finally the words came. He was well into the piece when the videophone buzzed. August Sumner's face appeared on the screen. The editor had looked worn and tired five hours ago when he'd called Christchurch to console Josh about Melissa. Now his face was a grim, grey mask.

'Josh, we've had a major development in the Antarctic crisis,' Sumner said without greeting. 'I have General James Lowe on conference call from Washington. I'd like him to join our conversation.'

'Of course,' McCoy said.

The screen split diagonally, and the head and shoulders of General Lowe appeared in the bottom triangle. McCoy noticed that Lowe was in civilian clothes.

'I believe you know the general, Josh,' Sumner said.

McCoy nodded. 'One of the few men I've interviewed in Washington who always gave straight answers. Hello, General.'

'Hello, Mr McCoy.'

Sumner said, 'General Lowe, would you please tell Mr McCoy what you've just told me.'

The officer's eyes were pained. 'I've resigned from my country's service, Mr McCoy. Resigned so that I might speak out as a private citizen. You and the *New York Times* have been the victims of a monstrous deception. A deception that now has half of the world poised on the brink of war.

McCoy listened incredulously as Lowe told him that the American laser threat was a lie, a hoax, a desperate bluff devised by Samson Fisk. The security adviser had deceived the *Times* publisher, Max Chadding. The White House had never intended to use the lasers.

Sumner shook his head sadly. 'Every journalist must expect to be used at one time or another, fed a story fabricated towards someone's end. Still, you never get used to the feeling you've been stabbed in the back.

McCoy seethed. 'Doesn't Wollcott realize his laser threat has convinced half the world that there's not going to be any tomorrow? There are governments out there that believe world order is about to disintegrate and the only way to ensure their own survival is to strike their enemies now, while they still have the power.'

'The president and Fisk are both intransigent,' Lowe said. 'That is why I have come to you. I'm asking the *Times* to get out the truth. Tell the world there will be no American laser attack. No war. There is time to reason differences.'

'I'll get out a bulletin immediately,' McCoy said.

Sumner said, 'It was a courageous act to resign and oppose the White House, General Lowe.'

'I hope I have saved some lives, Mr Sumner. Thank you both. Good-bye.'

The picture flicked to a full-screen image of Sumner. 'Lowe's news is a godsend, Josh,' the editor said. 'The end of the laser threat will calm the war hysteria and allow time for peaceful voices to be heard.'

'The laser threat may be over, August, but we've still got to sweat out an eruption from that Ross Sea volcano,' McCoy said. 'If that submarine mountain blows, both the Shelf and a vast area of the West Antarctic Ice Sheet will melt into the sea. Every coast on the planet will face the same fate as the flooded shores I've just flown over.'

'Have you talked to Waldo?'

'Thirty minutes ago. The latest satellite readings are ominous. The pressure within the cone is nearing the critical level. There's no question that volcano's going to blow. Waldo's assuming Christchurch will go under in the next few hours. He just sent Charlie Gates inland to Sheffield to set up an emergency satellite monitoring post.'

Sumner shook his head morosely. 'I'll let you get out that bulletin. Talk to you later, Josh.'

McCoy put the tsunami story on hold and typed BULLETIN into the word processor.

ABOARD *TIMES TWO*: THE AMERICAN THREAT TO USE ORBITING LASERS AGAINST SOVIET TROOPS OCCUPYING THE ROSS ICE SHELF ENDED ABRUPTLY AT 12:30 GREENWICH MEAN TIME WEDNESDAY, WHEN GENERAL JAMES LOWE REVEALED THAT THE US ULTIMATUM WAS A BLUFF.

GENERAL LOWE RESIGNED TODAY AS CHAIRMAN OF THE JOINT CHIEFS OF STAFF AFTER A POLICY DISPUTE WITH THE WHITE HOUSE OVER THE ANTARCTIC CRISIS.

LOWE REPORTS THE LASER PLOY WAS A STRATAGEM OF THE NATIONAL SECURITY ADVISER, SAMSON FISK, CONTRIVED IN AN UNSUCCESSFUL ATTEMPT TO PRESSURE THE SOVIETS FROM SEIZING THE SHELF.

'THERE WILL BE NO AMERICAN LASER ATTACK. NO WAR,' THE GENERAL SAID IN A STATEMENT TO THE *TIMES*.

IT MUST BE ASSUMED THE KREMLIN WILL NOW PROCEED WITH PLANS TO BREAK OFF AND FORTIFY SECTIONS OF THE SHELF AND DEPLOY THESE 'ICE STATIONS' OFF THE PACIFIC COASTS OF THE PACIFIC POWERS. THE RUSSIANS ARE EXPECTED TO LAND PERSONNEL ON THE ICE IN A MATTER OF HOURS.

THE AMERICAN BLUFF WAS NECESSITATED BY THE CRITICAL SHORTAGE OF US LONG-RANGE TROOP TRANSPORT PLANES, WHICH MADE A CONVENTIONAL MILITARY REACTION TO THE SOVIET ANTARCTIC THRUST IMPOSSIBLE.

WHAT WASHINGTON'S RESPONSE WILL BE IN THE FACE OF THE RUSSIAN OCCUPATION OF THE SHELF — AND THE ARMING OF SELF-PROPELLED ICE STATIONS THAT IS LIKELY TO FOLLOW — IS A MATTER OF CONJECTURE AT THIS TIME.

CERTAINLY, AMERICA FACES A DRASTIC REASSESSMENT OF ITS DEFENCE POSTURE AND A REVIEW OF WHAT ARE BOUND TO BE SHIFTING INTERNATIONAL ALLIANCES THROUGHOUT THE PACIFIC OCEAN BASIN.

THE END OF THE AMERICAN LASER THREAT DOES NOT, OF COURSE, REMOVE THE DANGER OF A MASSIVE MELTDOWN OF ANTARCTIC ICE SHOULD THE ROSS SEA VOLCANO ERUPT AND BATHE THE WESTERN CONTINENT IN FIERY FALLOUT.

EVACUATIONS ARE CONTINUING FROM LOW-LYING COASTS AROUND THE WORLD.

McCoy made some final changes, then keyed the computer and sent the bulletin out.

He felt an emotional, almost a physical release as he sank back in the cabin chair. To be able to expose the monstrous lie was a catharsis, a purging of part of the tension that had gripped him for the past three days.

Yet the relief was a surcease only. Rankin had judged the chances the Shelf would escape a massive meltdown as a thousand to one. McCoy doubted even that remote hope existed. The inexorable geological forces surging beneath the tortured coast of Antarctica would not be stilled.

The volcanic cannon was loaded and pointed directly at the ice of Antarctica.

NORTHDRIFT
434.2 Nautical Miles

Sonarman First Class Dale Brown started forward in his small chair in the control room of the USS *George Washington Carver,* his hands coming up instinctively to cup his earphones. He listened intently for a minute, then turned to the captain.

'Sir, I'm picking up a propeller. Very weak.' Brown paused. 'If I didn't know we were in Antarctic waters, I'd swear it was a small inboard.'

Captain Christopher Carol's brow furrowed as he watched the sound waves pulse on the sonar screen. Brown was right. Whatever the mysterious craft moving across the freezing surface above them, the motor had a ridiculously small screw. Lieutenant Commander Gerald Travers studied the sonar contact on the screen. 'One for the books, Captain. No question that's an inboard moving slowly about eight miles off the ice cliffs.'

'Any guess as to what the hell a small boat is doing chugging around in the middle of the Ross Sea?' Carol asked.

Travers shrugged. 'There are only two possibilities in these waters, sir. One, it's some sort of research craft from our McMurdo Sound Station about eighty miles due south of our present position.'

Carol shook his head. 'I think we can rule that out. It's too early in the year to launch a boat from McMurdo. The shore is still hemmed in with pack ice.'

'Then it's got to be a lifeboat, Captain.'

'Which means a ship has gone down somewhere in the area. But what vessel would venture this far south?'

'Don't the Japanese have an Antarctic Krill Fishing Fleet down here this time of year?'

'Yes, they do,' Carol said, 'a mother ship and three trawlers, as I recall.'

'Maybe one of the fleet struck the Ice and they had to abandon ship.'

'That's possible, but where are the other three ships? They would have started a search. We should be picking up propellers crossing and crisscrossing the area.'

Travers's eyes widened. 'Good Lord, Captain, you don't suppose the entire fleet . . .'

'Put yourself in the place of that Japanese fleet commander, Mr Travers. The Ice Shelf is four hundred miles across. Now if you're captain of a surface vessel and something that large appears where your charts show open ocean, what would you think?

'I'd assume it was meteorological, maybe a dense weather front.'

'Exactly. Ice crystals, for instance, would show up as a solid mass.'

'But wouldn't they have spotted the ice visually, Captain?'

'Not necessarily. A berg in the open sea is frequently surrounded by fog, covering the water for several miles out from the ice,' Carol said.

'Once they discounted the radar, the poor bastards wouldn't have had a chance,' Travers agreed.

'We're going up, Gerry. Whoever's in those boats can't survive long in these waters. Prepare to surface.'

A claxon sounded shrilly through the huge submarine and several minutes later the *George Washington Carver's* periscope broke the surface of the freezing Ross Sea.

Captain Carol squinted into the eyepiece and began a slow scan of the waves. 'Broken pack ice. Seas two to three feet,' he said to the officer of the deck beside him. 'Thick fogbank off the starboard bow.'

He was three quarters of the way through the sweep when he suddenly froze, his finger adjusting the focus. 'Good God!'

'Spot the boat, Captain?' Gerald Travers asked.

'Boats, Mr Travers, boats! There are eight of them roped together. Japanese, all right, I can see the Rising Sun below the gunwales.' He stepped back. 'Down scope

Take her up easy. Some of those ice blocks are big enough to do us damage. Let's just let them slide off the sides as we rise.'

Ship's cook Yoshio Konuma checked the fuel tank of the lead boat once more. His heart sank. It was almost empty. When the engine finally coughed and died, they would begin to drift. If the seas took them up against the ice, they would all be dead within a matter of minutes. He could hear the waves breaking angrily at the base of the massive white cliffs hidden in the fog. Time was running out.

An insane shriek came from one of the boats lashed behind. Someone was screaming about a sea monster. Delirium is setting in, Konuma thought. He turned towards the cries, his eyelids frozen half shut, and saw the black shape pushing up through the ice floes 200 yards away.

His mouth worked wordlessly. The adrenaline pumping through his body made him heady. A submarine!

The long cigar shape of the *George Washington Carver* broke the surface, the freezing Antarctic seas cascading down from the sail onto the black steel deck plates of the giant sub.

'Crack the hatch,' Carol ordered. A spray of ice water caught the men below, dripping off their heavy parkas. 'Lookouts above.' Two sailors shot up the ladder, followed by Carol and Travers. The captain focused his binoculars on the lifeboats. 'The poor bastards,' he said, shaking his head. 'I wonder how long they've been out there?'

He picked up his bullhorn as the Japanese boats turned and moved slowly in a string towards the *George Washington Carver*.

Thirty minutes later the forty-nine surviving fishermen were wrapped in blankets in the sub's mess, bowls of hot soup in their blue hands.

Carol turned the conn over to Travers and went forward to the mess. Despite their ordeal, the Japanese stood as he entered. He waved them down.

Konuma remained standing. 'Captain, I, Yoshio Konuma, ship's cook. Off trawler *Wakasa*. We owe our lives. We are most grateful,' he said with a stiff, painful bow, using the Pidgin English spoken throughout the Pacific basin since the early nineties.

Carol nodded. 'It's fortunate we were in these waters. Can you tell me what happened?'

Konuma lowered his head, ashamed of the tears brimming in his sunken eyes. In halting words he described the death of the entire Japanese Krill Fishing Fleet. Then, as the American captain listened incredulously, the cook told him how Takahashi, Ushiba, and Aoki had set out to climb the Shelf. Just as Konuma finished, Carol was summoned to the compartment phone.

'Captain, tower lookouts report a diffused green glow above the ice cliffs to the southwest. Artificial light of some sort. They estimate the point of origin at six to eight miles. We're picking up a pulsing radio signal from the same distance.'

'Flare beacon?'

'I think so, sir, and more than one. Definitely homing devices of some sort.'

'Crank her up and head for those lights, Mr Travers. Three of the Japanese set off to climb the Ice. It could be them.'

'Aye, aye, sir.'

Slowly the bow of the huge submarine came around, and the *George Washington Carver* cut through the freezing waves towards the eerie green glow beckoning from the Ross Ice Shelf.

The mountain stabbing through the polar sea began to tremble as more and more molten magma surged upward from the plume and coursed through the honeycomb of dikes within the rising cone.

Like the branches of a leafless tree, the dikes fed off the main conduit leading to the summit crater. Almost a day and a half before, the last of the Ross Ice Shelf had drifted over the submerged peak and there was nothing above to suppress the frenzied gases and steam that rose from the volcano in hissing columns.

Harmonic tremors pulsed incessantly now from beneath the volcano, and the mountain no longer erupted at intervals but continuously. The tortured skies above the Ross Sea were heavy with ash and smoking cinders.

As if at war with the polar continent, the mountain fired salvos of spinning lava fragments called volcanic bombs towards the blackened shores of the bay. The bombs arched over the sea, leaving behind white trails of cooling steam as they whistled through the air.

Above the summit, violent updrafts of air caused whirlwinds and waterspouts, and lightning bolts lit the hellish tableau with brilliant flashes.

Then suddenly, for the first time, the cratered peak thrust up through the surface of the Ross Sea, and angry waves crashed and churned against the steep slopes. As the hours passed, the volcano pushed ever higher, growing several feet a minute, building with each eruption until the summit yawned 600 feet above the level of the ocean.

Without warning the strongest tremor yet raced along the fracture, shaking the mountain to its roots deep within the crust. Abruptly the magma discharge stopped, the throat of the main conduit blocked by a shift of super-heated rock set in motion by the quake.

Trapped within the cone, the maddened gases and steam pushed inexorably against the lava plug above. Tiny cracks began to appear in the block as the pressure mounted.

The rock glowed red as it began to disintegrate. It could not hold for long.

Choppy waves broke off her stern as the USS *George Washington Carver* moved at slow/ahead through the cold sea 400 yards off the white line of cliffs that faced the Ross Ice Shelf.

On the bridge Captain Christopher Carol and his officer of the deck scanned the high rim of the Shelf with binoculars, searching for the source of the strange green lights.

'There they are!' Lieutenant Commander Travers yelled suddenly, focusing his glasses on a spot on the summit of the frozen wall a quarter off the starboard bow.

Carol swung around and zeroed in on the human figures waving their arms frantically at the top of the shelf almost 5,000 yards away. There was no question they were Japanese, but there were only two men, not three.

Travers lowered his binoculars. 'How in hell are we going to get them off there?'

Silently Carol turned from the Shelf and surveyed the sea behind the *George Washington Carver*.

A moment later he saw what he wanted and pointed with the glasses. 'Give me an eyeball estimate of the size of that ice floe about two hundred yards off the stern, Mr Travers.'

Travers adjusted his binoculars and studied the pancake of drift ice that had departed from the Antarctic shore with the spring thaw.

'Around thirty-four hundred square yards, sir.'

'Think we can move it, push it ahead of the *Carver*?'

Carol explained that the violent surf at the base of the ice cliffs would prevent them from getting in close enough with either the sub or a rubber dinghy, to receive men coming down off the frozen white walls.

He told Travers to watch the swells as they approached the ice floe. The waves rolled smoothly under the floe, the size of a football field, rather than crashing against its sides, as they did against the cliffs.

'We've got a lot of nuclear horses on board this boat, Mr Travers. We'll push that floe up against the cliff and maintain just enough pressure with the engines to keep the ice pinned between us and the Shelf face.'

Travers grinned. 'The floe will ride up and down on the waves like a floating dock, rising and falling with the swells!'

'Exactly. Those men managed to climb up the cliff. Rappelling back down shouldn't be that difficult. Once they make it onto the floe, they cross the ice and transfer onto our bow. I think it'll work.'

At the top of the frozen escarpment Takahashi and Ushiba stood transfixed, staring with gaping mouths at the huge black submarine moving through the ice-capped sea below.

The *Carver's* bullhorn crackled sharply to life and the two marooned fishermen were startled to hear the voice of their shipmate Konuma pulsing up at them from the dark shape of the sub. They listened incredulously as the cook from the *Wakasa* told them of the American rescue of the dories and Captain Carol's plan to get them off the Shelf. Their dumbfounded silence continued several moments after the bullhorn had quieted.

'They're Americans,' Ushiba managed finally, his voice faltering.

Ushiba's words snapped the first mate out of his shock. His face flushed with joy. 'Yes, yes, they're Americans! And they're going to take us off this cursed Ice,' he screamed, his hands flying to unwind the coil of rope around his waist.

As Ushiba watched, Takahashi kicked the ash and snow off a patch of frozen surface ten feet back from the lip of the precipice. Then he took his lifeboat hatchet and began to hollow out a thin circular channel twelve inches deep and almost four feet in diameter. Finally, the first mate cut a straight four-inch-wide ditch from the cliff edge back to the rim of the sunken circle, looped a rope around the ring, and played the line out through the straight channel and over the brink of the yawning white palisades. Gingerly at first, then with mounting force, he pulled against the nylon, the rope closing tightly against the inner edge of the channel until it held fast without giving.

Below them, the huge Carver slowly nudged the pancake of drift ice up against the foot of the Shelf face. As the floe made contact with the Shelf, Captain Carol ordered the sub throttled back just enough to keep the two bodies of ice in contact.

On the cliff above, Takahashi demonstrated the use of arms and body to feed out line and how to brake the descent with the rope. He showed Ushiba the way to push off and how to flex his legs to absorb the shock as he swung back in against the cliff face.

Then the first mate backed out over the rim of the Shelf, playing out rope in careful increments through his hands, and kicked out into space, describing a graceful arc that brought him ten feet down the cliff.

Fearfully, Ushiba made sure his own rope was secure, then repeated Takahashi's manoeuvre, at first managing only a timid hop over the edge and a stiff-legged landing.

Twice more Ushiba kicked away from the cliff, determined to make it, to live now that rescue was so near, his confidence growing with each awkward but gainful jump. Takahashi kept close as they lowered themselves, shouting across words of encouragement to his companion, and together they worked down the cold face of the Ross Ice Shelf towards the floe bobbing in the waves below.

Twenty-five feet above the wave tops the first mate called a halt and they drove two harpoon heads into the ice with their hatchets, winding their ropes securely around the steel holds. For several moments they rested while Takahashi studied the floe's lift as it rode up the cliff towards them, the breaking waves flattening beneath the frozen slab

Obviously the floe was making contact with the cliff somewhere down below the water, for there was an eight-foot gap between the edge of the drift ice and the Shelf face.

He waited until he was satisfied he knew exactly how far up the spray-slick cliff the floe reached at the summit of its climb. Then he lowered himself carefully until the surface of the floe was only ten feet below him at its highest rise. He used his last harpoon tip to secure himself and began furiously to hack out a small ledge. He was just finishing when the tail of Ushiba's rope brushed against him. A moment later his young shipmate bounced awkwardly onto the narrow step beside him, a proud grin of accomplishment dissolving the mask of fear he had worn during the descent.

An incoming swell rolled under the drift ice and the floe rose towards them like a huge white freight lift serving the cliff. Takahashi stabbed for Ushiba's gloved hand. 'One . . . two . . . now!'

They leapt in unison, the slab coming up to meet them as they plunged feet first into the soft snow layering the surface. They rolled over once like a team of circus acrobats, then came to rest on their backs, sprawled in contoured pockets of ash-darkened powder. They were on their feet in an instant, yells of incoherent joy streaming behind them as they raced towards the American submarine.

'Make ready to get under way, Mr Travers.' Captain Carol ordered, smiling as he watched the Japanese run with wild abandon across the floe towards the bow of the *Carver*.

He turned to gaze at the glowering sky off the vessel's stern. A chill crept over him as he looked up at the angry clouds etched with seams of fine black and grey volcanic ash.

'We'll be well out of these waters,' Carol said, the smile fading to a grim compression of his lips.

Twenty minutes later, with Takahashi and Ushiba aboard, the top of the *Carver's* sail disappeared beneath the freezing waters of McMurdo Sound.

'Take her deep, Gerry,' Carol ordered. 'Deep and fast and north.'

August Sumner keyed a request for the latest international news summary into the computer terminal beside his desk, then slumped back in his chair feeling exhausted and drained.

He wondered if his mind were sharp enough to absorb the news. For days he had been going on adrenaline, unwilling to rest and miss even part of the biggest story the world had ever known.

One by one, summaries of the foreign press began to crawl up his computer screen. The reports from London, Paris, and New Delhi echoed one another. The international media had seized upon Joshua McCoy's bulletin exposing Washington's toothless laser threat, and General Lowe had quickly verified McCoy's story at a tumultuous press conference.

In the command centres of the superpowers, fingers uncurled from thermonuclear triggers and orders for the mobilization of millions of military reserves were rescinded. In the reprieved countries of both East and West, people emerged rejoicing from urban fallout shelters and the refuge of rural mountain caves.

Yet if the thunder of worldwide war had dissipated, its echoes still reverberated through the capitals and guerrilla camps of a smattering of Third World countries, where fanatical leaders had used the Antarctic crisis to whip their followers into a frenzied lust for revenge against real and imagined enemies.

In a swift and unprecedented manifestation of common resolve, the United Nations Security Council met and voted, with the single abstention of the Soviet Union, to send teams of neutral diplomats immediately to the troubled regions of the world. The UN teams brought with them the carrot of promised help in fairly resolving disputes both old and new, and the stick of certain joint East-West military action against any regime or movement not abiding by the international body's mandate for peace.

The Security Council gave teeth to its resolution by quickly establishing hemispheric spheres of defensive responsibility for the neutralization of any nuclear missiles fired offensively. Around the world, a multinational flotilla of planes carrying air-to-air missiles rose from the airfields and carriers of the superpowers to patrol the borders of the unstable nations. The United States guarded the skies of Central and South America, while planes from the European nations flew sentinel over the Middle East and Africa and the newly potent air force of the Republic of China circled watchfully above Southeast Asia.

Yet if the menace of global war had faded, increasingly ominous satellite reports that the Ross Sea volcano was in a final preeruptive stage had heightened fears that a worldwide ocean flood was imminent.

Waldo Rankin had put out a call for polar and marine scientists to gather in New Zealand to formulate a coordinated international response to the expected cataclysm. But there was nothing Rankin or anyone else could do to stem the worldwide conviction that the inundation of the earth's coasts was inevitable when the Antarctic meltwater surged north into the oceans.

In the United States, the population centres along the western coast were deserted. National Guard troops patrolled the empty port cities against looters, and only skeleton crews remained behind to keep communications equipment and power plants operating as long as possible.

As speculation mounted that the polar deluge was at hand, yesterday's nervous trickle of evacuees from the Gulf and Atlantic coasts swelled to a torrent. Sleepless Americans gathered up children and pets during the early dark hours of Wednesday and streamed inland from Houston, New Orleans, Mobile. The airlines sold every seat on flights leaving Florida. The highways westbound out of Washington, New York, and Boston were solid ribbons of light through the dark predawn as the exodus from the eastern shore cities grew.

Across the Atlantic, refugees jammed the roads of Europe. In the Netherlands, the Dutch government had ordered the evacuation of thousands of square miles of low-lying countryside behind their vulnerable western dike system. In England, King Charles led a corps of volunteers stacking sandbags around the cathedrals and monuments of a vacant London, while several heavily guarded truck convoys sped the city's movable art treasures to the safety of the midlands. On the other side of the channel, French railroads and highways leading to the interior were clogged from the Pas de Calais in the north to the Côte d'Argent on the Spanish frontier.

From the tip of Scandinavia to the throat of the Mediterranean at Gibraltar, Europeans fled the threat of the coming ocean flood.

The final two pages of the summary described the escalating retreat of coastal inhabitants from the shores of South America, Africa, and the landmasses and islands of the Indian Ocean basin.

Sumner finished reading and glanced at the large eighteenth-century globe of the earth that rose through its mahogany girdle in the corner of the room. While the rest of the world was bracing itself for the coming rise in sea levels, the tsunami-ravaged western Pacific had already suffered the first furious onslaught of meltwater from the drifting Ross Ice Shelf.

The editor depressed a remote-control button on the computer console beside him and a row of wall-mounted TV screens flicked on to the right of his desk. He punched in the monitor codes for the stations in Beijing and Tokyo.

Simulcast translations of the stories moved from right to left across the bottom of the screens. The faces of both the Chinese and Japanese newscasters were sombre as they reported the devastated port cities and uncounted thousands of deaths along the Asian shorelines.

The Chinese news agency Xinhau was reporting that the immense surge of radioactive meltwater from the broken tsunami had inundated the entire coast from the South China Sea north to the Gulf of Bohai. China's normally teeming harbours were deserted after hundreds of thousands of junks fled up the country's rivers seeking safety inland. The great port of Shanghai had emptied in hours, its vulnerable watercraft hurrying west up the mighty Chanjiang.

Near Beijing, the Yellow River was clogged from bank to bank with junks jammed to their low gunwales with terrified refugees. The flight of the coastal poulation inland, in turn, had sent alarm radiating out from the rivers to the towns and villages of the countryside. Chinese peasants had abandoned tools, tractors, and rice paddies and begun a frantic stampede towards higher ground.

Across the East China Sea, Japanese newspeople were reporting the crest of poison meltwater had washed the home islands with eighty-foot waves. Hundreds of the maritime nation's fishing boats, tankers, and freighters had gone down in the furious seas. To the north, the ocean had flooded into the portals of the Seikan Railway tunnel between the islands of Honshu and Hokkaido. The thirty-three-mile tunnel, the longest in the world, had filled with seawater, trapping a long passenger train. At least 1,800 people had drowned as the bullet-shaped aluminum cars were deluged 780 feet beneath the bed of the Tsugaru Strait.

Tokyo announced that the flight path of an oceanographic television surveillance satellite had been reprogrammed, and the station would now switch to a live transmission from the probe's TV cameras hovering in geostationary orbit 240 miles above West Antarctica.

Sumner stared transfixed as the immense flat expanse of the drifting Ross Shelf suddenly filled the monitor screen. He had vaguely theorized what a body of ice the area of Spain would look like. His mind had pictured it on a vast scale. But this, this gargantuan entity that dwarfed the highest waves, dwarfed the very sea, this was beyond any imagination.

The once-pristine white surface of the Ice was layered with a steaming cover of grey and black ash. Streams of filthy meltwater flowed out from beneath the warm blanket of debris and cascaded in towering waterfalls over the cliffs edging the frozen plateau.

As he watched, the satellite switched to a long-range camera and panned 275 miles across the sea to the Ross volcano rising through the middle of the horseshoe-shaped bay from which the Shelf had drifted. Slowly the television eye pushed in to a close-up of the steaming black mountain lava.

Sumner came forward in his chair, his eyes intent on the distended slopes of the volcano. He knew enough geology to realize the bulging flanks evidenced incredible pressure building below as magma from the polar plume vented inexorably up into the cone.

He watched absorbed for several minutes, then rose wearily and went to the window of his office overlooking Manhattan from the 115th floor of the ten-year-old Times Tower.

The city that never slept looked eerily lifeless without its normal constellation of lights. The power had been shut off in most of the tall buildings, and only an occasional flash of headlights stabbed through the dark canyons as the last stragglers sped uptown towards the bridges to New Jersey and upstate New York.

Most of the *Times* editorial staff had already moved to temporary offices in the city of White Plains, twenty-five miles to the north. It would be some hours more before technicians could finish tying the paper's vast data banks and global communications network into the computers in White Plains. Sumner and a handful of volunteers had remained in Manhattan to ensure unbroken coverage of the looming Antarctic cataclysm.

Behind him the voice of the Japanese broadcaster grew excited and he turned to look at the monitor. The satellite camera had zoomed in to a close-up of the volcano just below the summit. A section of the northern slope several thousand square acres in area began to turn crimson, glowing like the red-hot side of an overheated wood stove. Sumner didn't have to look at the simulcast translation to know that magma had eaten away the guts of the mountain and was now just below the swollen surface of the rock. Very soon now the volcano would erupt, and a hellish fallout of molten magma, fiery rock fragments, and hot ash would rain down, metamorphosing the Ice of West Antarctica into billions of tons of meltwater.

Soon, around the world, the coasts would begin to drown.

# NORTHDRIFT
479.1 Nautical Miles

Chauncey Dutcheyes stood staring out over the dark and vacant streets of Christchurch from the twelfth-floor solarium of All Souls Hospital.

Battered and partially flooded by the thirty-foot waves tipping the eastern flank of the tsunami, the city had been ordered evacuated by the New Zealand goverment ten hours before. The decision to abandon Christchurch came after McCoy appeared before a massed bank of microphones and cameras at Antarctic Conference headquarters and released an all-media bulletin from Admiral Rankin.

Chauncey and Miki had stood in a hospital lounge and watched McCoy on television. After a few moments the ancient seer had closed his eyes and tried to envision the scene described by the American.

Satellite thermovision indicated magma was continuing to vent up into the Ross Sea volcano from the plume below. The pressure within the cone from the rising magma and gases was in the critical range.

Admiral Rankin believed the final eruption would come within twenty-four hours. The molten fallout that followed would ineviably melt billions of tons of ice into the sea. The surge of meltwater from Antarctica would be titanic. The accompanying tsunami might reach 500, even 1,000 feet in height. The Pacific and Indian Ocean shores would be most vulnerable, but even the coasts of the North Atlantic could expect 100-foot waves as the crest of meltwater surged up from the south.

There had been a communal gasp from the reporters present when McCoy flashed Melissa's flood projection chart on an Antarctic Conference video screen. Many of the international correspondents lived in the regions tinted purple, the low-lying shores, islands, peninsulas, and river deltas that would disappear beneath the waves when the seas rose 26.5 feet.

During the rest of the news conference McCoy had fought to answer the frantic, shouted questions.

Chauncey lifted his gaze to Pegasus Bay. He could still hear McCoy's voice as he watched the steep swells furrow the moonlit surface of the water. That was the trouble. McCoy's voice kept reminding him that the flood of the earth was inevitable, an inescapable part of the future, but when he looked into the hours to come, he could not see the deluge. He saw something, but the meaning was murky. It had been troubling him.

Miki Dutcheyes appeared in the door of the solarium and came up softly behind him. She put her arms around his chest and rested her head against his back.

'You are tired, little one,' he said, squeezing her hand.

She yawned. 'Yes. Our people are resting comfortably. They don't need me any more. Still, I can't sleep. I keep thinking about Campbell. What will happen to the people when the flood comes?'

His voice was resigned. 'I wish I could tell you, Miki. I have had a vision of the great Ice Shelf. I could see its frozen cliffs soaring above the sea across the entire horizon. Then as I watched, towering clouds of ash rose before my eyes and all became black. When I could see again, the Ice was gone.'

'But your vision is complete,' Miki protested. 'You have seen the Ice enveloped by the eruption. After the meltdown, the sea will be empty again. What more is there?'

'There is more, Miki, I feel it.'

'Perhaps if you rested,' she said. 'Your visions often come to you in your dreams.'

'There is another thing,' he said. 'I must talk to the Americans: Joshua McCoy and Admiral Rankin.'

She came around and looked at him. 'I'll arrange it, Great-grandfather.'

His strange violet eyes were far away. 'Say that I have a story to tell.'

Miki searched his parchment-like face. 'What story, Great-grandfather?'

'I have watched a volcano die, Miki. I shall tell them of the death of Krakatoa.'

Joshua McCoy scanned the list handed to him by Waldo Rankin and blew a silent whistle through his lips. 'There must be twenty Nobel laureates on here, Waldo,' he said, recognizing most of the names of the polar experts and marine researchers arriving in New Zealand in response to Rankin's call for scientific volunteers.

'Almost all the top people are here or on the way,' Rankin said. 'People are arriving from every technologically advanced nation but one.'

McCoy looked at the list again. 'No one from the Soviet Union. Have you heard from the Russians at all?'

Rankin shook his head. 'Not a word.'

The screen of the international media monitor in Rankin's office blinked to life, and McCoy crossed the room to read the incoming story.

'Flooding has started along the California coast,' he said to Rankin. 'Thirty-foot waves are battering San Diego and Los Angeles. Record seas are funnelling through the Golden Gate. The Coast Guard estimates San Francisco Bay has risen almost three feet in the past couple of hours.'

Rankin nodded grimly. 'The bathtub effect. The meltwater the tsunami piled up against the shores of Asia is levelling out, surging east across the Pacific towards North America.'

Rankin's intercom buzzed. 'Yes, Peg?'

'Chauncey Dutcheyes and his great-great-great-granddaughter are at the security desk, Admiral. And Charlie Gates is on line six.'

McCoy started for the door. 'You take the call, Waldo. I'll clear Chauncey and Miki through.'

Rankin flipped on the videophone. 'Hello, Charlie. How's it going in Sheffield? You set up yet?'

'Just about, Waldo. The satellite systems are in place. We'll be able to monitor the volcano with thermovision, infrared, and TV cameras. We'll also be receiving GRAVSAT readings direct from the Goddard Space Flight Center in Maryland.'

'When will you be operational?'

'They're laying the last of the transmission cables now. We should be on line in about half an hour.'

'Anything you need?'

Gates blew out his cheeks and exhaled a tired breath. 'Time, Waldo.'

Rankin looked up as McCoy returned with Chauncey and Miki.

'I'm afraid that's something I can't give you, Charlie. Let me know when you have the systems up.'

'Good-bye, Waldo.'

Rankin came around the desk and McCoy introduced the ancient seer and his great-great-great-granddaughter.

The mystical face and gaunt frame of Chauncey Dutcheyes looked oddly out of place, unsynchronized in time against the computer terminals and video screens of the modern room.

'How are the hospital patients you brought from Campbell?' Rankin asked as they sat down.

'Thank you, Admiral, they are doing well,' Chauncey answered. 'They were evacuated inland just before we left.'

McCoy turned to Miki. 'There's nothing more you and Chauncey can do at the hospital. You'd better think about leaving the city yourselves. I can arrange transportation if you need it.'

Miki smiled. 'I appreciate your offer, but one of the doctors promised to make room in his car when he goes. He's picking us up here in half an hour.'

The videophone rang on Rankin's desk.

'Excuse me.' Rankin rose and flipped on the set.

The anxious face of Connie Anderson in Operations came on the screen. 'I think we're monitoring the beginning of the end, Admiral.'

'What have you got, Connie?'

'Both our satellite thermovision and NASA'S GRAVSAT sensors have detected a massive new surge of magma moving up from the plume through the seabed. We estimate the surge will reach the volcano in two to three hours.'

'The cone can't take any more pressure,' Rankin said. 'I'm afraid you're right, Connie. We're facing the final eruption. The monitors in Sheffield will be on line shortly. Leave your computer networks open and evacuate your department from the city. Tell your people for me, well done.'

'Thank you, Admiral.'

Rankin said good-bye and buzzed his secretary.

'Yes, sir?'

'Time to pull the plug, Peg. Notify the remaining staff to close their offices and get inland to Sheffield at one. Anyone without a car can take one from the motor pool.'

'Shall I have your driver come around?'

'No, I'm not ready to leave yet. But go yourself.'

'Very well, Admiral. I'll just clear my desk, then.'

'Good-bye, Peg.'

Rankin straightened and looked at his visitors. 'You heard. I'm afraid we've run out of time.'

His gaze lingered on the frail island prophet. 'I'm told you have the power of precognition, Chauncey.'

'Yes, Admiral. The gods have given me this gift.'

'Are you able to foresee what will happen when the eruption comes? Is there any chance the Ice will escape the volcanic fallout?'

'I can only describe the vision that has come to me, Admiral. I see the great plateau of ice drifting across the horizon. Then black clouds appear before my eyes. When the darkness lifts, the ice is gone from the surface of the sea.'

Rankin turned and stared vacantly out the window towards the south. 'You're describing the volcanic melt-down of the Shelf.'

'That is what I thought when Great-grandfather told me,' Miki said.

Chauncey slowly shook his head. 'I cannot say that this is to be. The future is clouded. Yet my vision of the past is very clear.'

'Miki said on the phone that you had actually witnessed the eruption of Krakatoa,' McCoy said. 'If I recall my history, that was the island volcano that blew itself apart off Indonesia in the late nineteenth century.'

Rankin turned from the window. 'It was the most stupendous explosion ever recorded on the planet, natural or nuclear. The sound was heard three thousand miles away, and the ash from the eruption paled the earth's sunlight for over two years. If you were there, Chauncey, I'd like to hear your account.'

The old man slowly closed his eyes and began to look back within himself, down the time tunnels of his memory to the days of his youth 116 years before.

He began. 'In the summer of my twelfth year I was out at sea fishing in a canoe with two companions. A schooner came over the horizon. The lookouts saw us and the ship dropped sail. The crew threw over a rope and waved us on board. We thought it a great adventure.'

He opened his eyes and looked at Miki. 'In those times human sharks still fed on the people of southern seas, little one. They called themselves labour contractors, but they were slave traders. They kidnapped islanders and sold them to work the European rubber plantations far to the north in Indonesia. We were overpowered and thrown in the dark hold.'

Miki reached out to hold one of his age-spotted hands, her eyes pained as he described the ordeal of a century before.

'Ten weeks after we were taken, the scent of Pele came to me on the sea wind.'

Chauncey lifted a bony finger to his deep violet eyes. 'These marked me from birth as a seer. The elders taught me in my early years to know when the earth whispered of change, to recognize the scent of Pele though it were faint on the wind. The next day a great noise like the boom of a huge cannon suddenly rocked the ship. We heard the crew running in panic across the deck above.'

The old man's voice grew stronger as he looked back on the vivid tableau of his youth. 'We thought the schooner was under attack. Ten of us prisoners tore a bench free and battered through the hatch to the deck. We expected to have to fight the crew, but they barely noticed us. They were lined along the port rail, their faces twisted with fright.'

Chauncey's thin hands described a rising motion before him. 'The blackest cloud I had ever seen towered in the far sky. It rose from the summit of a mountain so distant I could only see the peak above the sea.'

The others listened motionless as the ancient Maori told of the death of Krakatoa.

'Great bolts of lightning flashed within the cloud and sparks leaped from the metal fittings on deck. A terrible scorching wind rose, and I lashed myself to the rail. Then a great explosion rolled the ship far over on her side. When we righted, only I was left aboard. And the mountain of Pele was gone.'

Rankin came forward in his chair. 'Then Krakatoa wasn't destroyed by a series of eruptions? It was one single immense explosion?'

'Yes, Admiral. Where Krakatoa had risen through the waves there was a great hole in the sea. As I watched the hole became a funnel, its mouth spinning wider and wider.'

McCoy's voice was incredulous. 'A whirlpool? In the ocean?'

'A whirlpool such as the world has never seen, Joshua. We were drawn into the circling waves, and the schooner began to slide into the abyss. Then the dark sea closed over me and I remember nothing more. Two days later fishermen found me adrift still tied to the rail.'

Rankin's eyes gripped the seer. Can you estimate how far across the whirlpool was?'

'The fishermen told me they were catching fish native to the Great Barrier Reef far to the south. Later I learned the whirlpool had sucked dry lagoons six hundred miles from where Krakatoa had stood.'

Rankin was on his feet. 'Six hundred miles! Great God Almighty! That's the key! The irresistible force of a vacuum. If we can re-create . . .'

He left the thought unfinished and whirled towards McCoy. Josh, I need your help on the computer. Run a search of our geological data bank. I want to know how far below sea level Krakatoa blew. Did the detonation originate in the magma chamber?'

McCoy crossed to the computer terminal and keyed data retrieval.

Rankin hunched over his desk and punched the number for Operations into the videophone. The screen remained blank.

'C'mon, c'mon!' The ringing continued unanswered.

He was about to give up when the screen flickered and Connie Anderson appeared. A shopping bag full of personal effects from her desk bulged in her arms. 'You caught me going out the door, Admiral.'

'Connie, I need a satellite orbit change.'

'Which craft?'

'Ingrid's Own. I want her sent into geostationary orbit over the Ross Sea.'

Anderson's brow furrowed. Ingrid's Own had been the first of the laser-equipped satellites used in Antarctic mining operations. Its directed energy beam could bore a mine shaft through the continent's frozen crust at almost fifty feet an hour.

The satellite had been named after Rankin's wife when it was launched back in the late eighties. It had been deactivated in 1995, when the last of Antarctica's great subterranean mineral deposits were reached with vertical shafts and the boring of lateral tunnels was begun.

'Admiral, Ingrid's Own has been in park orbit over the central continent for several years. Her systems are mothballed. It may take a day to reprogramme and switch orbits.'

'No good, Connie. I need that bird ready in two hours.

You work on the flight path. I'll programme the onboard computers myself.'

'Two hours! You're asking the impossible, Admiral.'

'I know. You can reach me onboard the SR-96. I'll be taking off for Antarctica as soon as I can get to the airport.'

Anderson sighed and let the shopping bag drop to her desk. 'I'll verify when I've gotten the orbit changed.'

'Thanks, Connie.'

McCoy turned from the computer as Rankin hung up. 'There've been several geological surveys of the Sunda Strait since Krakatoa blew,' he said. 'Core samples indicate the magma chamber detonated taking the cone up with it when it exploded.'

'How far below sea level was the reservoir?'

'Approximately six miles, Waldo.'

Rankin stared across the room at a large wall map of the Ross Sea, the muscles in his face working furiously. 'It's possible! By God, it's just possible!'

He looked at Chauncey Dutcheyes. The two men locked eyes. 'I think you know what must be done,' Rankin said. 'What I am going to try to do.'

'Yes, Admiral. I know. Yours is a heavy burden.'

'A burden I'm not going to let you shoulder alone, Waldo,' McCoy said. 'I don't know what you're planning, but we'll face that volcano together. I'm going with you.'

Chauncey spoke before Rankin could protest. 'I don't believe you'll change our friend's mind,' he said, appraising McCoy's set expression.

Rankin's smile was resigned. 'No, I don't suppose I will.' He reached for the phone. 'I'll get us a car.'

Miki rose and crossed to McCoy. She reached up and laid her hand gently against his cheek. 'I want to thank you, Joshua, for flying our sick out to the hospital. You saved their lives. The Maori people are in your debt.'

'There's no debt, Miki. I'm glad I was there to help.'

'I don't know what it is you must do,' she said, 'but I shall pray to the gods to return you both safely.'

Rankin put down the phone. 'My driver will meet us out front.'

'Our car will be here soon,' Miki said. 'We'll go down with you.'

Five minutes later an electric Austin swung to the curb. They said good-bye as Rankin and McCoy jumped in.

Chauncey stepped to the open window. 'Very soon you will possess what men only dream of. For a moment, yours will be the power of the gods.'

The ancient seer staightened and the car sped silently away through the dark empty streets of Christchurch.

'Why do they go, Great-grandfather?' Miki asked as the Austin's tail lights dimmed in the distance. 'What is it they must do?'

'They are going to war, little one,' Chauncey answered, his violet eyes boring into the black night. 'They go to battle the earth.'

Captain Aleksandr Polenov opened the curtained alcove in the forward section of the command plane and gently shook the sleeping general. 'You asked to be awakened, Comrade General. We'll be over the drop zone in thirty minutes.'

Leonid Vlasov stirred and dug his fists into his eyes. He'd had a troubled, fitful sleep, waking again and again in the throes of the same nightmare. In the terrible dream, his men were descending over the Shelf when suddenly they turned to puppets dangling from the shroud lines, stuffed uniforms with doll heads grinning at him idiotically.

He pushed himself upright. He hadn't been told about the heat exhaustion rampant among the paratroopers of the 32nd Karelian until moments before the division took off from Mossamedes. By then there was little he could do beyond ordering the men be given all the liquids available aboard the transports and rested one section at a time in the aisles.

He could only hope the winds over the Shelf were moderate. In their weakened condition, his troops could have serious difficulties with the control lines as they descended.

The general rose and straightened his tunic. 'I wish to speak to the men.'

'Yes, Comrade General.' Captain Polenov took the cabin address phone from its niche in the forward bulkhead and turned to face the rows of paratroopers. 'Attention in the plane. Attention to your commander.'

The seated paratroopers stiffened perceptibly as Vlasov rose to take the phone. 'Men of the Thirty-second Karelian, this is our last briefing. We jump in a quarter of an hour.'

A buzz went through the ranks.

'If all has gone according to plan, at this moment a long-range helicopter from our Antarctic base of Mirnyi is setting out flares to mark our drop zone. Once again, red flares will mark the tops of the cliffs facing the sea. Green flares will be positioned in the centre of a safe landing area two miles in toward the interior of the Shelf. Jump for the green.'

For five minutes Vlasov briefed his men on the jump and their responsibilities during the early stages of the occupation of the Shelf. 'The success of our mission will bring glory to Mother Russia and, at last, socialist order to the entire world,' he finished. 'We must not fail. Do your duty. See to your comrades. And good luck to us all.'

Captain Polenov handed him a radio message as he turned. 'From Moscow, Comrade General.'

Vlasov read the message and scowled. 'From the KGB, Comrade Polenov. Comrade Duglenko himself. He's ordered me to arrest the scientists Cherepin and Chirikov. He doesn't bother to tell me why.'

Vlasov crumpled the message into a ball and flung it at the tiny desk in his alcove. 'Damn Duglenko! I need those scientists on the mission. Without them we can't even separate the ice stations from the Shelf, much less navigate the stations north against America. Duglenko must be mad!'

The general sat down fuming on the small swivel chair before his desk and penned his objections to the order. He tore the sheet from the pad and thrust it at Polenov. 'Get this off immediately. Inform Moscow I require confirmation of the order from Duglenko himself.'

Fifteen minutes later the captain handed the KGB reply to Vlasov. The arrest order was reaffirmed. Duglenko had added that if the general did not carry out the KGB instructions forthwith, he would answer personally to the Politburo.

Vlasov shook his head wearily. 'The fools. The damn meddling fools!' He sighed and rubbed the fatigued muscles in his face. 'Bring Cherepin and Chirikov up here.'

'Yes, Comrade General. Polenov hurried down the aisle and reurned several minutes later with the two civilians.

'That will be all, Comrade Captain,' Vlasov said, waving a and for the scientists to take a seat on the narrow bunk. He pulled the alcove curtain shut behind them.

For a moment Vlasov stared at them silently. Finally he said, 'I must inform you that by order of State Security, I am placing you both under arrest.'

Anya Cherepin sagged against Chirikov and closed her eyes.

'Arrest? What for?' Chirikov asked incredulously.

'The charge is high treason against the Soviet state,' Vlasov said. 'I have not been given the particulars.'

Anya buried her head in her hands, a sob from deep in her soul welling out between her fingers. Her life was over. She'd never see Joshua again, never know the warm embrace of his love. Ahead lay only prison and a bullet in the back of the neck.

'There has been a terrible mistake,' Chirikov started to object. 'Surely you're not going to carry out the order. Not until specific charges are brought, accusations we could at least attempt to answer.'

'I am not a judge, Comrade Chirikov,' Vlasov said. 'And in any case, my instructions are not open to interpretation. You will have to answer the charges against you in Moscow. The command plane will not land in Antarctica. Once the division has jumped over the Shelf, the aircraft will be refuelled in the air—and you will be flown directly back to Russia.'

Cherepin dug her fingernails into the fabric of Chirikov's coat, needing something to hang onto, to keep from tumbling out of control into the dark abyss before her.

'I don't intend to manacle you or lock you in the lavatory or take any such ridiculous precautions against your escape,' Vlasov said. 'If you wish to force a door and leap from the plane, I suppose there is little to stop you. However, I don't believe either of you is the suicidal type.'

Cherepin rocked slowly back and forth, her eyes tightly clenched, her tear-streaked face a mask of helpless, hopeless despair. Vlasov was wrong. There was nothing left now but to end her life. She vowed bitterly that when the command plane returned to Moscow, she would not be on it.

There was a knock on the bulkhead beside the alcove and Captain Polenov thrust his head through the curtain. 'The

322

pilots have picked up the radio signal from the flare bleepers, Comrade General. The signal is strong; however, there is a complication.'

Vlasov came to his feet. 'What complication?'

'Only the green flares are visible below, Comrade General. And the line of beacons is only half as long as it should be. There are no red lights visible at all.'

Vlasov cursed and pushed through the curtain. He barged into the pilot's compartment a few feet away and stared down through the Plexiglas cockpit windshield. 'Where are the flares?'

The startled pilot pointed to the left and down. 'Port side, Comrade General, at approximately nine o'clock.'

Vlasov's eyes strained down through the patchy clouds. He could see a diffused green line below. There was not a spark of red to be seen in any direciton.

'Dammit! Circle the area. They may be waiting for the sound of the engines before they ignite the other flares.'

Five minutes later they had completed a tight circle. There was no change below. Only the line of green lights was visible.

Captain Polenov spoke up hesitantly. 'Comrade General, there are two possible explanations.'

'Well?'

'The red flares, as you know, Comrade General, were to be placed along the cliffs of the Ice Shelf. It is conceivable violent updrafts climbing the walls could have torn the flares off the edge of the plateau and blown them into the sea.'

Vlasov grunted. 'Yes, perhaps. What is your second guess?'

'The helicopter could have experienced engine trouble. They may have had time only to position the green flares. We've had a report from Mirnyi. That volcano rising through the Ross Sea has spewed ash over a wide area of ice and ocean below. The volcanic dust may have fouled the helicopter's engine.'

'Go on.'

'If they were forced down and had to distribute the

323

flares on foot, they may have had time to lay out only one short line. They would naturally choose the green flares, knowing we would aim for these when we jumped. A loss of power would also explain why we have been unable to reach them by radio.'

Vlasov mulled over what his aide had just suggested. It seemed plausible. In any case, he would have to accept the reasoning. They were committed.

'Instruct the other transports to jump on the green flares as soon as they see us go,' Vlasov ordered as he left the compartment.

He dressed quickly in the heavy polar clothing, zipping his jump suit on over his insulated coat and trousers. Finally he pinned the military decorations of a thirty-five-year career on his chest.

In the cavernous troop section of the transport, the Mongolian paratroopers completed their preparations.

The general walked to the rear of the plane. 'Buckle up,' he ordered through the intercom system. The men instantly attached their rip cords to the steel cable running the length of the cabin.

'Clear away the door.'

A blast of frigid air swept through the transport as the large jump door yawned open.

'Stand in the door.'

A burly Mongolian sergeant poised at the lip of the exit, one hand holding the rip-cord wire taut, the other gripping his Kalashnikov rifle to ensure that the weapon cleared the exit.

'Go!'

The sergeant tumbled from the plane. One after another behind him, the paratroopers shuffled quickly down the length of the cabin and threw themselves out into the swirling mist.

Several thousand yards behind them, the other twenty-four Antonov troop transports emptied in smooth sequence, leaving a wake of 5,000 white canopies bobbing above their human cargoes in the cold polar air.

When the last of the stick had gone, Vlasov returned

forward to the command compartment and called the radio officer from his set.

'There is something wrong with the flare pattern below,' Vlasov said, casting a glance at the silent Cherepin and Chirikov. 'It may be nothing but I have had a foreboding since Mossamedes. I shall be jumping with a radio pack. You will keep the frequency open and monitor my observations as I descend.'

'Yes, Comrade General,' the officer said, and returned to his seat.

For a long moment Vlasov stared into the forlorn faces of Cherepin and Chirikov. Then he spun on his heel and walked back through the empty troop compartment of the circling plane. He strapped on the radio, hooked up at the door, and leapt out into the freezing Antarctic air.

Far below, the first of the Mongolian soldiers to jump descended towards the diffused light of the green flares Takahashi and Ushiba had placed along the cliff tops of the Ross Ice Shelf. The Mongolian sergeant strained his senses downward, trying to decipher the unfamiliar sounds of the waves breaking against the frozen palisades hidden in the patchy sea fog beneath him. Then a gust of wind cleared the swirling mist and for the first time he saw the ice-choked waves pounding against the face of the Shelf.

For a moment, wonder played across his face. Then horror contorted his features as he realized the angle of his descent would carry him beyond the surface of the Ice and into the freezing ocean. He clawed at the air with his hands and feet, as if trying to swim through the emptiness to the solid safety of the Shelf. Then he realized what he was doing and steadied, reaching for the control lines of his chute.

He had begun to spill air from the canopy above when a terrible expression of pain twisted his face. He let go of the lines, crossing his hands over his chest to grip his upper arms, his fists clenching and unclenching repeatedly. At almost the same moment his knees jerked spasmodically up into his stomach. His muscles, weakened by the heat exhaustion in Africa, could not stand the physical demands of the freezing jump.

He reached towards the lines again, faltered and fell back. It was no use, he knew. His strength was gone. He could not control the chute. His body went limp as he accepted his fate.

Inexorably the sergeant drifted down beyond the lip of the Ice, his hopeless black eyes burning towards the faithless flares that had lured him to what he knew now was his imminent death. Moments later the Mongolian disappeared beneath the overhang of the Shelf, a final, long trailing scream echoing off the ice cliffs below.

Above him, the contorted bodies of thousands of his comrades withered in the agony of cramps and muscle spasms. Through the swirling mist the paratroopers caught sight of the ice floes crashing and grinding against each other in the hostile sea beneath them. Frantically they pulled on their guidelines, struggling desperately to manoeuvre their descent towards the safety of the Shelf top. Like their sergeant before them, their efforts were useless, their muscles unresponsive. Their strength had been dissipated in the humid heat of Africa. Terrified screams and soul-rending wails tore from agonized throats, a hellish concert from a doomed choir.

Then, finally, it was over.

Five thousand young Mongolian men died in the most hostile sea on the face of the earth.

General Leonid Vlasov checked his wrist altimeter as he drifted slowly down. He pressed a hand against the throat microphone beneath the insulated neck of his jump suit. 'I'm at three thousand feet,' he reported to the command plane. 'Still descending through fog.'

Cherepin and Chirikov listened distractedly to Vlasov's voice coming through the alcove curtain from the cockpit speaker. 'Fifteen hundred feet. I can see a faint green glow from the flares now. The drop zone is still obscured.'

Several moments passed, then, 'One thousand feet. I hear something . . . artillery fire! The Americans must be . . . No, wait. Wait! It's not shelling. It's waves breaking!' For the first time an edge of fear crept into his voice. 'There are waves breaking below me!'

Anya Cherepin came forward in her seat, her eyes locking with Chirikov's startled gaze.

'Five hundred feet. The fog is breaking up. I'm almost clear. I can see – ' A primordial gasp of horror tore from the loudspeaker.

'Comrade General!' The voice of the radio officer was frantic, 'Comrade General, what's happened?'

There was a long pause, then they heard Vlasov's voice again, now suddenly and strangely calm, as if he'd relinquished his will and already accepted the watery fate that clutched at him from below. 'My men are dead. Drowned. All of them drowned. Their bodies litter the waves. The flares have betrayed us. They are set on the cliffs. The division has been lured into the sea.'

There were several seconds of agonized silence, then, 'A hundred feet now. The sea will be cold. Very cold. Tell them in Moscow – '

There was a burst of gurgling static, then the radio went dead.

President John Stans Wollcott stared red-eyed across his Oval Office desk at the national security adviser, Samson Fisk.

'I assume you've seen the latest intelligence, Sam.'

'I was briefed by my staff ten minutes ago, Mr President.'

'Then you're aware that by now the Soviet occupation force has air-dropped onto the Ross Shelf. The Ice is theirs, with all that portends.'

'The laser ploy was a gamble, Mr President. It's regrettable it has come to nothing. However, the Soviets are still vulnerable. We could apply military pressure to their satellite allies in Central America; perhaps threaten to supply China with our new electric tanks.'

'I find it curious you believe I could ever again make any creditable move internationally,' Wollcott said. 'Or haven't you read that *New York Times* bulletin issued several hours ago?'

'I had no idea General Lowe would go to the *Times*, Mr President.'

'I've been caught bluffing with nothing in my hand, Sam. The resolve behind my future positions will be forever suspect. Your ploy has succeeded in emasculating me as president. I want your resignation. On my desk within one hour.'

Fisk sat stunned. His fortune, his family, nothing mattered measured against the power that flowed to him as the right hand of the president. To be stripped of office, forced to resign ignobly, would leave his life meaningless.

'Mr President! We have great work ahead. You can't let this one – '

'That's all.'

Fisk came heavily to his feet. 'You are tired, sir. Distraught. Perhaps if you gave yourself time to consider – '

Wollcott exploded up out of his chair. 'Get out!'

Fisk drew back instinctively. Then he turned and bleakly left the Oval Office.

For a moment the president stood behind his desk, the muscles in his blood-gorged neck rigid strands, his body rocking in rhythmic rage from toe to heel. Then he regained control and slowly lowered himself into his chair.

There was a discreet double knock on a side door followed by the appearance of his appointments secretary. 'Your helicopter's waiting on the lawn, Mr President. The Secret Service is quite insistent you evacuate.'

Oceanographers had warned that a sudden surge of meltwater up from the South Atlantic could inundate Washington. The Army Corps of Engineers had been ordered to surround the White House with a fifty-foot-high ring of rock and earth.

'What about the staff?'

'Most of them are already on the way to Camp David, sir. The rest of us will be going up when you leave.'

Wollcott rose and for a moment stood staring around at the Oval Office. Was this the last time he'd stand here, the last time any American president would govern from this room? He lowered his head and followed the aide out.

The president paused halfway to the huge Marine helicopter squatting on the lawn and looked back at the White House. From several entrances workmen were removing furniture, crated paintings, barrels of china. To his right, beyond the spiked fence, he could see large earth-moving equipment from the Corps of Engineers. As soon as he took off, the giant machines would begin piling earthworks around the executive mansion.

He finished crossing the lawn and boarded the helicopter. The olive-green craft rose in a swirl of autumn leaves and swooped out over Washington. He stared down at the empty streets. With the city flooded, they'd have to move the capital inland: St Louis, Chicago, perhaps Dallas.

Wollcott turned from the window, a maddening frustration washing over him. He was the most powerful man in the world and he could do nothing, nothing, to save Washington and hundreds of other coastal American cities and towns from disappearing beneath the cold rising sea.

Wearily the president closed his eyes. Technology had made the human species arrogant. No more. The Antarctic upheaval had shattered man's illusion that he controlled his world.

The planet's six billion human inhabitants had been brought face to face with a sobering reality. As the third millennium dawned, it was nature, not man, that reigned on earth.

NORTHDRIFT
505.2 Nautical Miles

The earth was a global village in the year 1999, shrunk by the communications revolution of the past decades, and news of the imminent flood looming over the oceans of the world had reached the most remote corners of civilization.

Outside the Nepalese capital of Katmandu, in the snowbound Himalaya Mountains north of India, an ochre- robed high lama emerged from his monastery cell to preach to a throng of anxious Buddhist followers.

He had gone into the forbidden Cave of the Wind beneath the soaring slope of Swayambhunath Mountain, he told them. There he had read from the sacred book held in the mummified hands of Pratap Malla, a seventeenth-century king of Katmandu. The ancient writings had revealed the end of man's reign on earth was near.

As word of the prophecy spread, Buddhists throughout Asia prostrated themselves in prayer, their fingers clutching 108-bead rosaries. The religious fervour swept to the Middle East. Muslims trekked east from North Africa, west from the Persian Gulf, millions heading on foot across the scorching Arabian desert towards the holy city of Mecca.

In Israel, Tel Aviv and Haifa emptied as Jews swarmed into Jerusalem, standing shoulder to shoulder in the plaza before the Wailing Wall.

The Christian churches were seized by the conviction that these last days of the second millennium after Christ had been foretold as the time of judgement, when Jesus would come again and the earth give up her dead.

Three quarters of a million faithful jammed Saint Peter's Square to be confessed *en masse* by Pope Clement XV, and from Westminster Abbey a continuous chorus of Protestant hymns drifted across the vulnerable Thames.

God be merciful. God save his sinners. The pleas intoned endlessly from hundreds of millions of throats in churches, temples, and mosques.

In every language and dialect spoken by man, the world prayed.

Anya Cherepin felt a surreal detachment as she stared down at the ice fields of Antarctica passing beneath the command plane. She had made up her mind to die.

A quiet peace had flowed over her the moment she'd accepted the thought of death. If there were another world, another level of existence beyond this, she'd be with Joshua then. If not, at least the pain without him would end.

She stole a look at Volodya Chirikov deep in an exhausted sleep in the seat beside her. Volodya was a good man, a humane man. What she must do would wound him grievously, as it would shatter Joshua, and she hated the thought of that. She could only hope they would both forgive her, understand that for her there was nothing left but death.

She rose and looked down at Chirikov's drawn face. 'Good-bye, Volodya,' she whispered. 'Thank you for being so kind, so caring. You have been a father to me.'

Anya turned away, tears in her eyes now, and started down the aisle of the deserted cabin. She reached the jump door and stood studying the instructions stencilled above the locking mechanism. There were two handles to lift in sequence.

She reached forward tentatively and touched the first handle. The metal was ice cold, as cold as the Antarctic wind waiting for her outside. She shivered and pushed the handle up. A red ready light glowed above the door.

One more. She forced her hand forward. Her fingers curled around the cold steel and she felt a sudden rush of adrenaline. She tensed to push.

'Comrade Cherepin, please pick up a compartment phone.' The voice from the cabin speakers startled her, sucking the breath from her lungs, and she fell back against the bulkhead, a hand at her throat.

She stared first at the speaker, then at the door. One shove up on the last handle and she'd be gone, free in death as she'd never been free in life.

The voice of the communications officer came again from the cockpit. 'Comrade Cherepin. You have a priority one call from Moscow. Please pick up a cabin phone.'

Her resolve cracked. Later, after she'd taken the call, she'd have to rebuild her courage. She took a deep settling breath, pushed the first handle back into the lock position, and walked several steps to a phone in the tail section.

'This is Director Cherepin.'

'Hold please,' the communications officer said. 'I'll patch you through.'

A moment later she was startled to hear the voice of Mikhail Romanov.

'Much has changed since we last spoke, Anna Yegorovna,' the general secretary said. 'Savin's mad scheme has cost Mother Russia five thousand sons.'

'So many have died for nothing, Comrade Romanov,' she said. 'So many young men.'

'The soldiers of the Thirty-second Karelian did not die for nothing, Anna Yegorovna. We have reason for optimism. Their sacrifice has provided a cause around which the moderates in the Presidium have rallied. A crusade against our adventurist foreign policy has begun. There is a groundswell of opposition to the use of our armed forces beyond our borders.'

Cherepin closed her eyes, numbed by all that had happened, numbed by the words she was hearing. 'With you to lead the moderates, Comrade Romanov, perhaps we can hope our country will now enjoy an era of peace at last.'

'I shall not be here to lead,' Romanov said. 'No matter I opposed Savin's plan, still I was the party general secretary and the blame for the debacle in Antarctica must ultimately come to rest on my shoulders. I have submitted

334

my resignation to the Presidium. It takes effect at midnight tonight.'

'Oh, no!' Cherepin protested. 'Russia needs you more than ever, Comrade Romanov.'

'My removal is not so catastrophic as you might think, Anna Yegorovna. The hardliners are in disarray, discredited in the eyes of the Presidium and in the hearts of our countrymen. Oh, I don't pretend the militarists are gone forever from the helm of Mother Russia. But for a time, at least, the Soviet Union will be led by men of moderation and peace.' Romanov's voice lifted. 'Far more than me, it is you, men and women of science, the world needs now. When the oceans flood, the earth will undergo the most profound changes since the last ice age. You and your colleagues must lead the human race through the difficult months and years ahead.'

'Surely you do not include me, Comrade Romanov. You must know the KGB has ordered my arrest. When I return to Moscow there will be a trial. I will be found guilty and –'

'There will be no trial,' Romanov said. 'As leader of the Soviet Union, I cannot condone what you have done – going to the Americans with state secrets. Yet faced with the great evil Marshal Savin planned, I do not see you had a choice. In any case, it would be rather difficult to try you when you are ten thousand miles from a Russian courtroom.'

'I don't understand, Comrade Romanov.'

'The American Admiral Rankin has called for the world's polar scientists and oceanographers to gather at Antarctic Conference headquarters. He is forming an army of scientists to join ranks against the cataclysm ahead. Russia shall join in that battle. As perhaps my last official act, I have ordered the command plane to change course. I am sending you to New Zealand, Anna Yegorovna.

Anya's knees buckled and she slid slowly down the bulkhead, her hand grasping the phone with tight, bloodless figures. She tried to speak, but couldn't. Her shoulders heaved and she began to cry.

'Do you know what comes at the end of next month, Anna Yegorovna?' Romanov asked gently.

Cherepin fought for control. 'Do you mean . . . do you mean the millennium?'

'Yes, the year two thousand, the millennium. It has been prophesied as a time of great transition for the world. And so it shall be. The fate of mankind is passing from the hands of statesmen to the shoulders of scientists. You have been called to serve, Anna Yegorovna. Serve well.'

'I shall, Comrade Romanov,' she whispered. 'I shall.'

'Farewell, Anna Yegorovna.'

For several moments Anya rested against the bulkhead, not trusting her legs. Joshua's face floated before her. Then she pushed herself up and started forward down the aisle, the joy welling wildly through her. 'Volodya!' She began to run. 'Volodya, we are free! We are free!'

From the mountain of Pele came the dirge of death.

The pounding of the magma trapped within the tortured cone sounded the slopes of the volcano like a stone drum, a primal lamentation for what was to come.

Two hundred and ten miles away Waldo Rankin watched his cockpit video screen flick to life as the SR-96 hurtled south 70,000 feet over the Ross Sea.

Charlie Gates's face appeared. 'How's your flight, Waldo?'

'Milk run so far, Charlie. What's the status of Ingrid's Own?'

'That's why I'm calling. Connie Anderson just finished her computer magic. Ingrid's Own went into geo-stationary orbit over the Ross volcano five minutes ago.'

'Thank God!' Rankin breathed. 'To be honest, I wasn't sure Connie could do it in time. What are the satellite coordinates?'

Gates gave him the figures, and Rankin switched on the computerized radar. He punched in the numbers, then watched as a white blip appeared behind the sweeping radius at the two o'clock position.

'We have radar lock,' Rankin said.

'We're ready in Sheffield,' Gates said. 'The last of the monitoring systems went on line twenty minutes ago.'

'Good. I'm going to leave this channel open. We'll be ready to take control of the satellite in a few minutes.'

'Talk to you then, Waldo.'

Rankin hit the intercom to the rear cockpit and told McCoy of the successful satellite switch.

'Josh, I promised you before we took off I'd explain our mission as soon as I was sure my plan was more than just theory. Now that Ingrid's Own is in position, I can tell you.'

McCoy listened incredulously as Rankin talked.

'We're going to re-create the detonation of Krakatoa, Josh. To do that we have to blow the magma chamber. The explosion will vaporize the floor of the bay and the water above it. If I'm right, a huge vacuum will form where the Ross volcano now stands. That vacuum will become a whirlpool within seconds.'

'The Shelf!' McCoy said, suddenly seeing what Rankin and Chauncey Dutcheyes had seen. 'It's just off the mouth of the bay. When the sea is sucked into the whirlpool, the Ice will be drawn back with the water! Good God, Waldo, is there a chance it will work?'

'Theoretically, yes,' Rankin answered. 'Once set in motion, the Shelf's momentum should carry it far enough into the bay to ground itself again.'

McCoy let out a long breath. 'I can't fault the theory, but how the hell do you propose to blow the magma chamber?'

'By using the volcano's own energy, Josh. We'll send a pulse of laser heat into the magma reservoir from the mine bore beam aboard Ingrid's Own. The violent temperature increase will force the volcanic gases to expand rapidly. In the confined space of the chamber the explosion should come nanoseconds later.'

'That magma chamber lies under six miles of salt water and seabed surrounding the cone, Waldo,' McCoy argued. 'How do you hope to penetrate to the reservoir with a small mine bore beam?'

'A narrow laser ray is exactly what we need, Josh. It would be futile to try to reach the chamber through the seabed. I intend to fire straight down through the central magma pipe into the reservoir.'

McCoy whistled. 'Even with the computer guidance, that's a hell of a shot.'

'I know Josh. And we only get one.'

'How will you target the satellite?'

'We'll make a run over the volcano to fix our heat

sensors onto the entrance to that magma conduit. I've programmed our onboard computer to monitor the sensors. We have Ingrid's Own on radar lock. The instant the pipe mouth is detected, the computer will plot the angle of fire up to the satellite. As soon as Ingrid's Own is locked on target, I'll order her laser to send a full power burst down the throat of that mountain.'

The SR-96 began to buck and yaw as the aircraft entered the ring of torrid air swirling above the volcano's summit.

'We have to go in low, Josh,' Rankin said. 'It's going to get a little rough. Hang on.'

The stick jumped and fought against Rankin's control as the black jet sliced towards the smoking cone. A moment later the SR-96 flashed across the peak and the words THERMAL TARGET LOCK appeared on the computer screens in their twin cockpits.

'Sensors on, let's get the hell out of here, Josh!'

Rankin yanked back on the controls and the aircraft climbed again, fighting up through the tumultuous atmosphere like a kayak battling through white-water rapids.

'Waldo, you two better get out of there,' Gates's excited voice came through their helmet speakers. 'Thermovision shows a second magma surge rising rapidly from the plume. That volcano could erupt any minute!'

Rankin's gravelly voice was calm. 'Easy, Charlie, I've got the throttle full out. We'll be beyond range of the worst of the fallout in four or five minutes.'

Thirteen miles below, the Ross volcano trembled in the throes of 1,400-degree gases. Like a kettle whistling on a stove, the vapours within screamed for release from the furious cauldron of the cone.

'Satellite seismographs are monitoring strong submarine tremors, Waldo,' Gates warned.

McCoy looked back down as the SR-96 climbed through the violent polar sky. A vivid streak of red had suddenly appeared beneath the heaving waves off the northeastern quadrant of the mountain.

'Good God, Waldo,' he said. 'It almost looks as if the volcano is bleeding into the sea.'

Rankin glanced down. 'A quake must have split the base of the cone. We're running out of time.'

Below, a firey tongue of hissing lava spread across the sloping bottom of the bay, turning the waters into a bubbling cauldron. Billions of krill were instantly cooked alive in their filmy exoskeletons as the water temperature leapt to 200 degrees Fahrenheit.

A pod of fifteen baleen whales shot through the boiling sea in a frenzy, the heat fast breaking down the fat of their blubber. The oxygen in their blood gurgled, their great lungs steamed. They hurled their immense bodies in crazed leaps into the nightmarish air desperate for breath, balancing above the waves on huge, thrashing tails. It was fruitless. The black froth of volcanic ash and gases hovering above the wet spray had little more oxygen to offer than the tortured sea.

The lungs of the great marine mammals burst within minutes, and one by one they sank slowly into the raging depths, huge clouds of crimson bubbles trailing behind their lifeless hulks.

Four hundred miles away Rankin brought the black jet into level flight and looked down at Gates's face on his cockpit video screen.

'Ready to take control of Ingrid's Own, Charlie.'

'Roger. Switch over on one,' Gates said. 'Five, four, three, two, one.'

The words SATELLITE CONTROL TRANSFER COMPLETE appeared on Rankin's computer-terminal screen. 'Systems linked,' he said. 'We've got her.'

'Do you want to run through the test sequence, Waldo?'

'No time for rehearsals, Charlie.'

He hit the intercom to McCoy. 'We'll fire the laser as soon as our sensors have fed the target data to the satellite computers.'

The jet bucked viciously in the swirling air currents over the Ross Sea.

'You've got your hands full just flying this bird, Waldo,' McCoy said. 'I'll monitor the satellite feed.'

'Thanks, Josh. Let me know the moment Ingrid's Own is targeted.'

McCoy flicked on the computer terminal before him. The words DATA TRANSFER IN PROGRESS slowed white against the background.

He felt the sweat trickle down his chest as the seconds passed. The screen blinked and the message TRANSFER COMPLETE: SATELLITE THERMAL TARGET LOCK appeared.

'We've got the target lock, Waldo.'

'Just a few seconds now, Josh.'

McCoy's eyes ached as he stared intensely at the computer terminal. He blinked away the strain. When he looked again the screen was flashing FIRE MODE . . . FIRE MODE . . . FIRE MODE.

'Now, Waldo!' McCoy yelled through his throat mike. 'Now!'

Rankin punched the three-digit fire order into his cockpit computer and the command flashed to Ingrid's Own high above. The SR-96 was suddenly bathed in a surrealistic glow as a ray of intense light from the orbiting laser stabbed down through the ash-blackened sky like a shaft of sun through a thunderstorm. The beam pierced the volcanic summit below and flashed down through the central magma conduit. In milliseconds the laser ray had reached the lava- and gas-filled chamber deep under the floor of the bay.

For a moment empty of time, Pele held her breath.

Then, with an apocalyptic explosion audible in New Zealand, the Ross volcano disintegrated into an awesome pitch-black cloud that shot upward in ebony billows forty miles into the polar stratosphere.

A pyroclastic shock wave, a mixture of 1,000-degree-Fahrenheit gases, dust and volcanic ash, drove the cloud before it with the force of 10,000 one-megaton hydrogen bombs. The searing shock wave lifted the SR-96 and carried the plane before it like a kite on a gale wind. The twin cockpits of Rankin and McCoy were plunged into sudden darkness as the black cloud enveloped the madly rocking jet.

Gates's voice through their helmets was frantic as the thermovision screen in Sheffield showed a polar sky strewn with molten rock and pumice.

'Waldo! Are you all right? Waldo!'

'We're still in one piece, Charlie,' Rankin said as the aircraft steadied. 'Keep your eye on those monitors. We're going to dive again.'

'No! It's too soon!' Gates protested.

'We have to get below the ash,' Rankin said. 'We've got to know what's happening to the Shelf.'

He turned on the intercom. 'The moment of truth, Josh. We're going in.'

'I'm as ready as I'll ever be, Waldo.'

Far below them a curtain of black volcanic dust had been drawn over the raging sea as if the earth, appalled at this venting of her fury, would hide the devastation from the eyes of the gods. Where the lava tower of the Ross volcano had risen through the angry waves, a six-mile-deep void now pocked the bay from shore to shore.

For an eternal moment the waters of the Ross Sea hesitated at the mouth of the empty bay, as if the waves could not believe the presence of the sudden cavity yawning ahead. Then the over-mile-high wall of water began to cascade down into the immense gaping hollow.

In less than a minute centripetal force turned the vacuum into a huge, foaming whirlpool that sucked insistently at the great volcanic cloud hovering above. The searing flotsam of fiery lava, pumice, ash, and gases that threatened to dissolve the ice of West Antarctica into an earth-girdling flood of dirty meltwater was being sucked back down into the depths of the shattered magma chamber in a towering, black, insanely hissing funnel.

McCoy stared dumbfounded at the heat-sensor monitor before him. 'Waldo, the fallout! What the hell's happening?' he shouted as the screen showed a hail of fiery cinders corkscrewing back down into the depth of the bay.'

'We'll know in a couple of minutes, Josh,' Rankin said as the SR-96 rocketed down towards the blackened Antarctic coast.

Two minutes later the jet broke through the ash cover and levelled off 1,000 feet above the shore of the bay.

'My God!' McCoy said hoarsely as they gaped down at the huge whirlpool spinning furiously below.

'We're halfway there, Josh!' Rankin said, banking the jet. 'Let's see what's happened to the Ice.'

Far out to sea beyond the mouth of the bay, the Ross Shelf brooded like a shadow on the horizon.

McCoy saw it first as they neared. 'Waldo, the cliffs! Look at the cliffs!'

A white band had begun to appear at the foot of the ash-blackened walls of the Shelf as the waters of the Ross Sea were sucked inexorably away into the bay.

'I'm going to come around,' Rankin said, putting the SR-96 into a wide turn.

As they watched from the circling jet, the sea began to retreat rapidly down the landward face of the Ice. Within minutes almost half the Shelf had been undermined. For a long moment more the Shelf resisted the pull of the river of seawater rushing towards the vacuum of the bay. Then gravity prevailed and the Ross Ice Shelf began to slide towards the Antarctic coast.

The Ice rocked madly as it was drawn with gathering speed back towards the semicircular gulf where it had formed thousands of centuries before. A furious wall of spumous seawater shot 1,000 feet into the air as the Shelf reached the mouth of the bay and the spinning rim of the whirlpool smashed into the forward cliffs. As the centripetal force of the vortex died against the implacable Ice, the liquid sides of the funnel collapsed in a sudden deluge into the vacuum centre. The Shelf hurtled without pause through the filling depression, advancing on the inner shore of the gulf like a colossal white blunt-nosed ship.

Moments later the cacophonous scream of ice scraping across rock tore through the polar air as the frozen plateau rode up and over the rim of the bay, crushing the earth and glacial ridges of the shore into powder. The Shelf's inexorable momentum thrust it forward over the lip of the continent, gouging out the earth and ice in its path. At last, the monstrous block shuddered, slowed, and ground to a halt, the landward flank of the Ice now gripping the polar surface fifty miles inland from the sea.

The largest single entity ever to move across the face of the earth stood anchored to the broken Antarctic shore.

A mile above, Rankin and McCoy stared down silently as the SR-96 circled the motionless Shelf. Rankin spoke finally, the emotional and physical strain of the past three days in his voice. 'We've done it, Josh,' he said, his words falling off to a whisper. 'We've done it.'

McCoy sank back into his seat. 'Chauncey was right,' he said, the parting prediction of the ancient Maori seer flashing through his mind. 'We've known the power of the gods.'

They circled slowly, wordlessly, once more. Then the black jet banked and rocketed north from the bottom of the world.

Below the angry polar waves broke impotently against the still cliffs of the Ross Ice Shelf.

# NORTHDRIFT
0.0 Nautical Miles

Anya Cherepin stood silently with Joshua McCoy on the balcony of Admiral Rankin's Christchurch office watching the grey swells from the Pacific roll across Pegasus Bay below.

She turned towards him finally and caught the faraway look in his face. 'You're thinking of Melissa,' she said gently.

'Yes,' he said, his gaze still on the sea. 'It's so damn hard to accept what happened. The submersible was sinking fast when Melissa went back down that hatch. She must have known she didn't have a chance. Yet she chose death with her research over life without it.'

His pained eyes met Anya's. 'Why? Why did she do it?'

'Did Melissa ever really have a choice, Joshua?' Anya said. 'Or was her work so consuming that her fate was never really in her own hands?'

McCoy nodded. 'I want to believe that. I want Shea and Kate to believe it, that their mother gave her life not because she loved them less but because for her science, knowledge was more than life. I hope they'll understand. I hope I'll come to understand.'

'Josh, Anya, you two ought to see this,' Rankin's voice came from the open door behind them.

They walked back in. Rankin was holding his granddaughters on his knees and watching the international television monitors with Miki and Chauncey Dutcheyes. The screens on the wall were showing a world in tumultuous celebration.

Just twenty-four hours after Joshua McCoy's bulletin from the SR-96, port cities and coastal settlements were filling rapidly with evacuees joyous at their return to homes they'd thought destined to disappear beneath the sea.

McCoy grinned and pointed at one of the sets. 'Who said the British were staid?'

The screen was showing a BBC broadcast from London. The camera was panning slowly across teeming Trafalgar Square, where cheering tens of thousands had gathered in a spontaneous outpouring of joy.

A second monitor pictured 600,000 frenzied citizens of Rio de Janeiro clogging the broad Avenida Rio Blanco in a scene of rejoicing unrivalled by even the greatest Mardi Gras of the city's past.

Rankin switched one after another to television stations in Stockholm, Bombay, Cape Town, New York, San Francisco. In city after city, in daylight and dark, people came together in common exultation.

'I wish Mommy could be here,' Shea said, tears running down her cheeks as she stared sombrely at the scenes of celebration. 'Everyone's happy. Everyone's happy and alive but Mommy.'

Kate began to cry, and Rankin drew his granddaughters to his chest. 'Listen to me, both of you. Your mother sacrificed herself working towards this moment. She's at peace now in a better place we're all going to some day. Mourn her, miss her, we all will. But so long as we keep her memory alive in our hearts, your mother will never die, not for all of us that loved her. Promise me you'll remember that.'

The girls nodded and hugged their grandfather.

The broadcasts from Shanghai, Sydney, and Manila were far more sombre as the monitors showed the devastation wrought by the Antarctic tsunami. It would take a year or more to clear away the low-level radioactive debris and contaminated earth left along Asian shores by the giant wave.

Yet even along the sea-ravaged coasts of the western Pacific, optimism prevailed. Millions of volunteers in protective clothing were already at work cleaning, salvaging, preparing to rebuild.

From New Zealand north to China and Japan, a thousand coastal cities and settlements would rise like the phoenix from their ruins.

Rankin eased his granddaughters down and crossed to a

computer console on his desk. He keyed in a request for the latest radioactivity levels from NASA satellite scanning the seawater off the Asian shores.

He went through the readings on the screen and turned to the others. 'Ocean radioactivity levels are dropping off rapidly in the western Pacific. They'll continue to go down as the meltwater disseminates through the seas.'

'I don't suppose we've seen the last outbreak of volcanism in the Ross Sea,' McCoy said.

'Far from it, Josh. The detonation of the magma chamber blocked the throat of the plume with hardened lava, but inevitably another surge will force its way to the surface.'

'How long have we got, Waldo?' McCoy asked.

'There's no way to answer that, Josh; maybe a year, maybe a hundred. A century is only the blink of an eye in the life of a plume. However long, we must start preparing now to redirect future magma surges before they can penetrate the seabed beneath the Ross Shelf.'

McCoy's eyebrows arched. 'Redirect? A magma surge!'

'Yes. I'm going to propose to the Antarctic Conference that work begin immediately to angle a tunnel down from the Antarctic interior into the plume pipe. Instead of venting up through the sea floor overhead, the magma could be siphoned up onto the surface of the continent.'

'But Antarctica is covered with ice and snow, Grandpa,' Shea McCoy objected. 'Won't the magma melt the glaciers?'

Rankin smiled. 'Few people realize that Antarctica is not entirely snow-covered, Shea. There are regions called dry valleys, which are swept continuously free of snow by gale winds.'

McCoy asked, 'Then you intend to pipe the magma into these dry valleys, Waldo?'

'That's the idea. The magma will cool into hardened lava the moment it's exposed to the subzero polar temperatures. Those valleys are large enough to store the upsurge for decades. Long enough for science to learn how to tame a plume.'

'An ambitious project, Waldo,' McCoy said.

'Ambitious! I haven't told you the half of what I'm planning Josh. When we tap into that plume pipe, we tap into limitless thermal energy from the earth's interior.'

His face became animated. 'Think of it! Heat and light for domed cities fed by crops raised in huge greenhouses. Non-polluting power for industry. Homes and work for a growing population! A new productive, independent future for Antarctica.'

Chauncey Dutcheyes spoke for the first time, his violet eyes impenetrable as he gazed out of the window towards the south. 'The admiral sees truly. Cities will rise in the land of ice. What now is snow and cold will be earth and warmth. Trees and children will grow at the bottom of the world.'

Rankin's intercom buzzed. He flipped on a remote speaker. 'Yes, Peg?'

'Mr McCoy's pilot is calling. *Times Two* is ready for takeoff.'

McCoy rose. 'Please tell Captain Russell we're on the way.'

'We must also go,' Chauncey said as Miki helped him to his feet. 'A Red Cross helicopter is flying out to Campbell with relief supplies. They have offered to take us along.'

Miki bent and took the hands of Shea and Kate. 'You must come again to Campbell.'

'Will you show us some more hidden beaches where the seals come ashore?' Shea asked.

Miki laughed. 'Yes, and secret caves and berry patches and lots more. We'll explore for hours and hours.'

Kate looked up hopefully at her father. 'Could we, Daddy?'

McCoy smiled. 'Maybe next summer we'll all come down and visit Grandpa and save a week for a vacation on Campbell.'

'Good-bye, my friends,' Chauncey said. He looked from Rankin to McCoy. 'Fate follows men such as you. Like a lamb.'

'Thank you, Chauncey,' Rankin said. 'For opening my eyes.'

'I told a story, Admiral,' the ancient seer said. 'Nothing more.'

Rankin turned to Anya as Chauncey and Miki left. 'There're going to be some exciting things happening in Antarctica once we get that plume harnessed. I could use a mind like yours. Care to come aboard with me at the conference?'

Anya smiled. 'Perhaps some day, Admiral. But for a little while at least I'm going to be selfish and spend every moment I can with Joshua and your granddaughters. And I must learn to be an American, too. When the time comes to resume my work, I'll apply to one of the universities in the San Francisco area. Berkeley and Stanford both have excellent earth science departments.'

'When you're ready, let me know,' Rankin said. 'I have a few academic contacts in the Bay Area that might prove helpful.'

'Thank you, Admiral,' Anya said with a smile.

Rankin knelt and gathered Shea and Kate in his arms. 'I expect a letter a week from you two. And a phone call every once in a while wouldn't hurt.'

'I'll write real long letters, Grandpa,' Kate promised.

'Will you come and see us sometimes too?' Shea asked.

'Of course I will,' Rankin said. 'Every single chance I get.'

McCoy put out his hand. 'We'll hold you to that, Waldo. Remember you've got a family in San Francisco.'

The two men shook hands warmly. 'I'll remember, Josh,' Rankin said. He turned to Anya. 'Take care of these three for me.'

'I shall, Admiral,' she said. 'For you and for Melissa.'

Rankin embraced her, 'Thank you, Anya.' He took the hands of the girls. 'C'mon, I'll ride out to the airport with you.'

Forty-five minutes later *Times Two* lifted off above Pegasus Bay and banked north towards the first refuelling stop in Pago Pago.

From the rear of the plane Josh McCoy could hear Anya singing the girls to sleep with a lilting Ukrainian folk song. He smiled softly and closed his eyes. It was over. The cold seas would not rise. They were going home.

Twenty-two hundred miles south of the climbing jet a lone black and white figure waddled laboriously up the side of an Antarctic ridge and stared out across the glaciers towards a distant blue line of seawater.

Konge let out an exultant cry at the sight of the ocean. The long columns of penguins halted below erupted in a joyous chorus as they recognized the call that meant they would all soon return to the nurturing sea.

Konge slid down the ridge, and the march of the colony towards the coast continued. Hundreds of the flightless birds had perished on the tortuous three-day trek. The colony had lost a generation of eggs. Their rookery was gone.

Still, the beaches were full of pebbles for new nests. Next spring nature would compensate. There would be twice as many hatchlings. Konge quickened the pace. Food and the future lay ahead. They had survived.

Life would go on at the bottom of the world.

# Fontana Paperbacks Fiction

Fontana is a leading paperback publisher of both non-fiction, popular and academic, and fiction. Below are some recent fiction titles.

- ☐ FIRST LADY Erin Pizzey £3.95
- ☐ A WOMAN INVOLVED John Gordon Davis £3.95
- ☐ COLD NEW DAWN Ian St James £3.95
- ☐ A CLASS APART Susan Lewis £3.95
- ☐ WEEP NO MORE, MY LADY Mary Higgins Clark £2.95
- ☐ COP OUT R.W. Jones £2.95
- ☐ WOLF'S HEAD J.K. Mayo £2.95
- ☐ GARDEN OF SHADOWS Virginia Andrews £3.50
- ☐ WINGS OF THE WIND Ronald Hardy £3.50
- ☐ SWEET SONGBIRD Teresa Crane £3.95
- ☐ EMMERDALE FARM BOOK 23 James Ferguson £2.95
- ☐ ARMADA Charles Gidley £3.95

You can buy Fontana paperbacks at your local bookshop or newsagent. Or you can order them from Fontana Paperbacks, Cash Sales Department, Box 29, Douglas, Isle of Man. Please send a cheque, postal or money order (not currency) worth the purchase price plus 22p per book for postage (maximum postage required is £3.00 for orders within the UK).

NAME (Block letters) _____

ADDRESS _____

_____

_____